W9-CKI-466

STORMY ISLES:
AN AZOREAN TALE

Original title: *Mau Tempo no Canal*. 7th ed. In *Obras completas*.
Vol. VIII. Introdução de José Martins Garcia.
Lisboa: Imprensa Nacional - Casa da Moeda, 1994.

Vitorino Nemésio

STORMY ISLES: AN AZOREAN TALE

Edited, translated, annotated, and with an Introduction by
Francisco Cota Fagundes

GÁVEA-BROWN

Acknowledgment

This publication was made possible in part by the generous contribution provided by the Direcção Regional da Cultura (Department of Culture of the Regional Government of the Azores).

Original Title
    Stormy Isles:
    An Azorean Tale

Cover and Design by
    Álamo Oliveira

Published by
    Gávea-Brown Publications
    Department of Portuguese and Brazilian Studies
    Brown University
    Providence, Rhode Island 02912

Distributed by
    Luso-Brazilian Books
    538 State Street
    Brooklyn, New York 11217

© 1998 by Francisco Cota Fagundes. All rights reserved.

Library of Congress Catalog Card Number: 98-073358

Printing and finishing
    SerSilito-Empresa Gráfica, Lda./Maia-Portugal

Depósito legal 131001/99

ISBN 0-943722-24-1

CONTENTS

INTRODUCTION

Vitorino Nemésio Mendes Pinheiro da Silva (1901-1978), novelist, short story writer, poet, scholar and university professor extraordinaire, and for a time popular radio and television personality, was born on the island of Terceira, Azores, his permanent home until his late twenties. Although Nemésio's parents belonged to the Azorean working middle class (his father being a small merchant), the writer himself claimed to be, on his mother's side, the tenth grandchild of the navigator Álvaro Martins Homem, who was also first donatary of Nemésio's native town of Praia da Vitória (today a city) and founder of the island's capital, Angra, later renamed Angra do Heroísmo. This interest on Nemésio's part in nobility and genealogy is going to be reflected in the novel translated here. The middle class to which he belonged also receives ample treatment in Stormy Isles. *Nemésio had a somewhat idyllic Azorean childhood–a lost paradise that he will forever pursue in his creative works–during which he claims to have had much social interaction with children of the lower classes, particularly fishermen, a group less prominently featured in the novel but still paradigmatically represented, as are farmers, who in reality comprise the overwhelming majority of the Azorean population (about 70%). Most of Nemésio's long life, however, would be spent in mainland Portugal, with a three-year stint as lecturer in universities in France and Belgium. He also visited several other European countries–England, Germany, Holland, and Switzerland, and traveled repeatedly and extensively in Brazil.*

Living at a distance from the Azores might have led to a weakening of Nemésio's island roots. Instead, his residence in the mainland seems to have strengthened his bonds with the native archipelago. His travels abroad, his long experience as a professor at the University of Lisbon (1933-1972, full professor since 1940) and his celebrated intelligence and erudition provi-

ded him with the experiential and intellectual wherewithal to lend a broad, deep perspective to his açorianidade ("Azoreanity"), a key concept for Nemésio. He coined the term in a brief essay published in 1932 in the Azorean review Ínsula. Açorianidade is reflected in much of his poetry and practically in all of his works of fiction, especially Stormy Isles.

Except for the first few years of his life, as already noted, Nemésio had a turbulent youth, marked not only by the bankruptcy of the family business and by his father's death in 1923, but also by his own failures as a student (as often happens, the future great writer and professor was not always an exemplary student), difficulties in choosing academic disciplines and a career (priesthood? the military? medical school?), considerable financial insecurity as the young Nemésio tried to make his way, academically and professionally, in the Portuguese mainland. Nemésio's professional and creative golden years, however, were marked by a seemingly uninterrupted series of major triumphs, both literary and professional. Despite all his personal difficulties, Nemésio's creative flow was never interrupted, and at times swelled to astounding proportions. And few professors have been more loved and admired, even adulated, by so many of their students. Some of them–notable writers and critics in their own right–continue to this day to refer to him as "Master." Nemésio is also recognized as the founder and director of the ephemeral but culturally significant Revista de Portugal (1937-1940). He was honored with the directorship of the Faculdade de Letras of the University of Lisbon. He was the recipient of doctorates honoris causa from the University of Ceará, Brazil and the University of Montpellier, France, and numerous other academic honors and prizes. His creative achievements were crowned by two important awards: the Prémio Nacional de Literatura in 1965, and the highly prestigious Prémio Internacional Montaigne in 1974.

Vitorino Nemésio's fame as a writer, recognized by some since his earliest mature publications but acknowledged and celebrated by many only in the last twenty-five years or so, rests primarily on his fiction and poetry, although he successfully,

*and often brilliantly, cultivated many other genres: biography,
travel literature, history of culture, literary criticism, journalism, and theater. Among his most important works of fiction are
the volumes of short stories* Paço do Milhafre *(1926; Buzzard's
Palace) and the revised and expanded version of this work* O
mistério do Paço do Milhafre *(1949; The Mystery of Buzzard's
Palace);* Quatro prisões debaixo de armas e outras histórias
(1971; Four Prisons Under Arms and Other Stories), containing eight revised stories of O mistério do Paço do Milhafre;
Casa fechada *(1937; The Closed-up House), a collection of
three novellas; and the novels* Varanda de Pilatos *(1926;
Pilate's Veranda), and the work that is generally considered his
masterpiece in any genre:* Mau tempo no canal *(1944; literally
Bad Weather in the Channel), which is translated here as*
Stormy Isles: An Azorean Tale.

*Nemésio also published over a dozen volumes of poems,
which for convenience's sake may be divided into three phases:
juvenilia, middle period, and later period. The juvenilia–Canto
matinal (1916; Morning Song) and* Nave etérea *(1922; Ethereal
Ship)–wherever republished by the poet. The middle period–one
that the critic Jorge de Sena considers the poet's most important–is initiated, interestingly enough, by a volume of poems
written in French,* La voyelle promise *(1935), followed by*
O bicho harmonioso *(1938; The Harmonious Animal), and
concludes with* Eu, comovido a oeste *(1940; I, Deeply Moved in
the West). To this phase, which Sena characterizes as thematically and formally oriented toward European modernity, we
may add* Festa redonda *(1950; Dance and Song on the
Occasion of the Holy Ghost Celebration), a work whose content
and form draws inspiration, as most of Nemésio's fiction would,
from Azorean, as opposed to Portuguese mainland and
European, sources (to the extent that these are separable), as
the subtitle of the work clearly indicates:* Ten-line Songs and
Improvised Songs Offered to the People of Terceira by Vitorino
Nemésimo, a Native of the Island. *What especially marks the
last phase of Nemésio's best poetry–the portion of his lyrical
production that he himself considered his highest achievement*

in the genre–is his religious crisis in the early 1950s, a crisis which, in his case, means a reconversion or recommitment to Catholicism. (Nemésio had had an early religiously rebellious phase and in his student days had actually become a freemason.) The three works associated with this religious crisis–and whose very titles bespeak the poet's metaphysico-mystical drama–are Nem toda a noite a vida *(1952; Life Not All Night Long),* O pão e a culpa *(1955; Bread and Guilt) and* O verbo e a morte *(1959; Death and the Word). In a poem included in the latter book, Nemésio writes: "From the old I extracted a new man / Like one removes a thorn from the foot / I gave tidings to all / And in faith washed my blood and the pus of life."*

*Nemésio penned several other important works of poetry, including many examples of circumstantial verse inspired by various places visited–*Violão de morro *(1968; Shantytown Guitar) and* Poemas brasileiros *(1972; Brazilian Poems); a volume whose title,* Limite de idade *(1972; Age Limit), embodies the poet's protest against the retirement laws that forced him, a still vibrant educator, to exchange his teaching for a (financially precarious) life of journalism, which he nevertheless carried out admirably well into his seventh decade; and another volume of verse that, thematically and formally, comprises a final tribute to his beloved island(s):* Sapateia açoriana *(Azorean Sapateia [a round dance and popular song]), published two years before the poet's death.*

Some of Nemésio's best-known works in genres other than fiction and poetry include his doctoral dissertation, A mocidade de Herculano até à volta do exílio *(1810-1832) (1934; Herculano as a Young Man up to His Return from Exile), a biographical work on the Portuguese Romantic writer, and* Isabel de Aragão, Rainha Santa. Vida. *(1936; Life of Queen Saint Isabel of Aragon);* O segredo de Ouro Preto e outros caminhos *(1954; The Secret of Ouro Preto and Other Travels),* Corsário das ilhas *(1956; Island-Trotter), and* Viagens ao pé da porta *(1965; Travels Close to Home);* Portugal e Brazil no processo da história universal *(1952; The Roles of Portugal and Brazil in Universal History) and* Vida e obra do Infante D. Henrique

(1959; Life and Work of Prince Henry the Navigator); and Conhecimento de poesia *(1958; Living Poetry).*

Published in 1944, Stormy Isles–*a generic blend of Azorean saga, family novel, historical novel, novel of manners, regional albeit universal novel, and novel with a classic tragedy plot, as Vasco Pereira da Costa convincingly argues–constituted a surprise, which undoubtedly accounted for the relative critical silence with which it was treated at the time. (Although the novel received the Prémio Ricardo Malheiros, critically it was greeted with what has been termed a "conspiracy of silence.")* Mau tempo no canal *evoked all of those typological categories, and perhaps others (Óscar Lopes, for example, opines that* Pilate's Veranda *and* Stormy Isles *together comprise a* Bildungsroman); *but it was* not a social or proletarian novel! *The plot actually revolves around a story of unrequited love due in part to the hatred between two warring families: one, a decadent aristocratic family with roots dating back to the founders of the island and more recently to English merchants; the other, an economically ascending urban middle class family with lots of ghosts in the closet and with pretensions to aristocratic privileges. The "common" people is the least prominently featured group in the novel, although the author, as stated earlier, was careful enough to include paradigmatically representative examples of fishermen and farmers. But all these elements of* Mau tempo no canal–*the rich and integrated typological mixture, the plot, the absence of class struggle (the class oppositions in the novel have been called, quite correctly, I think, "class animosity"), the presence of "heroes," even though the male protagonist is clearly an* anti-*hero and the female a highly problematic "heroine," the relative lack of prominence accorded* the *people–were anathema to neo-realism, the literary movement that prevailed in Portugal, parallel to other movements or tendencies (the existentialist novel [Vergílio Ferreira], the* "psychologistic" *novel [José Régio and João Gaspar Simões], for example), from the late 1930s to the 1950s and, with some ideological and many aesthetic modifications, to the next decade.*

The ideology of the neo-realist movement was admittedly

and ostensibly leftist, its aesthetic a modern reincarnation of representative 19th-century realism. The writer Nemésio, politically apathetic–or, as Heraldo da Silva calls him, a "political spectator"–seemed to have little in common with this committed literature. Although neo-realist fiction was officially "born" in Portugal in 1939 with the novel Gaibéus *(Migrant Workers), the movement had its national precursors, in the case of some of their works decades earlier: Aquilino Ribeiro (1885-1953) and Ferreira de Castro (1898-1974). The fiction of the revolutionary Aquilino Ribeiro, whose early works–for example,* Jardim das tormentas *(1913; Garden of Storms), depicting the life of peasants in his native Beira province–was much admired by Vitorino Nemésio and admittedly inspired in part the stories of* Paço do Milhafre *and* Mistério do Paço do Milhafre. *Ferreira de Castro, in turn, had published two of his social novels,* Emigrantes *and* A selva *(The Jungle), as early as 1928 and 1934, respectively. Both of these writers, in other words, had already published works that fit well into the category of* engagée *literature, even though they did not necessarily subscribe to the more stringent ideological program that the neo-realists themselves would follow.*

In the novel, Portuguese neo-realism is primarily although not exclusively associated with Alves Redol (1911-1969), Soeiro Pereira Gomes (1910-1949), Manuel da Fonseca (1911-1993), Fernando Namora (1919-1989), and Carlos de Oliveira (1921-1981). By 1944, all of these neo-realists had launched significant works of fiction: Alves Redol had published four novels, including the aesthetically wanting but historically important and already mentioned Gaibéus; *the ill-fated Soeiro Pereira Gomes (he is rumored to have been killed in prison by the Portuguese fascist police; what actually happened was that he was very sick in prison, and the PIDE discharged him to go die at home, which he did: he died at the home of his brother-in-law Casais Monteiro) had published his* Esteiros *(1941; Salt Marshes); Manuel da Fonseca had launched* Cerromaior *(1943); Fernando Namora had published* Fogo na noite escura *(1943; Fire in the Dark of Night) followed, one year later, by the still more socially oriented and politically committed* Casa da malta *(1945; Tramps' House); and Carlos de Oliveira, who among the group went on to write some of the best fiction and incontrovertibly the best poetry, had already published his ideologically correct and aesthetically well-wrought* Casa na duna *(1943; House on the Dune).*

The flourishing of the social novel in Portugal was due to many factors, among them the impact of the Spanish Civil War and World War II, and the socio-economic-political situation in Portugal under the Salazar dictatorship. Ideologically, neo-realism was also a reaction against the estheticist and socio-politically "uncommitted" presencismo, *a term derived from the review* presença, *the organ of the second modernist movement (the first having been launched in 1915 by Fernando Pessoa [1888-1935] and others) founded in Coimbra in 1927 by José Régio (1901-1969), João Gaspar Simões (1903-1987), and Branquinho da Fonseca (1905-1974). Among the foreign "causes" for the appearance of the social novel in Portugal were the prestige and popularity of the Brazilian novel of the Northeast (social novelists like Rachel de Queiroz, José Lins do Rêgo, Jorge Amado, and Graciliano Ramos) and some of the better-known American social novelists of the 1930s and 1940s (who, as we know, had ancestors and early examples in Dickens'* Hard Times, *George Eliot's* Middlemarch, *and Upton Sinclair's* The Jungle): *John Steinbeck, John Dos Passos, and Erskine Caldwell (one of Carlos de Oliveira's acknowledged masters).*

Vitorino Nemésio was for a time associated with the presença *group, even though when it came to literary movements he was and would remain essentially an independent. There is no denying, though, that Nemesian and* presencista *fiction have more in common with each other than either has with neo-realism. To see the affinity between Nemésio and the fiction of some* presencistas *or one-time* presencistas, *one need but think of the tellurian and archetypal regionalism of a Torga; the psychologism of a Branquinho da Fonseca, a José Régio, and a Gaspar Simões; the aesthetic (and, in the case of Torga, humanitarian, as opposed to a stringently ideological) commitment on* the part of all of them; the stream-of-consciousness technique, borrowed from James Joyce, who was introduced to the Portuguese by presença, which informs some of the best presencista fiction and is exquisitely handled by Nemésio in Stormy Isles: An Azorean Tale.

Vitorino Nemésio–whose novel, as Heraldo da Silva puts it, "aspires to a narrative synthesis of açorianidade"–defines this term in part as a "type of drunkenness caused by isolation.... Five centuries of existence on volcanic tuft, under clouds looking like birds and birds looking like clouds, constitutes a respectable chunk of time." "For us [Azoreans]," he states later in this brief and impressionistic essay (Nemésio's applied "Azoreanity" would prove greater than his theorizing of it), "geography is like history, and it is no accident that our written memories are about fifty percent comprised of accounts of earthquakes and floods. Like mermaids' ours is a double nature: we are made of flesh and stone. Our bones have deep roots in the sea." As the concept has been applied to the study of Nemésio's fiction, "Azoreanity" has meant the identification and study of "Azorean" physical, historical, social, and religious elements represented in Nemésio's works, such as Stormy Isles.

The nine uninhabited islands of the Azores were known to exist since the 13th century but were "discovered" by the Portuguese in the second quarter of the 15th (the date usually given is 1427) and soon thereafter (starting in 1439) colonized by them. Whether Azoreans constitute a group sufficiently different from their Portuguese-mainland brethren to warrant the regionalizing/particularizing term açorianidade, has been a hot topic of discussion among many Azoreans–and far fewer mainlanders. Nemésio based the term on hispanidad, used by the group of writers and intellectuals in Spain known as the Generation of 1898. As it would turn out, açorianidade anticipated, for example, caboverdianidade, a concept with which the mid-1930s generation of Claridade in the then-Portuguese archipelago of Cape Verde tried to affirm their uniqueness vis-à-vis not only the European mainlanders but the continental Africans under Portuguese rule.

Although many Nemesian critics have dealt with the nature of "Azoreanity" and universality in his works, in my view no one has surpassed Heraldo Gregório da Silva in the treatment of this topic. The concept of "Azoreanity," broadly conceived, had been dealt with in an essay that has acquired the status of a classic in the subject: Subsídios para um ensaio sobre a açorianidade *(1964; Contribution Towards an Essay on Azoreanity), by Luís da Silva Ribeiro. The essayist Onésimo T. Almeida also has written extensively on the subject, both theoretically and in relation to Vitorino Nemésio. Da Silva's* Açorianidade na prosa de Vitorino Nemésio: realidade, poesia e mito *(1984; Azoreanity in Vitorino Nemésio's Prose Works: Reality, Poetry, and Myth), although it makes an extremely valid contribution to Nemesian literary criticism as such–its value in this case residing primarily in the analysis of the "Azoreanity" and of the mythic/Jungian dimension of the female protagonist, Margarida Clark Dulmo–is an especially invaluable geographical, historical, and sociological contribution to the overall understanding of those aspects of Azorean reality that constitute referential support to the fictive world of* Stormy Isles. *He singles out the elements of the physical environment represented in the novel (volcanism, seismic activity, flora and fauna of both land and sea, climate); he sketches key aspects of the history of the early inhabitants of the archipelago evoked or represented in the novel (Portuguese, Flemish, English); he dwells on more recent historical happenings that impact on the world of the novel, such as the loss of Portugal's independence to Spain at the end of the 16th century and the coming of Liberalism in the second quarter of the 19th; the author then moves on to a discussion of the Azorean society through the centuries, focusing particularly on the temporal setting of* Stormy Isles *(1917-1919), although we could claim that much of the history of the archipelago is "packed" into this short span of time. In the chapter dedicated to religion, Heraldo da Silva focuses on two distinct but related aspects: the author's religious stance–which da Silva once again rightly terms "ideologically spectatorial," given that* Mau tempo no canal, *begun in 1939 (the year in which the first chapter of* the novel appears as short story entitled *"Um Ciclone nas Ilhas"* *[A Cyclone in the Islands] in Nemésio's own* Revista de Portugal, *7) and published in 1944, anteceded Nemésio's "religious crisis" by roughly a decade; and the religious traditions represented in the novel, ranging from what da Silva terms "religiosidade apavorada" ("terror-inspired religion")–largely derived from the experience of natural disasters, such as calamitous earthquakes and volcanic eruptions–to a less terrific conception of the deity and saints and a more cheerful attitude toward religious practices, as prototypified by the Holy Ghost celebrations recreated in some detail in* Stormy Isles. *Nemésio gave serious consideration to the physical as well as temporal setting of the novel. Contrary to what might be expected, only half of the last chapter of* Stormy Isles *takes place in Angra, the capital of the writer's native island. Only one chapter has the mainland (primarily Lisbon and environs) as stage. The main physical setting is the city of Horta on the island of Fayal, with secondary but still important stages on the neighboring islands of Pico and São Jorge. Among the possible reasons for Nemésio's choice of physical setting, the following may be pointed out. (The narrator himself refers to the main setting of the novel with stage imagery: "From the seaward windows one also commanded a full view of the channel and of Pico. The city was a front-row theater box to that year-round stage" [Chap. II.]) This setting encompasses more of the central group of Azorean islands than any other Nemésio could have chosen. Admittedly, the author had little first-hand acquaintance with São Miguel, the largest and most populous island in the archipelago. Neither this island nor Santa Maria, Graciosa, Flores, or Corvo are directly or extensively featured in the novel. The fact that these islands are not represented directly does not mean, however, that they are forgotten. São Miguel, for example, is given historic and far-reaching symbolic representation by extended reference to the 1552 catastrophic earthquake in Vila Franca, an element that Nemésio carefully weaves into the overall economy of the novel. In a sense, the novel's subject matter is the history of the Azores and its people, represented by the microcosmic stage and actors inspired in part by those aspects of Azorean reality that Nemésio knew best.* Stormy Isles *achieves, therefore, epic proportions. It would be no exaggeration to say that the novel is the Azorean counterpart of Luís de Camões'* The Lusiads *(1572), in the sense that the history of the Azores as a whole constitutes* the *subject matter of* Stormy Isles, *just as the history of Portugal has been viewed as comprising the subject matter of the national epic poem.*

Another reason undoubtedly weighing in favor of the novel's three-island setting (Terceira, as I said, is featured as important stage only at the end of the novel and the mainland only appears in one chapter) is the fact that it represents a geographical ensemble unique in beauty and variety of referential material: "feminine" Fayal with its little cosmopolitan city of Horta and world-famous harbor; majestic Pico clearly visible across the channel or passage between the two islands, rising seven thousand feet into the Azorean sky. A key source of thematic and imagistic material in the novel, Pico is the home of its intrepid whalemen and fishermen. (Nemésio, following an opinion expressed by Raul Brandão in the book on the Azores from which one of the epigraphs for Stormy Isles *is taken, also expresses the view that the sons and daughters of Pico constitute the Azorean cream of the crop.) Sleepy and bucolic São Jorge and history-drenched, decadent-aristocratic and festive Terceira comprise the third and fourth Azorean settings of* Stormy Isles. *The heroine Margarida Clark Dulmo descends to the floor of the Fayal caldera, climbs to the summit of Pico, crosses the Fayal and São Jorge* channels *under the most dramatic of circumstances, roams in the mountainsides and sleeps in a cavern in São Jorge. At the end of the novel she attends a bullfight in Angra do Heroísmo, Terceira—and afterwards heads out to sea, where the novel comes to an end, in the wide "channel" somewhere between Terceira and São Miguel (but tellingly within the Azores and closer to Nemésio's island than São Miguel!).*

All the while, the characters in the novel are under the spell of the Azorean climate: from the raging hurricanes (called "cyclones" in the Azores) that lend the novel its title to the sti-fling humidity (and insularity) that allegedly lends people and animals a feeling of torpor to the fertile rains that bestow on all the islands the "Azorean green" and on the sea the "Azorean blue" (alternating with the "Azorean gray" that Raul Brandão and several foreign writers have perceived throughout the archi-pelago). Finally, Nemésio chose Fayal because he spent about a year there in 1918, completing his fifth year of secondary school. His immensely detailed knowledge of Fayal, Pico, and São Jorge is largely based on and seems to belie that short stay. According to José Martins Garcia, a Picoese himself, only Pico is not drawn to precise geographical and topographical accu-racy. (It is true, though, that Nemésio returned to São Jorge in February of 1943 to make sure that he avoided the "dangers of inverosimilitude" in the soon-to-be-published novel.) Add to all this the fact that–as tradition has it, and as an article by David Mourão-Ferreira of 1988 seems to conclusively demonstrate–the partially autobiographical "love story" and the majority of the main characters of the novel are so recognizably Terceiran that the author felt compelled to transfer most of the action in the novel to the three western-most islands of the Central Group. And it is a good thing that he did. One can hardly imagine this novel–even with the same plot and characters–attaining its dra-matic and poetic intensity in any other venue within the Azores.

In his article "Novos Elementos Sobre a Génese de Mau Tempo no Canal" *(New Elements About the Genesis of* Mau tempo no canal)*, David Mourão-Ferreira demonstrates what had long been suspected: that the "love story" between João Garcia and Margarida Clark Dulmo was, in fact, autobiographi-cal; and that a Terceiran by the name of Maria was the model for the novel's heroine. (The full name of the person and the cir-cumstances of Nemésio's encounter with, love declaration and implied rejection are all mentioned in Martins Garcia's* Vida e obra *[Life and Works], published in 1978.) Mourão-Ferreira refers to and quotes extensively from nine of the many letters and postcards sent by Vitorino Nemésio to the addressee (the nine were sent between 1940 and 1944). For purposes of this*

Introduction, suffice to quote the introductory paragraph of Mourão-Ferreira's study:

> *A fortunate series of circumstances is responsible for the fact that I am now in possession of an extremely important corpus of letters and postcards graciously made available to me by their addressee. These were sent by Vitorino Nemésio during a period of forty years–between 1939 and 1977–to the extraordinary Lady who was, at least since 1924, the great love of his life and the main source of inspiration for his works, so much so that she actually served as the principal if not the only "model" for the female protagonist of* Mau tempo no canal, *the incomparable Margarida Clark Dulmo... who, as is obvious, in real life was called neither Dulmo nor Clark nor Margarida. (6)*

In an excerpt quoted by Mourão-Ferreira, Nemésio writes to Maria: "I have spent my life 'inventing you.' You're the blood doll [bonequinha de sangue] of Mau Tempo no Canal" *(10).*

Temporal setting is also extremely important in the novel. In 1917-1919, Horta, then the Azorean crossroads of internationalism, was well suited to be the backdrop of a work of fiction featuring a heroine–and what a character she is, both "humanly" and literarily speaking–who takes it upon herself to do battle with the tempestuous forces of patriarchy, with all that this term implies in a geographically tiny, culturally limited, and socially archaic insular world. By Azorean standards, Horta had experienced an economic boom as a port of call and supply station for hundreds of American whaling ships starting in the second half of the 18th and extending through most of the 19th centuries. The cultivation and export of oranges, primarily to England, was so economically important that a period of Azorean art is known as the Orange Business Period (1760-1830). Because of its excellent harbor, Fayal benefitted greatly from the orange business until its collapse in the second quarter of the nineteenth century. It is in connection with the orange business that the Clarks of the novel come to the Azores.

Nemésio's conception of his heroine as being in part English, gives his "historian-narrator," as António Machado Pires has quite rightly called him, an opportunity to shed fictive light on that important period of Azorean history.

The Dabney family of Boston, American consuls and ships' agents from beginning to end of the last century–in addition to being philanthropists and true friends of the Azores–invested a significant portion of their wealth in the construction of attractive little palaces and generally raised the cultural level of the island. They were responsible for introducing the coastal-whaling industry in the Azores, an activity prominently featured in key chapters of Stormy Isles *and of major overall importance in the novel. Around the time of the novel's action, Horta was still the principal Azorean port of call for Europe-bound ships from America and had important meteorological and coaling stations. Most of all, Horta was the Azorean capital of the Trans-Atlantic telegraph cables. It was through Horta that the isolated Azores were connected to the world. And for the first time in history (excepting the role played by the islands, especially Terceira, during the period of Portuguese maritime discoveries), a good chunk of that world was partially tied to the Azores by lines of communication. And so a few miracles happened in this little land of storms, darkness, silence and torpor. The presence of foreigners, both resident and in transit (including visiting foreign naturalists, travelers and literary luminaries, some dutifully acknowledged in the novel)–from England, America, Germany, France–meant the influx of some ideas and traditions, and new possibilities for social norms and fashions that profoundly affected the Fayalese, especially the Hortese. What Francis M. Rogers writes in his* Atlantic Islanders of the Azores and Madeiras *about Horta at the turn of the century applies equally well to the period of time encompassed by* Stormy Isles:

In any event, the advent of English-speaking and German personnel at the turn of the century to join the English employees and families already there, combined with the Bensaúdes and their shipping interests, with the heritage

from the earlier Dabney dynasty, and with whatever meteo-
rologists and oceanographers were either stationed or visit-
ing there, made of Horta a true cultural nucleus. Indeed, a
well-known Azorean literary figure has written that at the
end of the nineteenth and beginning of the twentieth centu-
ries the Fayalese city was the principal center of Azorean
intellectual activity, that Walt Whitman, Balzac, and Henry
Wadsworth Longfellow were being translated by local intel-
lectuals, often earlier than in Lisbon. (183-184)

It is against this background of economic, cultural and
social effervescence (a tempest in a teacup, but a hurricane by
Azorean standards) that Vitorino Nemésio weaves his fictional
web. But, as indicated above, if his physical setting privileges
only four of the nine islands, his temporal palette is broad
enough to encompass much of the five centuries of Azorean his-
tory, including those portions of it buried in old chronicles, folk-
lore, and myth. Nemésio's professional interest in and knowl-
edge of history might explain, at least in part, the considerable
amount of historical "atmosphere" that envelopes his plot and
characters, particularly his heroine. On her father's side, as
previously noted, she has ties to 19th-century English orange
merchants. The Dulmo name, on the other hand, is a
Latinization of the Flemish Hurtere–from Josse van Hurtere,
who supposedly lent his name to the city of Horta and to sever-
al slightly different family-names, as the heroine will explain.
As happens in the novel, the history of the Flemish presence in
the Azores is largely enveloped in mythico-historical mist. On a
few facts, though, historians agree. King John I (ruled 1385-
1433) and Philippa of Lancaster's only surviving daughter
Isabel, in 1430 married Philip the Good, Duke of Burgundy, of
which Flanders was a part. As a result of the Hundred Years'
War (1337-1453), many Flemish families were scattered and
dispossessed. As the last decades of the war coincided with the
peopling of the Azores, Isabel prevailed upon her brother,
Prince Henry the Navigator, charged with the affairs of the
recently discovered archipelago, to allow a number of families

(by some estimates about 2,000 individuals, by other estimates far fewer) to settle in the Azores. Vestiges of the Flemings are limited today to a few place-names and a considerable number of family-names primarily on the islands of Fayal, Terceira, Pico, São Jorge, and Flores. In the novel, however, the Dulmos are descendants of an almost mythical fifteenth century Fernão Dulmo, "captain" of Terceira in 1486 and also credited with the attempt to discover a "hypothetical island north of Terceira." And so Nemésio, through his character's family names–and, as the reader will see, toponymy associated in turn with the historical economy of the archipelago (Pasteleiro=an area named after a Flemish settler associated with the dyer's woad industry; Flamengos=parish of the Flemings; Urzelina, São Jorge=name derived from "cudbear," another important plant in the dyeing industry)–weaves myth, geology, history, geography, economy, flora and fauna, art, religion, folklore, to mention but a few, into a tightly woven fictional fabric. Nemésio performed a miracle of sorts: he came as close as any novelist ever has to creating ex nihilo. *So rich a book from so small a world! That is why the writer has to bring every conceivable little building block he finds, every speck of scoria, leaf of indigenous faya* (Myrica faya *'candleberry myrtle', which supposedly lent Fayal its name) or cedar, every twig of auracaria (or Norfolk Island pine, introduced into the Azores by the ubiquitous Dabneys) to the construction of his fictive world. In one of the Nemésio's letters to Maria, the model for Margarida, quoted by David Mourão-Ferreira, Nemésio himself states, referring to the novel: "From the whales of Pico to the hydrangeas of São Jorge, besides a thousand and one particularities of climate, humidity and the [Azorean] soul, everything about our islands is in there" (16). This opinion is confirmed by the critic Nuno de Sampayo. That the novel is a world built of words is self-evident. What may be less self-evident is* the extent to which Stormy Isles *is a world of words, as suggested by Nemésio's use of three different names (and he did not exhaust them) for "gull":* gaivota, ganhoa, *and* garça. *The latter literally means "heron," but in the Azores refers to the more prosaic gull, which in turn, following a bit of*

delusive etymology on the part of the novel's male protagonist, allegedly lends its name to one of the two principal families in Stormy Isles: *the* Garcias.

Vitorino Nemésio is eminently a storyteller. Stormy Isles: An Azorean Tale *is, after much consideration, the title I chose for this first English translation of the novel. I will admit, though, that it fails on one count: the novel is not a tale; it is* a series of tales within a much larger tale, *a seemingly endless Chinese-box-of-tales that go on being spun within a fictive world that might be described as a spawning ground for tellers of tales. Nemésio took the art of the interposed narrator to new heights in Portuguese literature. Nemésio is the creator of two major interposed narrators for other works of fiction: Mateus Queimado (a regional name for "buzzard" which, mistaken for the* açor *or goshawk, gave the islands their name, or so goes one of the several theories concerning the name of the archipelago) and John Derosa, a Portuguese-American residing in the Azores (Portuguese-Americans will find in* Stormy Isles *much upon which to feast!). These characters have been called "heteronyms," the designation that the poet Fernando Pessoa invented for the poetic personae he created. But there are, as the reader will discover, a multitude of more or less important "narrators" in* Stormy Isles, *several of whom sometimes usurp the role of the main narrator. Embedded stories are legion in* Stormy Isles, *several of which constituting* mis-en-abîmes *of the main story, as the critic Adelaide Batista and others have pointed out. But* all *the stories-within-the-main-story bear some sort of relationship to some other story or some other constituent element of the text.*

One thing on which most critics agree is that, as Martins Garcia has put it, Stormy Isles *is "a work in which everything relates to everything else, in which everything is balanced, in which everything acquires a structure similar to a succession of swells, endlessly transforming themselves"* (Vida e obra: *83). Spiders, for example, provide the writer with one of the richest thematic and imagistic fields, as a glance at the table of contents will readily show. Although the spider supplies much of the* negative imagery with which Nemésio's unabashedly biased narrator negatively portrays some members of the Garcia family, the work of spiders–the web–is a most appropriate metaphor to describe Nemésio's own integrative procedures, as themes and images undergo linkages (and transformation) throughout the novel and blend with one another often with iridescent surrealistic effects. Another semantic/imagistic field of great consequence is music. The interrelations of the arts–in decreasing order of importance: music, painting, cinema–has hardly been critically scratched. Although J. M. Bettencourt da Câmara has alluded to a number of parallels between music and the novel–for example, its more or less obvious ABA or sonata form–much more remains to be said regarding the importance of music and the other sister arts in Stormy Isles.

Transformation or metamorphosis is perhaps the best way to describe what happens to the numerous thematic fields and strands of imagery (but not only themes and imagery...) related to animal (the spider being only one example) and plant life, disease (the plague being the most prominent, but by no means the only disease operative in the novel), music, painting, numerous intertextual relations to works of erudite literature, folk literature, historical works, atmospheric conditions, the sea, and, to make an almost inexhaustible list short, the cone of Pico–rocky, solid, eternal (though in the depths of its bowels a tenth Azorean island might already be stirring), even as the clouds around its neck and the puny humans at its feet are lulled into torpor or violently tossed in the now ominously calm, now frighteningly stormy, Nemesian "channel."

Although this is hardly the place to elaborate on the function–thematic, ideological, imagistic, symbolic–of disease in the novel, I would nevertheless like to say a couple of words on the most important example of all: the bubonic plague. To start with, Vitorino Nemésio had a first-hand knowledge of this disease, as his father contracted it when the writer was about seven. Nemésio left us vivid descriptions of the horrifying experience in the literary portrait of his father, included in David Mourão-Ferreira's "Um Inédito de Vitorino Nemésio." From an intertextual viewpoint, the reader will undoubtedly relate certain moments of the novel to Boccaccio's The Decameron, in which a group of elegants abandons the city for the mountains to escape the black death. Some readers might, on the other hand, look forward rather than backward, say to Albert Camus' La peste, published three years after Stormy Isles. It seems to me undeniable that Nemésio's novel, especially the chapters having to do more emphatically with the plague, may be read in part as existential. As will happen in Camus' novel, there are those who are committed to helping humanity make the best of the human condition symbolized by the plague, while others–including those who will eventually commit themselves–flee, literally and metaphorically, from human(e) responsibility. This dimension of the novel may be worth pondering, especially in light of the fact that Nemésio's "ideological commitment" has for so long been questioned.

A final far-reaching thematic, ideological and imagistic field is comprised of the numerous games–from hunting to sailing to billiards to card playing and card reading, to mention but a few examples. Destinies are decided, love is metaphorically won or lost at the billiards table, at the outcome of a round of bingo–or at the shot of a gun that kills an Azorean wood pigeon. Hunting, as Óscar Lopes points out, constitutes another important source of imagery and symbols in Stormy Isles. Contrary to what happens in much contemporary fiction, however, in Nemésio's novel games are still taken very seriously indeed. The thematic and formal roles of games in Stormy Isles is another aspect of the novel awaiting critical attention.

A brief note on the translation: As often stated, translating is reading/interpreting. And so my translation is my reading/interpretation of Vitorino Nemésio's novel. Although I will readily admit that no work of theory has helped me translate a single paragraph of Stormy Isles: An Azorean Tale, I subscribe in principle to I. A. Kashkin's conception of realist translation as paraphrased and cited by Lauren G. Leighton in Two Worlds, One Art: Literary Translation in Russia and America (Dekalb:

*Northern Illinois University Press, 1991), without regard to the Marxist-Leninist ideology on which it is based: "Realist translators do not traduce, because their translations are faithful in three ways: 'fidelity to the original, fidelity to reality, and fidelity to the reader.'" (74). This is the ideal I pursued, knowing full well that it is an ideal and that it is not up to me to judge whether I succeeded. Here is, in very simplified terms, what I understand by these three types of fidelity. Fidelity to the author is faithfulness to his conceptual and affective meanings, to his diction, his syntax, his style-*but only *to the extent this is possible without betraying my perception of the grammatical, syntactical, stylistic and artistic exigencies of the target-language. In other words, I do not believe that a literary translation should be a paraphrase of the original but at the same time extreme literalism or a word-for-word rendition should be avoided (except in the case of obvious explicit meanings). In* Stormy Isles, *"faithfulness to reality" is understood as an especially careful attempt to capture as many nuances as possible of Nemésio's "Azoreanity"–from an effort to find the exact English name for an Azorean plant or bird to striving for appropriate vocabulary to render an event as foreign to Anglo-American experience as the Holy Ghost celebrations. Finally, faithfulness to the reader does not mean a trying-at-all-costs to make the English version read like a contemporary American novel. A foreign novel will, to a large degree, sound foreign if there is an honest attempt to remain faithful to the author's semantic meaning and aesthetic truth, to loosely paraphrase the theorist Peter Newmark* (Paragraphs on Translation, *Clevedon, England: Multilingual Matters, 1993). And I do not think there is anything intrinsically wrong with a foreign novel sounding foreign. How could one render a chapter on bullfighting into English without sounding foreign, even with a Hemingway as model? It is true, however, that if the cultural, conceptual and affective meaning of the original can be conveyed without defamiliarizing the English language (in this case American English), so much the better for the reader and, I believe, for the writer.*

That is why, in practice, a translation needs to be two *trans-*

lations (although, hopefully, with many, many versions in be-tween): a translation of the original (the translator being as faith-ful to the source-text as is possible: some particularly difficult passages of the starting version could even be a 'crib'); and another (or many) translation(s) *of this translation, this time the object of fidelity being the reader's language: making sure, for example, that dialogues come out sounding natural, not wooden as they inevitably will sound if preserved, like insects in amber, in the original* literal *version(s). I single out dialogues because these, in my view, present one of the greatest translation chal-lenges from the standpoint of the target-language. Descriptions–although they constituted one of the crucibles for this translator of* Mau tempo no canal–*were rendered with a higher degree of literalism. A description of a landscape or seascape embodies a degree of linguistic timelessness–and in the case of Nemésio, poeticity–that a dialogue between two lovers or two bullies does not. In the former case, I leaned more heavily on the source text; in the case of dialogue, I strove for naturalness, trying always not to forsake the source-text. Needless to say, two inher-ent components of naturalness are idiomatic language and appropriate register–the latter of which can vary widely be-tween Portuguese (with its inherent affinity for latinisms) and English (with its "phrasal words... its non-abstract, Anglo-Saxon monosyllabic strength," to quote Peter Newmark).*

Sometimes being faithful to both the author and the reader means compromising. And that is what I have done in many cases, as I translated this novel that recreates a reality–physical, historical, social, psychological–that is generations removed, and in some particulars never existed at all, in the personal and cultural experiences of the American reader.

For the sake of economy, I will provide but three examples of compromise: the translation of the novel's title, forms of treat-ment in Portuguese versus English, and punctuation. Among the literally dozens of titles that I and friends and colleagues who read the different "stages" of this translation came up with were the following: Inclement Weather Over the Passage, *and* Tempestuous Weather Over the Archipelago. *Let us take up the first of these titles, one syntagma at a time. I gave up on "Inclement Weather" because, to me, it lacks the poeticity of the Portuguese "Mau tempo." I could not fully explain why this is so (and in translation, "theory" or "logic," as important as they may be, sometimes have to* and should *yield to feeling and hunch). Perhaps it has to do with the overuse of the noun* weather *in the U.S.–from* weather *reports (newspapers, radio, television) to* weather *satellites. If the reader adds to this the fact that in Portuguese* tempo *commonly means both "weather" and "time," he or she begins to get the idea that* weather *for* tempo *is no ideal solution. As far as the second syntagma, "Over the Passage," the problem here has to do with* canal *or "channel" in the original Portuguese. Using "channel" would, at first, probably be somewhat confusing to the reader, for whom "channel" is, it may be safe to assume, usually associated with* the *English Channel, in the North Atlantic, at any rate. But using "passage" as a substitute for "channel" could also lead to association with "the Northwest Passage" or some other equally familiar "passage." The French translator of Nemésio's novel, Denyse Chast, seems to have had similar difficulties in translating Nemésio's title. That is probably why she entitled the novel* Le serpent aveugle *(first edition, 1953–this title being a literal translation of the first chapter of the novel: The Blind Serpent) and* Gros temps sur l'archipel *(second edition, 1988; Bad Weather over the Archipelago). The remaining problem with Chast's second solution, I would venture, is that the potential French reader who does not already know something about Vitorino Nemésio or the Azores could not possibly know, by merely reading the title, what archipelago is being alluded to (the cover of the book contains a reproduction of Morel Fatio's* Scène de chasse à la baleine, *which could suggest many places besides the Azores; only the blurb on the back cover, penned by Jean-Charles Gateau, indicates what archipelago is being referred to). My second title was discarded for similar reasons: the vagueness of "Archipelago" and, also, the (to me) overly Shakespearean "Tempestuous" (although in some aspects* Stormy Isles *will probably remind the reader of another*

Shakespearean tragedy, of which it might indeed be considered a modern parody). *My definitive title,* Stormy Isles: An Azorean Tale, *aims at two things: avoiding the hackneyed English "weather" by substituting for it the semantically kindred but (to me) more poetic "stormy"; and identifying the major referent of the novel by using "Isles" and "Azorean," respectively in the title and subtitle. As for "Tale," it is doubly intentional: on the one hand, it is an obvious allusion to Hawthorne, Poe and Dickens, which seems to me highly appropriate (Nemésio's heroine has been viewed in part as Romantic by critics like Gaspar Simões, Óscar Lopes, and Maria Lúcia Lepecki); and Nemésio's "realism," especially his use of description to speed up or slow down dramatic tempo, reminds me of Dickens: hence, "Tale," as in* A Tale of Two Cities. *Moreover, I hope that "Tale" also calls attention to the fictionality of the novel, without detracting from the referentiality of "Isles" and "Azorean."*

When dealing with a translation from Portuguese into English, the translator/facilitator inevitably has to come to terms with the second-person pronoun (equivalents of "you") and polite/respectful/subservient forms of address, also usable in Portuguese as "pronouns." One easy–but, in my view, unacceptable–solution is to render as "you" every single, tu, você, o senhor/a senhora/vossa senhoria/Vossa Excelência. *But, needless to say, this semantic simplification would play havoc with the rigid social stratification represented in the novel and a key component of a broadly defined "Azoreanity." I decided to compromise, by sometimes syntactically and lexically recasting the original in such a way that "Vossa Excelência," for example, could be rendered as "you" while using that form of address at least once, thus preserving its cultural and ideological import. The (sparing) use of "Godmother" as a form of address is part of my desire to be faithful to the writer. The concept "Godmother" is much too important in the novel to be substituted by, say, "Nanny," whose denotation and connotation, needless to say, do not fit Nemésio's fictional world. The use of the honorific* Senhor/a *and* Dona *(title of respect, used in the Azores and continental Portugal for women of social promi-*

nence, unlike in Brazil where it is used for any woman to whom one wishes to show respect) I hope will not be too intrusive. And many other examples of such compromises might be mentioned. I strove to preserve the original linguistic and cultural flavor–and thus remain faithful to the author; but at the same time without going to the extreme of excessively taxing and alienating a modern American reader.

Portuguese uses punctuation marks, especially the comma, the semicolon, and the exclamation mark much more than does modern American English. These were respected in the translation to the extent that they do not intrude upon my perception of acceptable practice in American English or interfere with clarity of meaning or rhythmic flow. These compromises are inevitable and are probably practiced, to a greater or lesser degree, by all translators. Nemésio, however, offers the translator a particular challenge having to do with punctuation: his unusually liberal use of the ellipsis mark. As the Harbrace College Book (9th edition) teaches, one of the several uses of ellipses is "to indicate a pensive or thought-filled pause, deliberate hesitation, or an intentionally unfinished statement (not an interruption)." Nemésio uses the ellipsis mark for all these–but he also uses it as an expression of açorianidade. Regarding the Azores, he writes in Corsário das ilhas (Island-Trotter), a work published twelve years after the novel but its kindred in "Azoreanity" (I faithfully reproduce Nemésio's punctuation):

Closed ports, islands in sight... Between us and the World that portion of salt that preserves the earth... Sometimes movement and force; at other times, tranquility and wonder... Vastness... vastness... (And, no matter how much we may dislike ellipses, these typographical spasms, they are necessary... One can only express oneself in this exact blend of exaltation and halting syntax...) (44)

Stormy Isles: An Azorean Tale uses ellipses to express not only the feeling of awe before the awesome power and grandeur of nature, but also to accentuate the notion of incompleteness or *postponement that is at the core of the novel's many dramatic turns; to suggest the self-expressive insufficiency of some minor characters (such as servants before their employers) or of major characters (the male anti-hero, for example) or the excessiveness of personality of other characters (the heroine). The ellipsis mark is also one of the means at Nemésio's disposal to poetically/impressionistically* suggest *rather than describe–even though Nemésio is one of those authors kindred to nineteenth-century realists, i.e., perfectly capable of overwhelming a translator with his descriptions (of physical settings, atmospheric phenomena, moods of the sea); descriptions, I might add, that are seldom, if ever, used for mere ornamental purposes. He also employs ellipses to help create the sense of mystery that pervades the novel, even as its outcome, as in classic tragedy, is foreshadowed well ahead of the conclusion. To my knowledge, no modern work of fiction uses ellipses so liberally and consistently, even though Nemésio has poetic precedents in the aesthetic use of this poetic device: Raul Brandão, whose* As ilhas desconhecidas *(The Unknown Islands), from whom Nemésio took one of the epigraphs for the novel, had a considerable impact on Nemésio's novel. As a translator, I tried at all costs to remain faithful to this obviously ideologically expressive use of punctuation. However, in my desire to spare the reader the annoyance of these "syntactical spasms," I eliminated about a third of them. It is for the reader to decide whether I should have eliminated more–or whether the examples remaining serve the author's and translator's stated purposes.*

Acknowledgments: *I wish to thank several people whose assistance made this translation and publication possible. First of all, my gratitude to Onésimo T. Almeida, who commissioned me to translate the novel. I also want to express my deep gratitude to my wife, Maria Deolinda, for her unwavering moral support and for the lengthy sessions in which she, a native of Flamengos, Fayal, traced and retraced with me every single inch of this long Nemesian journey, either reading aloud every word of the translation while I followed the original to make sure no crook or cranny remained uncovered, or reading the original while I recited aloud–for accuracy, rhythm and naturalness of speech–my English rendition(s).*

I also wish to thank Dr. José Blanco, Administrator of the Calouste Gulbenkian Foundation, Lisbon, Portugal for the generous grant that helped make possible the preparation of the manuscript.

Finally, I express my deepest gratitude to the friends and colleagues who read and critiqued the several incarnations of the translation: George Monteiro, Nancy Nash, and Peggy Louraine. A very special debt is owed to Kelly Washbourne, whose painstaking copy-editing was instrumental in making the final translation what it is now. Any errors remaining, however, are solely my responsibility.

F. C. F.

BIBLIOGRAPHY

Included in this highly selected bibliography on Nemésio are works cited and recommended, in the latter case only those having to do, totally or to a significant degree, with *Stormy Isles: An Azorean Tale* and/or the concept of "Azoreanity."

Almeida, Onésimo Teotónio. *Açores, açorianos, açorianidade: um espaço cultural*. Lisboa: Signo, 1989.

_____ . "Açorianidade: equívocos estéticos e éticos." In Onésimo Teotónio Almeida (ed.), *Da literatura açoriana: subsídios para um balanço*. Angra do Heroísmo: Secretaria Regional de Educação e Cultura, 1987: 303-314.

_____ (ed.). *A questão da literatura açoriana: recolha de intervenções e revisitação*. Angra do Heroísmo: Secretaria Regional de Educação e Cultura, 1983.

_____. "A Profile of the Azorean." In Donaldo Macedo (ed.), *Issues in Portuguese Bilingual Education*. Cambridge, Mass.: National Assessment and Dissemination Center for Bilingual/Bicultural Education, 1980: 115-164.

Batista, Adelaide. "*Mau tempo no canal*, ou 'a luz intermitente.'" *Insvlana*, 50:1 (1994): 7-21.

Bettencourt, Urbano. "Mau Tempo no Canal - mulheres cercadas." In *O gosto das palavras II*. Ponta Delgada: Jornal de Cultura, 1995: 91-101.

Câmara, J. M. Bettencourt da. *Sobre 'Mau Tempo no Canal.'* Ponta Delgada: Eurosigno Publicações, 1990.

Cordeiro, Carlos, et al. *Açorianidade e autonomia–páginas escolhidas*. Ponta Delgada: Marinho Martos Brumarte, 1989.

Costa, Vasco Pereira da. "Lendo o trágico em 'Mau Tempo no Canal.'" In *Conhecimento dos Açores através da literatura: Comunicações apresentadas na IX semana de estudos dos Açores*. Angra do Heroísmo: Instituto Açoriano de Cultura, 1988: 115-137.

Garcia, José Martins. "Introdução." In Vitorino Nemésio, *Mau tempo no canal*. 7th ed. Lisboa: Imprensa Nacional-Casa da Moeda, 1994: 9-24.

_____. "O 'Drama Camiliano' de Vitorino Nemésio." *Colóquio/Letras*, 119 (Jan.-Mar. 1991): 136-143.

_____. "São Jorge–dos apontamentos de Raul Brandão à ficção de Nemésio." *Arquipélago: Línguas e Literaturas*, 11 (1990): 67-84.

_____. *Temas nemesianos*. Angra do Heroísmo: Secretaria Regional da Educação e Cultura, 1981.

_____. *Vitorino Nemésio: a obra e o homem*. Lisboa: Editora Arcádia, 1978; this work was reedited as *Vitorino Nemésio: a luz do verbo* (Lisboa: Vega, [1988]).

Gouveia, Maria Margarida Maia. "Vitorino Nemésio–'Ilha ao longe.'" *Arquipélago: Línguas e Literaturas*, 10 (1988): 63-83.

_____. *A viagem em Vitorino Nemésio*. Ponta Delgada: Universidade dos Açores, 1986.

Lepecki, Maria Lúcia. "Sobre *Mau tempo no canal*." In *Críticas sobre Vitorino Nemésio*. Lisboa: Bertrand, 1974: 167-175.

Lopes, Óscar. "Vitorino Nemésio." In *Críticas sobre Vitorino Nemésio*. Lisboa: Bertrand, 1974: 198-225.

Maciel, Maria de Jesus. "O Pico na prosa de Vitorino Nemésio." In *Conhecimento dos Açores através da literatura: Comunicações apresentadas na IX semana de estudos dos Açores*. Angra do Heroísmo: Instituto Açoriano de Cultura, 1988: 103-113.

Moniz, António. *Para uma leitura de Mau Tempo no Canal de Vitorino Nemésio*. Lisboa: Editorial Presença, 1996.

Moura, Vasco Graça. "Nemésis ou l'équilibre inexorable." In Vitorino Nemésio, *Gros temps sur l'archipel*. Roman traduit du portugais par Denyse Chast e préfacé par Vasco Graça Moura. Paris: Éditions de la Différence, 1988: 7-15.

Mourão-Ferreira, David. "Novos elementos sobre a génese de Mau Tempo no Canal." *Colóquio/Letras*, 102 (Mar.-April 1988): 6-17.

_____. "Um Inédito de Vitorino Nemésio: 'Retrato do Pai.'" *Colóquio/Letras*, 102 (Mar.-April 1988): 26-34.

_____. *O essencial sobre Vitorino Nemésio*. Lisboa: Imprensa Nacional-Casa da Moeda, 1987.

_____. "Introdução." In Vitorino Nemésio, *Mau tempo no canal*. 6th edition. Lisboa: Livraria Bertrand, 1980: 7-19. Mourão-Ferreira's "Introdução" is followed by ten excerpts collectively entitled "Critical Opinions" by as many critics, some of the studies excerpted in this edition of the novel being featured in this Bibliography.

_____. "Sobre a obra de Vitorino Nemésio." In *Críticas sobre Vitorino Nemésio*. Lisboa: Bertrand, 1974: 114-136.

Nemésio, Vitorino. "O açoriano e os Açores. [1928]" In *Sob os signos de agora*. Obras completas. Vol. XIII. Lisboa: Imprensa Nacional-Casa da Moeda, 1995: 88-101.

_____. "Açorianidade." In Onésimo Teotónio Almeida (ed.). *A questão da literatura açoriana*. Angra do Heroísmo: Secretaria Regional de Educação e Cultura, 1983: 32-34.

_____. *Corsário das ilhas*. Lisboa: Livraria Bertrand, 1956.

Pires, António Machado. "Nemésio e os Açores." *Colóquio/Letras*, 48 (Março 1979): 5-14.

_____. "Marcas da insularidade no *Mau tempo no canal* de Vitorino Nemésio." *Arquipélago*, 1 (1979): 79-90.

Ribeiro, Luís da Silva. *Subsídios para um ensaio sobre açorianidade*. Informação preambular. Notas. Bibliografia por João Afonso. Angra do Heroísmo: Instituto Açoriano de Cultura, 1964. Rpt. in *Obras completas*. II. História. Angra do Heroísmo: Instituto Histórico da Ilha Terceira/Secretaria Regional da Educação e Cultura, 1983: 515-556.

Ribeiro, Orlando. "Três romances das ilhas [Baltasar Lopes' *Chiquinho*, Nemésio's *Mau tempo no canal*, and Teixeira de Sousa's *Ilhéu de contenda*]." *Colóquio/Letras*, 53 (Jan. 1980): 35-40.

Rodrigues, Maria Idalina Resina. "'Mau tempo no canal'–o homem e o destino." *Brotéria*, 108:2 (Feb. 1979): 205-211.

Rogers, Francis M. *Atlantic Islanders of the Azores and Madeiras*. North Quincy, Massachusetts: The Christopher Publishing House, 1979.

Sampayo, Nuno de. "Um Grande Escritor Português–Vitorino Nemésio." In *Críticas sobre Vitorino Nemésio*. Lisboa: Bertrand, 1974: 180-197.

Sena, Jorge de. "Vitorino Nemésio." In *Estudos de Literatura Portuguesa-I*. Lisboa: Edições 70, 1981: 217-221.

Silva, Heraldo G.[regório] da. "O português oral dos Açores na prosa de Vitorino Nemésio." *Arquipélago: Línguas e Literaturas*, 1 (1985): 127-169.

_____. *Açorianidade na prosa de Vitorino Nemésio: realidade, poesia e mito*. Lisboa: Co-edição Imprensa Nacional-Casa da Moeda/Secretaria Regional de Educação e Cultura - Região Autónoma dos Açores, 1984.

_____. "Açorianidade em Vitorino Nemésio." In Onésimo Teotónio Almeida (ed.) *A questão da literatura açoriana*. Angra do Heroísmo: Secretaria Regional de Educação e Cultura, 1983: 275-282.

Simões, João Gaspar. "Mau Tempo no Canal." In *Críticas sobre Vitorino Nemésio*. Lisboa: Bertrand, 1974: 70-77.

Trigueiros, Luís Forjaz. "Vitorino Nemésio e a festa de escrever." In *O prélio solitário: temas e tópicos de literatura portuguesa*. Lisboa: Instituto de Cultura e Língua Portuguesa, 1992: 35-42.

INSTRUCTIONS TO CAPTAINS OF STEAMERS CALLING
FOR COAL, PROVISIONS OR REPAIRS

The Coast being very bold throughout, may be approached with safety within any reasonable distance.

Pilots are always in attendance to anchor Steamers in a suitable berth for coaling at the anchorage.

Pilotage is compulsory.

TIME SIGNAL–A time Signal by means of Electric lights is made daily from the Meteorological obs.y on Monte Mosso. The light is switched on at $20.^h$ $57.^m$ $00.^{sec}$ corresponding to $22.^h$ $58.^m$ 00^{sec} G. M. T. After an interval of one minute the Signal is repeated. The light being finally extinguished at $21.^h$ $00.^m$ $00.^{sec}$ corresponding to $23.^h$ $00.^m$ 00^{sec} G. M. T.

> *–Charts of the Anchorage and Breakwater of Horta and Fayal Channel* (Reproduced from the Admiralty Chart by permission of the Hydrographic Office.)

AZORE SAILOR (Ascending, and pitching the tambourine up the scuttle): "Here you are, Pip; and there's the windlass-bitts; up you mount! Now, boys!"

> –Herman Melville, "Midnight, Forecastle," *Moby Dick*

Des vents d'ouest, entremêlés de calmes, retardèrent notre marche. Le 4 mai [1791], vers les 8 heures du matin, nous eûmes connaissance de l'île du Pic; ce volcan domina longtemps des mers non navigués: inutile phare la nuit, signal sans témoin le jour.

> –Chateaubriand, *Mémoires d'outre-tombe*, L.^{e} IV

Já percebi que o que as ilhas têm de mais belo e as completa é a ilha que está em frente–o Corvo as Flores, Faial o Pico, o Pico São Jorge, São Jorge a Terceira e a Graciosa...

(I now realize that the most beautiful thing about these islands, and what makes their beauty complete, is the one island just ahead: Flores completes Corvo, Pico completes Fayal, São Jorge completes Pico, and Terceira and Graciosa complete São Jorge...)

> –Raul Brandão, *As ilhas desconhecidas*

Chapter I

The Blind Serpent

"But you won't be back soon..."

João Garcia promised that of course he would.

Margarida's eyes, deep and blue under the bold arches of her brows, betrayed a yearning for lands faraway, a momentary spark of hope. She lowered them for a moment and went on:

"And I'm supposed to believe that?"

"It'll only be a while, I promise! The course for commissioned officers will be over before you know it; in the infantry, only three months! If applications for general secretary to the civil governor are still being accepted, I'll apply. I know there are only three openings and more than a hundred idle university graduates applying, but I'm not afraid of the exams. I only need a few weeks to know my stuff."

He went into detail. Margarida listened to him somewhat absentmindedly now, her eyes on the clouds as if she had a kink in her neck. Her hair fell free, receiving the full light of the lamp, causing her face to reflect the play of shadows in the wind.

They were so close they could almost feel each other's breath: she, leaning on a volcanic wall; he, standing on the graded patch bordering the road that divided the strip of small quintas[1] stretching from Angústias up to almost the end of Pasteleiro and muffling the trot of the horses drawing the victorias of Horta. From where they were to the entrance of the Dulmos' quinta ran a loose-stone wall draped with creeping vines. Some twenty

---

[1] The term *quinta* may signify a country house, a villa, a farm, a fruit-tree plantation or garden. The term is of sufficient currency in English to warrant its use.–Trans.

meters away rose the high wall and the large green gate with the thick lintel which, on account of poorly planned spacing, when opened all the way struck the rim of the small bell bought at the auction of a wrecked sailboat. Leading away from the city, the road traced a curve along the walls bordering small checkerboard fields. There, in summer, the chirping of crickets seemed the lamentation of the oppressed island over which now hovered a torpor relieved only by the sea. Off in Porto Pim the lights on the fishing-boat nets made the massive volume of water, made choppy by a subsiding but still strong wind, even dimmer. Inside the quinta the Dulmos' dog, a few meters behind Margarida, intermittently strained at his chain and snarled.

"*Açor*[2]! I shouldn't even be talking to you so late, with Grandfather so ill. Father is getting suspicious as it is, you know."

"What's the big deal? Isn't this the last time we're going to meet?"

"The last time? I can't believe you! You talk as if everything were over between us. Even if Lisbon makes you forget all about me, we're from the same island, practically neighbors, despite what's happened. From Grandfather's Granary, I used to see you walk by the big wall every day. Yes, even before the idea of anything between us had ever crossed my mind. I had no idea then. I just can't be cooped up inside for long, though. I feel like I'm going to suffocate. Even in the Vineyards house in Pico. I feel the same way there."

"I don't know how many times you've told me that. I'm sure the reason you came here today was so that you wouldn't feel shut in," João Garcia said, smiling and recounting a litany of picayune grudges which were the high point of a relationship in which they had spoken to each other but four or five times.

The dog was restless, threatening to drag his doghouse to where Margarida stood. He was a mastiff, a curly-tailed breed

---

[2] Portuguese for *azor*, or goshawk. This bird, or a similar hawk, possibly the buzzard mistaken for the azor, is responsible, according to a popular theory, for the name Azores.–Trans.

from Terceira, a kind of bulldog, stocky and wheat-bran colored. João Garcia saw his stiff slit ears from inside the quinta, as the dog swung like a pendulum exposing his parts, unsteadily following João Garcia's every move: standing on the dirt incline, at turns slipping and finding a foothold, trying not to lose contact with the edge of the wall. The wind was beginning to stir up the faya and cedar leaves. From where João stood, it became more and more difficult for him to understand what she was saying up above at the wall. Margarida rushed to the animal.

"Knock it off! Go lie down, *Açor*! Lie down!" She placed her open hand on the animal's square head; he stuck his useless watchdog's tail between his legs.

João Garcia steadied his footing on the slope and grasped at the wall, pulling himself up like a stevedore. The dog's fury instilled in him a nervous daring, as if Margarida were in danger or wanted to test him by creating for him a weaker enemy. But now it was *Açor* who perceived João Garcia, if only his head and elbows, as being on the attack. Incited by the shadow, the dog bounded on top of his owner to attack her, his gullet strangled by the collar. Thrown off balance by the impelling force, Margarida fell. Quickly grabbing the gray coat she had put over her shoulders, she stood up to the dog, subduing him. João Garcia had sprung to her side.

"Look out! He could bite you!" cried Margarida. But noticing the dog's cowardice and realizing the danger of speaking loudly, she said: "Never mind, then... somebody could see us! No, it was nothing. I just tore my skirt." She brushed the dust off her clothes. But the rapid sequence of events made her forget that João Garcia was inside the quinta. She let him hold her hand, which she had scraped during the fall, and which he looked after like a professional nurse. "It's nothing, nothing at all." Still, there was a little trace of blood. She turned to the dog: "Stupid dog! Didn't I tell you to lie down, brainless?!"

Açor did indeed seem to have shed his watchdog's skin, his startled eyes fixed on the couple mysteriously brought together, a quiver in his thick-set, droopy, drool-dripping lips. How his

5

field of operations had changed! The enemy shadow was within the confines of the place he was under orders to guard from all solitary forms that passed that way, though he was not relieved of duty when in the presence of his owners. And if he still yearned in his loins and ached in his nostrils, dissatisfaction that became a growl that the wind echoed, it is because an engine always takes some time to stop completely after being shut off.

Margarida soon began to realize the situation they were in. Finding herself in close physical contact with João Garcia, she felt as self-conscious as when they were strangers.

"Go! Somebody could see us from the road."

"No, they couldn't. If I stand in the road it's even worse. Now that we're going our own ways, I do grant you we've been a little careless. Folks in this neighborhood are gossipmongers. But what do you expect from them? When I come back it's going to be different. If I apply... If I'm appointed.... Even if I end up third in the running. The person who comes in third will have to go up to Bragança, where it's so cold. But then, that's a year from now... right?" He waited for some kind of answer and tenderly took Margarida's hand. But now she was listening to him as if from afar and only slowly could be drawn into the warmth of his plans.

"God only knows what's going to happen to us until then." And once again finding herself between João Garcia and the still mistrustful dog, who now was scratching an ear with his paw, she walked to the wall and listened for voices coming from the road: "There are always people walking by."

On tiptoe, João Garcia went to check. Two individuals were rounding the bend of the road, their distorted shadows trailing behind.

"My uncle Ângelo and Pretextato. They're going for their usual stroll. But the closer we are to the street lamp, the worse off we are!"

Upon hearing Ângelo Garcia's name, Margarida lost the feeling of agitation brought on by her sweetheart's presence and the dog's nerves. The thought of the homosexual awoke in her the Clark family's arrogance: that important, nauseated, and somewhat cynical feeling that had helped see Januário Garcia fired from the office of Clark & Sons, an event which had enveloped the Garcia family in a disdain born more of snobbery than hatred. She pictured Ângelo with his curling-ironed moustache, his little girl's cheeks, his grayish and honey-colored hair under his derby, dragging his little limping foot as he made the rounds of Horta. The thought of her grandfather at home, always ill, merged with that brief and repulsive image. Her father was always out. Her mother, wrapped in the shawl she wore on those long nights, was forever sitting by Grandfather's armchair in an irritated mood, one to which her romantic disposition lent an out-of-tune note typical of people who laugh or cry for no reason. Margarida looked at their large house. Swallowed by the darkness that had fallen on the quinta, it was barely visible by the beam of light coming from Grandfather's room and scattering on the parlor window. A gust of wind shook the fayas and cedars, lifting the edge of Margarida's coat and a lock of her hair.

João Garcia was again holding her hand; but that interruption made it seem severed from Margarida's arm. Beckoned by the urge to go home, she was again going to tell him to leave; but then she felt his warmth there next to her midst the trees and at a distance that made the impending Lisbon trip heart-rending and endless. João Garcia seemed to have understood her unresolved feelings, and soothed her:

"Don't be afraid. Aren't I with you? And aren't I coming back in just a few months?"

"But we've been together for such a short time and you entered the quinta when it's already so dark! Suppose someone saw us."

"Your father comes home late."

"Sometimes he comes in through the lane gate."

"I'd jump over the wall."

Again the cedars made a sudden rustling noise; the gusts of wind came up again, and taking perfect aim, unleashed a test of endurance on the trees. For a second, the trees traced full circles like spinning tops slowing dizzily to a stop. Between two heavy squalls, the quinta fell into darkness and everything grew dense under a gentle breeze.

The Dulmos' quinta consisted of a strip of land tapering off to a point, with both an unprosperous fruit orchard and another small grove of trees farther on intersected by wide raised walks extending between little checkerboards of volcanic rock where centuries-old cedars, fayas, and some wild aloe sank their deep, scraggy roots. Old Clark had ordered the walks laid right after his daughter's marriage to Diogo Dulmo, whose old mortgage he had paid off. The walks were then paved with a layer of hard-packed red argil, now worn away. It was along these walks that Maria das Angústias, half housekeeper and half wet-nurse, used to push the rubber-wheeled baby carriage that grandfather had ordered from London for his first granddaughter. Ten years later, Margarida resumed the voyages of circumnavigation of her early childhood but this time mounted on a thick-maned colt, the type that farmers used for carrying large milk cans to Horta. The fodder fed to the colt at the quinta had made his hair less dull, his hamstrings more flexible. It was when she fell off him in the fig tree orchard that Margarida suffered the deep cut that left her with a scar. At home, whenever the family spoke about events that had happened seven years previous (and in the islands, seven years can be a very long time), her mother would tell her to pull her hair back and show her scar, and Margarida, assuming an ironic and distant look, would submit to the inspection. "See? Scarred for life."

Now it was João Garcia's turn to discover the scar, which she showed like the necessary disclosure of a natural landmark as they walked through the fig tree orchard. They had come toward the ravine that skirted the quinta from the road to the sea. The terrain was now by degrees reduced to bare rocks strewn with the remains of sea-singed grapevines, wild fig trees, a mat of balsam, and the first shore boulders. A wall, blending in part into the ruins of the ancient fortification encircling the island, was barely adequate now as a divider between the property and the boulders upon which seagulls came to flap their wings and squawk. João Garcia could slip through there in case they heard someone coming from the house or if Diogo Dulmo should suddenly come in through the lane gate. But Margarida no longer felt apprehensive about anybody's showing up. Deep down, João Garcia probably felt less secure than she. It was Margarida who sought to keep him close at hand as they made their way in the dark. They had already strayed far away from the light's reflection that extended over *Açor*'s doghouse, from the lamppost to the trees, and gradually distanced themselves from the speck of pale light that shone from the grandfather's room onto the enlivened parlor window. They made their way, nevertheless, as if looking for the brightest spot in the night, as much to not be seen as to say their good-byes with the ease of two people who meet in a public square at rush hour and say what they have to say to each other, hiding nothing, fearing no one. João Garcia was the only one who now seemed hesitant, hardly uttering a word. Margarida, who was sensitive to the wind and the night, drew herself so close to him that he felt his arm around her.

Almost without realizing it, they found themselves sitting on a bench made of lava and brick and bearing a ruined tile panel depicting fragments of biblical scenes and crude hunting motifs. The two seemed to have much to say yet hardly spoke. With identical posture, each leaned slightly toward the other. João Garcia had let go of Margarida's waist and hand; she now occupied herself by twisting her serpent-shaped ring between her fingers.

"I've asked Father so many times to let me go spend a few months with Aunt Teresa in Lisbon."

(Aunt Teresa, married to a naval officer, was Diogo Dulmo's sister.)

"Where do they live?"

"In Junqueira. My uncle is assistant manager of the Cordage Company."

"I wish you were there now."

"I still remember their house in Pampulha, where I went when I was a child. It was like Fayal. I don't like Lisbon, except for sailing with Uncle Saavedra in the shipyard's tugboats.

Downtown Lisbon is a madhouse: cafés filled with smoke and nasty-looking guys, all just office buildings and stores everywhere, lots of briefcase-toters." She stared at João Garcia. "Did you ever think of becoming a naval officer? My cousin Corina told me something about it. Let's see... when was that?"

"Yeah, at one time I was gung-ho to join the navy. You could get in with five years of secondary school plus some prep business courses." He gave some details about how the school worked. Margarida said "sure, sure" to the different number of bars; she knew all about rank in the military. But João Garcia was already talking about the naval secretariat corps, the corps of engineers and conductors, the corps of assistant helmsmen. Her head was in the clouds again. He continued: "It was the year of the influenza. I went so far as to send my papers in to the recruiting office, but the epidemic struck. The papers didn't get there in time." João Garcia became melancholy and withdrawn: "A university graduate is always a bit of a bore, don't you think?"

"Don't be silly! I brought it up apropos of Uncle Saavedra, who's a good friend of mine. You should see him. At fifty, he's like a kid, always thinking about boat races and tea parties on board with lots of girls. But I prefer the sea to tea parties. What about you?"

They heard the pounding of the surf, hitting the shore with the assurance of a thousand men levering a boat to sea.

"Me, too," João Garcia replied, as if he and she were ritualistically repeating a phrase said to both.

"I actually sleep better when the sea is rough."

"Does your bedroom face this way?"

"It's in the 'little towers.'"

"Where the light is?"

"That's Maria das Angústias' room; mine is the one next to it."

"Ah."

"Do you want to see my ring? It's in the shape of a serpent." With his trembling thumb João Garcia felt for the serpent's head on Margarida's finger. "It has green eyes. No, you can't see one of the eyes because an emerald is missing."

"Margarida!"

"Please, don't!"

The wind blew with that mysterious rising force that fills the lost moments. It started whistling by the dwarfish fig trees and grew more intense a way off in the distant ones, which doubled over with loud cracking sounds and prolonged rustling.

"Let's go, then," said João Garcia, slowly getting up. "It looks like the tail of a hurricane. It's the season for them."

Margarida arranged her hair and picked up her coat, which had fallen into the weeds, wrapping herself tightly. A dust storm, peculiar in that dirt-free area, burst upon them, a real cloud of sandy dust loosened from the path they trod and mixed with curled leaves made rough by milk from the fig trees. The arums, ferns, and other plants in the ravine, despite being short and sheltered in lava banks carved by torrential currents, swayed with the force of trees being shaken to the core. Between the snapping trees of the quinta and the now heavy seas covered by a cloak of darkness, they remained for a moment, suffocating, unable to walk, flipped backwards like inside-out umbrellas, gasping for any breathable air, their ears lashed by the wind and sand.

All along the ravine ran a lonely, deep-rutted road. Starting there, the Old Road girded the island like a huge ring, as if someone had laid an ashen snare for catching seagulls. It was only broken by boulders, small chunks of a fortification wall, an occasional coast guard post, the dock, and the city. Despite its being used almost solely by the Porto Pim fishermen out crabbing, the Port Authority had installed a street lamp near the Dulmos' quinta. When they had reached the shoreline boulders, João Garcia and Margarida became visible in its flickering light.

"Looks like someone's coming," said Margarida, trying to make out who it was.

"It's probably nobody." But João Garcia clearly saw the shadow of a man struggling with the huge collar of his flapping overcoat. The lamppost was swaying. A huge wave, with greenish reflections, rushed towards the shore, its white crest turning to foam after the loud crash.

"It's my father!" said Margarida, holding down her skirt suddenly blown up by the wind. One could not tell whether the bright tidal glow loomed from the sea itself or from the patch of sky pierced by a single star. "Good Lord! I can't see far enough to take another step!"

"I'll go with you up to the cedar grove," said João Garcia.

"No, no! You'll waste time if you have to come back."

"Watch out now, you're going to fall!"

The human shadow by the lamppost walked back and forth, then headed in the direction of the Old Road and the main road, keeping close to the wall. Soon after, nothing could be seen but the bobbing shadow of an overcoat.

A window partition slammed shut in the Dulmos' quinta, followed by the sound of shattering glass. Maria das Angústias was trying to secure at least the shutters. She had left the kerosene lamp on a small card table next to a roll of wire that the men who were repairing the electrical system had leaned against another package of wiring and some ornamental glass tulips. She was in the "big living room," the one with the triangular-truss ceiling and a dais leading to the chapel. A poorly anchored ladder slipped, shattering the lamp. She screamed. Her hands dripping with kerosene, Maria das Angústias fought the shutters. The package tore to pieces, some tulips broke, and the fibers of the raffia palm rushed along the wall and vanished out the window.

"The wind's blowing everything away, Godmother!"

"Call Chica!"

But the kitchen maid had decided to go nosing around the courtyard to see where the clouds were headed; and now, her unfurled shawl flapping in the wind, she struggled furiously with the door. *Dona* Catarina came running wrapped in her shawl.

"Chica! Go help Maria das Angústias. She's broken the lamp! Can you believe this storm?! She just went to the living room to close the window. You, my dear, leave it open all night!"

"Help me push the door shut, madam!"

"I can't hear you, woman! In the big parlor..." But the maid would not give up on trying to close the door, and was now putting her shoulders to the door beams. "So now suppose you tell me what you were doing out in the courtyard in weather like this? And *Senhor* Clark needing hot water! Where has Manuel gone off to? *Senhor* Dulmo's still out and no sign of the girl. Any idea where she's hiding?"

The lamp on the hearth, though sheltered by the arch of the chimney, flickered and went out. Now the only light in the kitchen came from the dying embers swallowed up by the furnace. *Dona* Catarina finally put her shoulder to the door. In that darkened corner one could hear her labored breathing, both from the effort and her anger. Short-fused, she would fill the house with her insolent presence, performing in a minute the work that several people together would take hours to do; afterwards, she would collapse in one of the oversized armchairs in her father's room and, at turns laughing and crying, would vent her hurt and shame under her shawl.

Right now, however, her outbursts were for naught. The door had been fastened with a necklace tree cross bar, which made it look like one of the walls of the quinta or the latch of the safe kept in the Granary the morning Januário Garcia (it was rumored) clumsily tried to open it, though it was so stuck it wouldn't yield. A locksmith had come to pry it open. "So, Januário, you can't even remember the combination anymore, can you?"

Dona Catarina hurried to call Manuel Bana, the quinta caretaker, who was sitting in the foyer bench, smoking. It was his habit to wait there until his boss came home for the day, and when there was "news" to report (and quite often there was "news"), he called him into the big family room.

"Try closing the kitchen door; we can't close it because of the wind. This is some hurricane! And Margarida?"

"I'll go look for her."

"See to the door first. Holy smokes, what a hurricane!"

"We are at God's mercy," said the caretaker.

Dona Catarina went into her father's room to secure the old hinged and peep-holed shutters. Old Clark was reclining in his plant-fiber armchair next to a card table, which stood lengthwise almost at arm's reach and was cluttered with medications, boxes of cigars, the whiskey bottle (to feed the fantasy that he

13

still liked a nip), and a pile of untouched copies of *The Times*. It was hard to make out his features, consumed as they were by his fan-shaped, snow-white beard, now lit up by the green-shaded kerosene lamp. He had hardly spoken a word for days. Once in a while, Maria das Angústias would come to him. Holding him–she on one side, *Dona* Catarina on the other–they helped him change positions and fluffed up his pillow. The old man turned almost imperceptibly to fix his glassy eyes on his daughter, and managed only the weakest gesture with the hand that rested on the heavy Scottish quilt covering his knees. His legs stretched down a sloping mountain of cushions.

"It's a hurricane, Father. It looks like it'll blow the house away!"

The old man did not complete the gesture. Had he been able to move better, his gesture would have meant: "Among the dead and wounded, some will come out unharmed." Although chronically ill, he was strong-spirited: the type of individual who wouldn't be fazed in the slightest by seeing in flames the room where he lay dying. Even Dr. Nunes envied him his strong heart.

The door leading from the old man's room to the family room squeaked. Maria das Angústias came in.

"I couldn't close the shutters. I had to grope my way down the hall. In the chapel, it sounds like people are rolling something."

"It must be the wine cask," said Manuel Bana, resting against the door leading from the master bedroom to the entryway.

Dona Catarina had not even noticed him. Poking her head out of the shawl, she turned in her armchair.

"What do you mean, the wine cask?"

"The cask that's missing a stave."

"In the *chapel*? You mean to tell me you store the wine casks in the *chapel*?"

A violent, roaring peal of thunder was heard, and at once was absorbed by the house, which shook from the roof to its foundation. The cedar girders creaked. Then came another, more muted rumble, sounding as if a truck-load of dock dredge was thundering down the road. A brief silence followed, punctuated by the fleeting rattle of a mirror. Against the wall between the windows, the statue of Venus remained unshaken.

"Good Lord!" White as a ghost, *Dona* Catarina had stood up; and the old man breathed a sigh of distress, as if someone had disturbed him in the depths of his grave. "It felt like an earthquake! Manuel, where is the girl?"

The caretaker was not able to formulate an answer. His hand on the doorknob, he retreated as if to make way for a chased animal. Margarida burst in, brushed aside Maria das Angústias who stood in her way, opened the parlor door, and was swallowed into the darkness of the house. Starting with the gray coat that fell from her shoulders, she left a trail. *Dona* Catarina unconsciously picked up the bundle from the floor, as if that were absolutely necessary before going after her daughter. The coat reeked of weeds and sea breeze. Her husband's figure loomed in the parlor doorway; he grabbed her by the shoulder and pushed her aside almost calmly, as if he were opening a farm gate. Blind with fury, he was wearing his overcoat and holding a switch in his hand.

"Diogo! Diogo!"

The door slammed against *Dona* Catarina with the same blind force with which the wind had resisted Manuel Bana's efforts to close the one in the kitchen. Screams followed, muffled by the lashings of the switch against Margarida's clothes.

"Please, Father! For God's sake, Father!"

"Open up, Diogo! Open up!"

The switch made a swishing sound. One could hear chairs being dragged and the sobless gasping and deep exhalations of a person who accepts her inferiority and yet fights, calling on justice and physical strength to defend her.

"Please, stop hitting me!" The switch was humming. "Father, for God's sake, stop!" More lashings. The chairs jostled again, having become like barricades at the end of the room. "Let go of me, Father! Please let go of me!"

Chapter II

The Awakening

It was almost December and daylight was long in coming. Margarida woke up late. Pushing back the sheets and slipping into her robe, she felt with her foot for the slippers on the floor, and then made her way to the window. The quinta looked as if it had been ploughed up by fantastic rigs with high blades. The cedars were decapitated, two or three of them split, showing their heartwood and soaked fibers. Here and there in the orchards, faya branches swam in huge pools. Stretches of walk had slid away, forming deep gullies and exposing clumps of crumbling red argil cut into furrows by the currents. Looking beyond the shoreline boulders under water at high tide, one could see the still-raging Fayal Channel against the backdrop of the dark, conical Pico. Smoke billowed from the stack of the *Funchal*, anchored halfway along the dock between a tugboat, a dredge, and a gunboat. Margarida noticed that the ship had something missing: half of the foremast had been blown away by the hurricane.

Maria das Angústias soon came in with tea and cookies. She tried both to console Margarida and to downplay what had happened. ("Wet-nurse" was how the family referred to Maria das Angústias, despite the fact that Margarida had refused breast milk. She had been raised on the milk from a goat with a heavy coat of yellow hair and teats large enough to fill Manuel Bana's hand.)

"You just pay it no mind now, Bidinha; don't let it gnaw away at you! Your dad has his temper. Still, going to see that young man that late, knowing that your family can't stomach his kind! Come on, let's get you some breakfast."

The morning tea, the Clarks' famous black tea, flowed golden into the large English teacup. In Maria das Angústias' hand, the long-spouted teapot looked like the first duck testing the waters after a storm. Margarida broke the silence.

"To beat me like that, as if I was a dog!" She sobbed, but tearlessly and hard-hearted. Sitting at the tiny round table, she opened her nightgown and rolled up her sleeves. She had a welt on her left leg and near her hip, a dark spot the size of a large coin. Maria das Angústias kissed her brow (when she was kissed it was almost always on the side of the scar). "But they are sadly mistaken if they think they can beat me into giving him up. They'll get nowhere. We're lovers because that's how I want it! Such conceit, such presumption, their thinking they're among the first families of Fayal when they're no more than savages! I know... Father thinks his daughter's relationships should be handled like his lover's on Bishop Alexandre Square."

"Bidinha!"

"Don't Bidinha me; it's the truth! That's why mother is always going around like a bundle of nerves, and Grandfather's old before his time because of the grief he has endured. They say it was because of his stroke. Really! His grief is what's going to send him to an early grave. The Flamengos Creek pastures sold off, the office in total disarray, the whale fishery steeped in debt, everything is the stroke. The real reason is that they fired the only person who dared to disagree with Father. Father called him 'Crook.' Naturally. But Father's ruining of his father-in-law's and his own children's fortune isn't theft: it's being the 'twelfth son of Fernão Dulmo, *the discoverer of a hypothetical island north of Terceira*, and the grandson of the Commander of the Militia Diogo Dulmo, who housed in his home King Pedro IV'."

With sarcastic emphasis, Margarida recited the noble ancestry of Uncle Mateus Dulmo, her grandfather's brother–the only old Dulmo still left in Horta. But on recalling the old gentleman, her wrath abated. She was standing by the window now. The receding high tide had by now left half of the shore boulders exposed, as well as the whole stretch of fortification wall that ran along the quinta and over which João Garcia had disappeared the night before. Uncle Mateus was a good friend of hers, a great conversationalist, a real nobleman. And what a fine smile, mock-churlish under his rimless glasses. He even spoke to her about marriage: "Over love and heat, don't pull the sheet." He would take her to the backyard to see his chrysanthemum collection. In May, the bowers almost collapsed under the weight of the burgeoning roses, Mateus Dulmo's famous climbing roses. Her uncle had just finished playing the harmonium, whose pedals he pressed alternately, his brow furrowed, like skis on some mountain of dreams amid tree branches drooping with ice–the fir branches smelling of plum pudding and the *couché* paper in her grandfather's magazines. He would always clip a bunch of roses for her with his Rodger pocketknife, and that blade click and his way of putting the pocketknife in his vest pocket were more "Uncle Mateus" than the upstanding gentleman who went to the dock for his customary stroll. "My little enchantress...." From her father, all she got were beatings.

Maria das Angústias was beating the folded mattress.

"And how did Grandfather's night go?"

"Very peacefully. I watched him so your mother could get some rest. If I didn't get any shut-eye, it was because of the storm, not your grandfather. You wouldn't know he was there, the poor guy. Manuel is the one who snored like a chain saw. He slept on the floor in the parlor."

Margarida took advantage of her father's departure from the house to go kiss her grandfather. *Dona* Catarina called her into the living room and they remained alone in there for a long time; but the tone of the conversation was low, subdued. They discussed the old Clark grudges held against the Garcia family, recounted by *Dona* Catarina with that caste-inspired rationality which belied one's notion of her hot-blooded temperament. Under any other circumstances, she doubtless would have exploded; but there were particular motives urging her to be gentle, something more powerful than her continuing her support of her husband's power play against Januário Garcia, carried out so many years ago: her lioness' love for her daughter and that unassailable pride that tolerated no brutality and made her hold her head up like a strutting dove. Her arguments were

18

simply based, therefore, on those people's low-born status—not to mention their special circumstances relative to her family. Her romantic temperament appeared collected now, without those impulses that, indeed, never altered her ladylike manner, so conscious was she of social propriety. In her reprimand, besides a kind of passive tenderness awakened by her daughter's obstinacy, there was a certain affectation—a lesson in good breeding proffered *in absentia* to her husband.

Margarida listened to everything as she leaned against the windowsill, her features inbred with that delicate sensuality (a little like her mother's) over which stood guard two trustworthy eyes, which lent her serenity and a certain solemnity. Looking out over the dais leading to the chapel, she saw the panel of Our Lady Mother of Man, whose head was turned toward the ladder left by the electricians the day before, as if the Virgin were awaiting the ascent of someone. The *Funchal* was already leaving the dock, trailed by a whitish wake that parted the channel in two. It was a gray, melancholy day.

She went up to her room and alleging an aching body and head, did not come down for lunch, having asked the wet-nurse to bring up a cup of milk.

Ever since she was fourteen she had slept in the "little towers" in the room next to Maria das Angústias'. The "little towers" were not exactly an attic, but a kind of floor shorter than the full length of the house and resting on the four corners of the great trusses of the roof. From a back window one could see the main road, but not fully—only the rooftops of the charabancs and the ears of the mules that in the afternoons would trek to Castelo Branco and points beyond by way of Feteira. From the seaward windows one also commanded a full view of the channel and of Pico. The city was a front-row theater box to that year-round stage.

Margarida spent part of the day lolling in bed. She was absorbed in pacing back and forth between the windows and the Honduran mahogany bureau, in whose secret drawers she kept colored stickers, a set of little Chinese boxes that a pharmacist had given her when she was a little girl, and an inch-thick copy

of *The Lusiads*, a present from Uncle Mateus. On top of the
bureau lay novels by Júlio Dinis[1], two or three by Camilo[2],
English history books in sea-green bindings, and German textbooks. She had taken German lessons with Fräulein Wartel.

Margarida was not very sure about what attracted her to
João Garcia, who at that moment was undoubtedly already
beyond Velas. He had arrived from Coimbra a little less than a
year earlier, having recently finished his baccalaureate. Still
young, they had initiated their courtship in church. But how
long ago that had been! More than her soul, her body held from
that Sunday Mass something formless and nameless and so far
removed from him that it acquired in her a life of its own. That
something grew in her, not asking anyone what purpose it
served. Then she had seen him again while visiting at the Peters'.
As always, she had asked the old ladies to accompany her to the
spot by the chestnut tree. It was August, and the rooms in the
house felt stifling under their apple tree ceilings. The rooms
were huge but cluttered with Indian chests piled up under portraits of all the family's first born male heirs, the *morgados*. In
fact, the ladies had left their visitor standing in the garden to
come and greet her. "A visitor whom I do not know whether
we...,"–*Dona* Corina Peters had said, with her enigmatic smirk.
She was a bluestocking, very fond of mysteries, and a backer of
bookish pursuits. Her sweet little eyes spoke of the woods of
Atala, and she displayed a saucy innocence, under a head of
grey hair.

To Margarida, João Garcia seemed pleasant, well-mannered.
He really was not her ideal type of masculine beauty–too skinny,
disconcertingly shy, something not quite together about his
whole appearance. He had a habit of putting his left hand under
his crossed right leg, was not very well dressed (even though he

---

[1] Portuguese novelist (1839-1871). His Romantic-Realist novels reveal an
optimistic view of life; his happy-ending love stories make him a favorite with
the young.–Trans.

[2] Camilo Castelo Branco (1825-1890). Portugal's most prolific and renowned
Romantic novelist.–Trans.

wore a tie that revealed good taste), and tugged at his chin when he talked about pranks in Coimbra and about historical things of the island, for example, the discoveries and the convents. His eyes sparkled with enthusiasm, and he had very expressive hands. If he referred to something round, he would cup them as if he were peeling a fruit. He had a fleshy, somewhat sweaty nose; but he had an attractive forehead and a nice head of hair. (An odd sort of fellow!)

The newspaper *Insulano* had said as much as possible about a local boy who certainly did not belong to the island noblesse. Whenever a recent university graduate arrived, the paper published half a column of praise. In his case, there had been almost a full page and his faded picture. (He had stubbornly insisted that it be that picture; unfortunately, the most clearly visible part of the photograph was a pedestal and vase. Defamation of character!) The paper mentioned that he had been president of the student association, the author of the valedictory, and that he had sent the *Diário de Notícias* some very important articles on the administrative autonomy of the Azores islands. She would ask Uncle Mateus about the matter.

Moreover, she knew that when he was a freshman, he had published a drama in verse; but Margarida did not like poetry. That is, she liked some poems when she felt bored, for example, "Jesus in Nazareth," by João de Deus [3] (*Once as a child, he was walking along... The outskirts of Nazareth...When, lo, he spotted in a bush...*) and certain passages of Guerra Junqueiro's *The Simple Folk* [4] (*You, who art so young, with eyes the color of hope... whither art thou bound?...*). But she had been bored silly with poems by island poets-"tender petals," "I love you in the afternoons." And so for her, "poet" had stuck in her mind as the

---

[3] Portuguese Romantic poet, João de Deus (1830-1896) is especially well known for his Cartilha or 'Primer', used in Portugal until quite recently. Several of his lyrics, including "Jesus in Nazareth," are included in children's textbooks.–Trans.

[4] Realist poet, Guerra Junqueiro (1850-1923) is especially known for his satyrical, religiously irreverent verse and for his later poetry extolling the virtues of country life, *Os Simples* (The Simple Folk; 1892) being a good example.–Trans.

vague equivalent of imbecile and stunted creature. The poet she really liked was her cousin *Dona* Corina, but without her *Leaves in the Wind.*

After the meeting in the Peters' backyard, she did not see him for some time. She had spent the end of August at the grape harvest in Pico, in the vineyards that Grandfather still owned in Campo Raso between Candelária and São Mateus. In September, she had fulfilled her life-long dream of climbing Pico to the summit, even though it was not the best time for it. One had to spend the night halfway up the mountain in a cavern. In the morning she had drunk warm milk from the cow her father (in this he was a good friend!) had Manuel Bana milk, having had the animal brought up the day before so that it could arrive rested and as close as possible to the sleeping area. The day was not very clear; but she had watched the sun come up over Terceira, all bloody in a sea of lead, a sea she had never seen before, fresh and with nothing to break its unmoving limitlessness except for the dark islands shimmering in the mist. In the direction of Flores, a sad-faced moon was about to die. But she felt happy to see the sun slowly rising towards her; she waited at the rim of the dormant Pico crater, holding a metal-tipped walking stick in her hand. The bulky mass of São Jorge, stretching from Point Rosais to Topo, looked like a ship made blue by the very smoke of its passage toward the "hypothetical island" of Fernão Dulmo, the island that before any other saw the birth of the sun.

In October, she spent a few weeks in the city in Grandfather's Granary. João Garcia would stroll by in the afternoon, a cane hanging from his arm, accompanied by Dr. Luís da Rosa, who looked like a beanpole. Margarida usually embroidered on the terrace with her cousins Lemos; at other times it was with Maria da Paz, but with the latter, she did not attend to her embroidering, but joining in laughing themselves silly and eating pears, skin and all.

All this entered her mind like the sea slowly seeps into a grotto, gurgling its way in without direction or resistance–a mere drifting of waters. Just those thirteen months, so like any others after all! His letter was kept in the drawer along with many other letters of the same type; Margarida went to get it. Decidedly, it was simply this: the palpitation elicited by a paper that laid so many things before her (the letter ran to four sheets of paper!) without stirring her passions, and gave her the same impression she gathered from looking at the sea from the summit of Pico, a desire to let the water rise without knowing the reason why. Was she fond of João Garcia? She had never been fond of any man. She sensed an ill-defined feeling welling in her that could well have been the memory of boys, but when they were near the feeling swelled, its pleasure turning to pain in her breast. Whatever the feelings were, they were no more powerful in the presence of João Garcia than of any other young man. Perhaps even less so. But if those feelings did not light the fires in her that, for example, Álvaro Bettencourt did when he departed for Africa, they now took possession of her by way of a door that had never been opened in her before, a secret entry, not providing access to the great desire to be swept away, as she had in Bettencourt's case, but to remain who she was, locked away in her room with that switch-inflicted welt on her body.

It was five o'clock when she heard a voice calling hastily:

"Bidinha! Bidinha!" A little girl was in the doorway, decorating it with her springy golden locks and china-blue eyes. A schoolbag hanging across her shoulder, she stood there like a player who awaits the shout "I see you" in the game of hide-and-seek. "Mother said to come eat." The little girl started to close the door behind her, her initial joy waning: "What's the matter? Have you been crying?"

Margarida dried up her grief-laden, soulful eyes. She stood before the mirror at the washbasin in front of the bureau, in whose marble bowl a vase holding blue flowers thrust out its belly full of water.

"What a silly idea, Cecília! Bidinha never cries, you know that! The one who cries is a certain little girl I know, when *Dona* Cremilde orders her to go stand in the corner."

"Naah, naah! But today I didn't get punished. I had two C's! Bebé Lemos is the one who got hit with the pointer."

"And why was that?"

"Well, she starts saying silly things, like Titó is her boy-friend, and instead of copying the wine jug, she gives him chestnuts and chocolate wrappers behind my back. *Dona* Cremilde sent her to the board; she was explaining that stuff about the triangle that looks like a gourd... what do you call it?... the one that has the sides all messed up?"

"See? See?" said Margarida sweetly, breaking into a grown-up smile, arching one corner of her mouth. "A *scalene* triangle, silly! You are the one who is all messed up.... Look how you've got your cap!" She straightened it. "Come on, let's go downstairs... Take all that off! The schoolbag stays here so we can have a look at your math later."

They went downstairs. Their father was seated at the head of the table, slowly sipping his soup. Margarida gave him a very reserved kiss and sat to the left of her mother. At the opposite end of the table was Grandfather's place, left vacant months ago. With her back to the window sat Maria das Angústias preparing Cecília's steak. Ever since her brother Pedro had gone away, the little girl had laid claim to a larger area of the table.

"A letter from your brother," said her mother.

Diogo Dulmo handed the letter to Margarida on the very tips of his fingers, which he then used to wipe his moustache with a napkin. He had a red moustache, the same color as his heavy brows, so that one could not tell he was in a bad mood if not for his scarcity of speech. Otherwise, his whole person breathed that air of easiness and self-importance typical of those who lead an unencumbered existence and don't stand for nonsense.

Margarida kept reading, feeling as if she had come upon an unexpected chair at the far end of the garden. Her eyes shone brighter, her nostrils flaring from her breathing.

"Your soup is getting cold."

"I don't feel like eating anymore, Mother." The paper rustled.

"Even when you don't feel like doing something, you do it anyway, for that very reason," said Diogo. "But if you really don't feel like it, don't. Far be it from me to go against people's wishes where that's concerned. *I* know what would boost your appetite... a good tennis match. Speaking of which, Pedro says that your rackets always got mixed up. A likely excuse for his losing.... He comes in on the next ship." Margarida kept silent. "Didn't you read that?"

Diogo Dulmo had uttered "Didn't you read that?" looking straight at his daughter, indicating that he considered the silence already a little too long.

"I'm sick and tired of playing tennis."

Her father let a few moments go by, raising his eyebrows like someone who has not the least intention of flying in the face of another's wishes.

"Well. You can do something else. Sewing, for example. That's not a bad idea for a change. You don't vary your activities much."

Dona Catarina was beginning to show signs of frayed nerves.

"Cecília, tuck your elbows in! *I* see to Margarida's sewing." "Of course!"

An embarrassed silence fell, punctuated by the comings and goings of the servant clearing the table. And then Maria das Angústias, who ate slowly and with impeccably good table manners learned in twenty years of working for the family, set her silverware on the plate and ventured:

"I hope that this year Pedrinho gets the same riding instructor. The poor dear, he was so afraid his teacher wouldn't be back to the boarding school!"

"And why is that?" asked Diogo Dulmo, annoyed. His son's education was a subject he only thought about twice a year: in October to send in the first thirty milreis, and in June to have the last thirty sent, along with the fare for the boy to come home on vacation.

"So you don't know that his riding instructor's an officer who was going to be transferred from Lisbon?"

"Really? They'll get another one. And who could I transfer in to pay the bills?"

It was an old argument. Diogo Dulmo favored the school in Horta, which boasted easy access to bars, ferry trips to Pico, the Fayal Sport Club (he was a founder), and employment at Trans-

Atlantic Telegraph Cable Company, where the Clarks' firm was a grapevine of fat juicy contacts. But *Dona* Catarina had cast her vote for the elegant tradition of Colégio Arriaga (which bore the name of an islander, that of a former president of the Republic). Her father-in-law had supported her, being unable (at the end of his life) to do for his grandson what he had done for his son Roberto, that is, to send him to London–a great huge land that could drink up all the Dulmo blood circulating in the veins of a Clark.

"I'd like to learn how to ride a horse too," said Cecília, making galloping noises with her tongue. "When Bidinha was my size, she had a teeny-weeny horse."

"And you have a cardboard one that Uncle Saavedra sent you," replied Margarida, who, having folded Pedro's letter, was absentmindedly staring at her sister.

"Yeah! But that one doesn't walk. Yours was for real. He kicked you." She pointed to the scar on her forehead: "There it is–'the rooster!'[5] Cock-a-doodle-doo!"

"Don't be silly. It wasn't a kick!" said the mother.

Margarida, aroused by Cecília's liveliness, came out of herself:

"Hold your horses, munchkin. One day we'll go riding together." She blew on the hot chestnuts; she enjoyed bouncing them from hand to hand until their shells cracked. Then she removed the last thin skins with the quickness of a monkey.

Their humorous interlude cheered up Diogo Dulmo:

"All you have to do is say so. I'll have Jewel brought up from the communal pastures. Eight days of stable fodder and her coat'll look like a thoroughbred's. For Cecília, we'll borrow Pintado's tame pony."

"Yes, dearest, you really should bring Jewel!" protested *Dona* Catarina, who had an aristocratic conception of horseback riding. (The Dulmos, despite descending from the first inhabi-

---

[5] In popular language, a bump or protuberance on the forehead is referred to as a *galo* 'rooster.'–Trans.

tants of the island, rode unbroken, wild horses.) "Besides, Margarida's riding outfit isn't ready to go."

"I aired it out yesterday," said Maria das Angústias. "Since that ride that Alvarinho Bettencourt organized, Bidinha hasn't worn it. And it looks so cute on her. Unless she's still against wearing her derby."

Dona Catarina coughed. It had been her great dream to marry Margarida to Álvaro Bettencourt as soon as the girl came of age. Álvaro was so high-born, so refined. And a good person, as was to be expected of any son of Isabel! Both Isabel and she had attended Mónicas private secondary school in Ponta Delgada. The year was 1890. Count da Milhã on Pêro da Ponte Street, his frock-coat pockets full of custard tortes; she with a little crush on one of the Botelhos de Teive boys, Isabel already committed to her Jorge de Bettencourt. Then Fayal, the king's visit, Isabel's death from tetanus! And that ball in Amor da Pátria....

"What a sad lot, the way things turned out for Álvaro!" she thought. And for a long time she looked in the direction of a painting depicting a downward-facing deer, its very noble antlers standing high up above its glassy eyes, a trickle of blood running from its nostrils.

Margarida likewise was absorbed in what she was doing: making the chestnut shells crackle under her thumb. Stiffly, Diogo Dulmo got up from the table, went to wind the tall clock, and said to Maria das Angústias:

"Manuel Bana may close the gate at nine o'clock. I'll be coming home late today."

Chapter III

A Close Family

In winter, dinner at the Garcias' was served with the lights on. Januário was in the habit of closing his office at four but remaining inside working alone. Through the glass door, on whose lintel hung a wooden signboard that read SOLICITOR AT LAW, one could see his elephantine frame busy at a desk lit by a pull-chain bulb. He wore his hair cut in bangs. In Cathedral Square, the light afternoon traffic was thinning out; the first store lights stirred the shadows; the big, squat Jesuit church extended on one side to merge with the balconies of the Civil Government building. Januário rose heavily from his chair, went to the safe, and struggled to pull out his jumble of keys from his back pocket, the shadow of his frock coat growing larger on the wall. As he tried to pick out one key, they all became tangled, as always. Finally, the dark and slow bulk of his frame headed out in the direction of Jesus Street, leaving the office windows in cold darkness.

The Garcias' dining room had two glass doors leading to a small boxwood garden with a rosemary shrub at the center. The lightbulbs over the table, adapted from an old chandelier, cast a yellow glow on an ashlar staircase, whose iron railings, in the manner of those bordering graves, extended from the garden down to a ground floor storage room. When Januário raised his head from the plate to look outside, however, he saw a wine cask, boxes, and a mattock.

"It seems that Emília has been feeling very ill," said Ângelo. "Pretextato heard in Alexandrino's pharmacy that she's got the plague. She has a tumor on her neck. They're the worst kind; for, you see, those in the groin, according to Dr. Mesquita...."

"May she rest in peace, since all she brought us was grief," interrupted Henriqueta Garcia, emphasizing the insensitive epitaph.

"There you go talking prematurely about the girl's death!" said an annoyed Ângelo Garcia, arching his eyebrows oddly. "Neither one extreme nor the other, for Christ's sake."

"I've told you time and again that as far as we're concerned, she might as well be dead already! You needn't try and sell me on her." (Januário was staring at Ângelo) "nor sing prayers for the souls of those who may or may not need them." He crumbled a biscuit.

Henriqueta chewed slowly, savoring her pork. Her slender little body struck the only note at that table of a life filled with common pursuits, connected to one another by well-cherished moments, good and bad. Ângelo was full of life and had a saying for every occasion. He extracted conversations from the most far-flung corners of meaninglessness and silence. He cautiously stole upon a topic like one catches a mouse by the tail; then, drawing back and feeling radiant, he let the mouse kick about. In this he was very much like his sister; what set the two apart was that Henriqueta's courageous and strident ill humor was in the bachelor closer to annoyance and indifference. Seated at the table one in front of the other, they were like two counter-tuned violins of prodigious virtuosity. At the head of the table, Januário made his bass strings vibrate, every so often with decisive changes in tempo.

There was a brief silence. Then he read from the paper:

"*Lately, on the neighboring island of São Jorge, there have been a few cases of the plague, especially in the town of Calheta. Dr. Manuel José Nunes, the honorable Secretary of Public Health, has taken all measures warranted by this situation, there being no cause for alarm.*' Januário folded the newspaper. "This damned plague doesn't leave the islands!"

"St. Sebastian, help us in the name of the wounds of your blessed body!"–*Senhora* Maria Florinda whispered at the end of the table. Mother of those three, she announced her presence with a ringing and harmonious cough, like those heard in church during silent meditation. Stooped and trim, only her white hands could be seen against the blotch of her merino shawl.

"Despite it all, we must give thanks to God. Don't you remember the plague in Terceira, in 1908?" Henriqueta reminded them.

"That's what I call a tragedy," said Ângelo. "In only a month, more than a hundred people died. And not only that. With the pneumonia cases, all they did was wrap the victims up in a shroud and toss some lime on top!"

"The government should make provisions, and they don't," Januário remarked. *There being no cause for alarm!* As if last year in Pedro Miguel people hadn't dropped like flies, and all those poor wretches without serum... without medical attention... stuck in one another's homes!"

"Low-life people who sleep with the pigpens right under their noses."

"Come now, Ângelo! Where would you have them put their pigs? All they have are tiny shacks with only a door and a peep-window, just miserable hovels...." And Henriqueta stooped to suggest the low ceilings in Pedro Miguel. "Those poor people!"

"But the civil governor is the one obligated to look into these things like in Terceira, where they summoned Dr. Sousa Jr. and founded the League Against Rats. What good is the money in the Charity Fund? To give a job to some bum living high on the hog?"

Ângelo remembered his former goal of becoming a clerk for the Fund in order to get away from his brother's office and out from under his thumb.

"No. They've got their hands full over there. Pretextato's cousin, a self-assured lad and soccer player, does a good job of keeping the books." (Ângelo was the only one who pronounced Pretextato's name with the proper Latin harshness; the others just let it flow rapidly: Protestato.) He became pensive. "I always heard that the Fund was very well administered."

"That's just idle talk from Pretextato, who is buddy-buddy with Nunes."

30

Januário started to complain bitterly about the oranges. He was sick and tired of telling the workers in Fern Lane not to pick them from the trees, that first they should gather the ones on the ground. Henriqueta explained that these four were out of a dozen or so that she had ordered picked for *Dona* Carolina Amélia's preserves, which took peel and all.

"That marmalade from the Clarks' recipe, the stuff the English eat for breakfast."

"I know very well what it is; the Clarks have nothing to do with this.... What we're talking about is oranges. It's only right that we should send the preserves to *Dona* Carolina Amélia: it has always been traditional to do so on the day of Our Lady of Conception. But if you thought eight oranges were enough, why did they pick a full dozen?"

"All right, Januário; next time we'll send for only eight. How was I supposed to know!"

"Did you see the basket of camellias that Belina brought from Fern Lane?" asked Ângelo, who was crazy about flowers. He always wore a violet or a carnation on his lapel.

"Nobody pointed it out to me."

"Come on, now! When you arrived, it was time for us to have dinner," remarked Henriqueta. "They're right there."

Januário raised his double chin to look at the centerpiece, heavy with leaves, in a striped, greenish glass container.

"They're beautiful!"

"They really are!" said Ângelo, arranging the camellias. The pointed and sturdy leaves covered his hairy wrists. "Dulmo doesn't have this kind in Pasteleiro; only if you gave him a stake...." He smiled.

"The real stakes are the Flamengos Creek pastures I just bought this morning from Manuel Frade, from Salão parish, who in turn bought them off the Dulmos. The deed has just been signed."

"The *Americano*? The one who loaned the twenty thousand to that scum?" asked Henriqueta. "So you really bought the Dulmos' pastures? That's my brother! That's the way to give it to 'em!"

31

Henriqueta's exclamation rang with the tone with which listeners of cloak and dagger novels celebrate the demise of the traitor. Only Ângelo, who was still tending the camellia buds, seemed disinterested. Besides, he had been present at the signing of the deed. Januário savored his triumph.

"It's true. That beautiful stretch of pasture! The broken up areas produce corn; there's a depression where the grass sprouts right at the beginning of winter–and no easement to anybody." He got up full to bursting, and filled with a happiness that floated on the surface of his words. "If João is lucky, maybe he'll come back as Secretary General of the District of Horta. We'll celebrate with a cattle-branding party. I bought the Frade livestock. Beautiful place for a country festival whenever a gunboat is in the dock! So that these so-called blue bloods can see that the rest of us know what we're about."

The old lady got up from her chair, pushing her glass of milk aside. Stretching her pointed and toothless jaw, she clasped her hands:

"In my prayers, I only ask of God that He preserve your good hearts, my children. And that He pay you back, Januário, for all the good turns you've done me.... You are a true son of that saintly and honorable notary Severino!"

"There goes Mother," said Januário, turning his huge frame seated on the side of the glass door leading to the storage room staircase.

"May I live a thousand years, my dear son!" And kissing the three Garcias, she disappeared into the kitchen, hunched over and wrapped in her shawl. One could still hear her wishful words: "Yes, one thousand years.... And everybody at peace! Everybody at peace!"

Januário went down to the foyer office, as he was wont to do. There he neither worked nor received visitors, but he always had papers to take out of the safe and sometimes a letter to write. Henriqueta finished clearing the table and went to give orders in the kitchen, which was full of steam and plumes of smoke from the dishwater in the clay bowls and from the hearth. Ângelo went up to his room, a toothpick hanging from his mouth. Later they all met in the family room. Henriqueta sat on the couch and Ângelo on Carlota's piano stool, making it swivel. They were waiting for their niece, who had gone to dinner at the Honórios'.

"So, tell me, how's Emília?"

"She's in bad shape."

"Is it life-threatening?" Buried in her dark skirts, which felt soft to the touch of hands roughened by the crochet needle, Henriqueta opened her eyes, waiting for an answer from her sulking brother.

"You talk as if you cared! After the grief she brought us? A little late with your sympathy, dear old sister of mine...."

"Don't you come around with your insults! You know very well that what happened in this house wasn't my fault. If I warned Januário, it was because I had all the evidence right in the palm of my hand!"

"In the palm of your hand! What about the pried-open drawers? And the chair behind the powder room door? And your peeping over the doors?"

"You miserable scoundrel!"

"Don't go getting all excited...."

"You dirty rat!"

Ângelo had crossed his arms in his typical annoyed manner:

"Come on now, Henriqueta, let bygones be bygones. It's all water under the bridge. All I want to say is.... Well, I am not saying that you were not right in suspecting something. Emília was a little careless... always a little rash.... But remember what she did for us when Father died and Jacinto got married, when he refused to help us. He saw himself with his own pharmacy (Januário was stupid for loaning him the money!), and instead of working one or two years for Mother and you, who's been everybody's mother around here.... I'm not just talking about me–I was already set up in Meireles' notary office. He paid me badly, and I was still sleeping out of the house, at the Delma's boarding house. It was a living.... But what about the rest of you? What would have become of you if Emília hadn't convinced Januário to let you live in the house? Yes, we already had one albatross–Aunt Secundina. What would've become of you? Tell me. I'll tell you–you'd be in dire straights in Praia do Almoxarife, right next door to the rich sister-in-law of ours...." He sniffed. He was on the warpath against Henriqueta, his hands on his knees, propelled by his own incontrovertible logic.

Henriqueta looked through the sheer curtains over the window leading to Jesus Street, pondering that past. How hard it had been to walk down to the boat launch at Praia do Almoxarife, with the winter tide shaking the back side of that shady little house with only three windows and a ground-level storage room. Her eyes seemed to swing like a pendulum between the parish and Horta. They had yellowish rings caused by liver problems. But her lips knew how to wake her up and how to quiver. When at rest, her mouth was small but ugly. When she was speaking, however, everything came alive: sparks of saliva scintillated, a yellowish shadow flitted from tooth to tooth. Then she took a thread of logic, steeped it in her warmth, and ended up twisting it into an almost sentimental silence.

"In the name of our departed father, Ângelo! I swear to you that I never bore false witness against our sister-in-law Emília!"

"Will you excuse me a minute? It sounded like Mother's voice. I hope she doesn't fall down the stairs...."

Henriqueta got up and went to the living room. A jardiniere with a thick stand obstructed the way, forcing visitors and household members to trace a circular path around it. The cherry-colored draperies were stayed by large, golden curtain hooks with molded rings. Pleated and made of a deep, smooth velvet, they looked like ancient lancers' skirts cut in half. On the mahogany console table lay an arched glass case with the crown and scepter of the Holy Ghost–much worshipped in the islands–with surmounted doves fastened by screws. Henriqueta spruced the flower vases filled with camellias, snuffed the oil lampwick squeezed in its little capsule, and fussed about with practical intentions. Above the upholstered sofa in the opposite corner, there rose a vast frame with her portrait at thirty, her hair in curls, slim-waisted, her eyes with a touch of charcoal–by *Leoncio, photographer*. And she saw, suspended from that same cord, another picture: a sad and pretty profile with more char-coal on the eyebrows than hers, a round bust held by an enor-mous brooch, which her picture did not have. She trimmed the charred ends of the candles throwing light on the Holy Ghost but did not bow her head because her eyes were drawn to a beautiful enlargement next to the glass case–one of João Garcia, standing and holding his fifth-year student's briefcase.

"Aunt Henriqueta...."

"I'm coming."

Januário's authoritarian and insinuating voice was heard, followed by the Garcia women's good-night, which signaled the end of another full day. Henriqueta half-opened the family room windows but could only see the cobblestone street, the narrow sidewalk, and the corner lamp of the side street. The entry gate squeaked on its hinges.

"So, how was your afternoon?"

"Passable...."

"Did you eat all right? You're all skin and bones, Carlota; just look at these shoulders, here...." Carlota, seated at the piano stool, absentmindedly rolled back and lifted up the lid and then ran her fingers over the keyboard. "Come on, girl, can't you at least say what you had for dinner?"

"The soup was chick-pea." Out of the piano came the first weepy sounds of *The Blue Danube*. "Oh!... And meat-pie."

Henriqueta squeezed her shoulders gently:

"It's too late to play the piano, Carlota. Grandmother's al-ready in her room, and so's your father."

They all exchanged good-night kisses on the brows, which bore the mark of the destiny of each of them. Only on Carlota's hair did Januário's hand linger a little longer. Then it traced a heavy arch over his frock coat and came to rest on the knob of the door leading from the family room to his room.

The two single brothers, *Senhora* Maria Florinda, and Aunt Secundina slept on the second floor. One climbed up a narrow staircase, like those seen in pictures in which an angel has to ascend leading a soul by the hand. But the rooms were decent, quite wide, with windows toward the backyard. The rooms led

35

to a hallway that separated them from the garrets, which were filled with old junk: duck-bill shaped bathtubs, couch legs and old pictures, and cardboard boxes smelling of sweet mildew piled up under the skylights. Henriqueta and her mother slept in the same room, next to Aunt Secundina's, which had a window with a slit looking out over *Dona* Catarina de Ataíde's roof. "These are the deaf lady's bedclothes," the cook, standing at the washboard, would say whenever someone noticed in the middle of a conversation the sheets full of yellow stains being scrubbed with bleaching powder.

The deaf lady was the Garcias' great-aunt, sister of the "old notary public." She was rumored to be one hundred years old, tough and mean. She still remembered the waterspout that had leveled Pasteleiro and, along the shore, before the Old Road was built, left a row of one-story little houses bearing Public Works signs:

IN REMEMBRANCE OF THE 1832 FLASH FLOODS.
REBUILT AT THE EXPENSE OF THE ROYAL TREASURY

Aunt Secundina had not been out of the house in over ten years. She spent part of the day reclining on pillows, with her roving eye and her jugular veins prominent under her one strand of hair, dark as a parasite. Every morning she sent for Henriqueta to wash her face and part her hair in the middle.

Henriqueta went to check on Aunt Secundina before retiring. The deaf old lady had not slept part of the night, but she did not heave a single sigh of complaint. From the depths of her pillow, her charcoal eyes transfixed on the white belly of a giant statue of the Child Jesus. With the help of gestures, Henriqueta asked about her leg. How was it? It was all right. Her problem was a varicose vein twining her flabby muscles like the insignia of the Order of the Garter. Between her hip bones, where one could divine a possible blueprint for what would become Januário's torso, there was hidden a dried-up birthmark. Henriqueta turned down the bed clothes to ward off the stench of urine.

"Did Encarnação change you twice as usual?"

36

"Once.... She only did it once."

"But I told her to come upstairs before setting the table."

"She is a mean bitch."

"Please, Auntie! Let's not have those obscenities." But the old lady was speaking naturally, without hatred or in complaint, like an explorer who refers, using the correct names, to the species of animals of a country she is about to leave.

"But nobody can be constantly changing someone who lets herself go like that! If you made more of an effort, Auntie... if you only tried to hold it...."

"Hold it? Hold this!"

Henriqueta made a grimace, trying not to laugh. She knew the script. The old lady had to be a pain to start her day right. Afterwards she adopted a less harsh tone and became as playful and sharp as a bald-headed monkey.

"Well, I'm going to bed. Your blessing, Auntie."

"Listen, my dear, haven't you said the rosary to the Holy Ghost today?"

"No. But I placed new flowers that I just brought from Fern Lane: a basket full all the way to the brim, like this.... Besides, this isn't the time of year to be saying the rosary. Don't you know that it's almost Christmas?"

"Oh, my dear Child without His flowers!"

"We'll put them in tomorrow."

"Make sure to put them in tomorrow! My poor Child lying there all naked...."

Ângelo had come tiptoeing in to say good-night and, leaning against the foot of the bed, was listening to the conversation.

"He's been skinned alive, Aunt Secundina... skinned alive."

"Skinned by you, who stole the gold chain from me that I'd kept to put around His neck!"

Ângelo made as if he were pulling out the chain from the buttonhole of his vest:

"If you made a vow, Auntie, here it is. I had no idea. God forbid I should keep something that belonged to the Child Jesus! You never told me. I didn't steal it from you...."

The old lady pretended he was not talking to her. But one

could read in her eyes, which she lifted, raising the tension in her jugular veins, a denial of that pretense and the resentful pleasure she derived from the misunderstanding. Ângelo tried both to have some fun and exact his little revenge:

"I like this chain even more than...."

"What was that?"

"I said that I like this chain even more than Canon Borges did. Did you give it to him for one of his birthdays, or was it a present from Bishop João Maria when he came to Fayal?"

The old lady retorted cynically:

"Neither one nor the other. Canon Borges earned it with the sweat of his brow! I only gave him something that I wouldn't give to you, you can rest assured."

Ângelo was beaming. Henriqueta intervened:

"Don't go saying nasty things, Auntie!"

"Nuts to you! What did I give Canon Borges that you shouldn't know about? I gave him my virginity, the flower of my youth! I was made a woman at thirteen!"

"There she goes again!" Ângelo said.

Henriqueta insisted:

"You do have a gutter mouth, Auntie!"

"Look here, my dear, I used to say these things in front of your sister-in-law Emília, and she neither laughed nor lectured me. You make like you don't enjoy them but you're always coaxing me into saying them."

Henriqueta's eyes pierced her, and her lips actually quivered. But she only said dryly:

"Lie down and go to sleep, okay?"

The deaf old lady propped herself up and supported herself on her immense breastbones, warding off Henriqueta's arms with a dark and cynical glance:

"Shit!"

"Bless the Child Jesus' little penis!" whispered Ângelo, all excited and happy, already standing in the doorway.

The old lady, stretched out in bed like a board and throwing him a fulminating glance, repeated the expletive.

Chapter IV

Nocturne

The Dulmos received a letter from England announcing the arrival of Roberto Clark in a month. Having found out that his father's illness had taken a turn for the worse, Roberto decided to return–a sad way to fulfill the promise he had made him, so many years earlier, that he would come back to the island for a while to exchange the hug that the more errant Clarks, from Montreal to Singapore, had given each other across the generations before dying, as opposed to the Clarks who had remained faithful to *home*, the Clarks of Ladlooke Grove. Unfortunately, now there were no Clarks in Ladlooke Grove; otherwise Roberto might have saved his fare. Apart from Roberto, the only Clark remaining in London, and notoriously still part of the family, was Dr. David Marr, the son of a female first cousin of the Clark residing in Fayal and therefore, as far as the family name was concerned, a bastard, a Scotsman. He had an office in Kensington; Roberto himself worked in a downtown bank. They only saw each other every few years but exchanged Christmas cards every year depicting cottages covered with melting snow, "with best wishes."

Dona Catarina received the news with lukewarm but sincere joy. They were in the sewing room: Margarida trying on a mallow-green silk dress that the seamstress, on her knees, slowly covered with pins; Maria das Angústias at the sewing machine, sewing a girdle with a reinforced front. *Dona* Catarina, basting and looking somber, said:

"I'm finally going to have the chance to get to know the only brother God gave me."

"How old was *Senhor* Roberto when he left for England?" asked Maria das Angústias.

"Let me see. It was right after Easter of the same year I got married. He's thirty-seven now. Diogo and I were engaged in January of 1896 and were married the following April. Ah, my poor head can't figure all this out!"

"Oh, Mother, spare us the melodrama! If he is thirty-seven and shipped out in 1896 and this is 1917... he was..., let me see..., sixteen." The seamstress, holding her open scissors, waited for Margarida to finish gesturing to cut about a centimeter from a seam along the hip.

"So young!" said Maria das Angústias.

"So, you must have found it difficult to say good-bye to him, especially considering you had only recently gotten married.... Wouldn't you say, madame?" respectfully remarked the seamstress, a recent arrival from the mainland.

"We didn't live together. *Senhor* Roberto Clark is an illegitimate son." And, changing the hollow tone with which she set everything straight, *Dona* Catarina added: "But he's the son of a very refined lady from a nice Fayal family. My father became a widower very early in life; I was raised in a boarding school in São Miguel. I guess he was just sewing the wild oats of youth."

The seamstress listened to her with extreme reverence, afraid she might be thought nosy. Margarida, turning about in vain so she could fix the bottom of her skirt, was, on account of that, growing impatient:

"If you take any longer, Miss Otília, I'm going to take this off. I don't want to keep *Dona* Corina Peters waiting."

"Young lady, you have plenty of time to go to the Peters'. What kind of hurry are you in? Especially today, with a seamstress in the house!"

"Come on, Mother! I promised..." Margarida became quite flushed, looking from under her bare arm at *Dona* Catarina.

The seamstress deftly pulled the pins from the dress, and one could hear the rapid undoing of the basted pleats. *Dona* Catarina assumed a condescending tone:

"Well... are you going to get dressed, then?"

"Of course I am."

"Not even knowing her uncle's coming keeps her at home,"

said *Dona* Catarina with the benevolence of a superiorly refurbished old age.

"Let her be, Godmother. Bidinha doesn't even know him, and there is a ship pulling into port today!"

Margarida returned to the sewing room to pick up her purse and gloves.

"Miss Otília, before I forget... I don't want this stitched very tightly here–I could choke."

They heard the sounds of the foyer door closing, followed by little footsteps down the stairs. She was leaving for the Peters'. *Dona* Corina had offered to allow her to receive João Garcia's letters at her address. It was an imprudent suggestion. But Margarida knew that things are either natural or unwise depending on conventional classifications, and although she was aware of protocol, that awareness seldom altered her purposes. And *Dona* Corina had done her the favor with the most innocent goodwill in the world. "It's so sweet, that an artist exchange letters with an educated young lady, isn't it?" Only João Garcia had shown a little reluctance, leaving the whole arrangement undecided.

Margarida found the Peters' living room in a state of continuous activity. The Lemoses and Maria da Paz were there; Dr. Luís da Rosa was absentmindedly leafing through an album. Standing there with his glasses pushed up to his forehead, was Uncle Mateus Dulmo. They all cheered Margarida's appearance. *Dona* Francisca Peters, oldest of the Peters, wanted Margarida to join her in her corner. But since Margarida had leaned on the chair where Alice Lemos sat telling her a story concerning Cecília and a Lemos sister at school, the old lady, feeling a little resentful, withdrew into her dreamy solitude.

They were discussing music. Mateus Dulmo was explaining his difficulties last year during Lent in having Baldi's Matins properly performed, especially the solo bass part, which he wanted Paim to have sung: *Omnes amici mei derinlinquerunt me*. In a fit of sacred romanticism, *Dona* Carolina quickly intervened:

"How does it go? Sing it, Cousin Mateus!"

"Come, Cousin Corina, I don't sing bass." But he cleared his

throat and intoned a falsetto: "*Om-nes! om-nes! amici mei....
Om-nes amici mei... de-rrreeliinque-runt... de-rrree-liin-queee...
runt me!*"

"How beautiful! How beautifully simple!"

Mateus Dulmo offered to translate:

"'All my friends have forsaken me.' This indicates the
Lord's great desolation and the force of obedience that compelled Him to consummate the sacrifice of redemption. But
derelinquerunt is more than *forsaken*: perhaps it's more like
spurned. No, no! *Spurning* is something else... 'forgot me,' 'cast
me aside,' like something worthless. *Derelinquere*: 'to cast
aside, to abandon totally.'"

"Exactly!" said Dr. Luís da Rosa, who was glued to the
album.

"Exactly, no. Latin is a very subtle language, all sounds and
concentrated meanings, averse to the grotesque periphrastic ten-
dency of our vernacular languages with their bent toward analy-
tical minutiae. The celebrated difficulties with Latin on the part
of the master-priests is nothing but a testimonial to their igno-
rance and laziness. My master of Latin studies in Liège was
absolutely right: 'Latin is not in the *Magnum Lexicon*: it is
something in one's blood.' It seems I can't help but still hear
him: *'La Louve tend ses tétines. Prends y ton bien.'*"

The Lemoses followed that erudite display with some difficulty, but they admired Mateus Dulmo's vigor, his prestige as
direct descendant of the discoverer of the 'hypothetical island
north of Terceira,' and his ruddy hands covered with golden
hairs, hands privileged enough to have held the bishop's train
when he made his pastoral visit to the western Azores. Mateus
Dulmo, despite being modest and bashful, had felt then as if he
were being carried in procession on a bamboo litter, like the
undisputed deacon of the old Fayal nobility.

"I'm really amazed at how *Senhor* Mateus Dulmo knows all
these things! What a memory!" exclaimed Maria Lemos, aglow
as always in her great beauty and little understanding.

"It's admirable how he discovers the intentions behind the
lyrics and interprets them so well, in line with the feeling of the

music! Everything in such good taste and refined artistry...." said *Dona* Corina Peters. "Cousin, why don't you play a little Chopin for us?"

Mateus Dulmo turned his eyes to the old Peters' piano, which was bereft of its "gown":

"Today I don't feel like my old self." He began to hum abstractedly, making the floorboards creak under the hard soles of his shoes: "*derreeliinque-runt... de-re-lin-quee... runt me!*"

For the third time Margarida raised her eyes to *Dona* Corina.

"Yes, my dear, in just a little while...."

"What little secrets are you sharing, Cousin?" Maria Lemos asked in an insinuating tone, her eyes lit by a desire to be in on their confidences.

Maria Lemos had the faded and transparent smile of someone who understood everything as a half-remembered story. Her pearly teeth were visible. *Dona* Corina mysteriously puckered her little mouth.

"It's nothing, my dear. Just grown-up talk."

Mateus Dulmo was now testing the high notes on the piano. Someone ordered silence. But the piano keys only limped along. Chopin became hesitant on the fingertips of the nobleman, who suddenly got up and became interested in the photo album that Dr. Luís da Rosa held. *Dona* Corina, then feeling sorry for Margarida and all excited by that little bit of mystery, took her into her room. João Garcia's letter was in the poetry chest on a bureau heavy with hidden teak drawers and dried myrtle leaves.

"It's for the two of us." She read: "My dear Friends...."

It sounded like a chapter from an epistolary novel, but despite that it maintained here and there the tone of a genuine letter with details about the trip and his plans for the future, and a few details about what was playing in the Lisbon theaters. Two pages spoke of Portugal's entry into the war and about the fuss over the recent Sidónio revolution.[1] Then there were passages

---

[1] A military coup of 5 December 1917 led by former professor Sidónio Pais (1872-1918) who was afterwards elected president of the Republic and ruled until he was assassinated on 14 December 1918.–Trans.

that seemed very interesting to *Dona* Corina, even though somewhat obscure. They referred to the stormy isles and to the "joy of feeling in one's hands a poisonless serpent." All in all, a beautiful style. Didn't Margarida think so? And the *beau geste* of addressing such a beautiful letter to the two of them, something so out of the ordinary....

Margarida was of the same opinion, expressing it in the same words: "very well written; obviously a refined spirit, soaring high...." How funny!... she had never really noticed the little Oriental figurines on the bureau: an Indian with an open parasol; then, amid the reflections of the inlays brightened by the lamplight (there was no electricity at the Peters'), always the same pagoda reflected on the mirrors inside of each of the little drawers. Was this Uncle Raimundo Peters' bureau? The present from the rajah? But *Dona* Corina preferred to call her attention to João Garcia's handwriting, so tiny and personal:

"Take the letter with you."

"No, Cousin, you keep it."

"So, does your father search through your drawers also?"

"No, that he doesn't do. That would be going a little too far. But still, it is a letter for the two of us. I already know what it says. Naturally, it was a great pleasure for me. Dr. Garcia had told me."

"So the two of you still treat each other that formally?"

"How, then, should we treat each other, Cousin?"

"Come now! Like sweethearts...."

"No, Cousin, between João Garcia and me there's never been anything more than friendship.... Something like mutual affection.... How should I put it? We're compatible. Perhaps, on his part, I don't deny that.... A flirtation.... But a flirtation that doesn't warrant the informal pronoun. No, such familiar terms would definitely be going a bit too far." Margarida's voice had a dry, conceited tone, as quick as the brick-redness that briefly flushed her cheeks. Then she laughed, lightening her features with a refreshing calm: *Dona* Corina still belonged to those times that saw love everywhere. Not so Margarida. She liked to have a good time, and when she offered a boy her friendship, it was as if he were one of the Lemoses, or if Cousin Corina preferred, as if she, Margarida, were strolling, cane in hand, through the streets. With a little malice, *Dona* Corina reminded her that, still, he and she had spoken a few times at night at the wall of the quinta in Pasteleiro. A disinterested friendship did not produce Juliets....

"What do you want me to say, Cousin? Don't you know that my family detests his? Do you want me to invite the young man for tea?"

"But you are not going to sever relations with me?"

There was a naïveté at once so mannered and so candid in *Dona* Corina's smirk that Margarida did not resist the temptation of running her hand through her hair. The elderly lady still kept the letter between the tips of her fingers, with the candor and shyness of a little bird turning its head before sipping at a flower, afraid of a branch, afraid even of nothing at all. Margarida's kisses made her feel more faint-hearted and dearly loved:

"You are such a love.... The pearl of Fayal!"

And they remained a while with their hands in each other's hair, their elbows resting on the bureau, gazing into one another's eyes like card players. *Dona* Corina's smile became diminutive and submissive; Margarida's glowed with a matronly maturity. It was *Dona* Corina who broke the spell to say:

"It's remarkable how much you resemble your grandmother, *Dona* Margarida Terra!"

"That much?"

"Everything about you." And drawing a live comparison, starting from the nearest to the farthest features: "The same hand gestures, the same width of shoulders, the same eyes that penetrate our hearts with such joy.... And at the same time so filled with a seriousness that tries to escape us.... with a certain something that seems otherworldly...."

Margarida smiled and filled her brow with a sad reticence, her round eyes with a far-away gaze. Then, fixing them obliquely on the ceiling, she took a deep breath:

"Yes, they say I look like grandmother, cut from the same

cloth. I hope I don't have to die as young as she.... That, I admit, I wouldn't like."

Dona Corina kissed her hand that she had since let go of, interrupting the lugubrious thought. They heard sounds from inside the house and came out on tiptoe: it was Mateus Dulmo who, having overcome his repugnance towards the piano, had begun to play the first strains of the *Nocturne*. Room was made for *Dona* Corina to step solemnly inside. And Margarida, not finding a chair, leaned against the Peters' bay window on the other side of the curtains.

The piano was an old, sad piece of junk, which *Dona* Francisca rarely awoke with a waltz or a mazurka. Its veneer lid, the color of tobacco, was chipped. Its pointed case, covered with a pleated pink padding, was faded from the sun and the silence, and seemed under Mateus Dulmo's bony fingers and forced by the remembered notes to exhale the cracking noises of the months it had spent covered up, gathering moisture and drinking in the presence of the dark furniture while its owners spent the summer in their Cachorro home, far off in the vineyards of Pico. Mateus Dulmo was not sure of the first measures of the *Nocturne*, which the low notes, somewhat plodding along, once in a while threw off course. But through the pianist's perseverance and as the music gained its course, the piano seemed to come out of its slumber and sound a sprightly tune reminiscent of the harpsichord or the spinet, imparting a slightly nunnish hesitation to Chopin's intentions.

The ladies applauded and the nobleman rose to his feet. No, Aunt Mariana's piano was not up to those knightly feats, Cousin Francisca would have to forgive him.... The old lady came out of her shell and stood up for the piano's quality. The Lemoses wanted to know if Aunt Mariana was the one with the grey coiffure next to the portrait of Uncle Raimundo Peters, the one who had died in Goa.

"Our grandfather's legitimate family," said *Dona* Corina.

Dr. Luís da Rosa raised the lamp to half the height of the two canvases and read:

RAYMUNDO PÓRRAS DA GAMA PETERS, NOBLEMAN KNIGHT OF THE ROYAL HOUSE, MEMBER OF HIS VERY FAITHFUL MAJESTY'S COUNCIL GOVERNOR OF DAMÃO (1799-1807)

"I know," retorted Maria da Paz. "He is the author of that book called *The Cultivation of Oranges in the Azores Islands*, which Dr. João Garcia is always singing the praises of. He says that the Lisbon second-hand booksellers are asking 5000 reis when they can get their hands on a copy. He is so keen on it. Why would that be, Margarida? Isn't it because it contains some stories about your great-great-grandfather Clark when he arrived from England and abducted the nun?"

"I'm not a big fan of that old stuff, my dear."

"It must be the Glória Convent abduction," confirmed Dr. Luís da Rosa. "But that was long before Ralph Clark's arrival on the island. Counselor Raimundo Peters wasn't one to confuse these things, even though Ralph Clark was the kind of man given to 'fatal passions.'[1] Counselor Peters was a very educated nobleman and a great statesman, the man who raised the tradition of the viceroyalty to new heights when he served as governor general and made an attempt at our colonial renaissance during the regency of King João VI. And this was long before the days of Sá da Bandeira."

"And some thanks the king gave him," reminded Mateus Dulmo. "Count de Barca and his shady doings!"

The ladies formed a halo around the lamp. The painting was but a stain the color of a corn cob, and from it emerged a hard countenance, Raimundo Peters' crooked nose, and his plump and energetic hand on the handle of his sword, twisting the baldric ever so slightly.

"What a handsome figure!" exclaimed Alice Lemos.

"The like of which you won't see around today!" chimed

---

[1] *Amores de perdição*, an allusion to the Portuguese romantic novel *Amor de perdição*, by Camilo Castelo Branco (1825-1890).–Trans.

Dona Corina, safeguarding with her pink smile the prestige of the family.

Dr. Luís da Rosa, not wanting to show any disrespect toward a relative of so illustrious a family, noted that even today there are persons of virtue (and he seemed to hint at the presence of Mateus Dulmo as proof) as great or greater than in the olden times. Time has lent the figures of the past a special charm, rendering them exemplary and inaccessible. Besides, not everyone could be a navigator, a warrior, or a governor in the Orient. There was the silent value of the arts, of literature. And even in the humble professions, behind a counter, or as a cash-box clerk, one could lead an active and honorable life and pave the way for future generations, from which would spring the creators of new forms of civilization and of culture.

Mateus Dulmo did not say much more, though his opinion seemed a little forced and skeptical. Dr. Luís da Rosa had set down the lamp. In the shadow, the ladies were still examining the governor's portrait.

"The one I really like is the brigadier, the little plump one," said Margarida, running her fingers over the keyboard on the other side of the room. "He has such gentle little eyes, and then that kind of *chèche* look with his hat set on top of his head...."

"Watch how you talk, dear! He's our uncle!"

"I'm sorry, Cousin Corina. When standing in front of a painting, I always forget blood relations. To me, they're all just paintings. What can I say? I find the plump little uncle ridiculous. What am I supposed to say?"

"Say what you feel, little one! Art, when it speaks the truth, removes the cobwebs from our minds. Our real family tree is a peaceful death, nothing else. Get it off your chest, dear. He is the plump little uncle, of course! And so what? When, by chance, the two things come together–I'm referring to noble blood and valor–then we have no right to forsake the roots whence we've come. You are the one who is the daughter of a Somebody and you forget it! (Sorry, doctor. The Dulmo pedigree is irrelevant here, but you know that I have a soft spot when it comes to this impudent niece of mine....)" He laughed and put his arm around her. "Impudence, yes, dear; for what you suffer from is impudence...."

Margarida had stretched out full length in a rocking chair and with her feet crossed and her head pressing against the back, was slowly rocking herself. The Lemoses smiled. *Dona* Corina, as always, took full advantage of the literary situation:

"Isn't it true, Cousin Mateus, that dressed in white, Margarida would make a beautiful woman in Chopin's time?"

"George Sand she's not!" said the nobleman, playing a card that called the others to their good senses. "Some George Sand!... a young lady who grabbed a wild cow by the horns in her father's pasture!"

"That was when we still had pastures, Uncle."

"Look, little one, when you want to wrestle a heifer, all you have to do is say so! Januário still hasn't bought up the entire Flamengos Creek area, so far as I know...."

There was an uncomfortable pause. One could hear the tugboat blowing its horn. They spoke about the passenger ship that, since it was not going to call on Corvo, should be arriving from Flores the day after tomorrow at noon. Margarida then excused herself for having forgotten the great news that had just come in the mail–the arrival of Uncle Roberto toward the end of January.

"Haven't I said that this young lady has gone soft in the head? Here her uncle's coming to Fayal and she says nothing!"

Dona Corina spoke of how charming Roberto was: a true English gentleman, judging from the portrait. Dr. Luís da Rosa confirmed his gentlemanly qualities: a very British disposition but also, in spite of it, something of the islander–perhaps his height, which came close to that of a Pico whaleman. Besides, the Pico character had something of the tranquil peace and childishness of the strong, a certain quality that was not quite Portuguese. How kind Roberto had been to him when, disillusioned with doctors from the three Azorean capitals, he decided to have intestinal surgery in London or Berlin! He had no need to go beyond London, that magnificent health clinic in Kensington. Dr. David Marr performed the resection of the colon and administered the anesthesia so well that he had not felt a thing. He had awakened with a nurse by his side straightening his pillows, a peach of a girl! He could still hear Dr. David Marr, after starting to vomit: *"You may be leaving us in four days...."* Roberto, very serious, was standing by his side holding a package of prunes.

"Are you referring to Mr. Clark's son, the one who plays the violin so well?" asked Maria da Paz.

"Admirably, my dear lady! I heard him myself," stated Dr. Luís da Rosa.

Alice Lemos reminded everybody that here was, at last, the opportunity to organize the great quartet led by Cousin Mateus Dulmo, who would be the pianist.

"I'm getting old, young lady! And I can't relate to today's music, Debussy and his lot. Roberto Clark must be one of them."

Dr. Luís da Rosa said he was not. On the contrary: very classical, with a very faithful interpretation, a very steady bowing. But there would be no harm in playing a couple of things by Debussy, who composed some pieces without all that symbolism, with a very simple structure.

Dona Corina had heard *Ce que dit le vent d'Ouest* played by Francisco de Lacerda at the Baron da Urzelina's home.

"Lacerda, there you go! Lacerda's the one who's good to play this new-fangled music...."

"Come, Cousin Mateus, don't say that! A European-class musician, the glory of the Azores, who directs symphony orchestras.... A man who teaches at *Schola Cantorum* in Paris.... A friend of Vincent d'Indy's!" Mateus Dulmo smiled, filled with secret pleasure at having been defeated. "I'm a very old-fashioned woman: just look how I like my Chopin; I cut my first teeth listening to Bach and Romantic music, and on account of that, I did not fail to appreciate Debussy as a talented composer. One sits next to a pianist with the *Vent d'Ouest* in front of him and gathers the impression she's listening to the wind in the trees... something precious, of such great tenderness, that the tears come to one's eyes...."

"If it makes you cry, it's not music!" said Mateus Dulmo, to keep the conversation going.

"And the *Cathédrale engloutie*? Do you have anything to say against the *Cathédrale engloutie*? Those bells sinking under the waves... that striking of hours in the tower clock, and all that left-hand action with the chords that seem like the rising of the cathedral, then to disappear under the sea..."

"Daydreaming!" persisted Mateus Dulmo, without conviction.

"Cousin, you're a barbarian today!"

Margarida had the same opinion as *Dona* Corina, although she excused herself for her lack of musical knowledge. Unfortunately, not all music spoke to her the same way. She found Bach, for example, a bit too like "church music"–and she made a naughty little grimace, shielding herself against Mateus Dulmo's little scolding which she guessed was coming.

"A silly little thing who never could sing the popular tune 'Margarida Goes to the Fountain,' which is the high point of her repertoire!"

"I know, I know, Uncle; but I am very frank: I don't say I like those things that I don't feel or understand. And the *Cathédrale engloutie*, I don't know why, stirs me to my soul." Then drawing aside the curtains and breathing deeply: "It's stifling in here! Today, there isn't even lighting worth a damn on the dock! The Municipality is saving on street lamps. The sea must be beautiful.... What a nice little breeze!"

"Mm, it is," said Maria da Paz, returning to Debussy. "I remember very well that when *Senhor* Lemos played the *Cathédrale* for us, Margarida became all upset and those big eyes of hers were like saucers... Dr. João Garcia was there, by the way. When she likes a piece of music, she'll rush to hear it like it's a matter of life and death."

"You and your crazy whims!"

"So, we're going to think about putting together the quartet as soon as Roberto arrives," said Mateus Dulmo. "He plays the violin, you the violoncello; I play piano...; Sigmalia, the flute."

A round of applause crowned Mateus Dulmo's decision. In

that expression of enthusiasm could be felt, besides a liking for music and a nice pretext for frequent gatherings, the pleasure that young people derive from seeing an old man play to the hilt his comedy of contradictions, and then, suddenly and all at once, toss all the bombs in his arsenal. Maria da Paz was filled with enthusiasm:

"The opening performance will be at the Fayal Theater, with a lecture by Dr. João Garcia on modern art! Right, Margarida?"

"It seems that Margarida will be the general impresario," said Mateus Dulmo, smiling. "Not a bad choice... She's good with figures, and can straighten out those who miss rehearsals." Margarida was rolling and unrolling around her fingers the fringe of a drapery with a big glass pendant. "But no melodramatic pedantry."

"João Garcia is an extremely well-educated young man," observed Dr. Luís Garcia.

"May it do him some good!"

"You never wanted to meet him, Cousin...."

"Who, me? I don't have anything against the boy. Besides, he seems intelligent. I read the articles he published in *Diário de Notícias* on autonomy for the islands. If I haven't yet spoken to him about that, it's because I haven't had the chance. I don't like arranged relationships...."

"Fine, but here's a person who'll introduce you to each other!" insisted *Dona* Corina. "Margarida and I will live to see, standing in our midst, two of the finest minds that Fayal has ever produced." And *Dona* Corina brought together uncle and niece in a hug made awkward by the distance that separated them.

The servant came in. She had come to announce that Manuel Bana had arrived with *Senhor* Diogo Dulmo's little carriage, that he couldn't wait long, that the mare, bathed in sweat, had just arrived from the communal pastures.

"The mare? So father has brought the mare to the city now? Well, good night! Uncle.... I don't offer to take you, Alice, because you're waiting for Cousin José de Lemos. Good-bye, Maria da Paz! Cousin Francisca...."

Dona Corina accompanied her to the staircase, all wrapped in her little silken shawl. The servant was holding a lamp.

"Good night, Margarida! You're not going away angry at me, are you?"

"The very idea! You look at things so differently from me, cousin.... You just wait: one day I'm going to come here and clear away some of those cobwebs in that head of yours. Long stories.... It'll be some afternoon when the weather is good, under the chestnut tree...."

"Come and visit whenever you like, dear! And will we answer the letter together in the same envelope?"

"Write to him yourself. Give him some excuse to cover for me, anything.... Let's get going, Manuel! We'll talk about it when I come to visit again. Watch your fingers...."

The front iron gate, with the pull-string and wooden handle that caused an arched bell to jangle on top, slammed shut. *Dona* Corina heard the mare's jog trot and the *charrette's* wheels bouncing on the cobblestones.

Margarida was leaving, feeling neither sad nor happy: she was bundled up in her gray coat, with the collar turned up. Manuel Bana, turning around in the driver's seat, explained the presence of Jewel by alluding to *Senhor* Diogo Dulmo's idea of wanting Margarida to ride her. The few lights on the dock dotted the sea. They rode past Walter Bensaúde Street with a noisy clatter. With just a pull on the reins, the mare would flaunt its fine features. She was a very sprightly dancer with croup bones in bold relief and could be, when well caparisoned, a beautiful animal.

To think of *Dona* Corina and her writing to João Garcia in the same envelope! For him to refer to marriage after his appointment to Bragança, and who knows what else.... Margarida straightened herself up on the seat cushion. Her eyes distractedly caught a glimpse of the billiard balls in a corner of the table at Yankee House. A group of young men doffed their caps: Margarida bowed her head slightly. Whenever she went by in a carriage, people not very close to the family never knew whether they should call out a greeting, as one does to a little girl, or take their hats off, as one does for a lady. Those who did not know her, and the mare herself, would decide. Margarida seemed taller whenever Manuel Bana cracked the poplar horsewhip, her dark scarves lending her a strong and precocious air. She wore an unabashed smile, a little distant. The clatter of the *charrette's* wheels on the cobblestones became noisier, and the riders could see a line of respectful simpletons forming, men who moments before had been discussing cows and women at the door of Yankee House.

It was there that João Garcia used to spend part of each afternoon, going afterwards for a discreet stroll along Ocean Street, passing by Grandfather's Granary. Margarida imagined his slow-moving, skinny figure vanishing toward the beginning of the dock where, every few months, one or two dreadnoughts came in blowing a salvo at the Santa Cruz fort. Now, instead of dreadnoughts, a ship, loaded with salt and under bare masts, rocked and creaked. The channel tide frothed over the seaweed-covered boulders. Then the same illusion that formed in her mind's eye the image of João Garcia moving away, brought back his shadow along the same deserted road that the big wall lamps filled with terraces of dim and dancing lights. Away in the distance, one could see a bonfire, at turns blazing up and dying down: it was brushwood burning on the hillsides of Pico. And then a tomb-like silence would fall, followed by the going inside the house, the getting into the bed that had belonged to Grandmother Maria Terra, the listening to the calm ticking of the English clock in the living room until sleep overcame her.

Right at the beginning of João Garcia's courtship would have been the time for her to cut all ties, not to allow herself to be drawn to the courtyard veranda. But she had fallen into her old habit of not turning away from anyone who looked at her imploringly. Afterwards, Maria da Paz filled her ears with how intelligent João Garcia was, how well-spoken, how worthy, how young.... And *Dona* Corina had, too. But now she understood everything that people said about her old cousin: how she secretly fell in love with all the talented young men, and the stories that involved the piano and clandestine trysts, with poetry readings mixed in. At the reading of the stupid letter–"it's to both of us!"–how exciting, like a little girl at her first communion, what belated naïveté in the way she had rolled her eyes! She had found it all so ridiculous, but also piquant, like something she never thought could happen to anyone. It seemed as if someone had put her, as in a play rehearsal, in the middle of a strange and topsy-turvy story. In all her girlhood experience (she had had a courtship with Álvaro de Bettencourt three years ago; then she had been courted by Cerejo, who was tall, charming, inside left in the commissioned officers team of the naval training ship *Sagres*; Dr. António Lopes gave her no respite at the Royal Club of Fayal, with his way of dancing very close, much given to mysteries and impossible love, and such nonsense...), nothing had prepared her for this; João Garcia did not fit any of those profiles.

They had arrived at the entrance to the quinta at the end of Pasteleiro. Wrapped in his overcoat, her father opened wide the gate for the *charrette*. The small bell rang with a dull vibrating sound, and then came the muffled crush noise of the wheels over the gravel.

"Good evening. So, what do you think of the mare?"

"What about the mare?"

"What I mean is that, in a few days, it will be good and ready for you to do with what you like...."

"Not for riding it won't be. I don't need to make a fool of myself."

"You're being foolish right now!"

But Diogo Dulmo's voice sounded viscous, incapable of engaging in a dialogue that put up the least fight. Margarida scrutinized him in astonished surprise by the light of the lamp in the front entry. She muttered:

"Yes, I can see that...."

"You can see what?" said Diogo Dulmo, raising his voice with difficulty. He caught his balance by propping himself up against a stone bench, as if the weight of the world had fallen suddenly on him.

"Can you see with half an eye in the dark of the night too?"

"Father, I think you better go to bed."

"You watch that little mouth!" Diogo Dulmo's eyes flashed with restrained fury. Then he tried to unstrap the mare's breast-plate, while Manuel Bana removed the cushions and the horse-whip from the *charrette*.

Margarida climbed the house staircase four steps at a time. Her mother was collapsed in the family room armchair. The door that led to old Clark's room was open.

"Did you see your father?"

"And a fine state he was in, too!"

"He spent all afternoon in the sewing room exhausting my patience. He had no shame! With the seamstress staring at us, and he goes on about this... and he rambles about that... spilling the whole kettle of fish about the Avelars and about the whale fishery: that they demand a partial payment on what we owe them, otherwise they'll seize the whaleboats and everything in the boat house. And I kept warning him: 'Dear, let's discuss it later! Thank God we can afford to pay...' (because, you see, the woman couldn't stop staring at us, a real disgrace, a person who had come here for only the second time!). Why, I had no choice but to hang out all our dirty laundry, lest the offense be even greater!" She exploded: "And you, why did you leave me here alone with that lost soul, that madman?"

"Mother, you're overreacting!"

"No, I mean it! And you don't care about me! You're just like him: you can't resist the first crazy notion that overcomes you! Now you're all given to the Peters girls, with little secrets and plans for the day the ships come in.... I hope all that enthusiasm doesn't spell your undoing!"

"Enthusiasm about what, Mother? Please, don't make my life even more miserable than it already is, at my age... I see nothing around this house but sickness and things that I'm ashamed of!"

"Shut up!"

Dona Catarina broke into a fit of quiet convulsive sobbing. They heard a kind of groan coming from the old man's room. Only then did Margarida realize that she was still wearing her evening clothes. The popping of buttons through the button-holes of her coat impelled her split-second decision to instill a little order into that disorderly home, where even the furniture, in spite of it all, kept its customary stuffiness. Ever since the hurricane, the electrical system had not been running properly. The switches did not always work; some of the light bulbs faltered, or as soon as they were turned on were reduced to a tiny wisp of flickering colored light that soon went out. As a precaution, a row of lamps was set up. At five o'clock, Chica was to trim the wicks and fill kerosene reservoirs. Margarida lit the three candles on the branched candelabra, kissed her grandfather, spoke a few words to him while she tucked in the heavy quilt around his knees, like one does a child. Then she herself went to the kitchen to ask the servant for the kerosene lamp. Cecília was in the little towers, in Maria das Angústias' room.

"Nurse, Cecília!... dinner is ready!"

Having convinced her mother to go to bed, she brought her tea and toast. *Dona* Catarina had snuggled up in her shawl and seemed to come to life as her daughter's footsteps filled the house. She was breathing rapidly when Margarida took her by the arm to her room and helped her remove the shoes from her wrinkled, swollen feet.

"My darling daughter.... Poor little child!..."

"Very good, then! Rest!"

At the table her father spoke not a word; he ate slowly, imparting to his head and torso a puppet-like movement. His protruding, glazed-over eyes swam in an almost idiotic smile. Cecília, quite panic-stricken and wearing a bib, did not feel like eating. But Maria das Angústias, promising she would tell Cecília a story afterwards, speeded up the meal on that side of the table, like a patron in a poorly frequented restaurant who anxiously awaits the last bite. She excused herself and rose from the table, taking the child with her. Margarida ate with her head lowered. Pensively wiping her mouth from course to course, she stared at the hunting scene of the deer with fallen antlers in the picture on the wall.

"So we are going to host *Senhor* Roberto Clark, the son of

that illustrious mother!" said Diogo Dulmo, finally. "I've already ordered the Granary rooms cleaned up; here in the house the only 'beef' I want to see is butcher block grade A!" Margarida kept her place. "He smelled an inheritance and couldn't wait.... He's going to find a lot to inherit!" Margarida straightened herself in the chair, looking toward the end of the table opposite where her father sat. "Right, the 'beef,' that son of a bi...g family. Come, pumpkin, you always take things the wrong way! I'm a good son-in-law.... I've always been a good son-in-law to Mr. Charles Clark.... *Oh, yes*! the great business-man... the 'well-respected industrialist!... ta-ran-ta-ra!...' *O reed, royal reed... who sent thee my way?*" Margarida made as if she were going to rise from the table. "Stay still! Listen, *Marrrgarida*!" He pronounced the *r*'s in his daughter's name with an exaggerated trill. He let the napkin fall to the floor, half-rose, then fell heavily into the chair whose legs he checked both on the right and left, as if they had committed the affront of not properly supporting his weight. "Dad is your friend. Dad beat you, but he's your friend...." Margarida stood up; he stood up also and, vacillating, grabbed her arm across the table. "It was on account of your strolling in the quinta with Januário's son, Angelinho's nephew... what did you want me to do?... Allow a low-budget aristocratic marriage in the moonlight?..." Margarida tried to break loose; but Diogo Dulmo's hand, full of hard sinews, had titanic strength. She kept pulling back her arm, her face revealing as much pain as if someone were crushing her bones. "Listen to your dad: Uncle Roberto is coming. I just speak for the sake of speaking.... Can't a person show his happiness? He's an upright young man, something that doesn't grow on trees; yes, because, from one moment to the next, our whole house can come crashing down around us... do you understand what I'm saying? All this..."–and with his free hand he made a broad sweep that took in the table, the bureau loaded with articles of silver, the old man's room farther on, the ceilings, the entire quinta, "all this could go up in smoke! Your dad's blunders!" He was on the verge of tears, the tears of a laughing drunkard remembering. He eased his grip on Margarida's arm and, with no need to support his body, blurted out: "Your grandfather was almost an old man when his son was born. His mother was nothing to you... do you get my meaning? If he makes you happy, so be it... marry him! That way, we keep it all in the family."

Margarida pierced her father with a steely, pained stare. She began to skirt the table, treading with steps that progressively grew quicker, causing a slight tremor of the furniture and the rattle of aged, sensitive windows. She stopped halfway up the staircase leading to the little towers, like someone who is mentally weighing something dreadful, climbed the rest of the stairs with the impetuousness of her whole being, and fell face down on the bed, head in hands.

Chapter V

A Spider and a Web

The news of Emília's illness had haunted Henriqueta's rest.
The daily household chores no longer sufficed for her, and she
decided, much to the dismay of the servant (who only a few
days earlier had scrubbed the floors and polished the furniture),
to give the house another thorough cleaning. The parlor chairs
were all piled into a corner, the table with leaves was shortened,
the trays and *bonbonnières* on the bureau were put away, and
the bureau itself was pulled away from the wall. The parlor draperies were slung over the balcony; and Aunt Secundina, to
facilitate the general scrubbing of the place, had been carried on
a stretcher to Henriqueta's room. The sheepskin that covered the
old lady's mattress was going to flap against *Dona* Catarina de
Ataíde's balcony–for the sky was overcast and the so-called car-
penter's wind was blowing through the dock.

In her room, Henriqueta proceeded with a type of inventory of
everything, she herself emptying the Scotch pine chest of drawers. But the old lady, who remained oblivious to the pounding on
the bottom of the pulled-out drawers, was bothered by the dust
and the musty smell; so Henriqueta, to avoid subjecting herself to
the old lady's curses, decided to lock herself up with all her possessions in Ângelo's room. *Dona* Maria Florinda, for whom
Secundina nurtured a tempered hatred, had made a little nest in a
corner of the family room, where Carlota was sorting curtains.

Henriqueta was going through her beloved objects, as if
being forced to perform a hard chore made inevitable by the
general disarray. She muttered to herself about Encarnação, who
ironed her nightgowns very badly: the straps came out all wrinkled! Then she opened the little chest where she kept her necklace and bracelets and forced the spring of the little cameo

with a picture of her and Ângelo leaning against each other, each with shoulder-length curls. She unwrapped the silk paper containing a lock of hair from João Garcia when he was six and, in a fit of maternal affection which seemed excessive even to herself, she kissed the little blue ribbon. All these operations transpired with such attention to detail that the time they took did not seem excessive. But there were in Henriqueta's eyes, yellowed by her liver illness, in her dexterous little hands, in the movements of her cinnamon-colored skirts from the Order of Mount Carmel, a momentum impelled her to go on. Finally, it was as if chance singled out a little metal trunk in one of the small drawers brought to Ângelo's desk; she opened it. She took out papers, sorted them, counted them. The first said essentially this: "*If you, respected anonymous person (who know very well who you are) hazard anything, dare not make any false assumptions. I love her, knowing full well the situation in which we find ourselves.*" Another read: "*I never dreamed she was so ungrateful. How cruel of her to disappear from the window when all I beg of her is the charity of a single glance upon me!*" And the last one: "*This letter has as its only purpose to prove that I am not a man who shrinks from a fatal attraction in which he always has proved himself a man of unassailable character.*"

The open windows made a tinkling sound: Ângelo had a fetish for weather stripping, but the installation was faulty. No: there was no possibility of a mistake! One could really think of a certain resistance on Emília's part; another possibility might be that upon her getting her hands on the letters, she might not have seen things for what they were and blamed everything on Mota's audacity, who, when it came to womanizing, paid no heed to the whos or wherefores of his prey. (Mota was a robust man. When he stood at the door of the cathedral, he used a stick to beat his gaiters, which made a squeaking sound. He had a dandyish and respectful way of raising his hand to his kepi.) Henriqueta folded the letters and adjusted her scapular, as if she had just finished bowing to someone who, after the respectful tip-of-the-hat, withdraws into a discreet and uncomfortable smile, all gooey sweetness.... Suddenly, the whole truth seemed to burst forth and grab her by the skirts: she had borne false witness! Emília lowered the curtains whenever Mota went by. It is true that she whiled away many hours at the window; that sometimes she left Carlota crying in her crib to go to the living room, that it seems she could not resist going to the little square-paned window. Henriqueta would follow on tiptoe, but she could not see Mota. And what about her? What compelled her to spy? Hatred of her sister-in-law? They had always gotten on well.... Emília, with the peaceful smile of a satisfied dove, always reveled in her *bon mots*, heeded her advice about running the household, let her do everything, decide the fate of everything.... And at night, with Januário secure at work in the foyer office, they let off steam about his bickering and about his constant hurry-scurry, which did not even allow him the leisure for a stroll or to go to the theater!

Emília had had a fun-filled childhood, having been raised by her Aunts Farias, who lived in *Dona* Joana's Corner. What had led Januário to court her–it was said–had been the old ladies' rumored wealth. He saw her from Meireles' notary office–all he had to do was lift his gaze from the stationery. He was still slim, dark, his torso revealing the little bulge that he had brought from the Angra Seminary (as shown in the framed picture of him wearing a silken vest), which girth had progressively filled out. Each morning, Emília lingered on the balcony, pensively raising the blinds with its little diamond-shaped segments. She had not totally broken off her courtship with Estrela.... And Henriqueta returned to her little tin chest, making a brusque sweeping motion with her Carmel skirt. Yes! It had been her jealousy of Estrela, her only love, which poisoned her relationship with Emília. How happy she had been when she found out that her brother was courting Emília! What hopes she had hung on that stroke of fate which distanced her beloved from the woman who would steal him! How active she had become in encouraging Januário! How friendly she had become towards Emília–she who, only a few months earlier, could not stomach her! And everything had turned out well, except for Estrela's resisting the plan that she, Henriqueta, had laid for him. Had it been because she was ugly? Ugly she was not: sickly, yes... sometimes quarrelsome and nervous, and on account of her strong feelings, which no one wanted to puzzle out, she came out with those spirited sayings that all cheered but which produced the same effect as spilling snuffing powder among a group of visitors. People laughed; Estrela laughed. They all ended up shutting her out.... They remained cohesive, assuming a happy and stinging indifference, as if their smiling lips had the taste of bitter lemons. Emília, on the other hand, was pretty and pleasant; she did not spoil anyone's state of peace or interfere with anyone's enjoying themselves at gatherings. And Henriqueta saw her pregnant with Carlota, with her hands resting on her lap.

She dressed quickly. She adjusted her hat in the dining room bureau mirror, which the servant and a part-time cleaning woman were pushing against the wall:

"Get a move on, Encarnação! When *Senhor* Januário arrives, everything has to be in order."

"Are you going to be long, madam?"

"No." She turned her head to answer Carlota, who was confused about whether the living room jardiniere was supposed to get the rug cover or the damask coverlet. "You, young lady, always have your head in the clouds! You know perfectly well that you're supposed to use the cover."

Her voice sounded so rude and the rebuke so unfair that Carlota, astonished and hurt, said from the top of the staircase:

"I'm sorry, Auntie!"

Henriqueta furiously slammed the front iron gate. She was turning her absurd despair against her own self. Her enemies, her arguments objectified in others, now came back to haunt her. For her, life was turning out to be hostile and insufferable. But at moments like this, she noticed with surprise that the ill will and the bitter taste in her mouth stemmed from her imagination and spread to others, returning to her laden with an unbearable weight. It was as if she were trying to clean a basket of feathers and the wind kept blowing them back, bent out of shape and dripping with mud, in her face. Her little heels pounded the sidewalk. She stopped in front of Rosendo's

63

shoe-repair shop. The cobbler leaned his huge tortoise-like body on the half door.

"Miss Carlota's shoes, master?"

"They're almost ready, madam. How is everybody at home?"

"Well, thank you. How's your family?"

"Avoiding the plague, thank heavens."

"But there's no epidemic!"

"Who knows...."

"Could there be that many cases?" She was about to ask: "Anyone I know?" but restrained herself from doing so and waited at the edge of the sidewalk, acting like someone who is in a hurry but does not want to be discourteous.

The cobbler spoke of the outbreak in Madalena–"and some other cases going around." He hesitated:

"It seems that on King Pedro V Street there's no improvement...." He did not finish the sentence, looking in both directions down the deserted street. One could only see his glasses, his cap and his hands resting on the half door: "Such sadness...."

Henriqueta cut the conversation short and left.

Now there was nothing to divert her energy, all concentrated in her heels. She walked in haste and straight ahead, almost without thinking. The impact of a destiny that was fulfilling itself almost physically and needed her to accomplish its ends impelled her through the streets of Horta; and the passersby, the thickset roofs, Pico's crater in the background with the ring of clouds around its neck, everything seemed to turn businesslike and tense within her. Although she seemed to be heading nowhere, she stopped at Alexandrino's pharmacy. The pharmacist spoke of his great pleasure and wonderful surprise at seeing her and asked for news of her brother Jacinto (even though Ângelo had just left there). Henriqueta answered with her eyes on the little bottles and a calm smile lingering on her lips. As if she were absentminded or grappling with a huge shopping list, she opened her purse, took out a little piece of paper, put it back in her purse. She wanted salicylate–what else? Incense and that powder that was so good for her mother's asthma. She made a show of perusing the large counter covered with filled prescriptions.

"We've got remedies for everything here, except death," said Alexandrino, tapping the tip of a spatula dripping tartaric acid on the rim of a little flask. Then shaking his hands, screwing the lid on, making the shelf glass door creak, and looking over his glasses, he commented: "With the way things are these days, there's no use getting attached to life."

"What about the plague?" ventured Henriqueta.

"There's no cause for alarm, but there are a few cases going around. As you know, on King Pedro V Street...." Henriqueta donned an inscrutable mask, as if she were holding in her hands the scale in the counter's glass case, and in her eyes, the certainty of a sale. Alexandrino drew near to her to avoid committing an indiscretion in the presence of two chatting cronies who weighed, with gentle maneuvers of their canes, the pale silence of the pharmacy: "*Dona* Emília Faria is faring very poorly.... She was given the last rites this afternoon. Forgive me, but under the present circumstances, I thought it my duty to inform you.... Time allows us to forget a lot of things, and of course mercy compels us to forgive those who have trespassed against us.... Something wrong, *Dona* Henriqueta? Sit down on this bench. Or come to my lab; there's a sofa there." Henriqueta had not fainted but looked very pale, her lips trembling. She pressed her temples so as not to lose her balance. The patrons in the pharmacy, now engaged in a discussion at the door, allowed Alexandrino to take her arm without causing a scandal: "Esteves, bring some ether! Better yet.... Bring the test tube with distilled water... just water.... That's what happens, my dear lady; old sorrows sink deep, painful roots...." He sprinkled water on her face. Henriqueta had stood up and tried to explain that she had not been feeling well for days: dizzy in the morning, her feet always cold.... Alexandrino said: "That's life.... We must forgive those who have trespassed against us! What an ugly world."

Henriqueta left the pharmacy, but not without Alexandrino's having first insisted that she rest a little longer; he could draw the laboratory curtain. But she even refused to drink the orange pekoe tea that the pharmacy attendant had brought her. Her almost pleasant impression of being swept by a fatal wind, in which she felt enveloped and whose danger brought her remorse and strength simultaneously, had abandoned her. Now there was something missing from her steps. And with her head lowered, feeling a little dizzy, she found that the cobblestones had a worn-down hardness that seemed to give her a stomach-ache. She turned down a side street, Misericórdia. But at the corner of King Pedro V, she was repulsed at the thought of having to turn left, although that is precisely what she wanted to do. She waited a while, soon discovering, however, that she was waiting only for herself. A hundred meters or so down the road, she could see Emília's house with its lengthy balcony and dull-paned windows and a boy standing at the door. Should she go? From the opposite side of the street, someone was walking toward the Post Office; they might see her.... She then made for *Dom* Luís Square, and sitting a moment on the ocher-washed wall, she heard the chain of the clock weights creaking. She came down by way of the garden. The trees blocked the view of the walkways; a Brazilian man, sitting on a bench, drew figures in the sand. Now she felt a haste that imparted to her skirts, always at arm's reach, a nervous pleating full of modesty and steadfastness. She would go home to fetch her mother's over-coat, and the rest she would leave in God's hands: she would sneak out down the back streets and go see Emília. She would, at least, feel from the staircase the commotion brought on by the illness. Encarnação's presence, as well as that of the part-time cleaning woman, irritated her. When she was going up to her room, she came upon Aunt Secundina's stretcher lying between the door and the wardrobe.

"Are we at Carnival?" grumbled the old lady, noticing Maria Florinda's overcoat being taken from its hanger. "Who's hol-ding a masked ball, for you to put on that outfit?"

"Oh, shush!" replied Henriqueta, furious.

"Well, my dear, have fun, for I'm not one to tell tales out of school. I never opened my mouth to accuse any woman of being a tramp."

Henriqueta held back a burst of rage and fastened with a brooch the front of her disguise–a sleeveless Fayal merino overcoat with a buckram hood, which lent her the air of a rooster astray in the fields. She hurried precipitately down the staircase to avoid raising any suspicions in her mother and niece, both busy at work. But at the corner of King Pedro V Street, two steps from Emília's house, she lost her nerve and felt her legs giving way as they did in Alexandrino's pharmacy. Instinctively, she dragged herself to the front gate, as if she only needed to sit for a while on the stone bench.

"What do you want here?" asked a man carrying spraying gear on his back, trying to find out who that woman was with her nose poking out of her hood.

"How is *Dona* Emília?"

"She's already gotten her fill of lime. They've just finished closing her coffin."

The very brutality of the news, like a clamp, riveted her to the spot. Still, she asked:

"Are there a lot of people up there?"

"They've all fled. They're scared stiff. As soon as they notice the swelling in the groin, they beat it! And if it's one of those who spits up rust, God help us! Not even a son or wife wants to get close to a patient like that! And I'm the one who is supposed to deal with it all, spraying sulphur all day long."

Like a thief, Henriqueta climbed the stairs on tiptoe. And seeing Emília's coffin lying there unprotected, with its unplaned boards, without a cross or anything, covered by the lime that stifled the room and caused two pious old ladies nestled in a corner to sneeze, she knelt a moment, covered her face, and then retreated.

Only when she reached Cathedral Square was Henriqueta able to breathe. It was a cleaning day for everything, at home and on the streets. Even a knee-high whirlwind swept up the pieces of paper and araucaria twigs lying on the cathedral steps!

At the door of his office, Januário was hauling his considerable girth into a victoria, which fit him like a glove.

Chapter VI

Another Spider and Another Web

Januário's day had been busy. In the morning, he had locked himself in his office with the two Avelars, father and son, to discuss a loan of twenty-thousand escudos to the Clark firm's whale fishery. He was not going to any other customers today. Ladeira and his office boy had been sent home. Ângelo, sitting in the back with his gray hair uncombed and pomaded, was slowly copying a deed, after having carefully bolted the doors.

The deal was a simple one, even though old Avelar, scratching his head, stubbornly insisted on making it more complicated with some peevish scruples. Was the Clark firm responsible or not for the whaleboats and for everything appertaining to the whale fishery? Were the ambergris balls in the firm's name or not?

"You mean the boat crew's?"

"No, sir! I mean the firm's... the Clark firm. CLARK & SONS, HEIRS."

"Very well. I propose we seize the whaleboats: Article 364 of the Civil Code, which applies wherever the Commercial Code does not, reads:

"*The creditor may also petition for embargo or seizure of sufficient property to guarantee a debt, provided he can prove: 1) The existence of the debt and 2) The justifiable fear of insolvency, occultation, or dissipation of said property.*"

"Let's establish one thing: does the debt exist, or not?"

"The letters are right there," said the younger Avelar, motioning with his chin as if he were throwing a stone.

"No doubt about it!" And Januário placed his hand, like a paper-weight, over the body of evidence. "Diogo Dulmo attests to the debt here. His father-in-law also signs it. All we need is a scribbled signature under a few words ('I owe so much to so and so') for the undersigned to have to bear the burden of the debt or, if he should be unable to pay, relinquish as much of his property as covers the debt. The Clark firm is a corporation bearing a collective name; this credit is chirographed...." said Januário triumphantly, regurgitating the lesson he had been careful enough to ingest in Leal's office, a reputable lawyer and his man of straw.

"Pyrographed?" muttered the older Avelar, who paid for pyrography lessons for his older granddaughter at Elvira Moules'.

"Father, please be quiet, *Senhor* Januário knows very well what he's talking about!"

"I hold and sustain that all we need is this little letter to force the gentleman to state his case. In commercial law, everything can constitute evidence at a trial. Therefore, 1: the debt exists. 2: 'the justifiable fear of insolvency,' 'or occultation,' 'or dissipation' also exists. Let's talk about insolvency. Or, better still: let's turn to the third requirement, 'dissipation,' which leads us straight to the point I'm trying to make. Is Diogo Dulmo a reckless squanderer, or not? Did he or did he not throw away the pastures in Flamengos Creek, which I ended up buying from Manuel Frade from Salão? Does he, or does he not, throw away his money out reveling at Mariquinhas Estragada's with José de Lemos?" Januário interrupted that torrent of evidence to allow for proper effect. The older Avelar scratched his sideburns. "The dissipation is a proven fact," exclaimed Januário, as if he were deducing a conviction from a jury's silence or were handing out a large plank at an auction in the Customs Building, there being no higher bidding. "All we're missing is 'occultation.' Is it true that Diogo Dulmo has the ambergris balls hidden in Bishop Alexandre Square, in his lover's house?"

"It's rumored...." grumbled the older man, always prudent and skeptical.

"It's not 'rumored'; I know for a fact! There are two witnesses. When the time comes, they'll come forward! Therefore 'occultation' has also been shown. Now, since occultation and

69

dissipation have been proven, the 'justifiable fear of insolvency' is also proven. Or logic isn't worth a hen's tooth! And article 365 states very clearly: *'He who petitions to take these precautionary measures, must supply in writing the bases for the request and must provide evidence.'"* And first hitting the letter lying open on the table and then his forehead, he said: "Here they are... and here... But let's continue:

'1) The evidence having been verified, and the bases having been sufficiently justified, the judge shall order the embargo or seizure, which will be carried out by the solicitor in charge of the trial accompanied by the bailiff.' And (of course!) since the most valuable property, the whaling equipment in dispute and the whaleboats themselves, is locked up in Calhau within the jurisdiction of the Island of Pico, it follows that the matter has to be decided by having the Most Honorable Judge of the Jurisdiction of Horta requisition it from his Cais colleague." And speaking to his most inner self, Januário added mentally: "Because it's there, in the Pico vineyards, that the son of a bitch still has his little pawns set up; I need to lay a checkmate on him."

Wisely, Januário still kept hidden from the Avelars, especially from the old man, the contents of Article 366 of the Civil Code, which subordinated the order of seizure to the signing of an affidavit of liability for damages in the event that the matter might be adjudged null and void due to "*occultation of the truth or unfounded allegation.*" The game would be up then.... The moment to lay all his cards on the table was for time alone to decide.

The younger Avelar, his fears of incurring high costs and lawyer fees allayed (for Leal was authorized to practice law in the two jurisdictions), found everything to be as clear as day, and expressed his opinion that they should proceed with it. He was a squat fellow with a thin little moustache who kept his hands open and away from himself, as if he had just been weighing codfish and did not want to dirty his suit. But old Avelar had a trace of a smile and without wanting to make waves, continued to lodge still more objections. Diogo Dulmo was a bad egg (he knew that). Old man Clark, however, was a man for getting the job done, a notable man. He was still alive and had the wherewithal to pay. To start legal proceedings against such a person would be a scandal. Businessmen in the marketplace would be irritated; people at the Bank of Portugal and Fayal Coal would not be pleased. Wouldn't it be better to threaten (just threaten) to seize the ambergris and the whale byproducts, of which everybody knew full well that Dulmo was in charge? (The old man had given him that as pin money, hence the rumor that he had ambergris hidden in Bishop Alexandre Square.) That, in any case, was old man Avelar's opinion–a well-thought-out opinion, born of the jurisprudence called "caution."

The younger Avelar became quite flushed and flatly contradicted his father. His tone was vicious, his sunken eyes harsh. Januário followed the movements of his two clients with the half-smile of one who does not lose sight of the obvious trump in his fanned-out hand of cards. Father and son exchanged glances, their arguments exhausted.

"Well," said Januário, "you're the creditors, it's all up to you.... So we'll try for the ambergris. Let's not forget that Pereira da Calheta de Nesquim still hasn't found anyone to buy his.... They say that you can make a killing on ambergris... but it all depends on the market. And it requires tying up a lot of capital."

Father Avelar reconsidered:

"Let's do whatever Chico wants; I don't want this on my head.... What I've earned is for him. Let him take the lumps!"

The younger Avelar wanted to draft right then and there the petition for the seizure of property as a guarantee of the twenty thousand loaned to the Clark firm. But Januário calmed him down for fear of upsetting the old man. He kept in his safe an 1880 vintage Pico wine, smooth as velvet.... It was before the phylloxera outbreak! He only had two glasses; but he, on account of his diabetes, could not drink.... And he spoke of the brilliant degree his son had just finished in Coimbra and of the nuisance it was to have a hiatus in his law studies on account of his having been drafted by the Academy of Commissioned Officers.

"He's so well on his way!" said Chico Avelar, sucking down his wine. "A boy who, not for being ahead of you, does his country proud." He raised his glass.

"To your son's health!" said the elder Avelar.

"To the prosperity of Avelar & Son!" toasted Januário, without a glass, gesturing like an orator with his short yellowed hand.

The old man, already won over, reiterated:

"Here, here! Like father..., as they say, like son."

Januário hid the glasses and the bottle in the safe and explained that João Garcia was, indeed, very talented but had no inclination for law practice. He was much more given to literature. But he would make a high government official, a great general secretary. The Avelars spoke of the chance of nomination, now that Dr. Urbano Prudêncio da Silva had retired, but Januário thought it better to drop the conversation right there and called Ângelo:

"Has José Mónica already gone to hitch up the mules? I need the victoria right away."

Ângelo followed the Avelars out, returning in a little while with the carriage.

Januário ordered the carriage to go to Carrasca Well. His bulk filled the seat of the victoria, which with its top folded down rolled along the street like a conch shell with a giant snail inside.

Dona Carolina Amélia had just arrived from Santo António Church. It was the right time to test the waters on the issue of her having co-signed for the six thousand borrowed from the Bank of Lisbon & Azores: four bills of exchange for fifteen hundred each, received by Diogo Dulmo. While he waited sunk heavily in a living-room chair for the elderly lady, he reconsidered everything. *Dona* Carolina Amélia was a tightwad, but she had a lot of respect for the illustrious families of the island. Her husband (there he was, at full length, in the portrait hanging on the wall, bearing his Order of Christ insignia) had been Civil Governor before the Baron de Roches. He had had an active role in the Pilar festivals along with the Terras and the Dulmos.

He had made his fortune in Brazil and, despite his illustrious standing, had taken a long time to get a foothold in progressive politics: they would always throw his humble origins in his face, his having been taken to Brazil by an uncle, Coicão, who ran a butcher shop on Ouvidor Street. All this, when one is rich, allows for certain indulgences toward pampered charges. *Dona* Carolina Amélia was very jealous of her husband's desires and memory. And here she was now....

"I haven't been able to take my eyes off the commander's portrait. What a loss for Fayal!"

Dona Carolina Amélia made herself comfortable in a corner of the sofa: *Senhor* Garcia's friendship made itself felt in everything.

"It's so good of you to come!" And she explained: she had gotten used to her procurator as one does a doctor. On the days she did not see him, she felt uncomfortable and always ordered the front gate closed later, just in case he might come.

Januário bowed a little, with his left arm out like a wing:

"You're exceedingly kind, *Dona* Carolina Amélia. And why haven't we seen you at our house? Henriqueta, about that marmalade jar...."

It was true! *Dona* Carolina still had not been able to go thank her for the orange marmalade. Her life was so hectic.... the renters in Castelo Branco....

Apropos of renters, Januário delved right into the issue. The deposits in the Bank of Lisbon & Azores were all up-to-date. The only thing still in need of attention was the Dulmos' bank payment, which had come due. He was in favor of filing a complaint for default. He knew very well how violently opposed his client was to taking any drastic measures, but his duty was to safeguard her interests. Besides.... And he told her, under attorney-client privilege, about the Avelars' decision. They themselves had come to him to initiate proceedings for the seizure of the Clarks' fishery–which had filled him with astonishment and exceeded the resources of his "private police force." In the marketplace, people were very afraid, in light of Diogo Dulmo's irregular behavior! A man from such fine stock.... Yes, and good-natured, for Diogo Dulmo did not have a bad character. He, Januário, who had been his victim, was being impartial.

Dona Carolina Amélia appealed to the consideration that her husband had for Mateus Dulmo, not to mention the favors, if memory served, owed to Charles Clark when there was that run on a bank in London, "where we kept our small change." Januário dealt with all of these considerations, reinforced them one by one, and even recalled other reasons for respect, such as the rumor that had been spread a year after the commander's death regarding the marriage of *Dona* Catarina Amélia to Mateus Dulmo. This, and the nobleman's statement: "Well, if I were the marrying kind, I would feel very honored! Not only is she a most respectable lady but in her day she was one of the most beautiful young women in Fayal."

Dona Carolina Amélia chirped a vague protest. One could see the medallion of jet-black interspersed with gold in her purple necklace. There was a sudden silence, in which each of them, looking vaguely about, tried to bring a little dignity back to the room.

"I feel very sorry for poor *Dona* Catarina.... They seemed like such a nice couple, with the little girl they have, who is already getting so grown-up.... And pretty! At seventeen, she already has such fine presence in society, in that proud, affable way–I don't know if she gets it from the Clarks or the Dulmos."

"The pride comes a little from both sides...," said Januário, keeping a penetrating impartiality, with his sword half-unsheathed. "But pretty, unquestionably pretty...."

"She has her grandmother's face, *Dona* Margarida Terra's."

"She does, there is a certain resemblance."

"A great lady!" said *Dona* Carolina Amélia. "And so unhappy.... Fayal has changed a lot. There isn't that old-time joy, that distinction anymore...."

"Yes, madam. There are a lot of libertine habits nowadays!"

"We even have girls who bathe in skimpy little bathing costumes in Porto Pim!"

Januário, seeing time vanish in the darkness of the araucaria blocking the view of the window, suddenly and coldly conceived a way to bring the errant conversation to a grinding halt:

"I was about to say... Never mind; I don't want to influence your feelings, *Dona* Carolina Amélia."

"Say it!"

"Those loose habits are the very reason that compels us to act prudently. Diogo Dulmo, unfortunately.... It's painful, but I have the moral obligation not to hide the truth from a client of mine." Januário was playing along with the curiosity and good faith of the old lady standing in front of him, who was a little set in her ways but vulnerable to a certain something, both solid and precise, that she seemed to be constantly asking of her procurator. He played his card: "Unfortunately, Diogo Dulmo is an improvident fool, spends everything on lovers...."

"Do you mean that affair at Bishop Alexandre Square?" interpolated the old lady. "Is that really true?"

"Worse than that, madam; unfortunately, much worse than that! Whole nights spent in the company of women in Mariquinhas Estragada's tavern...." He stood up and went to the window overlooking Carrasca Well. José Mónica, poor fellow, had not had his dinner yet, and he was used to keeping "rural" hours.... He pulled out his watch: five past five. Henriqueta also dined very late; mother was now a little worse, with her hernia.... Purposely, he had delayed looking again at *Dona* Carolina Amélia to allow his words their full effect. The old lady was standing, her chin held straight over her brooch. "I take my orders from you, *Dona* Carolina Amélia. As for the loan agreement with the bank...."

"Do what you think best, *Senhor* Garcia. You have both drive and a kind heart. Whatever your conscience dictates...."

"We'll do the best we can, my dear lady," said Januário, moving his arched spine under his deep frock, checking out its lining as if he were feeling for a pistol.

He ordered the victoria to head for home. But on the way, he remembered that Pretextato must have heard something about the rumors going around concerning Roberto Clark's arrival. Januário told José Mónica to go by way of the Weather

Station. Júlio Pretextato had just gotten off work and was pasting labels in his stamp album. Upon entering, Januário promised him a series bearing the image of Marshal Floriano Peixoto, which he had kept in his safe since the estate sale at Emiliano's. They were in Pretextato's home office, in the back of the station. Pretextato was a widower, the son of a colonel in the cavalry, which is why he had been able to get his only son, Bertito, into the Military School. On an old desk, there was a picture of the boy in uniform, and on the wall, a charcoal sketch of Alzira Pretextato, skinny and wide-eyed. In a picture frame with a lilac grosgrain ribbon, there was a seated portrait of Ângelo with a cane across his knees. The room exhaled ancient air that had a certain taste. Three bay windows overlooked a sunken backyard, where a thick water spout brightened and stirred the maidenhair fronds in the water tank.

Getting straight to the point, Januário said that he had come there to find out if there was anything new about the "beef." His diabetic, mask-like face shone with a brighter light; *Dona* Carolina Amélia was not there to force him to alter his countenance. Júlio Pretextato added little to the rumors going around Horta: Roberto was coming to see his father before he died and perhaps to try to save the part of the inheritance he had coming to him. Januário said nothing: he stretched himself out in the wooden armchair, made it creak, ground all the wicker joints under his solid and slightly fatigued girth. In his face, despite the ravages of his illness, one could read a profound inner tranquility and a perfect harmony with Pretextato's room. He had always felt good there among the half dozen delicate objects that held discreet positions on their respective pieces of furniture: the picture of the Prince of Monaco acquired on one of the study voyages of the *Hirondelle*, the piece of candle wax on a corner of the piano, the *Chansons de Billitis* bound in blue silk. An upholstered settee attested to Pretextato's frequent bouts with fatigue. His hands hung from his black dinner jacket, and he looked a little melancholy and wan.

Januário considered Pretextato's friendship with his brother a case of paternal and slightly ironic benevolence. Pretextato invited Ângelo for dinner, took him to Fern Lane in the flower- and grape-harvesting seasons, and consulted him about rose-bush grafting and seed selection. Pretextato had actually taken some courses at Polytechnic and had gotten the position of assistant at the Weather Station thanks to his vocation as an amateur naturalist who had a nodding acquaintance with stuffing birds, analyzing soils, and classifying fishes and birds indigenous to the island. Januário appreciated his classy ways and good manners and, regretting Ângelo's dangerous celibacy, saw in that inseparable friendship a means to keep his brother away from vulgar liaisons that might reflect adversely on his business. But there was more to Januário's complacency than that: he shared those interests with them about his rare tastes and got them to talk about the quality of different types of silk, ways to paint images of saints and to host gala parties, opinions regarding old family feuds (old ladies nursing their grudges), comparisons of the performances of Ferroni's tightrope walkers, and the *couché* paper that Pretextato showed to only a rare few. From time to time, he extended his tolerance to the point of showing up for teas held by Pretextato for a group of elegant and intimate friends.

"Januário, has it occurred to you that Diogo Dulmo, when he realizes his brother-in-law is going to find out the condition the business and his father-in-law's fortune is in, could find a way to make things difficult for Roberto?"

"How, if he's destroyed everything?"

"How should I know! Pulling a few strings. All he has to do is bewitch him... stick a woman in his face. Look at what he did to Major Caldeira, such a quiet man, so meek.... He got him together with Mariquinhas Estragada, then out in Pico, a few late-night dinners fit for a king; in no time, they were part of the same slew of lovers in Bishop Alexandre Square."

"The devil has a blanket that covers and another that discovers," said Januário, as if he were really holding in his hands the corners of a large blanket.

"A good match for Roberto would be his niece, Margarida. The bad news is that he's got a rival on his heels...."

"Who?" asked Januário with a spurious frown, in the depths of which played a twinkle.

"That's wanting to know too much...."

"Do you mean those fibs going around about my son, João? Let him sow a few wild oats, enjoy his youth! I also paid my dues to youth and don't intend to get in the way of the boy's little flings. At that age the more the merrier; it's like the poet Bocage [1] used to say: *'I dreamt that you, fine ladies, were flowers, and I the butterfly....'*" With a strange smile, Pretextato gazed with his chin glued to his shoulder. Januário resettled the full weight of his body with a deep breath and said, as if he were shooing away the rumor: "But *marry*? Nonsense! It's not going to be my father's son, who saw to João's upbringing, who's going to let him go and be the son-in-law of that scamp Dulmo." But there was in Januário's protestations a hurt and distant note, like that of a crystal glass that one unwittingly touches but whose ringing can be silenced with the mere touch of two fingers. He stood up. His frock-coat cast a half-shadow in the light from the stub of white candle wax on the piano. He extended his hand to Pretextato: "I'm going to have something to eat. Thank God, today I earned it."

"Very busy lately?"

"Fairly... fairly."

The distance from the Weather Station to Jesus Street was short, but the road was on a slight incline. The mules stretched the shafts of the victoria as they struggled to keep sure-footed on the cobblestones. Januário, boxed in the carriage seat, allowed both his belly and his thread of thought full freedom. For the next day, he had to draft another document concerning the Avelars' case and dispatch Ângelo to the bank. The mules were now trotting, and the idea of being almost home brought to his mind the prospect of his diabetic bran bread. The years weighed on him; the night, imperceptibly to him, had fallen on the city roofs and street lamps. Pulling out his watch, he reflected that

---

[1] Manuel Maria Barbosa du Bocage (1766-1805), Portuguese poet especially known for his personal and satyrical sonnets.-Trans.

it was still winter, short days... What he would really like was a little oven rice and a baked sweet potato. His sister could prepare such nice little dishes! And Emília.... But that was another story, something totally different....

"What in the hell do you think the reins are for?" he shouted to the coachman, after the carriage gave with a particularly startling jolt. José Mónica used the whip on the pair of mules; the victoria swerved and swayed as if Januário's body were made of cotton wool.

With diabetes! How could a man eat? Where was he going to put his belly and his leg with an open sore for two months now? (Would it never heal?) The office still gave him the illusion of a full day: he'd talk up a storm or scribble words on a sheet of paper..., use the other side of the sheet.... What a dog's life! Such a struggle, such a long run of luck! He was going to be fifty-two in March and had been without a wife for more than fifteen years.... He got out of the carriage:

"What's wrong with the mule?"

"The son of a gun is chomping at the bit.... The bastard! It seems like he's got his mouth full...."

Januário unloaded his anger on José Mónica:

"Couldn't you check if the mule was overfed before leaving the stables? Why didn't Pintado bleed him when he put new shoes on him? Is that how you look out for my property?..."

"Please, boss, it's not like that!"

"It's *exactly* like that: why didn't Pintado bleed him when he put new shoes on him?" And intently staring at José Mónica's unblinking eyes, Januário started toward his bay windows, pushing open the dark, thick gate.

One of the Clarks' mules had died from overfeeding; it was Januário who sometimes drove Catarina Clark in the break to the Flamengos Creek house–which now, glory be to God, was very much his. No, it couldn't have been Catarina.... No matter!

At the entryway, he pulled on the top of the iron gate: it did not open as before. Henriqueta came to meet him, and he noticed a strange air about her. She seemed to want to say something but was unable to speak; each of his sister's steps was thwarted by that soft impediment, the Carmel skirt. Januário kept going, a little sideways, through the doors leading to the dining room. There his mother, Carlota, and Ângelo, with the backs of the chairs in front of them, were awaiting the signal "Be seated!"–which was Januário's raising of the lapels of his coat at the head of the table.

"What an infernal smell of linseed!" said Januário, running his fingers against the edge of the sideboard. "Everything's greasy... everything smells of linseed!"

He sat down, turning his head to look at the four people at the table. Without understanding exactly why, he, along with his daughter, his mother, and his brother and sister, burst into an absurd, irrepressible chorus of sobs, which lent Henriqueta's features a beauty both comical and dark:

"Oh, the poor little thing, she died and we never had a chance to forgive each other!..."

Old lady Maria Florinda combed the fringes of her shawl, shook her head, and raised her hands in prayer:

"Lord, give her eternal rest and the splendor of eternal light!"

Januário, looking ashen, raised his napkin to his eye and wiped away a tear.

Chapter VII

Poor Tactic

The School for Commissioned Officers was located in the Junqueira area. João Garcia belonged to the infantry. Despite the fact that instruction and classes occupied most of his day, he had rented a room in Bairro Alto so he could be closer to downtown Lisbon and the hustle and bustle of the newspapers. Right away, he had become close to a young man from São Miguel, Alfredo Nina, whom he had met in Coimbra in his second year of law school and who had also interrupted his studies. Alfredo was extremely well-read; João Garcia's interests coincided with his. Also, his spiritual maturity, albeit a little utopian, and his profound humanity drew him to the real-life problems of society and man, stimulating and nurturing João Garcia's notorious apathy. Because they were complementary, they understood each other well.

Alfredo Nina lived on a side street in the Cova da Moura area. The two would meet on the Belém and Boa Hora buses, which crossed paths with the streetcars packed with workers from Arsenal and pale little seamstresses carrying lunch bags and all wrapped in their little shawls, which smelled of roasted coffee from their meager breakfasts. Lisbon's winter was harsh that year: floods in Ribatejo; Ribeira Nova and Alcântara turned into muddy swamps. The ships en route from Cacilhas sliced through a yellowish Tagus with cross waves that petered out at Ginjal and Mar da Palha. And Barreiro, still ballasted with lights at seven in the morning, reminded João Garcia of Madalena seen from Horta, though somewhat magnified in both size and sadness.

Because they were only fifteen days from examinations and field tests, instruction had intensified. Classes took on the air of office bustle: tactics notes, topographical sketches, models of orderly rooms, organization of night patrols.... The majority of the cadets took it all as a joke. They lined up at their benches, waiting for Major Rodrigues to reach his chair and open his briefcase. The teacher would give a lively tug at the bill of his cap, and they would sit down. "No. 63! What do you know about the duties of a mobile security patrol?... An arrow formation. Very good! And how do you protect the flanks?" Unobtrusively, *The Manual for Non-Commissioned Infantry Field Officers* was opened; the "cribs" anxiously elbowed the "brains," and all of a sudden, the Major came alive: "The 'blue party' was turning a corner and attempting to ford a river; but from the opposite bank, the enemy opened curtain fire, cutting off access to the bridge. No engineering.... The 'blue' terrain was level, sandy; the sandbags were filled and the individual shelters were dug with pickax. And then?... Turf, of course! And then?" Then, it was always the Major speaking, putting his pinky through the loop at the end of his stick. Some dozed off; others insolently spread out the newspaper *O Século* under the table; still others doodled Major Rodrigues' glasses in the margins of the *Manual*, initials, a fisherwoman....

But João Garcia followed the lectures with very serious attention, interrupted, once in a great while, by a thread of wily abstraction–born, for example, of the resemblance between Captain Parente and an Horta civil governor of some time ago... or of going to the window, high above Calçada da Ajuda, from where the river and the Other Bank could be seen... or of letting his imagination play for a while on the side of a lugger rocking in the high tide off on the horizon or on the funnel of an English collier slowly making its way into the Bar. He saw Margarida in a white blouse at the window of the little towers, a flight of gulls vanishing in the direction of Cascais. "... if we let *p* stand for propulsion, *r* for resistance, and *v* for velocity, it follows that the trajectory is directly proportional to...."

João Garcia was fond of the ballistics instructor's style but had difficulty following him in the certainty of his calculations, which seemed an extension of his trembling mathematical wrist, so incisive that it sometimes broke the chalk and reached out toward the audience in a kind of blessing gesture inviting confirmation of proof by evidence. Almost always incapable of subscribing to that kind of thoroughgoing reasoning, João Garcia seemed to decipher in Captain Parente's rictuses the mysteries of the bullet and the target. For whatever reason, that disembarrassment, that precision of words and gestures took hold of him, filled him with an indeterminate will to decide, to act. Suddenly interested in everything that was dynamic and visual in the figure of the instructor, his reeling imagination entertained itself by placing him wherever it wanted to: in Rossio beating his way through a crowd to go have a quick, after-lunch coffee; in the streets of Horta, on horseback; or, cross-legged and with a cogless spur clamped to his boot, explaining to a lady why the *mouche* needs concentric rings for it to be attached.

The call to break was heard: time for a cigarette. Nina leveled two curses against those boring theories and Major Rodrigues' bullheadedness: he was very clear when explaining his tactics but distracted when laying out a battalion column. The call to drill was heard and then to *forward march* .... There they went, knapsacks on their backs, along the Monsanto highway, forcing the peasants to move aside their loaded donkeys. In the solitude of the mountain range with its denuded slopes, the instructors' voices were heard marking rhythm: "One! two!... One! two!... Left!... Left!..." At the command to *at ease!*, everything ended up in stifled chitchat and unbuckled bootstraps. One cadet ran after another one who had pilfered his cigarette case and who reached the bivouac out of breath and without his kepi. The entire company fanned out along the edge of the highway, the long-distance antenna towers of Radio Monsanto punctuating the horizon.

By the *Funchal's* second return trip from the islands, João Garcia became convinced that Margarida would not write. The days of the ship's arrival were both a torture and source of hope. Generally, the ship arrived in the afternoon, its thick slow-moving prow practically razing the Tower of Belém. One felt as if one could touch the ship as it sailed by Rocha do Conde de Óbidos, already within reach of the tugboats dotting the Tagus, which killed their engines on approaching the vessel. From the Santos pier, one could clearly make out all the details on board: a seaman climbing the poop deck; the men in charge of maneuvers unrolling the cables at their posts; the line of passengers leaning on the rails and putting their binoculars aside, exchanging rapid words among themselves; and the smiles of those at last recognizing familiar faces and seeing waving white handkerchiefs.

João Garcia waited for the *passerelle* to be set up. His first movement, after determining that there were no more people coming from Fayal, was to follow the bags being unloaded and thrown into the post office truck, then to be received according to names of the municipalities screamed out haphazardly for verification: "Velas!..." "Lagoa!..." "Praia da Vitória!..."

João Garcia felt entangled in the crowd of onlookers on board. A group of chic island girls, who occupied a starboard bench, spoke with students who lounged in "sheep-footed" deck chairs and outdid themselves with pleasant and meaningless gestures. João Garcia walked around the deck, leaned over the mail hold. "Horta!..." Was the letter there? That one tied with strong padlocks was not among the largest bags. It was lifted by the crane, pressed against bulging suitcases from Ponta Delgada and Funchal, the slingful coming undone with a huge crash against the pier. His chest tightening, João Garcia came upon people he knew: merchants from Fayal on business in Lisbon or returning from surgery; an old fellow student just returning from months of exile on his first stint as public prosecutor; a well-known traveling salesman on holiday with connections in Horta, dazzling in his expensive suit. They caught him in the squeeze like a fish in a net. João Garcia answered the first questions absentmindedly; then, slowly, he warmed up and took great interest in the conversation, giving in to the indulgence of a beer in the smoking room.

On days like these, he did not look up Alfredo Nina, who had some ill-will, a little affected, against his Azorean homeland, who detested the gatherings in Santos, and who refused to read the paper, *Portugal, Madeira e Açores*. João Garcia simply asked to be excused from school. He took the Conde-Barão streetcar to Rossio, went up to Chiado, to São Roque Street, and then headed home to await the arrival of the mail. But if the ship arrived after three o'clock, there was no mail delivery in the afternoon; and night fell, prolonging his uncertainty. After dinner, he went to the Golden Key, looking for Dr. Sérgio Alves. It was he who had gotten João a foot in the door at the editorial offices of the Lisbon newspapers, recommending him to the tap brass. He was a representative from Pico who knew the entire Azores inside out; João Garcia sat by his side as if he were sitting on a boulder in Porto Pim or on a hydrangea-covered wall on the Caldeira roadway. Unlike Alfredo Nina, Sérgio Alves relished his acquaintance with individuals and things of the islands. He did not divorce himself from the recreated island milieu in the mainland, except in his vague experience of a broader lifestyle. His savory evocations had a minimum of criticism and perspective. And that is why he remained an average, down-to-earth guy, like islanders. Speaking with his island accent, he knew how to get the best out of colorful words, and he exaggerated the sugary sing-song of the Fayal pronunciation.

Sérgio Alves spoke to João Garcia about the cases of plague in Pico and those fewer cases in Horta. The topic seemed to preoccupy him, both for the tragedies occasioned by the calamity and for the excellent opportunity to act on behalf of the needy populations. He could secure a few dozen kilos of sugar from the Supply Center and look into the plan entertained by the deputies of the Popular Party of Horta District, dissolved by Sidonismo, to send two or three relief doctors–perhaps a mission like the one that had gone to Terceira in 1908. Sérgio had received news of certain gravity from his political informer, Mendonça of the Overseas Bank, number one on the list of Dr. Nunes' enemies. He needed to counterbalance the Secretary of Public Health's influence: oppose his electoral frenzy with a new doctor, an active and driven young man. (As soon as the ship arrived, Sérgio received a large package of letters and crates of canned pork products that came in the dispensator's hold.) He drank his coffee slowly, carefully examining the stained rims of the cups; the Golden Key was a great cloud of tobacco smoke and piled-up dripping dishes reflected in the counter mirrors.

João Garcia had suddenly lost the fire that the memory of the islands kindled in him. Alves was rolling paper for his cigarette:

"I'm going home. Rumors of a revolution have been floating around.... They've arrested some of the boys from the Group of the Thirteen that Sidónio had let out of prison."

It was after midnight when João Garcia took the Glória Elevator. The way home, starting from São Pedro de Alcântara, was sad and glutted. The cats in Boa-Hora alley howled as they devoured the fish bones in the trash cans. The street lamp on the corner of Atalaia Street gave off a greenish sickly glow. A sick prostitute kept the sheet hanging from her door and spied out at the passersby, begging for a penny. João Garcia always gave her one, asked her two or three serious questions, which carried a few hints about a change of lifestyle and a tenderness that brought out in the woman a sad and stupid smile and the desire to repay his concern in her own way. João Garcia gave her another penny and moved on.

He inserted the key in the lock. The staircase reeked of cat. He lay down but sleep would not come. The silence of Bairro Alto fell upon him like sentries coming on watch, stirring his remembrances and awakening him to a state of heightened alertness, as if the responsibility for saving the world rested on his shoulders. Actually, the world never seemed to him to be more alive; a quality represented in his bachelor's solitude by the very force of the silent night and of the exhaustion of a day spent waiting for a message from Margarida, a trial which two months had filled with a painful and ever more distant need. But the very intensity of that desire created in João Garcia the beginnings of a palpitation for what he awaited, as if the letter were his own fevered brain and as if the shadows at the end of the room, the wardrobe with mirror, and the cubicle that served as his study all covered with worn-out velvet and tiny red bows, all constituted a reflection of the paper on which Margarida had written.

How to explain her silence? Was it due to the letter having been sent both to her and *Dona* Corina–from his having addressed the two the same way, with the same confessions (stupid bashfulness!) cut away from the deep roots from which they stemmed? But he still kept it in his desk drawer.... ("For God's sake, don't lose my key!" He could still hear *Dona* Clotilde, the landlady, when she had rented him the room and had sung the furniture's praises: "Here's a good place for more private things... should you have, for example, checks or family letters.... Please, sir, be careful with open flames! And the rest... you know. My home is a respectable one.... I've had very upstanding people here: an airman... Moreirinha, who works at the newspaper *Mundo*, the one who was a Minister's secretary.... And no women! When it comes to that, I am very particular." And measuring him with a smile all mouth and eyes, a lingering smile: "Good sir, you have too serious a face for your age....") There, in the desk drawer, he kept the real letter, the one that he ended up not sending and to which, every time a ship departed, he added something new and pointless.

João Garcia could not explain the reason why he could not bring himself to send it. If he looked for objective reasons connected to his own will, he found the fear that Diogo Dulmo perhaps might intercept it in Horta, despite its being addressed to *Dona* Corina Peters. But then the recollection of the embarrassment he had felt regarding his way of combining his confessions to Margarida with the expression of affection prompted by the mediation of the poetess (should he send both letters loose in the same envelope? or protect Margarida's by sending it in a second envelope unsealed, of course...?) convinced him that he had been dissuaded for practically no reason, only a sheerly material reason that the minutes just past had made irreversible. There was, then, a type of paralysis in his character. Margarida lived stagnant within him like a water lily in a brackish pool enlivened by lethal moonlight. Moonlight–that fondness for feeling her always far away, suggested and desired without having a taste for her specially. Brackish pool–his life in the school... December and January, both spent in trolley trips... the

Cheribibi in Condes... the downpour of maudlin street cries–onions... oysters... keyrings a penny apiece... soooda pop.... That shower of vendors' cries seemed to well up from within him when he woke up in his room in Bairro Alto and was brought his coffee and newspaper, wet from the maid's run from the haberdasher's to the front door....

Three o'clock had struck and he could not fall asleep. Four o'clock (and an automobile horn), and from the vague fusion of half-sleep and the very strata of silence as palpable as hovering fog, he had ascended to a sharper, precise plane of consciousness. It was 5:30 when, hearing the swishing of the street-sweeper's broom, and seeing a bluish wanness pressing against the windowpanes, he finally fell asleep.

The maid came with the coffee tray to wake him up. She had to open the door, since no one answered it. She brought *O Século* and a pile of letters, the top one bearing *Dona* Corina's handwriting. João Garcia carefully ripped open the envelope, trying both not to tear the letter or to put off, even for a moment, this undoubtedly solemn gesture of destiny. He felt himself shaking. Finally–one measly page covered with Margarida's handwriting!

After "Horta, such and such a date"–without even a "Dear" or a "Good," not even his name!–he read the following:

> *It is very difficult for me to tell you the reasons why everything between us must remain at the level of a sincere friendship, which, unfortunately, we cannot display openly....*
>
> *Believe that* [informal pronoun crossed out]... *I have no regrets, not even about our having talked without thinking of the potentially disagreeable consequences, as we cannot expect anything favorable amidst deplorable hatred. I would be unjust if I did not preserve a positive memory of you and did not sincerely extend to you my sisterly friendship. Please accept it, and I ask that you not think ill of me* [transversely:] *MARGARIDA.*

João Garcia had no time to imbibe the last drop of that bitter drink, which to him, nevertheless, tasted like flowers from that fiery land where those whom you love the most hurt you the worst. Alfredo Nina came in, put his kepi and stick at the foot of the bed, and unbuttoned his mélange overcoat:

"Good day, Your Excellency! Anything come in the mail?"

João Garcia pointed to the still-unopened envelopes, and excused himself to read Uncle Ângelo's letter, which he recognized from the small round handwriting with looping scrawls. His downcast look, whose deep cause was camouflaged by features made indistinguishable from lack of sleep, became progressively sadder.

> *Dear nephew: I hope this letter finds you in perfect health, for ours.... Your Father begs to be forgiven for not writing, but, poor thing, he has been suffering from his regular ills, with more sugar in his urine and in a state of weakness that is also explained by what has happened lately, something nobody expected! Your unfortunate Mother died of the plague. At this very difficult time for all of us, I can only say to you, do not grieve. Let it be, for nobody chooses the parents who will give him birth and neither must we think ill of those who, departed and awaiting us, bore a heavy cross toward forgiveness of their sins! You are very young and have a beautiful career ahead of you, God willing. Believe it, that everything that happened in this house so long ago was not our fault nor perhaps that of my poor sister-in-law; it's all fate. Aunt Henriqueta, as you know, also has her temper, and no one is free from temptation. Well, it's all said and done; don't give it a second thought. It's been a vale of tears; everything comes at once, but your Father is recovering; I am the one who is heartbroken because my peacock in Fern Lane died. The peahen walks about so bobtailed that it frightens me! I put the feathers in the vase on the writing desk in my room, and they look so*

pretty with those silvery reflections and those little purple eyes. I am telling you this because here at home you are one of the few who appreciate these things, you and your Father when he is of a mind to. It seems that Carlota is going to write to you. The teacher says that she has a lot of talent for the piano. Your grandmother sends you many kisses and asks if you have already finished the cookies and the little bottle of hendaya. *Aunt Secundina is getting deafer and deafer, thanks be to God, and with that perfectly foul mouth that the Good Lord gave her. She is here, also waiting for the grave! Greetings from your aunt. Pretextato sends his regards and says that Ladeira and José Mónica are always getting after him to tell me to give their best to the doctor. A big hug from me, your uncle and sincere friend–Ângelo.*

"Man alive! You look as white as a sheet...." said Alfredo Nina, noticing João Garcia's increasing paleness.

"Do you remember that conversation we had some time ago about my mother? Well, she died...."

"Be strong, man!"

Alfredo put his arm, quotation-marked with golden stripes, around João Garcia's shoulder. João Garcia had set the tray and the letters on the nightstand so he could begin dressing. His feeling of closeness to his friend made it natural and human that he display all his black pieces in a chessboard of frankness, like partners silently altering their positions in the game.

"I understand your grief! But don't give yourself over to melodrama! A man like you has to be strong! As for all that family imbroglio, only the annoying aspect sticks in your mind, like your father's bourgeois cowardice. Having doubts regarding the behavior of the poor woman, he did not dare to do what his heart desired, which, perhaps, was to bring her home and forget the whole thing. That's what you must take away as an example for your life. You have, so to speak, to avenge your mother."

"My mother!... Sometimes I don't really know what that word means..."

90

"You, too... are a man without the strength of his convictions! If you wanted to know her better, why didn't you look her up?"

"To avoid complications...."

"This from an adult, a man old enough to shave! And did you speak to her often?"

"Two or three times...." said João Garcia, as tense for having struck up the conversation as he was for his irremediable cowardice. But like someone who cannot stop a car going down a steep incline and derives a certain pleasure from the certainty of the impending crash, he said: "My aunt Henriqueta was always suspicious... She never forgave my mother. And I knew that I would cause my father grief if I went to see her. Well... I just don't know! Sometimes it all looks to me like the machinations of unknown people... tragic people... And I feel so ashamed! I don't know how to rebel... That, above all, Alfredo! I can't go back to the past."

João Garcia's voice was filled with tears. Alfredo Nina put a cigarette in his cigarette-holder, quickly lit it, and threw the spent match into the wastepaper basket:

"May that remorse serve you as a consolation, man! What burns, heals...."

"You are right... Now I just feel this remorse... stuck here!" João Garcia had sat at the desk, with his head on his fists. "And to top it off, I don't even know how to cry!... That would at least bring me some relief! I search for my mother's face, and it's as if a stranger appears... just a lady who lived in King Pedro V Street with an old aunt.... Going further back, yes.... That one I remember! I don't know what happened. I don't *want* to know! I know that that one, as far as I am concerned, is rehabilitated."

"Rehabilitated?" exclaimed Alfredo Nina, suspending his pacing of the floor. "How can you talk about rehabilitation in a case like this! Let's suppose that it was true, that your mother had some kind of an affair and it went all the way. Do you dare condemn her?... Do you know the circumstances under which a woman yields?... Are you sure that they, after being rushed headlong into marriage... she, a child tormented behind those little green lattices used on our islands, which seem borrowed from a harem... was your father her man of choice...? Was he *her man*?" And Alfredo Nina pronounced "man" with the tone of an enlightened man, his blue eyes blazing and his teeth clamping his cigarette-holder. João Garcia looked as if he were about to attempt a protest, which turned cold in contact with the heated remarks. "Rehabilitate? Rehabilitate what?"

Perhaps Nina was right. And João Garcia remembered well the day his mother had gone calling on friends with him in his sailor suit. They had gone by a man standing at the door of Alexandrino's pharmacy, a military man. His mother had gone in to buy a pacifier for Carlota. The military man at the door made overtures to him: "Do you like chocolates?... Do you want chocolates?..." He had accepted right away. He felt like staying with that gentleman, who made squeaking sounds with his brown gaiters and carried such a pretty little whip. His mother paid for the pacifier, grabbed his hand, bowed to the gentleman, who had turned all red, and afterwards spent the whole afternoon making him an officer's cap with a cardboard bill. João Garcia then felt that a special meaning was attached to his little sailor suit (on which the military man, upon kissing him, had left the smell of cigar), whose white-trimmed collar his mother straightened and which smelled of *Mikado* soap and of a day of strolling on the dock lawn. Only now that Grandmother Maria Florinda had Uncle Ângelo ask him if he still had cookies and the little bottle of *hendaya* did he understand why the little old lady was the only person in the family who spoke to him about his mother, who had been thrown out of his house when he was nine: "Joãozinho, you must always respect your mother's name, for she's all alone in this world! But God forbid! in the name of His Five Wounds! Aunt Henriqueta must not even dream that I am speaking to you about these things.... And if your father should find out... God help you!..."

But João Garcia had never been able, from his grandmother's fragmented speech, to plumb the depths of that intrigue. The river flowed between the two steep banks, moving ever farther and getting ever murkier. Only with a kind of twilight awareness did he manage to grasp the ends of a memory: his mother nervously throwing her clothes into the open suitcases in the room; his father locked in the foyer office with his aunt; and Henriqueta, with a pale grin, as she held the door open and in her hands a pile of crumpled letters: "So that you, dearie, haven't the bloody gall to deny it!" "I swear! I swear!" Henriqueta's dramatic breathing was then heard as she made her way to the rooms upstairs, her righteous heels hammering the staircase. But then she came rushing down the stairs again, four steps at a time, as if she had forgotten the best part: "And tell Captain Mota that you are leaving all lively and full-breasted because you refused to breast-feed your daughter!... You shameless creature!"

João Garcia (remembering as if it were a death in the family!) saw his mother burst into an explosive and crushing fit of tears, wringing her hands toward the Garcias' smoke-yellowed Christ: "My God! My God! May I fall dead upon this floor right now if I had a drop of milk for my darling daughter!..." And her hands upon her breasts seemed to want to destroy that dried-up spring, while Ângelo's baritone voice was heard next door in the powder room, as he walked Carlota back and forth: "Oh, oh, oh.... Oh, oh, oh....

>	*Don't cry, lovey! Don't cry,*
>	*Mommy is coming for you...."*

Chapter VIII

Schermo

Under that ever-present hooded overcoat of clouds that Pico wore in ruffles around its neck, Horta had been living in the nightmare of the plague for two months. The epidemic's fury had strengthened. Still, it was not so much the body count in the city and its environs: it was the dreadful news coming in from the countryside; the disinfection teams' mules drawing the big carts under heavy lashings; many rumors arising from bars and druggists; and the mattresses being burned in the large abandoned building near the eroded boulders of Porto Pim, the place where they tried the whale blubber.

In Salão, a boy had developed a large swollen tumor under his arm, sores on his hips, and an earthen redness on his face and body. In the morning, he was unable to go to work; his mother applied vinegar compresses and strained his broth. He then started to spit up a rusty liquid and in a matter of three days was dead. His mother was already bed-ridden when the neighbors raised his coffin from the taboret and carried him, amid wailings and shawl-covered heads, to the grave. The following day, his pregnant sister fell ill in bed. Her husband, who had shrouded his brother-in-law, became ill not long after and also died. In a week, the inhabitants of four homes in Cabouco do Salão lay with their hands tied and covered with dirt, including the priest and the gravedigger. Dr. Rodrigues, called at the last minute, was in a state of despair. He entered the homes holding a swathe of cotton over his nose, ordering everybody out: "Out of here, you fools!" He did not want anybody to come in contact with a victim. The milk and the medication were to be handed to the patient from the doorway, as if the person were a rabid dog! Were the people supposed to just keep to their homes, with no one coming out to help them?... When the populace saw Pintado's landau at the entrance of the village, they received the doctor with a shower of stones and with their hoes ready to strike. A military detachment arrived, and for a day and a night, the four little thatched houses of Cabouco do Salão filled the Fayal skies with a blackened smoke seemingly filtered by the wind.

In Horta the old convent was transformed into an isolation ward. At night one could see the nurses' heads pressing against the windowpanes and the movement of lights and of white uniforms along the hallways. The local newspapers came out with screaming headlines requesting a medical envoy and lodging complaints against the government, which only thought of closing the ports to navigation, making worse, by paralyzing business, an already critical situation. The gunboat had departed for São Miguel for serum, but it was an old wreck and when its boiler broke it had to put into Terceira, where there were no adequate means to repair it.

However, except for those who had sick relatives and for those who gossiped in the club and in the pharmacy, everyone went about their business, trying to escape the epidemic as best they could. In the wealthy homes a lot of sublimate was consumed; and in the morning, the poor women of Flamengos could be seen coming down the hillsides carrying boughs of eucalyptus leaves to burn.

At the Garcias', Carlota had just finished giving her piano lesson and gone to the balcony. She could hear the trotting of horses climbing the steep incline but could only make out the rump of a horse and the flap of a riding-coat. She called Henriqueta. Who could it be? From Aunt Secundina's room, one could see *Dona* Catarina de Ataíde's well-kept backyard and, beyond some cornfields, the top of the hill. Aunt and niece quickly climbed the stairs and yanked aside the blinds in the deaf lady's room.

"Bring the binoculars!" Carlota went to Ângelo's room and, not wasting any time, leaned out of her uncle's window, quickly focusing the lenses. "Give them here, dear! You can't see anything from there...."

95

It was a lady, for sure. But what about the horseman? One could only make out a cap and a whitish coat.

"Perhaps it's the Baron da Urzelina's son and his sister. They arrived one ship late," said Henriqueta.

The riders were now galloping toward Vista Alegre.

Ever since Emília's death, the Garcias had kept their windows shut; only the family room shutters were kept half-open behind the small-paned and lilac-tinged windows. Henriqueta had expressed the wish that Carlota stop her piano lessons. But Januário had insisted stubbornly. Show respect, yes; break habits, no. He was a widower outwardly, but inwardly he was the same. In the afternoon one could see the piano teacher's black dress, followed by her hand pulling the half door behind her. A series of well-developed and hammered-out waltzes lingered in the muffled silence of the street.

Henriqueta came down to the foyer to fill in her nephew on the great afternoon news. Perhaps he knew who those horsemen were. He had arrived from Lisbon just a few days before, wearing a commissioned officer's uniform, with high brown boots laced all the way up. Once he had ridden with Captain Soares on a barracks' horse. (In Horta, most saddle horses belonged to the military.) But João Garcia's room was silent, its shutters pulled down. Henriqueta rummaged through some papers, put some books in order. Lying on the table were an open novel and a pair of gloves. Everything in the house now gave off a military air, from the shell jackets all in a row to the sword in the corner and the war-pistol cases opened on a chair. Henriqueta was bothered by the nephew's untidiness; but was excited by the novelty of the uniforms, the orderly awaiting orders in the kitchen, and the fact that João Garcia looked so dapper in his gray cape, tapping his stick against his gaiters. She put special care into the different components of his wardrobe and into the eggs that she personally fried before he left for guard inspection.

Since his arrival from Lisbon, João Garcia had gone for his customary afternoon stroll three times. He rode along the steep little alley down to Ocean Street; went by the Clarks' Granary, now with its windows open; and ridding himself of Dr. Luís da Rosa after a few minutes of chatting at the door of Yankee House, he took the Pasteleiro roadway. After reaching Escoto's grocery store, he began to see the Dulmos' quinta in the distance: first, the araucarias and the cedars covering the roofs; then the windows of the house that the setting sun, in the direction of Flores, divided and tinged with an orange glow. No sign of Margarida! Once, João Garcia had perceived the movement of a dress in a corner of the balcony, but then all he saw and heard were the chairs placed for conversation and the drone of random voices from inside the house. He walked by, keeping close to the wall, and caught sight of the little bell and string, the badly fitted gate, Cecília pedalling her tricycle, and the immense courtyard around the araucaria, whose top little ring of branches seemed tattooed against the sky. João Garcia hardly took his eyes off the strip of road; his heart was so constricted in his chest that to him it seemed to have no blood. What could have happened to make Margarida not come to the gate even a single time? So that epistolary farewell was definitive? That pledge of love he had finally sent her, laying bare his soul and handing it to her like a flower torn from its stem–had none of that been worth the effort?

He had barely caught a glimpse of her while disembarking. On board, his father, Uncle Ângelo, his sister, Pretextato, and the Honório women had surrounded him and asked to see his sleeping cabin. There was the luggage, which could not be unloaded right away. Januário had stood on the gangplank waving his arms, demanding a boat exclusively for his family. But the *Chalandra* could not moor until its turn came: the customs skiff was loading the luggage of Roberto Clark and Pedro Dulmo, who had left the boarding school. The elegant entourage trod the stair carpet of the official boat: Diogo and Mateus Dulmo, the Lemoses, *Dona* Corina, and Margarida, looking distracted and distant....

He had already gone by the Granary three times, three times along Pasteleiro, in the morning, in the afternoon, and again at night, looking at the house all lit up and enigmatic behind the wall, with the street lamp casting a yellow light over the road and a portion of the quinta down to the sea. What could have happened to the letter he had sent to *Dona* Corina's home? It had not gotten lost. He had received an answer from the noblewoman, regards from Margarida, an account of another night presided over by Chopin and the plans for a quartet. But everything so indirect and so cold.... Not even one line from her! At first he thought: perhaps she will send a postcard to soften the breakup. But not receiving the postcard had consoled him for weeks on end in the bustle of downtown Lisbon and the drudgery of school. For not getting a postcard was proof that Margarida had reconsidered and was not going to break up with him without a second thought. The other ship had not been long in coming. The gatherings of islanders in Santos had come and gone; the slingfuls of bags had been unloaded onto the big post-office truck. Then there had been the carefully executed stamping with signets at the door of Section 2 at Terreiro do Paço. More family letters, with long ones from Dr. Luís da Rosa; the pile of banal *Insulanos*, with typos on the coverage of dock traffic: "*Yesterday, such and such a ship entered the port, tugged by... a colleague of his.*" Maybe the following morning.... Sometimes a letter had gotten lost, the club voucher being received only in the afternoon mail delivery. But the mailman had picked up the two straps of his mail bag at the door of the haberdasher's, and João Garcia had returned, crushed and all alone, to his boarding house.

This afternoon he stretched out his stroll a little farther, to the first houses of Feteira. He was repeating the itinerary of his early courtship, when he had not dared to look back more than once, having left Margarida behind at the wall with Maria da Paz, or alone, eating a lapful of strawberry guava, or pacing back and forth memorizing the German declensions. Even today he had no explanation for his infantile bashfulness. He carried it within like the Host or a relic. He seemed to have no mouth, feet, nor the determination that everybody else had! Apparently, he did not approach the wall because he recalled his father's situation: dismissed from the Clark firm, and slandered by

Diogo Dulmo. The whole family was dragged through the mud of the public streets of Horta: his mother expelled from the house for adultery, Uncle Ângelo a fairy, Uncle Jacinto a village pharmacist, and Grandma Maria Florinda "an old woman with shawl and kerchief (the notary Severinino's mistress)." So one was born stigmatized by things that had happened to others? Was his love a public shame to feel sorry over and to keep quiet about? But no: Margarida did pay attention to him in full view of everybody; *Dona* Corina Peters had brought them into the fold of those silly poetess' evening parties (actually, only two or three times; but what about the chestnut tree? the afternoon spent reading Eça's *The City and the Mountains* aloud, with Tricas' stupid gramophone playing in the distance?)

> *If you see that I'm dying,*
> *Send for the Rescue,*
> *Send for them, for pity's sake...*

Margarida had made the rigmarole complete, despite the Lemoses' protests:

> *But I only want single men,*
> *Excepting bakermen,*
> *Standing by my coffin....*

Stupidly, João Garcia felt like one of those bakermen in the tune and repressed his love like something for which one only could find expression in another life.

Was João Garcia's life going to consist of nights spent at the Municipal Library and Cota presiding at the recital and marking the measures of the sonnets by striking his fingers against the end of the blotting-paper roll?... Or was it going to be his flesh-and-blood love: seeing her, marrying her, having her, and taking her off the island to Bragança, with him as Secretary General of the District of Horta and rid of that commissioned officer's cape, which guaranteed him only a place in the Royal Club of Fayal and the right to play whist on the corner opposite the *fau-*

teuils, where the insolent or elegant boys addressed with the familiar pronoun the thirty or so young girls of the upper-echelon families of Fayal?

At the public fountain of Porto Pim, a man had brought his mare to water. Manuel Bana! What if he handed him a letter? The last time it had turned out well. He saw the caretaker shrewdly pulling out his leather wallet all full of grease, smiling, removing the elastic band.... But Manuel Bana greeted him from afar and appeared reserved. The mare bucked and, making a wide circle, broke loose. Downcast, João Garcia started off in the direction of Pasteleiro. The lights of the dock were already on.

Chapter IX

Encounters

By nightfall the fields were covered with mist, and Pico rose dull and monumental out of the waters. From the direction of the Caldeira roadway came the sound of trampling, followed by a cloud of dust and a horseman in pursuit of a lady on a galloping horse.

"*Easy now! Let him go alone....*"

The horses fell into a trot and lined up side by side. Roberto Clark's horse was in a sweat, with a little foam on his belly and a hint of blood on the flank; Margarida's was dry and moved at a slow pace.

"Whew, I can't go on.... You spurred me on, Uncle, and then let yourself fall behind! That just won't do..."

"You just took off like a shot... I warned you: hold firm, then slack off... hold firm and then slack off.... And then you let him do the curve at full gallop with the other hand. *That's dangerous!*..."

Roberto Clark expressed himself fluently in Portuguese. He had only a slightly silly accent full of *ohs*, which amused his niece so much. Sometimes he hesitated a little, searching for certain words and snapping his fingers like one who lets slip away the very word he needs. He was a tall and broad-shouldered young man, and wore a sport coat and corduroy trousers à la Chantilly and a Scottish cap pulled all the way down to his red eyebrows, from under which peered two little eyes of no definite color, as if they were under water.

"How nice to gallop like this! And besides, this horse isn't like Jewel, who caught that disjointed way of walking from the *charrette*...."

"What? Your father's mare, the turkey?... *A half-breed...* I've already told your father that he must sell her."

"Oh! If you could only manage that, Uncle!..."

"For twice the price of Jewel, you can buy a good horse. I'll put up the rest of the money. It'll be my birthday present to you."

Margarida smiled but appeared reserved as she knotted the bridle reins a little and tidied her hair. She could not remember what it was like to have a birthday since her last one in the Vineyards house, when her grandfather could still move about and had insisted on going out into the channel. In February there were many days of rough seas, when the ferries nose-dived into the great troughs dug by the Guia wind. It took two people to hoist her grandfather off from the little pier staircase. Manuel Bana inside the ferry pulled him by his arm and the ferry collector standing on the pier steps stretched out his arm, braving the danger of slipping on seaweed. But Grandfather was stubborn. He would also drag himself to the window overlooking the fruit orchard, whose view was almost blocked by the table, and spread out a jigsaw puzzle on the carpet, the whisky bottle and a box of cigars by his side and whist cards fanned out on the floor. And there he would spend whole afternoons listening to the shears of Manuel Bana, who was pruning trees outside.

That year he had insisted on inviting all the families with whom they were friends to come to the Vineyards house–ferries upon ferries, the courtyard gate opened for the *charrette* and equipped with iron rings to tie the donkeys up to. They had dined in the storage room above the boat house in order to fit in more people. That was the last time they had decorated a cake with the roses she liked–Mateus Dulmo's first climbing roses, budding camellias from Pico that looked like little cups. And twenty candles burning amidst her dish set!

"You're getting old, eh?"

"Not really, but... time doesn't fly just for those who have traveled a lot, like you, Uncle. I wish I could too!..."

"Travel or get older?"

"Perhaps both...."

She felt like totally opening up to her uncle, to explain those two points that he had singled out so well apropos her remembrance of her birthday in Pico. But she could not find the right word, or at least words appropriate enough to be exchanged there from saddle to saddle in those beautiful fields. The crops were producing their first single flowers, while the tree buds remained discreetly closed. The dark green of the pastures, the Azorean green, hot and humid, stretched into the distance. The horses moved their long heads, causing their nostrils to vibrate every so often.

Perhaps she did not want to get older but would like to have a good span of time go by, like a stretch of blank film, and then be able to close her eyes for the entire duration of that sweet ride back and cover her ears like a person who has had a bad day and cries upon getting into bed, exhausted, spent.... And then wake up the following morning, but after a few years have passed, far away from Fayal, or in another Fayal, with only a road encircling the island, Pico laying before her... seagulls... and not a soul anywhere.

Her uncle had said: "Travel or get older?" Margarida, by way of reply, kept silence, staring at the horse's ears. At the edge of the road, there were some better homes with a long second floor above the ground storage floor and with ashlar stairs. Money from America. Every day those insignificant rural people cashed checks in Horta and bought up tracts of land. Pedro sometimes spoke about going to California, but he was a crazy guy: what he liked were American saddles, pocket-knives from *Betefete,* [1] and living like a cowboy. A couple of household servants, Jesuína and Garrancho, had sent him a picture: she, wearing a high-collared outfit and feathered hat; he, a pair of boots with swollen toes and *alvarozes.*

"'Alvarozes'?...!" repeated Roberto, intrigued.

---

[1] Term by which Portuguese emigrants and uneducated Azoreans generally refer to "New Bedford."-Trans.

"A type of dungarees, *overalls*. That's what they call them...."

"Yes, I know...."

Roberto then spoke about the sketchy plan of taking Pedro with him and finding him a job in the city. The fact that his English was poor was no problem: he would get him involved with his pals playing cricket and going camping; he would make something of him. Margarida asked whether foreign girls could find jobs in England, but Roberto thought it a shame to bury her in an office. In civil service, due to the war, yes. Nursing. Sorting mail in the prison camps and reeducating the wounded who, because of shell fragments in their heads, had lost their memories and even forgotten their names.... A friend of his, Mary Low, had joined the Red Cross and was leading a full and happy life.

It was getting late. The roadside shacks could be seen better with the supper lamps lit. Roberto worried about the plague. Margarida compensated for her earlier silence by speaking to him about her father's stubbornness in not allowing her to lock herself in a big isolation ward to care for plague victims, those who were left by the mercenary nurses to die of neglect. She spoke with the warmth of one who shares a secret that weighed on her chest, tightened by the riding-coat. The horses, smelling in the ground the nearby stables, stepped up their paces.

"Why don't you honor Aunt Teresa's wishes and go spend some time in Lisbon? Commander Saavedra told me he'd waited for all of you until October. Diogo said that he was going to take Pedro to the boarding school and then would leave you there with them...."

"Utter nonsense!" said Margarida. The thought of her uncle revealing romantic projects in which he himself had collaborated left her cold. "Father really tries so hard pretending everything is running beautifully, poor man! But you, Uncle, know very well... things have changed a lot from the time when Grandfather had everything in the palm of his hand. Ever since they fired Januário from the office... But our lives are no longer the same... Let's not talk about sad things.... "

Roberto kept silent. He reined in the horse and slowly lit a cigarette. His niece's seriousness impressed him. Her body's strong profile–not very secure in the saddle, albeit bold and mature–made him recall his mornings in England riding with Mary Low in the outskirts of the little town where he went to regain strength for his work in the bank. Mary was much older than Margarida but had a more childish air, a docility that was a little contrived and selfish. To speak in monosyllables and to have the courtesy of preferring the same things he did, to wish to go to the first teahouse that struck his fancy, and especially to a local cinema whenever he was not feeling well, was to him as good as whiskey with just a little soda. Mary was a pretty brunette, elegant even when wearing simple high-cut and pleated dresses that allow a woman to move in a smart way. And Roberto was tied to her in every aspect of his taste, even in his thirst for silence and conviviality, which was his heart's only excess or impertinence. For that very reason, his niece's presence filled him: she provided a contrast, proof of an extensive and difficult world, whose existence touched him and from which he did not mind keeping his distance. Her habits and her quickness had won him over. There was something naïve in Margarida's conception of certain trivial things in life. He loved, for example, to advise her to use certain restraints in her toilette. He gave her *Yardley* soap as if it were the most natural thing in the world to do, and she placed the bars in her wardrobe drawer, some on top, others at the bottom. This was as pleasing to Roberto as if he had been charged with the bookkeeping of a foreign banks consortium à la the Anglo-Spanish Bank.

They were reaching the first houses of Santo Amaro, still at a walking gait. Margarida had strained during that ride. And now that the descent did not require her to pay close attention to the trot, which her uncle had wanted to be rhythmic and with both horses abreast of each other, she smoothed out her dress and patted her horse's dark neck.

If only a lot of people were at the windows when they reached Vista Alegre! They had not gone beyond half the distance to Caldeira. And now that they were returning, Margarida pondered her uncle's words. She looked forward once again to seeing the still blossomless hydrangeas, already full of sap. An allusion Roberto made to the sale of the Flamengos Creek pastures seemed to her to carry his intention of helping to save the home. That idea caused Margarida pain. She recalled the insinuation made by her father at dinner: using her and her youthful twenty years like one uses a good-natured co-signer by marrying her to an uncle who had come to get him out of a bind. But Roberto had turned out to be a surprise to her. Nobody paid any mind to her opinions–and he, loading his pipe, listened to her quite seriously. He gave her his undivided attention and watched her with the curiosity of someone observing an insect. They would stroll through the quinta and spend hours in the ravine, untangling the blackberry thickets to pick *candeias*. The little flowers emerged from their hiding places looking like torn thumbstalls with black and white stripes. They looked like little widows dressed in Fayal-style hooded overcoats. Roberto, who had worked the miracle of training *Açor* by speaking to him gravely and with his hand opened wide, pressed his strong onyx ring against the dog's square head and squeezed two *candeias* into a crust of bread. The dog opened his thick lips, gulped down the piece of bran bread, and shaking his ears, spit out the chewed-up flowers all full of slaver. Then he ran and rolled on the ground. It was now time to go and chat for a while with the family in the dining room. Afterwards, Roberto would put on his top coat and take the *charrette* to go spend the night at the Granary.

They rode past Vista Alegre, already in the dark of night. An officer respectfully doffed his cap. It was João Garcia! Instinctively, Margarida dug her heels into the horse's flanks; but Roberto, who had stopped and whose backstepping forced João Garcia to make a wide turnabout, extended his hand to him:

"I don't need to introduce the two of you, I know...," said Roberto. "When are you going to come by the club?"

"I always go at night. These last few days following my return have kept me a little busier than usual...."

"But I've seen you in the Pasteleiro area. You're keeping up your fine shipboard habits, half the time by yourself...."

"Pasteleiro is Fayal's 'promenade of the downcast'.... All one needs is a few months away to miss all of this. Every time I return, I like to check on Pico, to see if it is still in the same place...."

"What's become of Luís da Rosa? I only spoke to him once, on board."

"He's rehearsing Sigmalia's troupe."

"It's true, Margarida! We forgot Sigmalia in my visits to my friends from the old days. Does he still play the flute? He instilled in me the habit of playing the violin. It's been more than twenty years! Do you feel cold, Margarida?..."

"No, Uncle. But the horses have worked up a sweat. Dr. João Garcia is in an uncomfortable position, with the lamp light in his eyes...."

Margarida's horse slowly traced a circle on the cobblestones, and the lovers' eyes met at the same time as their hands. João pleaded:

"At least one more time... Tomorrow, at the wall...!"

"*Good-bye*!"

When João Garcia heard his own steps on the cobblestones, there was no longer any sign of the riders. A few poor women, filling their water pails at the fountain, checked him out from top to bottom with a mocking curiosity. João Garcia dragged nervously on his cigarette and pulled up his cape.

Above the drinking trough and attached to a small hook, there shone a little yellowish, hesitant spider in the middle of a web. The water rose dark up to the iron bars that supported the water pails; the thick lead spout gurgled in the silence; and a cow's rump vanished in the darkness of the lane.

João Garcia walked aimlessly. He saw a footpath cutting through a ridge; his hand, free of the cigarette and holding the stick, begged for something to do. He headed that way, methodically whipping the tips of the bushes. Tomorrow she would show up, for sure. Margarida's eyes shone undaunted after that cruel remark about the light in his eyes and that aristocratic concern for the horses' perspiration. When shaking her hand, he had felt her tight glove. The farewell trot, independent of the actual and progressive distancing of the horses, still pulsated in João Garcia's wandering thoughts, as if that trot were his blood circulating in the distance. The loop at the end of his stick sent lopped-off tips of the honeysuckle vines flying.

Brusquely, he veered off the footpath, cut again toward the fountain, hesitated between continuing down towards the city or going up to the Lomba. But he ended up going around the monumental Clock Tower and then halted. On a park bench and half-hidden by the shade, he caught a glimpse of a soldier and an individual in civilian clothes. Only then did he notice that on the far side of the Tower there were two other people hiding behind the trees. Down below, the civilian seemed to be entertaining the private by whispering a story in his ear. "Weird...!" he thought.

He drew back quickly and taking advantage of the shadow cast by the Clock Tower, in no time gained the street. But the scene intrigued him. The anxiety felt in those last few days, his obsessive strolling along the Pasteleiro road, Ocean Street, and the side streets of the city made him forget that he had been on patrol only the night before. He felt his pockets for a pencil, thought about calling out to the soldiers, coughed. Suddenly, however, he heard the curfew call coming from the barracks and thought: "What right do I have to intrude upon these young soldiers' privacy in a public area, perhaps on leave for the night?"

But his curiosity got the best of him. He let a few minutes go by, then cautiously came down the Clock Tower's slope. One soldier quickly slipped away, and the other fled the scene like a shot. João then came face to face with a man with a huge black eye, his clothes in disarray, his hair flying in the wind: it was Uncle Ângelo!

"Uncle!..."

"Keep going, João. It was nothing.... I can walk on my own. It was nothing...."

But João Garcia charitably put an arm around him and helping him through the square and the streets, which luckily were almost deserted, managed to get his uncle into his downstairs room, after silently closing the front gate.

"God help you!...."

Ângelo lay stretched out in bed with his clothes on but without his tie. He had purple furrows on his face down to his slavering lips, and his breathing was labored:

"Make sure that the women upstairs don't hear us, João! Your uncle is a miserable wretch...."

Chapter X

Second Nocturne

Ever since Roberto's arrival Margarida had been shaken up. At home she did not feel as much her mother's sighing. Her father, a little because of his sense of honor and to win over his brother-in-law, was on his best behavior. He spent more time in his father-in-law's room and went by the Granary early in the morning to see if Roberto needed anything. *Dona* Catarina emerged from her shawl like a moth from its cocoon. The swelling in her feet and her tiredness prevented her from traveling to Horta, but she received news from Margarida about the big house in the city after it had been aired out and cleaned. She had picked out blankets and linens for her brother's bed by going through big drawers and trunks that had not been opened since she was single. At last she brightened up a little.

Pedro was not going back to Lisbon. Halfway through his first school term, he had received low grades. Since as punishment he was being forced to take special lessons in the old cafeteria of the convent where the school was housed, he got up in the wee hours of the night, packed his clothes and books, and moving on tiptoe through the dormitory half-lit by the Rossio lights, opened the shutters cunningly left unlocked the previous day, and landed right on the wall fence like a parachutist. Until the ship's departure, he had stayed at Commander Saavedra's in Junqueira. Roberto Clark also bought him ship fare and, upon their arrival in Fayal, managed to contain Pedro's father's anger with a healthy smile and a friendly hand on his nephew's already strong shoulder.

Margarida had helped her mother to accept things as they were. If the boy did not want to study, what was to be done? At eighteen he was no longer a little child. Time spent waiting for a job would go by quickly. There was the quinta. He liked to hunt. He dabbled in mechanics. Perhaps he could be talked into taking a course in America–something practical, not too intellectually demanding. Or else he could in due time become a telegrapher for the Trans-Atlantic Cable Company. But Uncle Roberto suggested the possibility of taking him to London. Who knows what future might await him there, especially the experience and the deep-rootedness that he did not enjoy now?

Pedro seemed the diametrical opposite of Margarida. Although no one knew why, he was dark. The Dulmos were redheaded and short; the Clarks, fair-haired. He was swarthy, with black eyes filled with cunning and leisureliness. He could close his left eye a little and, aiming only with the right one, cock the trigger of his gun, point the barrel–and fire! A few meters away, there would fall dead on the stubble a quail or a poor harmless blackcap that had been testing the height of the quinta cherry tree (which in May, Margarida watched in vain in the hope of seeing it covered with blossoms).

Since someone needed to attend to the household chores in the Granary, and one could not count on *Dona* Catarina for that, Margarida was the one who spent part of the morning hours there. Sometimes Manuel Bana, after milking the cows, drove her in the *charrette*. At other times, she walked. And since she liked to get up early, she stopped at Angústias Church to hear morning Mass. If she saw the Granary shutters still closed in the distance, she went for a stroll on the dock. On some days, an American submarine came in and was moored to the inner pier. One could see its olive-colored stern above the surface and the sailors wearing their little white "soup bowls" on their heads, with their overalls covered with oil stains. A garland of seagulls crowned Mount Guia. The shutters of Roberto's room, which looked to the sea, opened out. One could see his hand on his lathered-up face; a white face towel waved from there. Margarida, standing on the big wall, attempted to make her savage howl heard, the *ho! hi!* of the afternoon regatta races–the "password." But Roberto remained impassive, shaving. Margarida jumped down from the big wall to the pier and hastened her steps in the direction of the Granary.

Finally, the quartet Mateus Dulmo had dreamt up was organized, and rehearsals were scheduled for afternoons in the Granary. Roberto found his father's big house a little gloomy. He had thought of throwing a ball to reunite friends and relatives whom he had not seen for years. The quinta was far off; old man Clark would feel disturbed by gauntlets of open doors, the shaking of the floors under a never-ending parade of dancing couples, and their laughter. It was better to hold the ball in the Granary. But the plague upset everything. Sigmalia had fallen ill. A whole family in the neighborhood had come down with the disease. The house became isolated and smutted by formaldehyde, its seaward windows wide open over the gray waters of the channel.

Despite that, Margarida ordered the rugs in the salon dustcleaned at the far end of the Granary. To accommodate her uncle, only the rooms overlooking the dock had been prepared. The windows on the back of the house had been recently painted green and white.

One afternoon while she busied herself dusting the pendants of the chandelier, Margarida saw João Garcia far away, standing absentmindedly by the big wall–his foot resting on the bench. He was wearing a tie and pelisse and was with another officer. They could not see her; but for caution's sake, she moved back a little and closed the blinds.

The day before, she had not gone down to the wall as he had asked her. There was no reason to show up. She did not even think about him any more. Realizing how strange this lack of feeling was, she concentrated her attention for a while, trying to determine whether it was so; then she brushed harder at the prisms of the chandelier.

She had never been as interested in anything as she was in that huge dark room that had not been opened up in years. The walls oozed moisture from behind the hanging portraits, from which the subjects' features emerged through flaking tones. The furniture was pretty, though slightly mismatched. There were old knickknacks and clutter. Mariana from Pico, who had been Roberto's wet-nurse and who could do little more than make a bed or sweep the floor, had lined up everything in the hallways and kitchen. She was reinvigorated by her "little boy's" return. Margarida sorted things, rummaged through the drawers, and came to the balcony to blow the dust off the little Saxon boxes.

Despite the suspension of rehearsals due to Sigmalia's illness, Roberto wanted the big room set up within a few days. And one night, leaving *Dona* Catarina napping in the armchair in her father's room in Pasteleiro, he told Diogo Dulmo to have the mare hitched up. They would drop him off at the club; and Margarida, Maria das Angústias, and Roberto would spend the evening in the Granary, cleaning house.

In an old wardrobe cabinet, they had discovered a ball gown that had belonged to *Dona* Margarida Terra. Roberto insisted that Margarida try it on. It was Carnival time. The previous Thursday, there had been a masked ball at *Dona* Corina Peters' home: Roberto and Pedro had both worn masks. To avoid gossip, Dr. Luís da Rosa, wearing a milkman's costume, had come in a landau belonging to Pintado. Margarida had donned a black disguise, and to keep *Dona* Corina guessing, she had put on a visor that allowed only her eyes and the tip of her chin to show. Confusion reigned in the poorly lit hallway. Then in the parlor with the little green cloth-covered tables pulled to the center and readied for a game of whist, they argued about who had worn the best costume and whose voice was too distinctive to disguise; and due to the constricted, dispirited air that gradually had fallen upon all of them, they talked about supernatural phenomena for which there was no explanation but nevertheless happened. "I saw it!" "How can it be?" "I swear it! A whitish light, like skimmed milk, floated toward the back of the house. We were standing like right now but with only a candle lit in the middle of the table, this way...." Maria da Paz sprang to her feet and covered with her two hands the strong kerosene lamp that cast a full light on the tokens used for keeping score. "Father was dumbfounded. And Mother also. Damião Serpa couldn't get his hands off the table d'hôte and said: 'Wandering spirit, if we can help you, knock only three times!' And the leg of the table rose exactly three times!"

The elderly *Dona* Francisca Peters covered her eyes. *Dona* Corina believed that spirits did dwell within things but also was of the opinion that one should not meddle with certain powers. It was dangerous to play games with the invisible, to go beyond certain limits.

But a dubious round of whist had been played. They had to recapitulate who had opened, whose jack that was. "A jack? It was Margarida's! The jack of spades always ends up in Margarida's hands...." But it was the jack of diamonds, and it was finally ascertained that it had been played by André Barreto, the son of the Baron da Urzelina. "I was the one who broke with diamonds."

Tired of playing whist, they laughed a lot and spoke about other things. Mateus Dulmo opened the piano lid and flushed out a provocative waltz. André Barreto then offered Margarida his arm; Roberto bowed before Clarinha, André's sister, and for a few minutes the Peters' living room, with chairs pushed aside, shook under their feet.

Margarida was the first to stop dancing. Her black disguise had circled the dark corners of the salon, with its low stifling ceiling, more often than the other girls'. She went to the piano and spent the rest of the evening party convincing Uncle Mateus to play his entire Chopin repertoire. Roberto Clark consented to playing the "Ombra Mainfù," the *Largo* from Handel's *Xerxes*. The shadow of the violin was cast upon the canvas of Raimundo Pórras, Governor of Damão. Behind Mateus Dulmo's hidden form, Margarida's hand turned the pages of the score, bending the flames of the gutted candles.

Now, in the Granary, after a certain reluctance, she consented to trying on her grandmother's ball dress. Maria das Angústias adjusted the waist and the width of the skirt. Roberto went to turn on the switch of the chandelier above the jardiniere so Margarida could check the fit.

"Bidinha, you can't see anything there. That mirror has no reflection!" said Maria das Angústias.

But Margarida insisted that that was how she liked to see herself–in old mirrors. They removed the rawness from things and reflected the backgrounds so well.

"You look like a painting, a Reynolds," said Roberto naturally. His paternal and impassive look made him seem to be imagining the effect that Margarida would cause dressed this way at a carnival party rather than perceiving her image as reflected in a puddle.

"It's cute, no doubt about it!" said Maria das Angústias, taking a closer look and puffing up the silk ruffles on the shoulders. "She's her grandmother's spitting image. Don't you think so, *Senhor* Roberto? Godmother also looks a little like her mother, come to think of it. But she resembles *Senhor* Carlos Clark even more. Just as you do, m'lord. But the one who really takes after the Terra family is Bidinha."

"When one starts trying to find resemblances, she discovers what she *wants* to discover. With me, it's like this.... I am either all Clark, 'all of me!' or 'she really has that arrogant Dulmo look.' 'No! No!' replies another: 'What she is, is a Terra!' Yes: 'Earth,' just like everybody else is on Ash Wednesday. Let her be, poor Grandmother there in her picture frame!"

Roberto surveyed the big room from end to end. He seemed deep in thought during that conversational detour through hereditary resemblances, naively proposed by Maria das Angústias and presumptuously developed by Margarida. He recalled his mother stuck in a house on a Horta street since she was twenty-five, hardly even going to the windows that remained shut all day, as if its residents had abandoned the house or were suffering from the plague. Her Fayal-style veil took her to morning Mass and, rarely, to a store. Dead to the family! Her place in the Silveiras' theater box for the operetta premieres was always given to her sisters' friends.

Margarida went around the jardiniere to turn off the chandelier. Since the other bulb was weak, the big room with its drowsy furniture remained in the dark. The embers of Roberto's pipe shone by the window.

"Lieutenant Espínola!"

Steps and a voice, drowned by the calm, muffled broad rolling of the sea, were heard coming from outside.

"Come on up!"

"Thank you, but I've company."

Roberto hesitated:

"Very well, then. What about later? I don't go to bed early. Come over for a while! For a chat."

Margarida quickly took off the dress.

"Where did you meet Lieutenant Espínola, Uncle?"

"In the club. He was with a group of officers when introduced to me. He's an ace billiards player. Is he from this island?"

"Yes, he is."

"I told him to come in, not knowing whether you like him. Sorry about that."

"That's all right! Actually, he's a well educated young man and very much interested in history. He was Pedro's tutor and knows a lot about chemistry."

"Does he teach in the high school?"

"He teaches history. They say he has done very important research on the discovery of the Azores. He is preparing a new edition of *The Insular History of the Western Atlantic Islands Under Portuguese Rule*."

"You even remember the titles, *Sophia*?"

"What's the *Sophia* about?"

"*Because you are a thinker! You have a philosophical mind... a lofty mind.*"

"Only if you consider Father António Cordeiro a philosopher. You don't take me seriously, Uncle. Not only when it comes to horseback riding but to everything! You baby me and give me presents; but serious consideration, you give me none. That's exactly what I think!"

The emphasis she placed on her complaint carried with it a touch of contradiction. Roberto quietly bit his pipe; his bluish eyes became a little brighter.

He enjoyed feigning a certain indifference when it came to matters of the spirit, but he was intelligent and well-read. He had brought from London that superficial but reliable information found in encyclopedias, specialist manuals, magazines for all tastes, and the ponderous and summary discourse of the periodical *Spectators*. He especially enjoyed reading novels, jungle and sailing literature, Kipling and Conrad. One of his suitcases bearing a state-room label was half full of books. In France he had gotten a supply of Tauchnitz. Margarida devoured a little of all that.

Someone rang the bell. The staircase pull-string attached to the old arched bell had rotted. On the eve of Roberto's arrival, they had moved the big office bell to the upstairs rooms. That sound echoed brusquely throughout the house, which, despite the comfort and intimacy derived from its having been the Clark family's original living quarters, warranted, on account of its huge size and forlornness, the designation "Granary." The title actually came down to them from the time when the first Clark, Ralph Clark, had filled it with sacks of cereal and crates of oranges awaiting a sailboat for shipment to London. The firm's founder had slept downstairs in a corner of the office until marrying.

Maria das Angústias' voice came down from the top of the stairs; then, total silence. The wet-nurse called out:

"Who is it?"

It was nobody. Sometimes children went by, were intrigued by that little white button, and pressed it.

"Isn't it Macedo in the *History of the Four Islands* who tells of my great-grandfather, right after he arrived in Fayal, ravishing a nun from Glória convent?" asked Roberto, still turned towards the door with an impassive air.

"No. That's a very complicated story.... Uncle Mateus is the one who knows it well. It seems that there's a booklet by Raimundo Pórras about the exporting of oranges that tells the whole story. They say that Uncle Ralph was the perpetrator of the abduction; but Dr. Luís da Rosa insists that Raimundo Pórras... (the one who was in Damão... you know, Uncle?... the one in the picture at our Cousin Peters'–the color of ground coffee... we have a print of it).... Well, there's no doubt that an abduction took place; but it seems that the booklet doesn't mention our grandfather's name."

"Perhaps to avoid causing a scandal among half a dozen families. On the island, we are all related to one another. I seem to remember my wet-nurse telling me that story. Let's see.... Some Mother Superior, Rosinha da Glória.... But she confused the nun with the ballad 'Silvana Sitting in Her Garden.' I've always had a memory like an elephant! It's true! What if you were to call her?"

"Good idea! Mariana! Come here, Marianina! Your little boy misses you so much."

The old lady came down the hall, all embarrassed, with her hands crossed under her woolen apron.

"My grandmother used to tell me those tales about Sister Rosinha da Glória... stories from the good ol' days! But why do you wanna know, little one? Do you wanna make fun of me? May as many angels accompany me to heaven as the number of times I told you those stories to get you to eat your soup! 'Member? In Pico, after the death of our *Dona* Margaridinha, when your mother went to live with you in the Vineyards house... in that *desert*?"

"Tell us again!"

But the old lady stood meekly by the door, withdrawing her head into her coat, which had a row of black glass buttons. Her sharp chin protruded with her toothless laughter, an abrasive, innocent laugh, a kind of posthumous modesty.

"Go away! You're acting like your old devilish self! Come now!"

"Don't be silly, Mariana!" Roberto said in English. "Otherwise, I'm going to start speaking English with you."

"Oh, you hush your mouth! And this pretty little thing, my little pearl... also helping make sport with the old lady!

> *Young girl, don't you buy*
> *A rich man's sweet talk:*
> *It's like rolling boulders*
> *On the Pico Island shores...."*

Margarida applauded:

"Bravo! See, Uncle? Get ready now... When Mariana sings one of her songs, she doesn't need to be prodded anymore: she improvises on the spot the story of *Charlemagano* and the one about Empress Pigpen. All you've got to do is ask."

The old lady, small and sprightly, had ceased being intimidated by the presence of her young masters in that salon full of shadows and heavy runners. She fell into a chair and, with her little eyes afire as in a trance, began:

"A lot of water has passed under the bridge! My grandmother Joaquina had a squint in her eye, poor thing! God love her! She'd grab the piece of bamboo pipe she used for filling her pail at the public fountain, the one with the spout like a stiff horn (pardon my words!); I'd take her by the hand and she'd sit at the doorstep to while away the time, you know. She lived in Criação Velha, in the little house that belonged to my father, above the whalewatcher's stone. To call the men to the whaleboats, they'd blow the conch shell. What a time it was!"

"Come on already! What about the nun?"

"Sister Rosinha da Glória entered the old convent 'cause of something that happened to her. She had a boyfriend who treated her bad; her father didn't like the match. He was the first-born of Fanais, the son of a captain of the militia. My grandmother used to say that he put the fear of God in everybody. When he arrived in a bad mood, he'd start coughing...." And Mariana coughed. "His wife and the servants didn't know where to hide. The daughter was beautiful! Like an angel.... 'If you speak to him at the wall, I'll tear you limb from limb!', her father would say. In those days, men in Fayal used those big huge rods, like the poles they use in the procession of the Holy Ghost. In Criação Velha's public storeroom there are still two that were used by the festival organizers, as proof that I'm not telling lies."

"And then what happened?" asked Margarida, in a faint voice and with her elbows on the jardiniere.

"That poor little angel's body was all bruised from the lashings she got. Her father locked her up in the tower and fed her bread and water for a week straight. Her mother became so sad that she was all skin and bones. In the end, when the rage had passed, he said this: 'Joana, get all your daughter's things packed, because I'm gonna stick her in a convent.' Oh, the tears that flowed in that house! And everything she had was the best... panniers, gold chains... shirts upon shirts, the kind made on the loom like in the old days. Everything was tossed on top of the trunks and given to her cousins who lived by the main square. An auction! I used to lead grandmother on and she, one-eyed as she was, went on with the story: in the towers of the old convent, the bells seemed to announce somebody's death! The mother only said: "The bells are ringing right on my back, for the light's fading forever from these eyes of mine!' And her face was a stream of tears.... The church was chock full of people!... Robertinho, you remember... on turning the corner of the fire station, the old convent... where that what's-his-name lives.... I forget his name! The nuns all sang, corralled in by those window grates, while the priest blessed the poor little thing, all dressed in white with a train like she was getting married. Her hair cascaded all the way down to her heels... The Mother Superior grabbed a pair of scissors and cropped it all right off! It was enough to break your heart! Everybody started crying. Then the father burst in and shouted for everybody to get out of the place."

"What about the abduction?" asked Margarida, with a lump in her throat.

"That was three years later. The English gentleman came here to buy oranges and got into the convent's enclosure in a basket. Rosinha da Glória was a young thing.... One night, you know... the servant who let the English gentleman in pretended he was delivering big oranges to the Mother Superior, and so he came out with the basket, the nun, and everything...."

Roberto gave a forced laugh and shook his pipe. There was a moment of silence. The old lady continued:

"It's not nice to lead girls astray in a sacred place, but neither was it good to embitter the young girl that way. What can I say? Marriage and death are decided in Heaven. It's fate."

Attentive to the story, Roberto and Margarida had not even

noticed Diogo Dulmo. Taking advantage of the darkness in the big salon and in order not to interrupt them, he had walked in stealthily and leaned against the console table. His solid figure was immobile, his hand resting on the marble edge. His eyes, fixed but clouded by shadow, surveyed the distance between Margarida's elbow and Roberto's serene and attentive body. He seemed to be looking inward; but the preoccupation that furrowed his brow since his brother-in-law's arrival now lay many fathoms deep, beyond his ulterior motives. It was Margarida who, prompted by the lull, said:

"It's time for us to leave, Father."

"I came up to say that I think it's better that you stay here tonight. The *charrette* has a broken mortise, and I told Manuel Bana to go unhitch the mare. It's really coming down out there. Hear it?"

As if approaching the door of a shelter, they all drew near the windows. A heavy shower was falling outside in a compact rhythm without wind blasts, altered only, every so often, by some larger drops. The dock lights seemed veiled in the distance by the sheet of rain. The house, swallowed by silence, seemed larger and more deserted.

"I've already told Maria das Angústias to put more sheets on your grandmother's old bed."

"And you, Father?"

"I'm going to sleep in Pasteleiro. I brought my overcoat."

"You'll sleep in my room; you have the divan in there!" said Roberto.

"It's not worth it. Catarina can't stay alone with her father. Good night!"

Since the light bulb in the Clarks' bedroom was burned out, Roberto fetched a candle and struck a match. Maria das Angústias fluffed up the pillow. She seemed to be going back to her time as a robust dry-nurse making up the crib at nightfall in the little towers:

"Ah! Bidinha will be very comfy and cozy here. It's as if we had to sleep on the floor in Pico during the grape harvest."

"And where are you going to sleep?"

"We'll use benches to extend Mariana's bed. Go! Get ready for bed!"

Margarida had a hard time falling asleep. Now the rain was intercepted by an insidious wind which seemed to suspend it, only to drop it that much harder against the windows. She had taken a book to bed, but the candles were new and the stiff wicks resisted the flames. She snuffed them with a match and started to peel off meticulously the hot wax with her fingernails. Under an edge of the sheet lay the *Typhoon* with a folded page. Captain MacWhirr ordered that the halyard raise the flag of Siam, but Margarida was not in the mood for Conrad's storytelling. She blew out the candle and tried to close her eyes. The bed reeked of stale linen and burnt wick. The thought of Captain MacWhirr's wife lying in bed while her husband assumed the command of a ship in the China seas fused in her mind with that of Rosinha da Glória's cropped hair. Mariana told that story so well.... But it was gloomy. She needed to wash her hair and had brought no cap. Why had she stayed at the Granary? Could it really be the rain that had prevented them from going home? Brave the weather? With her father–of course!–there were always broken mortises in the *charrette*, pretexts to have it parked in Bishop Alexandre Square, with the mare draped in oilcloth. The length of the house was made apparent beyond the fanlights of the door leading to the salon, from which came a very faint beam of light from the room next to it. Uncle Roberto was retiring for the night. She heard something like footsteps, and sounding in her imagination sharpened more by the silence than her ear–the impression that clothes were being folded, the thick scraping, suddenly interrupted, of a chair across the floor. And what if her father had proposed that they sleep in the Granary to allow them some privacy? The opportunity that the devil takes by the horns? She lit a candle and picked up the book again. But the sensation of a body that stretches and finds a comfortable position on the mattress, followed by a longer silence marked by heavier rain, brought to her mind the image of Roberto lying down with the corner of his mouth marked by the habit of his pipe and that air of one who falls in a deep, con-

fident sleep. "If you're fond of him, let it be! Marry him!...
Keep it all in the family." And why shouldn't she? The last few
months she had felt disabled, as if she were something to disas-
semble and at last had only the central piece remaining, awaiting the others all scattered about. Even Lieutenant Espínola's
passing by with a friend (who? for what?...) had her wondering
how he would look with a wife by his side. She had never
brushed a pelisse. Now, when she again rode a horse, she would
do as Uncle Roberto liked: wear a sport coat and trousers, à la
califourchon....

With her eyes half-closed, she thought of her mother watching over her grandfather's sleep. She saw the entire quinta, the
ravine in bloom and filled with arum lilies, the araucaria dripping water, the stables. Jewel's sorrowful eyes first avoided the
chewed-up straw and took in with a glance the steel brush that
lay in a hollow; then they brightened up as she stiffened her
ears. Uncle Roberto had insisted that her father sell the animal.
With that knotty spine and without her tub of water, she would
surely die in the communal pastures! Now Baron da Urzelina's
son was also cozying up to her by showing her his three-year-
old horses. Her uncle had said that his birthday gift to her would
be the money still lacking for a good horse, counting what the
sale of Jewel would bring. She was almost falling asleep. But
Jewel was big and had good legs; in Manuel Bana's hands, she
nearly always broke into a full gallop. Jewel was the one who
had whisked her away from that spectacle of the simpletons
devouring her with their eyes at the door of Yankee House. She
would not ride her.... She turned in bed.

Grandmother Margarida's bed was cramped against the wall
and as narrow as a bunk. "The one she resembles most is
Grandmother Terra..." "Earth..." Rain. "That arrogant Dulmo
look...." Rain. She had gone to view the ship from *Typhoon*...
and was now sailing on the high seas.

Chapter XI

The Living and the Dead

A row of carriages had parked along the Dulmos' quinta. Voices and laughter rang from the courtyard. The bright figures of girls fluttered between the landing of the staircase and the vestibule. The mules pulling the landaus shook their bell collars and the flowers with which Roberto had patiently trimmed their headstalls. Cecília and Bebé Lemos were chasing each other around a victoria; an old coachman guarded a team of horses, his eyes on the wheel spokes. It was an afternoon in April. Pico's peak looked purple, intersected by a dark cloud.

Roberto had organized this outing to Caldeira against the wishes of his sister and grandfather. It was still very cold, and they had to pass farmhouses of people suffering from the plague, shacks burned down by order of the secretary of health after another outbreak of pneumonia. But Roberto insisted that there was no danger of contagion, except near the patients or by touching their infected clothes. On the contrary, the country air drove away the danger. Driving under the incense and poplar foliage filled the lungs with fresh air; the group would bring boughs of eucalyptus in carriages with the tops down. Besides, it was not a good idea to feed their terror by keeping young people locked up at home. They should lead a normal life–or else leave the city behind. People talked a lot about the air in Pico. In Madalena, there had been only half a dozen cases of the plague and all bubonic: two deaths in all.

The Lemoses rode in a landau with *Dona* Corina and a girl, Daisy Warren, from a neighborhood where the telegraph cable personnel lived. Maria da Paz, along with André and Clarinha Barreto, took another carriage. Margarida had wished to go in Roberto's victoria; but Dr. Luís da Rosa, always absentminded, had gotten into it first, and there was only enough room for two. His carriage had departed at a trot with a little freckled boy along for the trip. Pedro sat lounging comfortably in his seat and outfitted in his hunting gear.

Margarida tried to get into Cousin José de Lemos' carriage, in which Fräulein Wartel also was riding; but Roberto stuck his head out of the carriage and with a gesture that Margarida resignedly understood, pointed to the door of the landau in which the Baron da Urzelina's son and daughter were traveling: "Okay, let's get going."

Dona Catarina saw them round the bend where the quinta wall narrowed and where the empty road, under a canopy of cedar branches, muffled the sound of the carriage wheels and turned the horses' trot into a drum roll. She went to her father's room. Maria das Angústias was busy with the medicine bottles. The house was in silence, and from the back windows, one could see the channel, bereft of sails.

"When *Senhor* Mateus Dulmo arrives, tell him to come in here."

The sick man's nightstand was strewn with papers covered with numbers; wrinkling his brow, he was trying to decipher a copy of a promissory note:

"This isn't what I told Diogo I would sign. I was cheated. I see ten contos twice: twenty contos!"

Dona Catarina had nestled down on the rug at the foot of her father's armchair and, leaning her head over, caressed his arm and tucked the heavy quilt around his legs:

"Don't bother with that. Uncle Mateus will explain everything to you later. Roberto says that as far as he's concerned, he never thought of his inheritance after being declared legitimate."

The old man shook his head and put down the paper; under his wrinkled brow, his light eyes turned glassy as he spoke:

"My poor son!" *Dona* Catarina made a supreme effort not to burst into tears. "I lovingly paid for his college in London... He didn't even allow me the pleasure of continuing to send him his monthly allowance! And always those letters: 'During hard times, the firm comes first. Diogo has been down on his luck.' At 18, he was already tied to a desk, while the others were having a rip-roaring time! My poor son!"

"You're tormenting yourself, Father. Let it go... there's always a solution. I trust that Uncle Mateus will convince *Dona* Carolina Amélia. Perhaps the Avelars will not dare to.... Roberto enjoys the reputation of being rich. He's so well-liked."

"He's a Clark." And thinking about the whaleboats and the bare-headed whalemen with their eyes and ears on the whale-watcher's rocket, he raised his voice, already less upset: "'Is it the Granary? CLARK & SONS? Let's pay.' And now?... 'Dulmo, that poor excuse for a man!'"

"Please, Father!"

Mateus Dulmo, who had probably overheard the whole conversation, slowly came into the room:

"May God bestow his blessings on all you good people. How are you feeling, Carlos?"

The old man grimaced indifferently and removed his hand from the pile of cushions. Mateus Dulmo's arrival shut him up in his sick man's selfishness, behind his downy flowing beard. Mateus Dulmo walked to the window, glanced at his niece, asked about the caravan departing for Caldeira he had seen in front of Angústias Church. He spoke about gillyflower seeds; the purplish-red bed was looking very pretty. The room smelled of medication and flowers, despite the empty vases; along the hallway there were patches of sunlight and a smell of sea breeze coming from the terrace.

"Well, Carlos, things are going very badly... very badly. But there's no reason to give up ship. Roberto, of course, says that he wants no part of his inheritance; so you need not consider his share of the assets frozen."

"CLARK & SONS!" said the old man, emphatically. "A corporation signifying Anonymous Association of limited responsibility! That means the partners' personal estates are not responsible for covering the firm's liabilities, except up to the value of each one's share. Isn't that what it means? In my father's time, at any rate, that's what it meant."

"You're mistaken, Carlos," objected Mateus Dulmo with the patience of a night-school instructor teaching a course to remedial students. "Your firm is not a corporation; its responsibilities are not limited. It's what they refer to as a 'collective,' which holds the partners, along with all their personal estates, responsible for everything, both assets and liabilities. You know that the whaleboats are not just in Diogo's name; Catarina's share already went up in smoke. Besides, you have continued to be a co-signer for your son-in-law; the family's honor is at stake. As for me, I want to tell you something.... The pastures I inherited from my mother are worth about twenty contos. I had another twenty or so set aside for a rainy day. I'd thought of leaving them to your granddaughters, since Teresa has no children. Now I'm going to leave them to their father. And I'm not going to die of starvation on account of that. I still have my pay-clerk's pension and the hole in the wall where I live. As you can see, what matters most is protecting the good name of all of us, Clarks and Dulmos alike. Up to forty contos, all of you can count on me."

"'All of you,' no! Your nephew...."

"We can't accept your generosity, Uncle," said *Dona* Catarina, her eyes brimming with tears. "That would mean that you'd have to watch disappear everything you've worked for and labored so hard to save."

"Labored hard, nothing! I'll still keep my harmonium; I'll become a Kappelmeister."

"These Dulmos are like that!" said the old man as if he were talking to a doctor who had just finished stitching up a daredevil's head. "Diogo let everything come to this because of that confounded attitude of his!"

"Let's be reasonable, Carlos. I don't deny that that young man doesn't have his head on straight; but a good part of this mess stems from Januário's time, when you went to England."

"And who forced me–by telegram–to fire Januário? And who had set up that deadbeat José de Lemos, your relative, in the office by the time I came back?"

"You lay too much blame on family blood, Carlos.... What

the hell! We're childhood friends; I was like a brother to your wife.... I never offended you or hurt you in any way. I am an honorable man!"

Old man Clark had almost gotten himself up. One could read in his eyes, which, aided by the movement of his slim and nervous hands upon the heavy quilt, were searching for Mateus Dulmo's eyes, a mixture of confusion and rage. He seemed to want to retain half of what he was saying in the subtle furrows of his brow. A broad blush suffused his hollow cheeks. He breathed heavily, laboriously. *Dona* Catarina had stood up and was looking anxiously now at one man, now at the other:

"What about the Avelars, Uncle? What do the Avelars say?"

"I proposed an agreement among the creditors. I even looked up *Dona* Carolina Amélia, who was not totally averse to it. Then she seemed to change her mind. The older Avelar was entirely in agreement, and even the son proved to be less intransigent. But yesterday, I don't know what side of the bed he got up on; I went there with Dr. Nunes, who's rescued them from that flour deal gone awry. Avelar was inflexible. If you don't come up right away with at least two thirds of the whale fishery debt, they will forget the whole thing–and seize the whaleboats and the ambergris."

Forgetting the danger that the scene represented for her father, *Dona* Catarina walked around the armchair, opened her shawl and, raising her eyes, said:

"All this is Januário Garcia's doing! He's been plotting all this from the shadows! But I know his dirty hands: the marks are still there on the safe's padlock from when Diogo changed the combination and forbade him to touch anything that was secret. Those slimy hands he beats his chest with, like this....." She bent forward, and her small, milk-white wrist, a little swollen, elicited a hollow echo from her chest (for years now she had not walked up the transept of Horta Cathedral at the time the Gospel was being read with that air of distinction). (Only she and two or three of her cousins had stood, like the men, with a long and respectful clearing of the throat echoing through the three naves, where there was no room to fit even a pin.)

"The pretender to the hand of his employer's daughter and almost the father-in-law of his granddaughter!... who threw his wife out of her home to please his sister, that Garcia broad!..."

"Who are you talking about, Catarina?"

"... Januário, The Whale! I remember it like it just happened! I was just a little girl in pigtails, and he would drive me in the break to Flamengos Creek. So tender he was! So attentive! He would cozy up to me in my plaid outfit. When it rained, he opened that tent (the whitish umbrella that used to belong to the notary Severinino) and drew me close. I was an ingenue and had no idea. But when I came from the boarding school, already more savvy.... No! that wasn't natural. And a smooth talker... He became very zealous; he bent my ear with talk of all the good deals he had advised father to make. That the family was very rich... With him at the helm... all he needed was for us to give him a couple of years... when they came out with motorized whaleboats... a silent motor they used in the Shetland Islands. The profits would even be enough for pleasure trips! Should he get married, he'd do as Counselor Calapez does: visit the great European capitals every couple of years. That greaseball!..."

"Kate!"

"Let me get it off my chest, Father! Oh! He never dared to come straight out with anything. I would have eaten him alive! But ever since Diogo asked for my hand (he had already gotten married, and his bouncing baby boy had already been born), he never again looked us straight in the eye. Then, in Father's absence, everything was uncovered: the phantom profits that he didn't record; the lumber bought at auction and taken at night in barges to Praia do Almoxarife; finally, the bank account books stolen from the safe. A thief in every way! Those dirty, frog hands.... that in church he flaps his chest with!"

Old Clark had tilted his head back and closed his eyes. His hands were shaking:

"That's enough, girl!"

"Catarina, you're forgetting your place," said Mateus Dulmo gravely.

"It's because I remember who we are, Uncle, and because I remember that I ran the risk of calling that Garcia woman's nephew, the child prodigy, my son-in-law! And let's not speak too soon, we are not out of the woods yet."

"They're children and can't be held accountable for their parents' transgressions."

"So much has befallen us!" said the old man. And looking at Mateus Dulmo, like one who appraises the worth of an object he would like to buy, provided its owner could be reasoned with: "You'll have to forgive me, Mateus, but as far as the Dulmos are concerned... Your father saved his own skin, and right now you'd be wise to do the same."

Mateus Dulmo had withdrawn behind an offended smile, which cast a light on the world of his memories. They were like shipwrecked people who had missed the lifeboat while arguing about the most dignified way to grab hold of it, and Mateus Dulmo expressed his shame in rapid creative reconstructions and connections. His brother was a gambler and a womanizer; his nephew was a drunkard. But his beloved Charles William Clark was no saint himself. Cold, stubborn, that physical self-sufficiency stemming from his always having gotten his way, leaning for support on his collection of genealogical fruit trees and on his unimaginative cynicism spiked with shots of whiskey. And he had been as romantically inclined as his father, albeit never making any great blunders, only sailing through the business so long as someone else was at the helm.

"We'll end up in the poorhouse!" said the old man from the other side of his cushion barrier.

Dona Catarina, freed from her resentful mental block, attained that inner zone wherein discouragement refuses to take in anything else and seeks a modicum of a solution amidst the debris, opting for the best way out by pretending that things are not as broken as they seem:

"That we'll end up in the poorhouse is an exaggeration. Diogo did the figures. After all the debts are paid off, provided they don't force a sudden liquidation upon us, we'll have the vineyards and the quinta free and clear. If Diogo changes his ways, we can still save face. The wine still brings in a little income. They promised Diogo a position at FAYAL COAL. He still has friends there."

"And the poor little girls with no dowry... the boy with no career! Especially Margarida, at such a perilous age, with that pack of suitors always after her! But what tears my heart out is to see the Granary sold! To see my father's home in the hands of strangers!"

Poor old friend, who displayed no real warmth except in his rote routine and ostentation... He was paying dearly for his self-ishness. Margarida Terra, that exuberant and sensitive girl–"the pearl of Fayal," as she was known in Horta–his prisoner in the Granary! And not even the miserable excuse of jealousy or one of those stupid quarrels that poison the blood of those who experience them! A stupid isolation, because of her being socially snubbed by some. All that refined sociability, made of English utensils, expended on others; and once in a great while, a boisterous party thrown in the Granary or in the Vineyards; his wife then treated royally as if he were the Mikado and acquiesced to help the Empress of Japan come out of her *noli me tangere* of chrysanthemums and tiny blue eggs....

With his bony, delicate fingers, Mateus Dulmo absentmind-edly polished a whale tooth. He had picked it up from the window sill, where it was used to prop up the window. At the entrance to the channel there was a touch of twilight. A yacht was sailing away.

When Catarina was a child, he went by the Granary to watch her mother bathe her. Carlos came home in the wee hours; at other times, he did not even come home. Mateus Dulmo had tried to teach Cousin Margarida the triumphant opening bars of *Tannhäuser*, but her hands had great difficulty executing the severe and violent chords in which the pinky has to stretch a long distance to extract the sharp sound which the thumb must sustain and enrich.

The whale tooth stood upright on the window sill. The moon, almost full, rose from behind Pico.

"The children should be arriving," said *Dona* Catarina.

"Unless, since there's moonlight, Roberto takes them to Espalamaca and then they come home in the *charrette*."

"I just remembered something!" said Mateus Dulmo, who was coming down slowly from mental meandering to a solid stage. "There's only one person who can undo that scruple *Dona* Carolina Amélia has of insisting on having a creditor's agreement."

"Who, Uncle? Corina Peters? It's true they attended boarding school together. And here I never thought of speaking to Corina about it!"

"That wouldn't do any good. They talk but deep down they don't understand each other: *Dona* Carolina Amélia has that heiress's circumspection; Corina is all up in the clouds, a poetess. No. The one to win over the lady is Margarida."

"How can that be! She has seen her only half a dozen times, Uncle. The girl never went to Carrasca Well, except to ask for donations for the Ribatejo earthquake victims. She was a tiny thing... in that embroidered linen dress with a little pleated skirt...."

"Well, that's what brings out the soft spot in people. *Dona* Carolina told me that she had barged into the house as if she were a member of the household. All the other little girls were huddled together whispering, and she: 'What can you see with this lens?' 'Who is that gentleman with the badge on his chest?' 'What a lovely brooch! Is it made of jet?'"

Dona Catarina, finding the description perfect, confided:

"I really can see Margarida standing in the middle of *Dona* Carolina Amélia's living room, that museum...." Her hands seemed to be protecting a little glass case; her ironic smile vibrated in the wool of her shawl. "But we're hardly on speaking terms with her! On what pretext is the girl going to look her up? That she's capable of doing it, I have no doubts. She's been my angel of mercy, the poor soul!..."

"We have to think about it. Calapez says that he's going to throw a ball; he always invites her. Dr. Nunes promised me that he was going to meet alone with Avelar's son and try to get a reprieve. He even thinks that perhaps he could speak to Januário regarding his boy's candidacy..."

"Candidacy for what?"

132

"For secretary general of Horta District. Prudêncio has retired."

Dona Catarina lowered her eyes to the floor, as one who has resigned herself to everything:

"Secretary General and Acting Civil Governor of the District, with a right to occupy the tribune in the cathedral.... And that Garcia woman, with those dishpan hands, making sure that the damask bedspread doesn't fade.... Ah, me! Pity those of us who once were haves and are now have-nots!...."

Scenario: Mateus Dulmo's home in São Francisco Street. A wall and a green gate. A door knocker. Only the coachmen of Horta or some horseman going by can see the guillotine windows beyond the wall and above the rose bowers. Lights in the office. *Senhor* Matias, who lives in front, can also see the house because he has the time and the high vantage of the "little towers." Sensing some intelligence in someone, he always says: "He's the savant of Fayal!"

Mateus Dulmo's words to his old servant, when he returned from Pasteleiro:

"If anyone should knock at the door, I went out, got that? Bring the tea to my room."

Now in the room: a green satin lampshade focuses, on Mateus Dulmo's hands, that little burning orb fueled by the dock Power Station through a cable that supplies the city's evening electrical needs.

Before him lay these documents:

> "The full ownership of *so many* ares and *so many* centiares of pastures, equivalent to ninety acres of land, located in the area of Flamengos Creek, parish of Flamengos, Municipality of Horta...." (*To be set aside.*)

> "Au nom du Recteur Magnifique de L'Université de Liège, moi sous-signé... Doyen... Diplome d'études Supérieures décerné à titre étranger... Monsieur D'Ulmo, Mathieu... Mention honorable..." (*Drawer.*)

"REAL ESTATE CREDIT COMPANY. Case number *such and such....*"

MINISTRY OF THE TREASURY.... Voucher of Foreign Debt....

('... three, four, five, six...')."

"Here is the one I am looking for...."

"Jesus-Mary-Joseph. Horta, 16 March 1886.

My good Cousin Mateus. Thank you very much for your efforts in trying to make Carlos change his behavior toward poor Ana Silveira, for it suffices that he keep only one woman, me, walled in, and what's more, you remember what Uncle Terra's household was like and that joy of long ago in which we aunts and cousins got along like a cote of doves, with not the least ill-will! I don't recall us ever closing our door to anyone or that those who were alive lived as if buried in a grave. It's true that here in the Granary we don't live that way, and I think we even have picnics in Pico for, I believe, Catarina's birthday.

Next week I'm going to spend a few days in the vineyards. It's the best time of the year. Carlos just received some graftings from abroad, peach trees and Queen Claudias, and I want to see if I can still get some red camellias to put in the vases in my room, for come February's weather none of this is possible. But we're not going to stay long, unless Carlos decides differently all of a sudden. Why don't you join us over there, Cousin, after you get over your cold?

Yesterday they unloaded six large planks in Porto Pim, and Carlos ordered Januário, the office boy, to buy them at auction. It seems that they are of the best wood, even though they were all full of knotholes from the ship-worms. Perhaps they can be used for the two whaleboats they are building in Santo Amaro do Pico. I found all this out from the office boy, who is as sharp as a tack. I spent the afternoon looking at the lumber from the tower window. The tide goes out early, and nightfall is beautiful along the entire channel.

As for news from Belgium, I was glad to find out from you, Cousin, that they finally found the inscription on poor Francisco Brum's grave in the Oogenbom cemetery (check my spelling). Even if his ashes cannot be brought to Fayal due to the great expense, it's always comforting to know where they rest. And nothing else. It seems incredible that such a progressive people should treat the dead that way. To lie in a cemetery, all torn apart, as you told me, because of a case of expropriations for a railroad, and for so many months, everything in such a state! Anyway, they say that Belgium is pretty. I never made it past Antwerp. I stayed there on the return trip from Holland, a country of so many flowers, on the way to catching the ferry bound for Southampton.

Once again, thanks an awful lot for everything 'Lord Matheus, Esquire, Lord Cousin,' as Aunt Dona Maria Leocádia used to write (do you remember?). Oh, and still apropos of Carlos and Ana Silveira, just a few more words, that I want to tell you that I have no complaints, as you well know. We are not entirely unhappy unless we want to be. For is it not true that a little patience goes a long way?

I have run out of paper. Nothing else for now. Good-bye. Your devoted cousin–Margarida.

P.S. The group picture with Francisco Brum would not make a suitable copy. And it pains me a great deal. I like to see him there exactly the way he looks, with the vine that comprised the background already so faint. So many beloved beings gathered together there, whom God has already called to His presence!"

Mateus Dulmo's servant, at the gate, speaking to *Senhor* Matias' wife:

"Oh! Thank God that my master is very cheerful and very generous with gifts.... His home is always well supplied and filled with everything under the sun! Of course, he is very well-heeled. He does not waste it like Somebody I Know and Who Shall Remain Nameless, who throws everything to the winds..."

Senhor Matias' wife, speaking from high up in her little towers:

"... of course! as we all know, and why not? Everything he owns is for Bidinha, who will end up being very rich! And poor thing, she deserves it. A beautiful young girl! So tidy... And such *presence*! She is a sea of joy! Oh my, I must get going..."

Mateus Dulmo was already logging his half hour of practice at the harmonium.

Chapter XII

The Spider's Iris

The Fern Lane house, where the Garcias spent their summer, stood behind two big laurels that sank their roots in the court-yard. There were only three rooms on the upper level with fin-ished floors. One climbed down from one of them through a hatch to a kind of cellar where the wine press with its joist, stone weights and shaft was located. Three large Santa Maria earthen pots of descending size and hung on lead pipes seemed displayed there to illustrate the principle of interconnected ves-sels. In the wine-cellar hearth, a mere hole in the wall, Henriqueta and the servant cooked for six on broken trivets. (The deaf old lady did not leave her Horta lair as Ângelo called it and old Maria Florinda had taken advantage of that stay to go revisit her beloved Praia do Almoxarife, in the company of her son.) Henriqueta was angered by all that faya smoke filling the cellar; but Januário now spent the better part of his solicitor's vacation locked away alone in the Flamengos Creek house, and there was no way to convince him to put in a new ceiling in the kitchen. The cistern, still under construction, would probably have a fifteen-hundred gallon capacity. It was a cement tank that, given its tomb-like structure, seemed destined never to rise from the bowels of the island. Rare was the day that Januário did not go sleep at the Fern Lane house, but he arrived late for dinner, exited the victoria with baskets of pears balanced on the axle and bunches of hydrangeas carefully sorted: the blue ones in a basket, others covering the water in a large clay bowl and forming an arrangement the color of dried blood.

The Flamengos Creek house, which Januário bought from Frade of Salão, who in turn had acquired it furnished and every-thing from Diogo Dulmo, on the inside maintained the same appearance it had during the orange-harvesting season when the Clarks owned it: beds with twisted posts; the dining room downstairs; a few steps down, the table with feet in the shape of donkey's hooves; and grooves in the windows for the hooked latches. A big cedar trunk seemed to support the weight of the must emanating from the darkness and the emptiness. It reeked of something absent and pungent that after a few seconds one could identify: it was tangerine rind. From a worm-eaten bench with a drawer below the seat and missing one leg, one could see the remains of the orange orchard withered from blight.

In spring or on certain fall days when the sea did not let the boats from Pico draw near Horta and the wind blowing ashore from the channel covered the floor of the notary's office with twigs and dry leaves, Januário sometimes would order everybody out and send Ângelo to look for José Mónica in the bars and come back with the victoria. Januário would then go spend the night at the Flamengos Creek house. Complaining about his sugar level, he would bring with him his sack of bran bread and his slippers. As for eggs, they had them at the Creek. Only Henriqueta made mention of the eggs, while Januário got all worked up over them: it was precisely because of those beautiful chickens, and the isolation, that the Creek was good for him. There were no good fresh eggs except from his Leghorn hens, and his problem was his miserable diabetes acting up. He would leave a pile of coins on the dining room server. "Payment for the firewood that will be brought tomorrow." Despite the more or less veiled protests from the family, who contrasted the spaciousness and comfort of the Creek house with the sad Fern shack, all dark and ramshackle, Januário had always insisted that so long as it was up to him, the *Insulano* would never be referring to Flamengos as the site of the Garcias' *villegiatura*.

Stretched out in bed, Januário felt like a new man as he thought of his escape from the chicaneries of his Horta office and from the burden of his family. He spent hours reading *O Século*. From the bed's headboard hung a forgotten rosary with quinate beads. Januário used the margins of the newspaper to figure out the conversions, mentally reducing to acres the hec-

138

tares in the ads offering rural quintas; and suddenly and beatifically interrupting all this mental activity, he would slowly slip back into his true self, like water filling a bathtub.

They spent Holy Week in this fashion, to the family's horror. To bury himself in Flamengos Creek on those special days, he who took such pleasure in Holy Thursday morning prayers and in listening to Father Joaquim Maria in the role of Jesus in the Stations of the Cross, before the Magistrate consumed the Holy Host and night fell! But during those days he came to Horta. On Palm Sunday, at lunch time, he placed a package of Jordan almonds next to Carlota's silver place setting. They would be having black grouper for lunch.

Upon becoming aware of his son's interest in Margarida Dulmo, Januário's first reaction was one of foolish joy. Ladeira was the one who had told him, interrupting his copying, and with a courage gathered up from a safe distance through innuendo: deals about pastures, the vacancy for general secretary, and the sight of Honório's daughter, who went by the Cathedral Square looking ever smaller and prettier. "Now Joãozinho can always be found in Pasteleiro. That'll end up in marriage! And it would be a good match."

Ladeira's behind-the-scenes machinations bore a mixture of a kind of tactile knowledge of things and blindman's buff played with a firm hand, a hand short and stumpy from working with small-size stationery. He was not unaware of Januário Garcia's old secret love. He had watched, blow by blow, the campaign against the Clarks and the bribing of the Avelars over issues more important and sinister than those concerning the debt on the whaleboats, issues regarding which his boss held the key well-greased with influence and which he kept hidden away in the depths of his honey-tongued speech. Januário listened and kept quiet. He was busy all afternoon. On that day his employees left a little earlier; his apprentice was given permission to go and practice soccer on the dock lawn.

Here was his dream of seeing his son João married to a Clark! His bitterness of so many years dissolved by the young girl whom he watched through the office windows entering the cathedral or window shopping at the jeweler's, with a body already like her mother's, looking at her own shadow. What was her mother's name? What was it? "Kate!" her father called her. Januário knew a little fragmented English, all nouns. Since the time of old man Roberto, the firm had done no business with England; some imports from London were transacted between his employer and his absent son. Calendars, yes, and that ruined portrait of a young man wearing a high collar and fluffy coif, with his name at the bottom written in beautiful calligraphy: "*Ralph Clark*." In the half-light were the green lamp, the smell of tea, the jam spoon stuck in the drawer by the elder Clark, Catarina about to arrive. "Januário will be kind enough to take you to Flamengos in the break. The boy is needed here. Close the blotter!" Then Januário's eyes traced a proud curve connecting the mares' croups to Catarina's checkerboard corselet, which caught the attention of the middle-aged men of Horta as the break's wheels made the cobblestones jostle, while he held the reins firm in his hands.

Later, with a little luck.... All his life he had seen himself as a poor young man, well behaved, bound to marry his employer's daughter. They considered themselves noble on the side of the Terras, and had that prestige born of their fortune and first and foremost from the way they did business. There were no business people like them, except in the Bensaúde Company and FAYAL COAL: that office with armless cane chairs, an employer who did not have to watch what he spent and who rode horseback and attended the meetings of the Western Azores Savings Bank, with his tall hat placed on the same table side by side with that of Counselor Bettencourt. All this formed a defensive wall and nailed Januário to the seat of his chair at the desk, recording the outflow of exported whale oil and making the country louts, who were there to exchange a few dollars, wait in the hope that a telegram would arrive with the news of a higher exchange rate so that Januário could cash in by offering a little less. But Catarina was a good deal younger than he; a man also had to keep his word: Emília Faria had grown up first. The Clarks did not have any grillwork balconies facing

Meireles' notary office, nor that flower with silky eyes that graced the stationery of a poor copyist orphaned early in life who earned his daily bread with the tip of his pen. But to everything there is a season; it was all foolishness. But the foolishness had worked on him and had made the firm's entire operation dependent on his actions. When he became the firm's bookkeeper, the whole web of checks and whales cut up with large kitchen knives, tried in the pots to fill the barrels, then reduced to precious gray balls that he could hardly resist keeping in the safe wrapped up in policy forms, had seemed to him to be a system invented by and belonging to him, an emanation from the belly he was growing around the waist of his striped trousers. Catarina had returned to the private school in Ponta Delgada; the King and Queen had paid a visit to the islands. The Commendation of Our Lady of Conception had been bestowed on "the esteemed gentleman Charles William Clark," son-in-law to Baron da Terra.... Summers.... Winters... (the ship arrived; the ship set sail). He had worn a cutaway at his wedding. João–almost wiped out by diarrhea at age two and nights longer than a trip to Flores in a rowboat.... His mother and sister had moved to the city..... Jacinto had opened a pharmacy... (he had gotten married in the morning... because, as the saying goes, he had drunk the milk before buying the cow by impregnating his sweetheart...). And Pico continued in its hooded overcoat worn on grayish afternoons, when it seemed its clouds and one's nerves were connected.

It struck him like a whim of fate to have been kicked out of that office, like a dog, and now to be summoned, by that young woman's pretty bosom, back into the lives of his employer and of his daughter through a third party–that intelligent son of his, a lad well-mannered toward all, whose career was well under way. His life's bad turns were going to come to an end, and by his own actions. He had worked the land with the sweat of his brow. The seed was good: like Christmas vetchings putting forth sprouts in an enclosed space, then finding an opening and turning green and frizzled.

But suddenly he thought: "No!" It was all just castles in the air. Januário had the impression of having just come out of the egg of his crazy dreams with the white still showing. He had his life to attend to, his interests. He should use his head! Catarina and his youthful ambitions had not amounted to anything. To lay his sorrow to rest, he had dug up that worm's burrow and crawled inside. To each his own.... Some played cards, others collected stamps, had affairs. He had that foyer office, which was sacred. Whoever went by Jesus Street at night and saw lights on the windows could snarl to his heart's content: "There's Garcia plotting his shady deals...." Inside the office, something different was taking place.

He had bought his safe at auction in the aftermath of the fire at the Madalena Tax Office, when the whalemen had revolted against high taxes. It was a "box," as Ângelo put it, a transition between the "strongbox" and the "steel safe." The fire had twisted the latch next to the steel ingot bearing the combination grooves; and Januário, who had ordered the safe polished, stared, every time he opened it, at that bluish spot left by the locksmith after the expensive repair. The light from the bulb above the desk cast a shiny glow upon the top wad of pound notes in the safe. Januário grasped it with his fat, fleshy hand. But his eyes did not linger on the gold longer than the instant necessary for an instinctive inspection, a methodical strategy induced by other strategies, which solitude and the night combined to particularize. Having run his fingers through a pile of papers like a cardsharp ripping through a deck of cards, Januário's hand, glowing from the electric lights, delved into the safe's secret drawers, and pulled out a velvet box. The spring made the satin-covered lid pop open, and out came one of João's braids, a kerchief, and a small silken green bag. Januário went to the window, pulled back the curtain, observed the lamppost in front, dark in the deserted street. Occasionally a young boy walked by whistling or someone with a coat hanging over his shoulders; the sound of wooden shoes could be heard vanishing down the cobblestone street. On this moonlit night, the stone fence of a house in front seemed about to burst into flames: but it was only the live coals that a servant had scooped up from the hearth and emptied on top of the wall. Januário then left the window, closed the safe, and remained sitting at the desk for a long time, hesitating between those hanging keys and that piece of smooth silk he held in his yellow, swollen hand. Beside the tiny conch shells, which Januário seemed to be counting with his trembling thumb, he fixed his eyes on a little bouquet wrapped in green silk, the withered stems looking like those of violets. An almost faded perfume of blushing powder still emanated from the powder puff next to the flowers. To the side amid a pile of deed forms, Januário caught sight of a picture from which peered a little nose. It looked like the nose of a creature emerging from the depths of its burrow to the loose soil of the entrance, whose fear made its hair stand on end, and turned shadows into enemies on the prowl.

In front of Januário was a picture of Kate sitting on the cushion of the new break. The photograph was sharp. Januário's camera had a good lens, one of the three brought to Horta by Velez, he of the goatee à la Guise, and the traveling salesman for the Metal Company. Wasted money. Stupid move! Januário made an effort to understand himself at eighteen or twenty. In his mind's eye, he saw the garret in his father's Praia do Almoxarife house and Aunt Secundina bringing in Canon Borges' washbowl for him to develop the negatives. *C. & H. AUTUMNAL FLOWERS*. "Just like at the Clarks'! Just like at the Clarks'!..." And this effort to connect his past with his present situation right now in his office began to bring him into contact with himself, putting things back in proportion: his body wrapped in his dress coat, the price of the Zeiss camera in the window of the store Casa das Utilidades after the war... everything more expensive but earnings also up, mortgages went through the roof due to money coming in from America.... The silken bag began to close over the tiny conch shells and violets; the picture was returned to its place. A last caress of his wads of pound notes preceded the turning of the safe key in the lock of that stifling office on a Horta street. In the tower of the Carmo Church, the cracked bell took a long time to strike midnight: exactly one minute, by his gold watch.

In Flamengos Creek, if he stayed up late reading the newspaper, he could not fall asleep. Toward early dawn, a couple of roosters opened the morning round of debates. Januário thought: "If Canha's son, that scarecrow from Cedros, managed to get acquitted .... The process was in good hands. Dr. António Lopes was the best criminal lawyer in Horta; in civil cases, Leal was not far behind him, especially when it came to clever legal maneuvering." More roosters crowing.... And cold... silence... the sweet smell of citrus wafting from the orange orchard. "Eggs are really expensive...!"

On Holy Thursday, Januário was back in the city and appeared at the table looking fully alive, sounding off, telling bad jokes. Ângelo looked skinnier and displayed his tan. These days he always wore a globe-amaranth, prompting Januário to remark: "You must give me that for seed. Globe-amaranth tea is the best thing going for coughs...."

"Such the wit, aren't you, Januário!..."

Lunch went well; the light from the balcony windows brightened the tablecloth. João had to eat his dessert in a hurry because of the guard inspection: he had to report to his battalion in the daytime. He was already wearing his kepi and gloves; his father leaned one side of his face over toward him for a kiss and gave him the news:

"Tomorrow, Laura and *Dona* Carolina Amélia are coming over for dinner. If you could get away from the barracks for the morning ceremonies.... At least the end of them... Try to be here! These are days to remember...."

Chapter XIII

Feria Sexta in Parasceve

To João Garcia, the religious holiday spent in the barracks seemed like an island in the open sea of a colorless life stuck in doldrums. The call to order had sounded early; most of the soldiers were on leave or exempted. The day sergeant announced the daily routine with the bugle call: mess... lights out... detainees and convalescents... day corporal... soldiers on fatigue... mess. He carried his tray with the classic dish of beans, two smoking potatoes, a piece of pork sausage. He tasted it, feeling a desire to eat with the soldiers, do as they did: throw a potato peel at Damião Serpa's huge body. "Plenty of food and well prepared"–he would write in the report tomorrow. Locked in his room with his cape pulled up, eyeing the bowl of the valved washbasin and the pistol holsters, João Garcia felt the solitude of Carmo Convent weighing down on the old windows and opening up the city like easy and docile prey for his thoughts. Everything that intimidated him in his daily encounters–his family, his happy friends, the street corner shops with their display windows, the fleeting glimpse of Margarida in the *charrette* with Roberto and Pedro–stole upon him from the direction of the dock and of the rooftops overrun with trembling little weeds like something tangible that he could retain by means of a simple mental effort.

He would do as his father wished. He had already asked permission of the Commander to leave the barracks an hour early: Espínola, who would relieve him, did not care about Good Friday. Despite the state of war and the lights being turned off on the dock on some days for the purpose of a frightful practice battle against imaginary submarines, the routine at the garrison ran smoothly, given the soldiers' familiarity with the islands–and the work was well done. He would leave on time to attend part of the ceremonies. Margarida surely would not miss them. And in the cathedral, after Mass, with everything in the dark, he would find a way to speak to her. One word would suffice: at the storm door or near one of the aisles, taking advantage of the full church. He could already see her in her mantilla, making her presence known in the darkness of the church by her infallible Parma violet corsage: only two or three flowers at the end of her veil, lest she offend the solemnity of the day and custom. Would he at least have the time to show her his grief over that unfair coldness, to convince her, finally, to show up at the wall of the quinta or at the window of the Granary? It is true that he had exhausted all his strategies; she had dodged him in a most enigmatic way, one which seemed to him to conceal misunderstandings with an astonishing naturalness, born of blind or contrived circumstances, like a barrier being erected against her true will. That is why the outcome of it all was always postponed until a mysterious occasion, a future equally impervious to foresight and obstacles. Was that going to be his day? Who could tell? Should he find some other way?

João Garcia was walking around the barracks square when he noticed a guardsman coming toward him, adjusting his cartridge belt to ask permission to address him. Following the soldier was a barefoot little man whom he did not recognize at first.

"Kindly forgive my being so bold, sir."

Lo and behold, it was none other than Manuel Bana! He quickly reached for the arm of Manuel, who, embarrassed, held his hat against his forehead; one could see its pink lining soiled from the sweat of his mop of hair.

"What brings you here, Manuel? How wonderful to see you!"

"I came here to ask you a special favor. I have a nephew here in the service, our boy Chico; I don't know if you remember him, sir... 625 of the 5th; I call him 'Fifty Cents'.... And, to go on with the story, my sister is an unfortunate woman; she was left a widow a year ago. Her husband left her one measly acre of land and the house: a little shack.... But she does some

odd jobs in Capelo; she has a tab to pay at the grocery store....
They had some pastures rented from *Senhor* Mateus Dulmo; he
waived my brother-in-law's rent for last year. But my sister is
all alone now; she and her little daughter. Her only breadwinner
is that son of hers...."

"And what would you like me to do?"

"If you had a word with Captain Soares, sir, for him to allow
a few days leave... at least three days! It would be an act of
charity.... The corn is doing well this year; but what about
hoeing? And then there's the beans... the potatoes.... Everything
will be ruined if nobody looks after it. You know how it is, sir,
they're women; even if they try, they're only women. The fields
need a man's hand."

"Well, let's see what we can do." João Garcia pulled out
pencil and paper. "What did you say his name was?"

"Francisco Cardoso. Francisco Bana; that's our family
name. I didn't have the nerve to come bother you, sir; but then
the young miss told me right away: 'Go, Manuel, go see him, for
the *Senhor* Alferes is a very good man. If you want to, you can
tell him that I was the one who sent you.' I beg your pardon, sir,
but the girl was the one who said that... As for us, we are a
bunch of know-nothings; we don't even know our way around.
Good Lord! I use to carry that little one in my arms. A
teeny-weeny thing, she was..." Manuel Bana's hand measured
the height of the hardened ground of the barracks square, flex-
ing his muscles as when he was a recruit. A glassy smile overcame his cautious look.

"I'll see what I can do, I'll see," said João Garcia, adjusting his
red armband. "I can't promise anything, but I'll do what I can."

"Oh, sublieutenant! That would be an act of charity."

"We'll see."

Manuel Bana had done his military duty in Terceira; he was
an artillery man. In front of officers he kept his file posture, now
a little altered by his rural speech habits and by his frank humility
as a city dweller and a quinta caretaker. In his presence, João
Garcia felt the affection that country folk awoke in him with their
way of speaking, and also an irresistible curiosity, born of a tacit

solidarity with them, as if in remembrance of a half-forgotten and long-ago camaraderie. The idea that somehow Margarida was associated with this mission, this request for a leave, suddenly filled him with courage. He asked the servant to wait:

"Would you mind delivering a letter to the young miss? It's about some books I was supposed to loan her...."

"Just tell me what you'd like me to do!"

João Garcia went up to his room and took out a sheet of paper. To know the man was waiting was to feel the certain complicity of fate in at last telling Margarida everything; and there in isolation, the warmth of his true feelings and the immunity of distance imposed by happenstance, all excited him as if he were involved in some mysterious mission. In this convent-turned-barracks high in the hills of the city, overlooking a Pico purplish with sea clouds at nightfall, he felt in possession of a force arising from the remotest of times when the islands still had no trace of any human presence—no offices, no derby hats, no pianos sounding inside homes on the weed-covered side streets; nor that nameless restlessness that ate away at poor rural women without male breadwinners; no city girls shrouded in their mantillas and steered away from the paths that demand the naked truth. All this is more or less what he wrote in the letter that he handed Manuel Bana from the window.

"Sergeant! Is there anyone missing?"

The little lights of Pasteleiro were shimmering in the heat of the channel when the call *lights out!* was heard.

It being an almost clear night, João Garcia arrived at the cathedral on time. The ceremonies transpired with a grave and unalterable rhythm. Not the least sound was heard. The priests went up and down the altar set up in the transept. The change in the style of worship, bringing it closer to the people, made its tragic meaning seem more intimate and humanized in the celebrant, with his girded and tufted alb, remaining truly contrite in the chant preceding the sacrifice of the Lamb, who unleashed the wrath of the Most High and the representation of the end of everything.

In Horta Cathedral during Holy Week rites, only yellow candles were bought. The candles were dipped in a special solution as if to polish them. With the baring of the altars and the black draperies in the windows, their plaits already undone in expectation of the consumption of the Host, everything was in mourning; an almost palpable shadow fell, broken by the ritual words: *In spiritu humilitatis, et in animo contricto suscipiamur a te, Domine....*

Januário Garcia, kneeling at the foot of a torch and wearing his brethren of the Lord of the Passion habit, was slowly acquiring the color of the dirty candlewax. Ângelo stood next to Pretextato, languid and also in character; availing himself of the day's ceremonies, he began, with a disguised attention, to survey the church and congregation: the island of ladies in the nave chairs, the boys from good families occupying the lateral chairs. At the back of the church stood the commoners, from among whom emerged the hoods of the Fayal overcoats, Caneco's head, the moustaches of the young men, barefoot and flushed from being so tightly packed together. Close to the Lemoses, one could make out Daisy Warren's little blond head, more little books and hands, coughing... and *Dona* Carolina Amélia with her V-shaped grosgrain ribbon and her medallion twined in her black-speckled veil.

A small thread of smoke rose from a censer; a spoonful of incense released a white wisp. The church had the good smell of fine wool. Ângelo tapped Pretextato on the elbow:

"Fayal still has beautiful girls! Just look at those eyes...."

But Pretextato only saw the profile of Pedro Dulmo standing next to his frock-wearing father. On the former's dark, lean face the muscles twitched. Pretextato cast a sidelong glance at Ângelo. Both smiled, lowering their eyes. Then, filled with a sincere solemnity (which seemed to contain an internal mechanism to slow its pace), their eyes caught sight of *Dona* Peters' coiffure, her smiling face hidden behind a lilac veil. Margarida was kneeling nearby, behind her mother. Ângelo saw her tufted mantilla and her eyes lowered to the book. The acolytes went to kneel at the feet of the celebrant to receive his blessing. The Tract having finished, the acolytes, with wide stoles over the sleeves of their flaxen albs, opened the leather covers of their missals against the stands' metal frames and intoned the Passion according to John:

"*In illo tempore: Egressus est Jesus cum discipulis suis trans torrentem Cedron, ubi erat hortus....*"

Margarida tried to find the gist of the proceedings in *The Holy Week Explained*. But her mind was somewhere on the road to Caldeira, riding in a landau, fixed on that recreational trip organized by Uncle Roberto, which she had joined with such enthusiasm but which had finally degenerated into stretches of boredom and family squabbles. They had left the carriages up on the road and hiked down to the edge of the lake, which lapped the burnt heath thickets and the clumps of budding hydrangea bushes. André Barreto had tried and tried until he managed to wrest the two of them free from the thick of the caravan and make for a secluded cavern. The moonshine was like daylight. "Margarida, it seems to me you lead such a sad life.... I don't like to see you this way." She laughed in his face: "Who, me? Sad?" But André had become so panic-stricken and seemed so anxious to see in her the very things she herself did not have that Margarida regretted such an unthinking reaction. The incense trees were all damp from the dew and covered with that sugary flower to which the moonlight gave an unreal air. Margarida cut a little bough and put a leaf in her mouth. Were there any incense trees in São Jorge? Of course: São Jorge had everything. They spoke about cows. Margarida enjoyed branding festivals; she had been to Terceira. Roped bullfights[1] amused her, especially those people hanging from the walls and the bursting of the fireworks. "Listen, Margarida...." And the rest of it. The rest of it until fortunately Pedro came out of the brush holding the crinkled little feet of a long-legged bird in his hands: "A woodcock. I killed it with one shot!"

---

[1] Roped bullfights are amateur affairs in which the bull, instead of running loose, as in the formal bullfight, is fought on the village streets while restrained by a rope tied around its neck. Bullfights in general were introduced by the Spaniards and only take place on Terceira.–Trans.

Kneeling in the nave, Margarida tried hard to ward off these stray recollections by devoting herself to the booklet:

> Then they led Jesus from Caiaphas to the hall of judgment. It was early in the morning. And they themselves did not go into the judgment hall, lest they be defiled, and so that they might eat the passover. Then Pilate spoke to them, and asked: "What accusation do you bring against this man?"

But the deacon was already reading farther ahead:

> *Gens tua, et potifices tradiderunt te mihi; quid fecisti? C. Respondit Jesus: Regnum meum non est de hoc mundo.*

Still, the road to Caldeira pursued her, as if the ritual instructions in the little book, printed in blood-red ink, which she skipped as she read, needed to be replaced by the trip, the hydrangeas, the life and blood of those months of the plague and surprises since the arrival of her uncle. Her mother was seated two steps away, resting her arms on the *prie-Dieu*. Margarida thought about the silliness of that word her family used for the praying stools; but that's what they called them. It had been so ever since Madame Laborde's stay in Horta; it was the *prie-Dieu*. Half of her things had phony names like that. Or were her family members the fake ones? Her mother seemed to her more and more unsteady and aged. An irresistible tenderness drew Margarida's eyes to that mantilla into which her mother's vigorous head seemed to sag as if preparing itself for the final repose on the death pillow. But only for a second. She recalled the atmosphere at home, her father's nights out, difficulties, and her mother winding everything into one big skein and handing it over to her to untangle. She then felt overcome by a strange anger and hostility. Her mother was a selfish woman: a black moth wrapped in that nocturnal shawl, only thinking of debts and the family's good name.

Dona Catarina struggled to get up from her praying stool, crossed her hands on the velvet-covered *prie-Dieu*, and heaved a deep sigh from her chest, as if she meant it for the Christ who stood amidst the dirty candles. But she was her mother.... With those swollen feet! The poor dear!... Then her eyes came to rest on Clarinha Barreto's profile, with her veil pinned to her flaxen blond hair. She had the coldness of those girls who assume the nature of whatever they are wearing but who can also kneel in a church like marble statues by a baptistery, with a conch of holy water in their curvy little wings. But pleasant... so nice!... Whenever Margarida encountered André Barreto with his sister, her welcome to Baron da Urzelina's son was considerably warmer. She became more expansive, telling amusing stories and sayings she had heard from Manuel Bana. She sensed, beyond the words and beyond these guests of Horta, a potential family: a certain connection with Urzelina, with pastures, cow bells, a big house on a mountainside, and her sleeping alone in a wing of the house—a window facing north, voices in the hallway calling "Lady Baroness."

In the nave where the fine young men of Horta were kneeling, she could make out a group of officers, and particularly André's coarse and solid head. Margarida shook as if someone had tapped her on the shoulder, then fixed her skirt. It was all she could do not to pass out: doubtlessly, a result of that absurd fast that, despite Maria das Angústias' vast knowledge about papal bulls, had been imposed the day before. But in actuality the "baroness" of her daydreams appeared to her like a living, breathing person, the body of someone who was making use of Clarinha Barreto to manifest herself physically and either rested on the *prie-Dieu* her mother leaned on, or became part of it, lending her body a statue's stiffness under her mantilla.

Letting his eyes roam absentmindedly along the whole length of the nave, João Garcia fixed on her frozen, almost absent look. And Margarida buried her head in the little book to hide her tears from the world.

Chapter XIV

The Fine Art of Letter Writing

Margarida had just returned from Uncle Mateus Dulmo's house and, exhausted, had sat down on the veranda bench when she heard Manuel Bana's steps coming down the courtyard staircase. From where she sat, she could see, beyond the bower, the rim of Caldeira do Inferno crater crowning Mount Guia. The cedar branches broken by the hurricane were twine for the rolls of pearly waves heading to Porto Pim to peter out. At first, that sound of scraping feet, so familiar to Margarida, merged with that of the whitewash tide against the rocks; the foam of the breakers formed, together with her thoughts, a hazy and distant halo. But it was... it was he.

"Miss Bidinha!"

"What is it, Manuel?"

With an impertinent smile, the caretaker handed her a sealed envelope:

"I've been carrying this letter since yesterday. I couldn't catch you at a good time. I'm no good at this sort of thing. But he won't give me a moment's peace! If you want me to, I'll tell him to...."

"And what about Chico's leave?"

"He said that he'd probably manage it. When I told him that you had recommended I talk to him, he didn't say a word, like he was changing the subject.... But as far as the leave for the boy, I am to consider it done, unless they can't see their way clear to give it. You could tell by the way he looked, all serious. 'Well, let's see what we can do.' He sure thinks highly of you! It's a kind of weakness of his, an obsession.... And he said that the letter had to do with some books."

"That's right.... some books that he loaned Miss Daisy and that were left here. Give me the letter."

Without losing sight of the sea, which lent height and movement to the trees with their broken branches, she slowly opened the envelope. Manuel Bana started walking away, stretching out his moustache with his full hand along the wrinkles in the bark-like skin of his face until he joined the two well-measured ends on his chin:

"The *Senhor* sublieutenant seems to be expecting an answer..... What do I tell him, miss?"

Margarida, who was absorbed in her reading, gestured slowly toward the stairs with a wave of her hand. The servant disappeared.

Those words in small handwriting brought her a strange message–as if a general, having met with an adversary at a comfortable point along the front lines to discuss an armistice, had decided again to defer to befuddled negotiators with unilateral stipulations. Perhaps it was all necessary and sincere: that return address at the top ("Horta, Carmo Barracks"), again the evocation of their meeting at night in the quinta–and "love" and "my love" more than once. But try as she might to match the force of those words, it seemed to her like this was water under the bridge, with neither accountability nor effect. Why had he not told her just that on the street? He had interpreted that first letter literally and then there were her evasions, the avoided conversation the day of the horseback ride... her failing to appear at the wall in the afternoons.... But, then, couldn't he see her furtive steps along the quinta's walkways? the chair she had left on the veranda with her sewing basket? Wasn't that her living language, the "yes" that it was necessary to yank out of her by force, by a personal gesture? But the gesture was written all over that cowardly conceived page, in that report by an on-duty officer who derives pleasure from jotting down his vacillations in the pages of a diary. What kind of an answer should she give him? "I expect you tomorrow, at such and such a time." That was one option....

She stuck the letter in her bosom and hid her face in her hands. That second of meditated seriousness gave way to nervous laughter. She was overcome by the ridiculousness of it all.

154

In her mind's eye, she saw Uncle Mateus Dulmo's head at the harmonium and heard, for the thousandth time since leaving his house, these solemn words: "Everything you do for your family, you do for yourself." And again: "A woman like you ought to fear nothing!" It was horrible! Uncle Mateus said it standing still in front of her, with such certainty and calm. It was not as simple as befriending *Dona* Carolina Amélia and getting the promise of a truce out of her. Her uncle, who had suggested that to her in his attempt to find a way out of her father's financial difficulties, had finally agreed with her that such a mission was humiliating. She had spoken to him of marriage, love, her life of leisure, and the possibility of her going to England as soon as Uncle Roberto became convinced of the need to set up some-thing for her–including getting her in touch with her English relatives, the Marrs, and arranging for her to stay with them or to work as a companion to some rich family, even as a nurse.

Her uncle's attitude in calling her attention to the facts of the situation had seemed to her a little harsh and spoiled her image of the little old man picking his bending roses, his accompany-ing her to the dock or to Espalamaca and buying her chocolates on the way back. But they had gone so far in everything that a new world opened up before Margarida that afternoon, as if they had locked themselves away on São Francisco Street like mysterious shadows and thrown the gate key in Horta's face. Her uncle had revealed to her his resolution to place his fortune at the disposal of their creditors in order to shut them up; and Margarida, disarmed in her protests by the old man's calm and unshakable air, had leaned her head on his solid shoulders. He drew her close. Then he had shown her pictures of Grandmother Margarida Terra, a letter from her with a long postscript; he had related to her his triumphs in Liège; and without his alluding to anything that might be construed as love, Margarida had become aware of his bachelor's loneliness–the old maid patching clothes downstairs, the pile of musical scores for harmonium lying in a heavy pile on the scrubbed floor.

These ideas came to her dissociated from any forethought but rather as connected with the reading of the letter by a spontaneous contiguity, like two wind gusts blowing through and indifferently shaking a single tree. Absorbed in these matters, she became impassive, ready for anything. If João Garcia wrote to her from the barracks on a day of solemn resolutions, she would answer him with old resolutions rediscovered right there on the veranda.

Some people standing nearby on the shore caught her attention. Her mother was trimming the walkway hedge with Maria das Angústias, and Uncle Roberto was absentmindedly approaching with a pair of binoculars hanging across his shoulder, and a bouquet of flowers in his hand. From where she stood, she called the two notes of "the password." Roberto waved back to her. Judging from her mother's and the wet-nurse's movements, she perceived that they were coming toward her and went to meet them. Roberto chose two crimson gillyflowers and, after first trying them on her waist and then at her shoulder, ended up pinning them to her hair, after setting aside his unlit pipe:

"There we go.... They look best on you this way!"

Margarida straightened her hair and, with a hairpin between her teeth, quickly pinned both gillyflowers to her blouse.

"Do you have any plans for this afternoon?" asked Roberto.

"No, Uncle. I've just come back from São Francisco Street."

Dona Catarina inspected her daughter from head to toe, trying to discover in her the effect of the interview. She expected to find her downhearted or with that energetic tic that was in her a sign of repression–a silent reproach that from a daughter, a mother could not bear to hear because of its very wordlessness. But Margarida appeared to her to be inexplicably serene, as serene as she only saw her once in a great while: for example, when, after church, where she seldom went, she spent hours and hours praying or filling vases with huge bunches of flowers that Manuel Bana carried for her. Roberto, wearing an air of mystery, took her slowly by the arm, and together they climbed the stairs to the veranda.

"Sit here." Margarida allowed herself to be led to the stone bench, to which the purplish lichens lent a tone contrasting with the clouds that rendered the day dull. She felt Roberto's firm and open hand on her shoulder. "I want to tell you something.... You cannot sacrifice your life to the state of affairs into which your father allowed the family to sink. I don't want to hear about dealings with this lady of Carrasca Well, with whom your family doesn't even have social relations. And these suitors, these matchmakers.... Come, tell me: are you at least fond of him?"

Margarida kept adjusting the gillyflowers; she could still feel the sensation of the hidden letter in her fingers.

"I? Fond of whom?"

Roberto bent over her with a grave sweetness; his eyes had a penetrating, loyal shine:

"Tell the truth... I saw what I saw. On the ride to Caldeira... And at Warren's house; he couldn't stay away from you. Why aren't you frank with me? Am I not your friend? And what's the problem, if you are fond of him... He is an honest young man, pleasant, with fine qualities...." Margarida made a gesture of indifference. Roberto insisted: "What I can't understand is that other people are beginning to treat the conversations between you two as a kind of conspiracy, as if you were courting. All I hear about is André's fortune... the Baron da Urzelina's wealth."

"They're probably right, Uncle! In a land where everything is inheritances and business, what can a girl be worth? It's the dresses, the ball, the birthday, a festival that one attends... If they don't have anything to talk about, why not be a topic of conversation for them? Yes... let them talk; why not? I am a type of building that, by chance, became vacant. Much more than this is owed by a child to 'her progenitors' (isn't that what they call them?). Even more so if one is 'a mere female,' as Mariana from Pico puts it. 'The mere females are supposed to remain quietly at home, sitting on the floor by the window.' I have already received my first Communion; I have had my Confirmation.... We are approaching orange blossom season. Life is like the passage of the year at the farmer's: tilling, sewing, harvesting..... Haven't you heard what Mother says? 'This girl is not like the others; she doesn't know how to have fun! One of these days, I'm going to die and she'll be left without anyone to take care of her!' Do you know, Uncle, what 'without anyone to take care of her' means? Because, Lord knows, I'd like to know! Let them do with me as they wish; or else, just let me be! Just let me be!"

Margarida's voice was bitter and brusque. Roberto took out his tobacco pouch, shook the smoldering ashes from his pipe:

"A mother's words, poor woman.... My sister has been very unhappy!"

"Perhaps not as much as it seems.... She never knew how to stand up to Father. You must understand, Uncle, that these Horta ladies don't know what life is all about, except when it takes a turn for the worse. They grew up being catered to; they live only for the Royal Club of Fayal and the parties on board whenever a squadron arrives at the dock. That was mother's life. While the Granary still had something to export and the whale fishery was profitable, she allowed Father to spend his nights out; everything was considered perfectly natural.... And whenever the director of the boarding school sent word that he couldn't do anything with Pedro, the reaction always was: 'Poor little thing... Bring the little boy to the office; we'll hook something up for him at the Trans-Atlantic Cable....' But now that there are no longer whales or prospects at the Cable... well, my, oh, my, everything is falling apart!"

"This is a petty environment, no doubt about it... with closed-minded people! But look: Do you remember the conversation we had in Lomba when we went horseback riding?"

"We're never going to ride again..."

"... because you showed interest in getting a job in London, in getting out of this place?"

"I'd swear to it by drawing a cross on the pier.... Would I! for good!" Margarida took off a shoe from the foot of her crossed leg and hit its heel three times against the bench like the women of Feteira do. Her rosy face, in the light of the match with which Roberto lit his pipe, seemed all afire.

"I've changed my mind," said Roberto, rising a little to drop the burnt match from the veranda to the street. "I've been thinking... Marr has the clinic in Kensington; he's always hiring nurses, society girls. And even if it were in the office.... He performs operations on many Portuguese; there's a large Brazilian community spread all over Europe who will settle for no other surgeon. Only him and Dr. Bensaúde. You'd go there as assistant director; you would attend to the patients at the clinic."

"Why do you put such ideas into my head, Uncle?"

"As I've told you, let's think about it seriously. I could take you with me.... But I'm by myself. It's true that I'm your uncle, almost forty.... But it's not very natural; well, not common.... *Oh... shocking!* What wouldn't they say here in Horta! The serodio uncle's honeymoon; a little dish.... *Don't you think so, Margaret?*"

"What of it!" said Margarida shrugging her shoulders and shaking her hair. "Don't you have that friend of yours, Mary, in London?... Doesn't she live with a sister? You could put me up in her house."

Embarrassed, Roberto crossed his arms:

"Later.... Later.... First, I have to speak with Marr–or actually, write to him. I'm almost certain..... Or else you can go with me and stay in Lisbon for a while, at Uncle Saavedra's. Then I'll send for you.... It would be funny, wouldn't it? Me standing on the pier surveying the main rail, looking for you amidst all those heads, and you waving a long hello with a handkerchief... and the ship drawing close to land.... *Don't you think so, Margaret?*" asked Roberto in English.

Margarida eagerly hugged Roberto; and noticing Manuel Bana sneaking up the stairs, she ran toward him:

"You wait here, Manuel. Don't you move!"

In a hurry, she climbed the courtyard stairs four steps at a time; and, locking herself in the little room overlooking the thick and lichen-covered araucaria, in an instant she filled up half a sheet of paper:

> *João Garcia: I am engaged. I hope that, this time, you understand a situation that I myself cannot explain to you. I do not want you to be left with a bad impression of me, but, nevertheless, I think that a resolution like this, expressed in this manner and already made when I wrote*

to you in Lisbon, lacks something that only a meeting could, perhaps, clarify. It has not been possible.... The fault is neither yours nor mine. What can we do? But, again, I would like you to consider me, truly, your sister. I know that it is customary to say this on these occasions, and I regret having to act toward you in like fashion. But it's from the heart. Margarida.

Rereading the letter, she found it rang hollow; but she folded it, methodically moistened the edge of the envelope, pressing hard to seal it. And while addressing it, she felt seized by a stupid laughter, which shook and excited her as if she had lost the notion that she was a person and that her blood and the floor were slipping away from under her feet. "I am engaged." Only those words gave her a sense of self, of an identity which was, nonetheless, dubious and incomplete and which demanded some clarification at once. She was engaged to whom? To André Barreto? To Uncle Roberto? The idea of her lonesome life filled those names with a sad and ambiguous reality. An unknown force uplifted her as it did the araucaria out on the courtyard, an irresistible force, full of those green tentacles that enclosed the house with shadows. She thought of Uncle Mateus: "A woman like you ought to fear nothing!" So that's the way it was? Manuel Bana was waiting for her with his sly moustache, leaning against the veranda pilaster.

"Here's the answer." And turning to Roberto:

"Cousin Corina's things.... Another bazaar."

Chapter XV

Carnet Mondain

In the afternoon, the Royal Club of Fayal was the one entity in Horta not napping on the balcony or tending the Trans-Atlantic cable.

João Garcia hit the floor with the bumper of his billiard cue, made a creaking sound as he chalked up, resignedly looked at the counter, and said to André Barreto:

"Only four balls to go. Sink them one by one in the corner pocket. You're the billiard king!"

In fact, wielding his cue behind his back, André Barreto made two short bank shots, in preparation for a showy finish on the third shot in which the red ball, almost touching his, ended up striking the vertex of a difficult two-cushion configuration.

"Stack arms!" cried Lieutenant Espínola as he watched André put up his cue in the rack. João Garcia did likewise and, spinning his black-dotted ball, said:

"Since I lost the wager, I owe the house half an escudo and the champion a beer."

"It's good that the rookies should pay tribute to the masters," said Espínola.

André Barreto softened the remark:

"Rookie, no! He actually plays a good game, well thought-out."

"You're right.... What brings Garcia down is that scientific game of his. It looks like quantum mechanics!"

"I've never played all that well; but the truth is, it's been months since I've had my hands on a cue. Billiards demands constant practice."

"Hug the rails, man! Are you telling me you couldn't handle a shot like the one I made? Look... like this... see... just like that!" And Lieutenant Espínola, holding very tightly but with difficulty the three balls in his small left hand, roughly reconstructed the shot under discussion. "See? A head-on shot! Then you were basically in the same position to have a go as Barreto, and he made a good shot. Come on, do it again, André, so Garcia can see it."

But André's ball, despite being struck solidly, harmlessly ended up next to the red ball without touching it.

The waiter opened three beers; Lieutenant Espínola went to get a book, which he had left open, face down on a playing table:

"I was here bored stiff reading when Barreto came in. I thought you weren't going to show up... So how's your microbe? She going to die? Now *she*'s what I call a tough cookie!"

"She's been feeling better today. But she's breathing her last, poor woman."

Lieutenant Espínola explained to André Barreto that they were talking about an old aunt who lived at the Garcias' and who was over a hundred: *Senhora* Secundina. He had seen her once: she was like a piece of iron from a tool found on some excavation site, something that for the life of him he could not identify or know what to do with but which still held up and in working order:

"Imagine, she remembers the waterspout that leveled Pasteleiro in the time of the Miguelistas![1] when the proprietor João Dulmo had to replant the Calhau quinta with cedars that now have heartwood a century old."

André Barreto knew the cedars well. They must be the same age as those that his father still kept in Urzelina, in the Dentro woodland. No ax could penetrate them! Only when you lifted a piece of bark could you see what they were like!–hard, sweet-smelling, and as red as a billiard ball.

---

[1] Adepts of Miguelismo, Dom Miguel de Bragança's Absolutist party. The struggle between Miguel (1802-1866) and his brother King Pedro IV (1798-1834), defender of Constitutionalism, led to a civil war in Portugal (1832-1834).–Trans.

"What a tough old lady!" Espínola added. "When João led me up those stairs, which is like climbing up the winding staircase to the top of the Lajes do Pico Cathedral, she said to me right away: 'Young man, are you an idle dreamer, too, like our Joãozinho? Leave the books alone, and court as many girls as you can!'" But noticing João Garcia's painful and sickened look, Espínola hesitated: "No... I'm not going to say the rest. How naturally she utters those eternal words: 'itch!' 'bitch!'"

André leaned back on the chair, his shaking body enveloped in his cigar smoke. His facial muscles became contorted, which always happened when he was measuring the green cloth for a carom or reacting to a witticism. His slim and vigorous physique lent him a reserved look; two short creases furrowed his brow, and he gave the impression of security and goodness.

They spent the rest of the afternoon reading and playing checkers. The weather turned dour, it was overcast in Pico and at the entrance to the channel. The club was almost deserted; the mirrors in the reception room reflected faded scenes on old tapestry and the famous carpet of the Royal Club of Fayal. The piece had been bought at auction in the customs house from the property seized from a pleasure yacht owned by a Polish prince who had shown up in Horta with an American ballerina and had been unable to pay for their refreshments. Lieutenant Espínola took André to examine the workmanship of two candelabra and the brand of a Delft vase. In the silence and torpor of the street, a voice might be heard, or some loud laughter on a street corner, or the rattling of carriage hardware accompanied by the hooting of the coachman urging on his tormented mule. By contrast, the elegant and somber room, with its draperies and the golden, shapely feet of its credence tables, imparted to the clubhouse the appearance of a refined and free existence.

Counselor Calapez had hosted a ball only days before; the dancing had gone on until almost five in the morning. João Garcia, leafing through the pages of *L'Illustration*, recalled the parade of dancing couples on the other side of the glass doors, saw again the trembling chandelier laden with lights as if the waltzes and tangos merged with and scintillated in its crystals.

Melancholy and unoccupied, he had spent the next night in-
doors, regretting his folly at having allowed Dr. Luís da Rosa to
convince him to accept the invitation from the counselor, who
received guests at his home as if he were handing out commen-
dations. It was his father's fault, with his obsession to see him
shine and socialize, trying to ameliorate the discomfort of knowing that his brother Ângelo had been invited on account of his
flair for interior design. Another reason (and why not?) was a
certain hope of seeing Margarida again, perhaps to follow up on
that phrase in the letter: "something that only a meeting could,
perhaps, clarify." But the courage he felt in her absence on his
return from the sad, pointless strolls in Pasteleiro vanished
every time he saw her, like a soaked flag in an afternoon festival spoiled by rain. Sigmalia's waltz awoke him to the fine serv-
ers in Calapez's living room, the circle of seated ladies, the
first move of the boys eyeing the evening gowns from a distance, and then boldly approaching the partners of their choice.
On that occasion Dr. Luís da Rosa had seized him by the arm,
and he had experienced the sensation that someone had blind-
folded him with the two ends of a kerchief and dragged him
along like a sleepwalker: "Miss Margarida Dulmo... The two of
you haven't yet met, have you? It's taken a long time!" And that
indiscretion on the part of Dr. Luís da Rosa, resembling the conclusion of a game of blindman's buff, which had all of a sudden
placed Margarida's waist under his near-trembling hand! Then
that unspeakable sweetness sculpting her live head, the naked
shoulder a handspan away from his lips, and again that blind
serpent on her ring against his left hand holding her fingers as
one holds a feather. Not a single word filled those moments of
dancing, from which he only retained, as from a dream, the
memory of the couples' faces appearing and disappearing in the
crowd: Damião Peres' strong, starch-stiff chest; Alice Lemos'
smile upon her peach-colored face; the satin trim on Dr.
António Lopes' tuxedo, his smooth-shaven face, and his polished and pointed tango foot endowing him with the elegance
and malice of a wolf cornered in a cave.

The conversation behind the draperies had not furthered

anything. The speech rehearsed for weeks and weeks to the beat of drums in the parade of the School for Commissioned Officers, and during the trip, and back home, and in his bunk-bed, and during that month in Horta during which he filled his mind with visions of a male and a female horseback rider coming down from Lomba at nightfall–died there on the spot, along with the breeze from the dock coming in through the windows of Calapez's festive mansion, lit like a great luxury liner preparing to head out to sea.

How he had foreseen it all!–Margarida's resistance, his blunder in sending the letter jointly addressed to her and *Dona* Corina, his embarrassment now, and her silence then... and how he had provided a reasoned-out solution for everything, with her retreats being headed off by his love-inspired logic! But it was a design drawn by a timid person, a play of poles and nothing more. Love did not demand confessions at an open window. Nor did it call for literary allegories of a love conceived as the stuff of myth, a myth connected with the shores of the island and with stormy isles in the night. And thus he had lost his chance during the waltz, like one who obtrusively drops a worm at the feet of a girl who has another dance partner. Sad and alienated in his chair, João Garcia meditated. Now processed in the style of tactics theorems, his meditations began to weave a precious thought in his mind, one made of a hard substance, as if it were not a sentence: *The love of a myth is a pure myth.*

He was occupied with these ruminations and with *L'Illustration* when Margarida entered the club with Pedro. They were looking for their uncle. Lieutenant Espínola, with the promptness of a leading man and a little affected in his words (which were harsh here and there to mark his nonchalance and the disinterestedness characteristic of a fine young man) set out to look for Roberto. This somewhat ostentatious scene rendered even more uncomfortable for João Garcia and André Barreto the presence of that woman in their midst–as if both men felt apologetic for creating the appearance that they were rivals for her attention, something that was far from their intentions. André spoke warmly, rattling the stack of ivory pieces on the

165

checkerboard, which had been pushed aside. Had Margarida gone out riding the day before? He could swear that he'd seen her.... But, no; it must have been Daisy Warren. Margarida put two and two together, realizing that it was her English friend, availing herself of the confusion to show a certain indifference before such solicitude, who imagined every girl in Horta to be her in disguise. But her way of accepting André's intimate ways did not show irritation or boredom: it was, rather, a sportive and frank understanding between people of the same caste, a fraternal feeling, with a touch of coldness and of ritual.

João Garcia spoke of horses and showed his liking for the assistant manager of the Trans-Atlantic cable company, Mr. Warren. He had met the Warrens at Dr. Luís da Rosa's; Daisy had translated poems by Antero de Quental into English and borrowed books from him. Margarida indicated she was aware of this relationship and apologized for having kept Tolstoy's *Resurrection* too long. She was very interested in reading the novel and already had gotten through most of it. She was a good friend of Daisy's.

Her frankness in confessing that she had taken home a book of his touched João Garcia. Margarida, after all, was still interested in him, shared some indirect, vague interests with him–the indifference of someone who casually hands to another, under the edge of the table, the prize at the end of the game up-down. But did her speaking about it in front of André Barreto amount to her reducing the little secrets shared with the Baron da Urzelina's son during the ball to the frivolous proportions of a mundane comedy? Or did it amount to her acting, for the rich man's sake, immune to the possibility of any little "mysterious relationship" between herself and João Garcia? And what about the naturalness with which she was now speaking to him here in the club, standing next to her brother, as if nothing had happened between the Pasteleiro quinta and the Jesus Street gratings? As if Januário Garcia's campaign involving the Avelars and *Dona* Carolina Amélia was not, precisely now, at the height of its fury?

From the windows of the Royal Club of Fayal one could see

the office's glass door and the solicitor-at-law signboard swinging in the afternoon wind. With a little effort and that instinct so typical of islanders (which makes city people and activities predictable in both time and circumstance, as they perform their centuries-old acts like a Mass hidden from view but easily followed from the nave), they could perceive his father's movements on the other side of his desk and his immense frame commanding Ladeira's penstrokes and Ângelo's tics. Of course, all of Horta suspected João Garcia's desolation amidst the large spiders of his family: Aunt Secundina, moribund and monstrous in the attic; and Aunt Henriqueta paralyzing her nephew under her abrasive and lukewarm wing, airing out his uniform, imposing certain habits on him, summoning him into the fold of the Honório women like a hen impelling a chick toward a kernel not meant for it. But why isolate him so much from that unfortunate noose that his father Januário was tightening ever more around the Dulmos' necks? What kind of woman was that? Why didn't she flee from him?

Roberto Clark, who was playing whist at a table toward the back of the club, finally appeared, preceded by Espínola's steps. He kissed Margarida on the brow, patted Pedro on the shoulder, and started to order some cakes and ale. Paying no attention to his niece's haste, he arranged the chairs where, after the billiards game, the partners had gone from discussing the story of old Secundina to striking the checkerboard with their stone checkers, a game in which games are won or lost by centimeters.

"No, Uncle. We're leaving."

"What? Already?"

"And you're coming with us. We need to talk."

Margarida's hand, emerging from a gray suit coat, came to rest on Roberto's shoulder, looking even more feminine against that tanned neck showing both the tension of cricket and the friction of rough, practical collars. Roberto, who needed to lower his head somewhat in order to look at his niece, tried, with a smile, to figure out the hurry inscribed upon those eyes. With his hand, he caressed her hair:

"Not even a moment? Are you that busy? Indeed?"

But the ring of empty chairs, in light of Margarida's rejection, spelled a vain expectation. João Garcia and Espínola stood up and extended their hands to her. André managed to detain her one more minute with a story about Clarinha, an acquaintance whom the daughter of the Baron da Urzelina had made in Conceição. Her name was Odete Frade.

"I know her well. She is so stubborn!"

According to Margarida, one needed to be wary of meddlesome Fayal girls and to refrain from taking new faces too far into one's confidence. People might consider her foolish for thinking that way, but these overly pampered girls who pout and for whom daddies buy pianos and *liberty* silk dresses, were not her type. She preferred "our Rosa," Manuel Bana's niece.

It sufficed to hear her mention that name, in that manner, for one to see in Margarida the little girl from Capelo, with her head cocked and her "shut up, ya!," her roughened hands holding the hem of her homespun apron. André laughed heartily, that tranquil laugh that set all his muscles in motion. One could read in his enlightened face and in his eyes clouded over by a deeply drawn smoke, a look that said "understood" in that telegraphic code between elegant people who pronounce judgment on a city from the height of their amusement. João Garcia, who again had taken up *L'Illustration*, thought about the group formed by his sister and Laura and Odete Frade, inseparable in their afternoons at the window in Miss Elvira's studio–kermess and pyrography. Such a nice girl! Every night, she stretched her body over the edge of her balcony toward the pinpoint eyes of Zé Goulart, who worked at Italcable and played sweep for the Fayal Sport soccer team.

As soon as Margarida had left, followed by her uncle and brother, João Garcia ran to the entry, pulled up his cape and quickly headed for Carrasca Well. He had forgotten the dinner at *Dona* Carolina Amélia's home, to which the Honório women were also invited. And now that the disdain with which Margarida had referred to a friend of his sister's ricocheted in him, filling him with more an irremediable disappointment than resentment, his father's recommendation that he not miss the dinner sounded to him like a grave duty, a blood obligation. Despite Aunt Secundina's state of health, his father had insisted that they go. He viewed these invitations with the same degree of seriousness with which he summoned the family to the annual observance of the Paschal duty and with which he encouraged João not to miss attending the criminal trials at the correctional police headquarters. They were social and professional duties, tributes paid from a good attorney to his client and of a young baccalaureate-degree holder to the bar and to public opinion. One could not miss them for anything in the world; they were above all things! After all, Aunt Secundina had long since become a kind of astral measure of their family's life, a lifelong gauge of the Garcias' character. One went to visit her in the little towers pretty much like Pretextato climbed, every morning, the Weather Station turret to check the pluviometer for the amount of rain that had fallen on the soaked parts of Horta, which gave life to the weeds, cabbages, and to the Peters' chestnut tree. Sprightly or half-dead, Aunt Secundina was the pool of the Garcias' sap. Even uprooted, she still afforded them her unwavering support.

Chapter XVI

The Witch of Spades

Dinner at Carrasca Well took place in silence and uneventfully. Januário ate with an affected dignity, all stiff and proper. In his movements and parsimony, one could sense an important subject being pushed aside by the demands of a vast and delicate endeavor: considerations left over from Lent about "life's too short" and the ingratitude of men, "well-springs of pride and vanity." One phrase ("the sins of the world") contributed much to bolster *Dona* Carolina Amélia's accumulated astonishment. Januário elaborated on it with a quotation from the Mass: "Lamb of God who takes away the sins of the world."

"*Agnus Dei qui tollis peccata mundi.*" Ângelo, who from the very start of dinner had displayed on the table a great bouquet of pansies, stumbled in the middle of the phrase, which he had fancied repeating in his acolyte's Latin. But "*qui tollis*" at once reminded him of Quitolas, a stuttering classmate who ran errands and picked up cigarette butts from gutters. Unable to stifle a giggle, Ângelo spit out a mouthful of wine onto his crinkled serviette.

Januário's eyes blazed with anger:

"I won't stand for any shenanigans. I'll smash your face!"

A dead silence followed. The ladies seemed to wish to bury themselves eyes first in the bunch of bananas ripening in the fruitbowl. They devoured their dessert in a hurry, conscious of one another's presence. *Dona* Carolina Amélia could only say:

"Oh, *Senhor* Ângelo! Such an outrage in my house! And to provoke your brother like that!"

"Don't be surprised, madam.... It always happens, I'm sorry! I have to bear this cross to my grave." And Januário, in order to maintain a certain calm, had to take such a deep breath that his vest expanded like a balloon.

"Let's change the subject, Father!" said João Garcia, standing up.

"You're already old enough to know your place, at least to show respect for your nephew, for the position he occupies today. But no.... Always wagging that silver tongue of yours...." And with an expression that was, at once, full of pity and rage: "A cripple! Who doesn't even know his own defects.... I'll tear you limb from limb!"

"You'd be well advised to keep your trap shut until we get home...," said Ângelo, feigning a strange disgust. "I've always preferred to wash my dirty laundry in private."

"Uncle, will you please be quiet? That's the end of it."

Januário, who had regained his composure, looked daggers at his brother:

"I'm sorry, madam! I really apologize; and now, let's get down to our little business."

"Don't mention it, *Senhor* Garcia! Apologize for what? For God's sake! A quarrel, we all have them. *Senhor* Ângelo didn't weigh his words... that's what happened. You are always so sociable, all of you are such good friends!"

Januário's ingratiating voice could already be heard from the direction of the living room. A secret force seemed to take hold of his emaciated form, lending it an import at once solemn and sweet, which grew as he paced the floor. *Dona* Carolina Amélia, despite being accustomed to her peace and quiet and detesting rudeness, after the scene she had just witnessed, felt as if a neighbor had come to relate a story involving people of low station, to whom she wouldn't give the time of day. Januário stopped, as always, in front of the full portrait of the late civil governor, and shook his head solemnly. Then with soft steps, he bolted the door and installed himself in the armchair in front of the old lady, resting his hand on his hip as he had seen the great Pedro Cabral do on stage at the Fayal Theater. (Horta would never again see a theatrical company like that! *Gillette of Narbonne... The Blue Bird... The Bells of Corneville... Night and Day....*)

"Well, my dear lady, with respect to the co-signing...."

171

Laura and Carlota had calmed down João Garcia and tried to get his mind off the humiliation. Laura had a certain power over him, a sedative and pleasant influence, precisely to the extent that he was able to dissociate himself from the idea that she had been his childhood sweetheart. She had been a petulant little girl, rather pretty, blond, with a bent toward small intrigues and possessed of a haughty pride in her beauty, imparting an expression of distaste to her face and a corrosive malice to those eyes above that angelic mouth and those cheeks as red as the pips in the suit of hearts.

"Leave them alone, João! Your father gets all worked up over nothing.... There was no reason for such a scene. But you should have seen *Dona* Carolina's face."

"I, on the other hand, could have just died! How shameful!" said Carlota.

"Come, now! What do I care.... Let's go to the sitting room; the beasts are in their cages. And what do you say we go to *Dona* Carolina's pantry and swipe some marmalade?"

"No, we couldn't do that!"

"Okay, then let's go to the sitting room! João...."

The three made themselves comfortable; and Ângelo, who had gone out for a little fresh air and to see the geese, came in a little later. All that João Garcia needed was to hear his uncle at a certain distance from his father to feel won over by his colorful chattering and to dive headlong into the storyline he extracted from people like the author of a play composing in front of his audience, from the set to the tirades to the stage calls.

"Laurinha, my love! Have you already seen the Beef?"

"What beef?"

"The guardian of the Granary, the pipe smoker? They're shouting from the rooftops that he's engaged to his niece. They are going to live in London. He is going first to get money to save his brother-in-law (if boy Januário allows him enough time...), and then will send for her right away, all right! Naturally, they will marry by proxy. And, of course, we'll miss the chance of seeing that little dish walking out of the cathedral... that wide train sweeping the staircase.... Now, that is always a pretty sight. Oh, and I almost forgot the Beef's top hat, with its 'LONDON'-*Come on, yes*! silk lining. The guardian of the Clarks' Granary, the pipe smoker!..." Leaning on the back of a chair, Ângelo's face had assumed Roberto's expression leaning on the window facing Ocean Street. With a pencil in his mouth acting as a pipe, the channel tides seemed stretched before him and, in *Dona* Carolina Amélia's sitting room, the compact cone of Pico bore witness to his humorously furrowed eyebrows. The girls, sitting on the couch, were dying of laughter. "*Thank you, 'Màrgueréte'! Thank you....*"

Laura, overcome by a fit of laughter, sat rocking on the sofa; the tears ran down over the hands she raised to her eyes; she bent her head almost to her knees:

"But that's exactly like him!... That's the Beef!"

Ângelo, feeling very flattered, next removed *Dona* Carolina Amélia's sewing kit from the coffee table in the center of the room; with the crochet needles, a ball of yarn, and the poor lady's thumbstall, he made a puppet for a shadow show–a cat's head. Then, pulling out a deck of cards from the *étagère*, he started a game of solitaire:

"I'm up against a tremendous *'difficulty.... A b i g yarn!'*"

The girls had positioned themselves around the coffee table; Carlota adjusted the height of the lamp kept in suspension by a porcelain weight. But Laura, with an abrupt movement that exposed her moist and voracious set of little teeth, mixed up the rows separated by suits, and all electrified with excitement, shook Ângelo by the shoulder:

"You'd better read the cards for us, *Senhor* Ângelo! Come on.... let's see if the Beef is really going to marry Margarida Dulmo or if Carlota is going to be the lucky girl!"

"You and your crazy ideas, my dear!"

"Come on, *Senhor* Ângelo; read the cards for us! That's the only way to find out. And João also has to take part in this, no doubt about it! Just being involved in rumors isn't enough." She went to get João Garcia, who was in a corner drearily leafing through a book of patterns; she dragged over a chair, forcing him to sit down: "That's it! Carlota, queen of clubs... João, since he's a sublieutenant, the king of spades.... And the Beef...."

"The Beef's the king of diamonds!"

Laura clapped:

"Well chosen! He's really loaded... Bravo! That's an excellent beginning."

"And you, my love, are the queen of hearts! *'Golden parrot... Little Belgian canary...,'*" hummed Ângelo, stroking her hair.

"Hey! Get your paws off me!"

João Garcia listened to all this as if a thick fog had descended upon him, his uncle, his sister, and Laura, something opaque and unstable, dissolving lost people in a wide clearing. Theirs were voices and gestures that his hearing and his sight could hardly join together. Deep down inside, his vision of Margarida held fast, like an apparition fleeing from its earthly form, or a person who, sensing approaching steps, wraps herself up in a disguise. The lowered lamp, casting a golden glow upon Laura's head, arrayed in a mysterious pose those figures standing in a circle around the playing cards.

"The king of diamonds is in pursuit of the queen of clubs...." Ângelo summed up after a few seconds of concentration, during which his little moustache, moist with cream, shone and twitched:

"Do you see, Carlota? Here he is, because he always takes the steep narrow street when coming down on horseback from Lomba."

"... but the queen of clubs has her five senses trained on foreign lands, lands of plenty...."

"It's the *Americano* from Capelo, who courted you on the dock lawn, my dear! It's really him!"

"Meanwhile, the king of hearts shows up from this side..."

"Who is he?!"

"Quiet!"

"Why? So I am not entitled to know who my partner is...? My darling king of hearts?"

"... the king of hearts shows up now with the altar on his mind (it's a seven!), and the queen of diamonds turns to spades because of the king of spades. She is thinking of setting sail (six of hearts:

sailing vessel), with jealousy... suspicions... a matchmaker's scoffing remarks.... The queen of hearts goes on her way...."

"Now it's up to you, my dear...," said Carlota, with a smile of relief brought on by a game too complicated for her taste.

"Me? I've never gotten in anybody's way, thank you! I have better things to do than get involved in that pretentious bluenose's conquests!"

"And now...," said Ângelo, imposing silence solely with his gestures, like those of a fortune teller matching distant cards, "...now, the king of diamonds would get his lady, if it weren't for this doggone knight of spades, which I don't know what to do with.... Oh, no! Now there is even a seven of spades, which means death... And a codille. May the devil take these cards–I don't want any funny business here!"

During the slow and silent rounds of quadrille which prolonged the evening, João Garcia felt as if floating free of himself, absorbed by the game strategies and by the desire to see his partner get a good hand. His partner was Laura; and it was amusing to see her attentive to the slightest movement of the table, holding the cards with her tiny hand, whose fragility was thrown in high relief by her bauble of a bracelet. Her eyes were as cunning as a fox's, keeping, in the demands of the game, her opponents at bay, looking right and left for any signs of hesitation preceding difficult moves. Carlota sometimes complained that they could peek at her cards. Laura protested dryly, pursing her lips and checking the last hand, trying to remember what cards of what suits had already been played. And when it was João Garcia's turn to play, she stuck him with her piercing stare, like one who probes with a pin the softness of a rare fabric. Then as she looked down at the cards on her lap, the wrinkling of her brow accentuated the expression of her lowered eyelids, whose tawny little lashes had the sweetness of an angel's:

"To play a seven on the second round! What an idiot... what an idiot!"

After having gone by São João Street so Laura would not have to walk by herself, the Garcias headed back home in silence. High up on the drive, the Honórios' gate was open; Laura, wrapping herself well, did not want them to accompany her any farther and scurried home. Her sharp voice could be heard in the silence and lividness of the deserted street:

"Good night! See you!"

Avoiding Ângelo, Januário had quickened his step. João Garcia, walking by his slightly crippled uncle, watched that unhappy figure vanish along the strip of sidewalk, his derby fallen to the side like the crest of a blackbird or that of an old starling with ruffled feathers. The night was stifling hot; and João Garcia, going up to Aunt Secundina's room, found Henriqueta slumbering next to the kerosene lamp, whose wick was lowered and smoking.

"How is she doing?"

Henriqueta rubbed her eyes, still half-asleep, rearranging her shawl and making herself comfortable in the chair:

"She seems to be trying. This is one tough old lady!"

João Garcia went to the window propped open by a clothes-brush and raised it a little higher. A small piece of sky showed some stars. For a long time now, the deaf old lady seemed to have asked death's permission to linger there a little longer; life at the Garcias' went on as something postponed in part, the exception being that stubborn life that persisted in the little towers. João related to Henriqueta the incident that had happened at *Dona* Carolina Amélia's dinner table; he complained about Uncle Ângelo and about his father's imprudent behavior. Henriqueta shrugged:

"He has a short fuse! It's the Garcia temper, these outbursts of ours.... But what about Januário?... that shrill-voiced wonder.... He's the old notary's spitting image!"

The deaf old lady stirred and groaned. João Garcia leaned on the edge of the bed and looked at her ill-defined shape under the clothes, her chin whisker as plain to see as a comma. And by the yellowish kerosene light, Henriqueta noticed in her nephew's eyes an expression that seemed to convey both repugnance and resignation. João Garcia's jutting out of the chin toward Aunt

Secundina's cadaverous face pestered by flies summed up the meaning and the ending of a life.

"What's the matter with you, my boy? You look like you lost your best friend!"

But João Garcia, who had allowed his aunt to put her arm around him, brusquely pulled away. His now-measured steps made the narrow and steep stairs creak, like one who is hurrying down to carry out an act of heroism and then, suddenly, feels his courage draining from him.

Chapter XVII

Third Nocturne (Metapsychics)

Downstairs, in João Garcia's room, there was a chair on which he always hung his uniform and two wooden hangers where he put his swagger stick. In front of a table piled with books hung a portrait of Antero de Quental,[1] suspended from a cotton string. As he unfastened his shell jacket, João Garcia went over fragments of sonnets that popped into his head like a sudden fog rolling in, peering into his own soul by the light of those silent and noble features on the wall.

A book about the Franco-Prussian War, opened on top of his portfolio, reminded him of the lecture he was to deliver in the barracks two weeks hence on the subject of *Historical Aspects of the Struggle Among the Great Powers*. His commander had introduced such lectures as an innovation in the *Determinations* of the *Order*, *Lectures by officers on*: a) Tactics and ballistics; b) War strategy; c) Military organization and supplies. Each topic was followed by the list of lecturers. He and Espínola were in charge of a fourth category: d) History and diplomacy. For months, they had spoken of nothing else in the officers' room, in the barracks square, and in the cooperative. The sergeant major who presided at the "Brotherhood" had, with the help of the soldiers on fatigue duty, been preparing the chapel-turned-library: they had already placed a piece of canvas over a table's oilcloth cover and added a bottle of water with a single glass. In the sergeants' mess hall, there had been discussions about who

---

[1] Azorean-born Antero de Quental (1842-1891) is the major poet of the Generation of 1870, to which the novelist Eça de Queirós (1845-1900) also belonged. Antero is especially known for his philosophical and sometimes morbid sonnets. He committed suicide in a Ponta Delgada park.–Trans.

were the most intelligent officers in the battalion, the difficulties involved in gaining promotions, and whether a captain knew more or less than a doctor at law. João Garcia was the object of special admiration among those present who contributed to the newspaper *Marte* and who sought in books and in regimental festivities an oasis from the office and barracks square routines and the mornings spent in the drilling of recruits, when the heat extracted from the dry weeds a smell like drum leather and molding walls. When he was on duty, his red armband gave him away from afar; he leaned a moment to look inside the guard quarters: "Gentlemen...." The sergeants, sitting in groups on the iron bunks, shook bread crumbs from the blankets, turned the pillows in a hurry, and stood at attention in their duck shell coats: "Would you happen to have a book to loan us, sublieutenant?" João Garcia had given a lecture at the "Brotherhood," followed by a recital, and had encouraged them to organize a recital "to benefit the scholarship fund." It was said of him: "Now, that's what I call an officer! He is one of a kind!"

Recalling these comments, which he picked up from Uncle Ângelo or from overheard conversations in the kitchen between Henriqueta and his orderly, João Garcia sat at his desk amid papers scattered all about the room, feeling the need to impart to his lecture a strictly military and rigorously technical character. Being an officer was an imperative that he now discovered in the depths of his conscience, like a person who finds a toy while rummaging through a drawer aware he is past the age of playing with it, but who also realizes that his war toys had their adult counterparts. And why should he not take seriously the *Regulations for Field Officers*? the Firing Range? He liked military service. What for others amounted to the nuisance of the company with its paydays and depot duty was for him a serious pleasure, something filled with meaning, as if he were a monk. Espínola used to say, "You're a fool! You take everything so seriously! To carry out duties, fine; meet one's obligations.... But this hero-worship on the part of the recruits, these orders of 'right foot!,' the camaraderie.... Nonsense!" But João Garcia, when he was assigned the patrol of the garrison, went in all seriousness to the military command to get the password and communicated it, all excited, to the patrols in the city before going for a stroll along Pasteleiro. Now his great desire was to put the idea of Margarida out of his mind, to consider the Dulmos' quinta a mere chance occurrence in the terrain, with cartographic vines and cedars, a forsaken house where all of a sudden they had installed an observation post to defend against an enemy squadron. At night, recalling the pungent smell of the fishing ground breezes, the kilometers of dust and wind filtered through the foliage of the tamarisks, and the volume of the channel waters rolling in the shadow of Pico, he would halt at the regulation distance from the sentry, who would slap his calf-leather brogues together: "Who goes there?" "Patrol!" "Halt! To arms!" "When recognized, patrol may advance."

Espínola, who had become aware of the unction and seriousness with which he carried out this ritual that harked back to the depths of time (as if his sword met, in the corporal of the guard's bayonet, the steel of a knight wearing a true coat of mail), right from the start made a joke of it: "Always the poet, eh?"

No, today he did not feel up to the Historical Aspects of the Struggle Among the Great Powers. His pen got stuck on sentences like: *"The Rhine of the ballads marks out the multisecular battlefields between a people who conceive of the art of war as an intelligent and forceful defense of their territorial heritage and a people who experience war as an organic necessity, nurtured in poetic tradition and in the metaphysics of expansionism."*

He composed three, even four versions of it–four belabored versions. It was ridiculous and risky: they could even think he was a Germanophile. Captain Soares went from subordinate to subordinate, always with "notes" from the minutes in his hand: "So, when is the poet going to speak? When are we going to hear the poet speak?" Antero's portrait, with his impassive posture, dominated the far end of the room:

> *In your hand, gloomy horseman,*
> *In black battlements attired,*

In your hand shines a sword of comets
Piercing darkness with blazing light.

And as João, already stretched in bed, reached for the volume of *Sonnets*, one could hear the ruffling sound of the page being turned to the closing of the sonnet "Mors-Amor":

Fearless, the strange beast rides on.
The dark steed announces: "I am Death!"
The horseman replies: "I am Love!"

It must have been almost midnight. Outside, someone was walking along the deserted, cold-benumbed street with its wrought-iron balconies, a street imaginable before the first rooster's crow in the Horta backyards, reminding João Garcia of Aunt Secundina imprisoned under her sheets, which moved from the fetid bed to the soaking piles in the washtub. Hers was a life turbidly merged with that water running all night into the neighborhood water holes and feeding the frogs, discernible by their slight movements in the mud. One of these days, Aunt Secundina would be leaving through the gate, carried by four or six men, to go feed the plot of grass in the Horta cemetery. "OBITUARIES" in the *Insulano*: ".... The deceased is survived by Mr. Januário Garcia, solicitor-at-law, Mr. Jacinto Garcia, a respected pharmacist in Praia do Almoxarife, Mr. Ângelo Garcia, broker...." Such vocabulary for a page like the *Insulano* yet! Uncle Ângelo, "brokering!"

After he closed Antero's book, something fell on the rug, which made the book appear thicker: an envelope. João Garcia's name appeared to him to be concentrated in the *G* of Margarida's elegant and slightly sprawling hand, tied together by six letters which by an absurd collaboration of his conscious mental associations and her strokes of the pen (now coiled, now firm) represented for him her body and her being but nonetheless retained a meaning that was absolutely civilian, a meaning that could not be denied on that street and in that house: *GAR-CIA*. Why, after all, that reckoning of probabilities which had

181

Margarida as its object, like a solution underlined in chalk on a blackboard, when he was but that looping upon the envelope, that noun that seemed derived from the name of the "gull"–"*Garcia*"–used to designate an abstruse quality (perhaps the disease of gulls, birds of the wind and of the islands...)? He felt a welcome peace descend upon him, which seemed an offering from the floor overhead, where once in a while his father's vast bed, holding his huge body overtaken by a deathlike sleep, stirred up a rumbling or a creaking sound. Serving as ceiling for his father, another floor with other Garcias supported the weight of other beds and the roof frame, while from Aunt Henriqueta's room came the sound of a container being slowly filled. At that hour, Laura was sleeping or also getting up; and it would be exciting and mysterious, like watching an egg crack open, to surprise her at that brief moment when she surrendered herself to the darkness and to the silence, to feel her warm, small hands undoing her nightgown. And *passe-partouts*... statues of the Holy Christ from São Miguel within a purled frame... Uncle Ângelo's slippers with an embroidered butterfly... (what harm was there in that?) ... as well as the picoted oval picture of the Sacred Heart of Jesus pasted up behind the door, with 40 days of indulgences and the consecration of that entire household to those red flames. In short, it was a house like any other! A lifestyle like any other! In short, blood relatives, a family.... or were they?

At one in the morning, João Garcia, who had hardly slept, heard someone warily tapping on the window. He enjoyed falling asleep feeling the presence of the street, and so never closed the shutters. Only the large drapery, which was rolled back and secured to a hook, prevented people from seeing in from the outside. But lying on his bed, João Garcia could see the legs of the hurrying passersby or a little passenger carriage returning to the city from the countryside, shaking the street cobblestones. He now went to the window in his pajamas and came face to face with Espínola, who in order to penetrate the darkness and silence of the room had made his hands and cape into a kind of photographer's hood. He could not make out what

Espínola was saying, for the burning ashes from his cigarette filled his gestures with smoke. João Garcia, wrapping himself in his cape, went to open the door. Espínola was coming to incite him to go paint the town red. He still did not know exactly what they were going to do.... They could, for example, rent one of Pintado's carriages and go eat limpets in Bailabém's tavern in Feteira, or else go to Mariquinhas Estragada's for sausage and marinated pork–"What about it?"

Still startled, João Garcia paced the floor in his slippers.

"Come on, man! So late?"

"Don't be silly! Let's go!"

"But Bailabém's tavern is probably closed... It must be, for sure!"

"Closed *schmosed!* He lives right next to the tavern. I have often waked him up in the wee hours, and that's when he becomes a real frycook. And his pork sausage is really out of this world!" Espínola pinched his lips in appreciation: "Fit for a king!"

Giving in, João Garcia started to put on his civilian trousers. Damião Serpa, a great friend of both of them, had remained on the street corner on the lookout for Pintado's carriage, which should have been arriving from Flamengos with Dr. Nunes, responding to a plague case. He was a dark-complected young man, athletic and with a healthy outlook, and he had a soft spot for João Garcia. Childhood friends, now they only saw each other at Yankee House, or once in a great while, at Badela's. But between the two there was a camaraderie full of affection and verve, arising from the contrast between two people who, in a manner of speaking, complement each other.

Since Damião and Espínola could not agree on the night's spree, and João Garcia, drawn into it, could not help decide, they ended up by walking to Pintado's coachshed and stable at the end of the street, with its open, broad plank gate reddened by a capricious, gloomy light.

"Are we going in Pintado's victoria?" João Garcia, stopping, wondered aloud. "Where to?"

"Leave that to us. Just listen to this nobleman! You expecting maybe a coupé?"

But Pintado kept his victoria way inside the shed; it was difficult to get it out from where it stood against the wall under a candle lamp, a can of oil for the livestock hooves and a ram's horns forming a vast panoply. An otherworldly charabanc–called the "big carriage"–whose curtains had been removed, occupied the space reserved for the passage of the carriages into the interior of the coachshed, whence came the smell of manure and the calm pawing of the mules. Pintado, holding his lantern high, shed light on the movements of a kind of dwarfish individual standing on top of a footstool, stacking in the charabanc some boxes made of unplaned pine planks lying at the entrance to the shed.

"Coffins in this place?" exclaimed João Garcia, trying to pierce the darkness, as he stood behind Pintado's overcoat. "Are they for the plague victims?"

"Yesirree! Half a dozen are going to the quarantine. They've just arrived from José Taleia's shop... brand new from the adze. As the saying goes, he who wears these coats pays nothing at all to the tailor. Am I right or not, Perneta? Tell the good doctor here not to be afraid. For half a crown, you'd go in one of these to the door of the hospital, wouldn't you boy? I'm going to pull off your ear, you overstuffed dog!"

The light of the lantern hit the face of the dwarfish man who, to make that macabre load fit, was trying to bend some charabanc shafts supporting the roof. The effort creased his face. One could see, inside his crooked mouth, the redness of his gums and his teeth blackened from chewing tobacco. Pintado, opening the lid of one of the coffins, acted as if he were going to ring Perneta's neck and push him into the coffin:

"You scoundrel. This miserable plague is your ticket to Brazil...."

"Let's quit this fooling around," interrupted Espínola, annoyed, "and let's establish one thing: are you an undertaker now, or do you still rent carriages? Can we get a victoria to go to Feteira or not?"

"We'll take care of everything, lieutenant! Perneta is going to take a ride in this here coupé into 'joined-feet' country, and I'll drive Your Excellencies wherever you wish to go. You decide! The dead with the dead and the living with the living. Isn't that how it should be?"

Damião Serpa, encouraging the coachman's friendly disposition, helped the second coachman to turn the charabanc around and then took it rumbling down the improvised plank ramp to the sidewalk. He dressed well, never without his derby; and with his sleeves rolled up, thrusting an elbow against the teeth of the mule that was scratching himself against the pole and rejecting the headstall, he had a playful and smart air, which cheered up João Garcia. They got into the victoria.

"Go by Pasteleiro, Pintado! Then head toward Bailabém!"

> *Standing on a wooden leg,*
> *I've knocked them all down;*
> *Not a mackerel was left standing,*
> *Not even a single olive.*

It was a serene night, with the moon in its first quarter and whitish scales lining the sky. The bouncing of the victoria on Horta's cobblestones made the passengers giddy and enabled the little tune to raise their spirits, creating in that procession an atmosphere of gaiety which at first had seemed difficult to attain. The carriage headed slowly toward the countryside. The bouncing of the springs over the hollow macadam alerted them to the proximity of the cedars and the gate to the Dulmos' quinta; the victoria moved on, rolling over the sandy shoreline road. Then Damião Serpa ordered Pintado to stop and put down the top. He put an arm around Espínola's waist, another around João Garcia's, who had shrunk into a corner, smoking; then, very talkative, leaning back while the mules, at a slow pace, wound their way up the incline, he sang his favorite aria for moonlit nights: "Window, open up!"

Bailabém served pork sausage for three, limpets, *hendaya* and Pico wine. Despite Espínola's efforts, they spoke of nothing but the plague and other sad subjects. Even Damião Serpa availed himself of those depressing stories to present his own ideas on the soul's immortality. It always involved a romantic or adventurous case or a violent death in some shipwreck or ambush, which raised the question of our knowing whether the soul goes to heaven, purgatory, or hell–"as the priests maintain"–or whether it is something like an invisible insect hovering about the living and which people succeed in attracting towards a three-legged table and forcing it to explain itself by means of little knocks.

How mysterious everything was! He was a hunter and had lived in California for years. He remembered stories from the time of the Gold Rush, when they still rode covered wagons from New England to Sacramento and sometimes, when ravaged by hunger in the deserts, had to barbecue the drawing oxen themselves. In Boston, there was a Metapsychical Society, of which Damião had become a member.

"A "meta-what" Society?" asked Espínola, exploiting the picturesque nature of the things that Damião exaggerated.

"*Fiat lucas*.... M e t a p s y c h i c s: the study of the soul after death. It's a fact! They even have laboratories, scientific works on the subject. I can quote you some that I still have at home."

"'Metaphysics' I know something about," insisted Espínola. "It's one of the branches of philosophy: psychology, logic, morals, metaphysics...."

"You forgot aesthetics!" reminded João Garcia. "Are you trying to tell me that the beautiful has no speculative status?"

"I'm sorry! But there are those who deny the importance of aesthetics among the philosophical disciplines. In that case, we would have to consider other infinitely more important fields of human thought, for example, the 'theory of knowledge,' originating in Kant...."

"In aesthetics, I can cite the great work by de Guyau, *L'Art au point de vue sociologique*...," said João Garcia, already showing a polemical attitude, as if he were hurling a *distinguo*.

"But I'm telling you sociology is not aesthetics! It's a branch of ethics, a new science, almost an experimental one...."

"Quite right, my brothers-at-arms! That's how I like to see you! And what about that second order of pork sausage, Bailabém?"

Damião hit the table with the bottom of the empty bottle: "We want a jovial atmosphere! We're out of ammo."

The tavern had reached a saturation point under the cloud of tobacco smoke as well as that of the kerosene lamp blazing at full strength on top of an upside-down grain-measurement container. To this was added the aroma emanating from the sizzling frying pan on the other side of the counter inlaid with discarded coins minted, under the order of Angra's regency, from the church bells of half the archipelago. Looking out the window, one could see loose shore boulders under a sheet of water from a sea turned silver by the light of a sickle moon.

They were still arguing over the branches of knowledge and their respective importance. Espínola found great difficulty in explaining the purpose of the theory of knowledge, about which he was actually on fairly shaky ground. Damião kept hammering away at his point:

"So we don't know that what's true is true? That's funny! Two plus two equals four; prove to me otherwise! Postulates cannot be challenged."

"That's asinine!"

Besides, Espínola wanted him to stick to the issue of metapsychics; and Damião, noticing that he was being quoted, concentrated his attention, setting his fork on the plate:

"I can only say that I was a witness to the following: A young friend of mine, a Spaniard, had a girlfriend in Boston. The girl's father felt obliged to go out to California; he bought a dairy farm in Los Angeles and sent for the family. The girl liked him a lot; they went out alone. He would pick her up after closing the office; she was working in a pencil factory, on the other side of Boston. On Sundays, they'd take the subway and go have lunch in an oak-and-pine forest, a beautiful place! You have no idea what a forest is like in America! In the middle of it, one of those toll roads, an asphalt road, mind you... very modern, right smack through the middle of those woods that go on and on for miles... and the automobiles and the busses: vroom... vroom.... Larger than this island!"

"Ximenes took me along once. Over there, it's not like here, where a boy who has a serious courtship going always has to keep an eye on his friends. Over there, we are all pals! The girl was an American, her father was German. I can still see her... Grete [2]. How gorgeous.... And very outgoing! On our trips together, she'd pay as much attention to me as she did to Ximenes; everything so natural, nothing indiscreet.... Sometimes she'd grab my arm and we'd run off, with a finish line previously marked off and paced out, she and I.... We'd be off like a shot! She was really something... And what a gorgeous pair of legs!"

"Now I see!" said Espínola. "Your whole point was the girl's legs. Some metaphysician you were! And a groom's best friend at that!"

"Stop joking, okay? She was a respectable girl, I swear to God!"

Despite his need to continue satisfying his athlete's appetite with pork sausage (João Garcia was creating a mountain of limpet shells on his plate and drinking in silence), Damião had raised his fork with a genuine gesture, one as healthy as his rosy cheeks from the heat in the tavern and from the wine. Espínola, who had a serious disposition underneath his humorous dryness and who liked goading those with whom he spoke until he touched a soft spot close to home, looked at him with a frank smile:

"I'm joking. Tell us the rest of the story."

"Well. They were supposed to write to each other. Ximenes never found out what happened to the girl. A year later he received a letter, returned to sender from the boarding house where he had lived, a place owned by a Chinese rogue. The envelope was all full of rubber stamps: *Care of Mr. Chin-Lan-Fu, Lincoln Street, Boston*; *Raleigh, North Carolina*; *Pueblo, Colorado*; *Arizona*... chasing that little chinaman, who seemed to have dropped off the face of the earth! Poor Ximenes! He showed me the letter so many times that I even memorized the inscriptions on the envelope. What a pretty handwriting she had: *Grete Spiel*."

"And so?"

---

[2] *Grete*, diminutive of *Margaret(h)e* but also a full name in its own right, is the German equivalent of the Portuguese name Margarida.–Trans.

"He tried everything. He contacted consuls, private detectives, a cattle agency, a Boston firm that imported apples and grapefruit.... He found out, afterwards, from a foreman of the pencil factory, a co-worker of hers.... Her father had married her off to a business partner, some rich guy. A horrible story! The guy had a wife in France and hadn't told her. He fell in love with her and kicked out his wife. Grete's father, who had a financial noose around his neck on account of the ranch, locked himself in a room with her and brandished a pistol. He'd kill himself if she didn't come to his rescue. She had to choose...."

"Lord, there are such scoundrels in this world!" said Espínola.

"Ximenes, of course, knew nothing about all this. I did my utmost to make him forget the girl, went with him to dance parties, shoved ballerinas in his face."

"The ones you didn't want for yourself, of course...."

"You think I'm making this up, do you? It's a big country; everything is possible! Ximenes is the one who didn't want any part of it.... I used to drill it into him: 'Let bygones be bygones, man. Girls are a dime a dozen. Most likely she has some boyfriend, and here you are, worrying yourself sick over her....' He went around moping. Sad, sad as night, that's true. But she had given him her word of honor. He always told me the story looking very upset, lost in thought, as if speaking to a ghost: 'Mark my words, John! Dead or alive...' (poor devil! it was plain to see he was doomed to love her, fatal attraction, an obsession!), 'dead or alive, you'll hear from me.' And we did. One night, one of our 'mediums' received energy from a spirit so strong that it made her interrupt a conversation we were all engrossed in, stand up all bathed in light, and begin to shake. The spirit seemed alive! Ximenes could only say: 'Grete! Grete! *En la pantalla!*...'" Reacting to the disbelief he could read in Espínola's face, Damião protested: "I have the proof at home, man! *Reports of the Metaphysics Society*. A medium from Calcutta."

João Garcia, to the great surprise of both, had stood up; he raised his tray with a huge pile of limpet shells and, taking operetta steps, started to hum:

Window, open up!
Let me look at Maria!

Espínola and Damião started to push the chairs aside, shaking their heads, open-mouthed, and finally burst into an uproarious fit of laughter, the kind that takes a long time to taper off.

"Holy cow! What a load of bull!"

"Eh, brother! What's up?"

But remaining indifferent and performing a miraculous balancing act as he held the tray aloft, João Garcia went on singing:

How many sleepless nights you've given me!

"Yes, sir.... Lovely!"

Suddenly he stopped short, furled his eyebrows, as if gripped inwardly by an irresistible vision, and with hardly any drunken movements, he waxed rhetorical, his face lit up in excitement:

"I propose a toast to Grete and her fatal love! Where are you, who are fleeing from me? Don't you remember that night you walked, with your hair blowing in the wind, along the edge of a cliff?... My pale hands held your delicate fingers! Who broke the buzzards in the tiles in that nocturnal park in Arizona and forever blinded the bronze serpent, our confidante and accomplice?... Your light dress got caught on the brambles along the walkways.... You were a bride in the rain, which soaked your hair... and I was running in the dark and in vain called after you! The tree sap was borne by the wind that bore us. 'Grete! Grete!' 'No! No! Let me go. I shall return!...' *'Who tore, who soiled my linen sheets?...'* (Bad.... This is by Camilo Pessanha [3]!). *'Who broke (what cruel, simian fury!)'* the branch of the old orange tree that put forth the wrong blossoms?... Was it in Arizona?... In Pico?... Tell me, Damião, for God's sake! Speak to me about Grete! Now...!"

---

[3] Portuguese symbolist poet (1867-1926), Pessanha had considerable influence on the poetry of the chief modernist poet Fernando Pessoa (1888-1935).–Trans.

In a flash of lucidity, João Garcia sat and put his glass down; and revealing in his voice, now lower and discreet, the realization of the spectacle he was making of himself in the presence of a stunned Bailabém standing behind the counter, he said:

"You guys steady me; I feel a little dizzy... I drank too much."

With a little fresh air and ammonia which, on these occasions, Bailabém always brought out from the back of a cabinet, João Garcia got into the victoria and sat between Damião and Espínola, hatless and with his head leaning back. The victoria top was down; the night was serene, although a little overcast. When Pintado cracked his whip, Espínola and Damião started to whistle, feeling comfortable and full, and smoking cigars. Before a Pasteleiro hemmed in with cedars and slumbering by the boulder-lapping tides, they got off near a drinking trough. João Garcia took a ritualistic ablution, with his feet standing on the two iron bars. Damião looked at him askance:

"How goes it? How do you feel now? Better?"

"A little better. Man! What a feeling! Everything was moving in circles...."

"Big surprise! Bombed like that!"

"It seemed that you were making a farewell gesture," said Espínola.

"You poured almost half a bottle of *hendaya* into the red wine. And to make matters worse, it's Bailabém's wine, which goes straight to your head."

But João Garcia was feeling so well or so bad and Espínola was in such good spirits that Damião succeeded in dragging them to Mariquinhas Estragada's, by way of the side-street door leading to a little room with a partition wall. Written on the white-washed wall was PEACE AND QUIET, in the stenciled-lettering style used on wine casks. Damião ordered coffee and Benedictine to calm them down. Mariquinhas Estragada, wearing wooden shoes, served them personally. Keeping a hand on the half-opened door leading into the deep storage room which was separated from the barroom by an arch supported by the main wall, she watched the goings-on at the tables, which were hardly visible under a cloud of unbreathable smoke and a bevy of beer mugs with which sailors off an American torpedo boat were slamming their tables as they fraternized with a group of Fayal workers from the Trans-Atlantic cable company and with soccer players:

"It's those sailors. They've been raising cain around the place!"

Mariquinhas' sharp, harsh eyes were especially trained on the group of "lovelies" and on an older individual bickering with a foreigner. His pasty voice could be heard, and he was patting one of the women's thighs with his open hand.

"Shut your peephole, my dear lady!" said Espínola. "We don't want any trouble here. Who is he, anyway?"

"He's an old customer," Mariquinhas answered in a mysterious tone, sniffing and closing the door after herself. "It's a female thing. It has to do with Mémé.... He's always bringing the girl down; but one of these days, he's going to bite off more than he can chew!"

Mariquinhas' low, thick voice helped them to distinguish her long-necked and slim frame in the shadow of the partition. Her skirt, short and skin-tight at her belly, revealed her ankles, hard and rough as a man's. Her mouth was a stab wound under the soft peach-fuzz on her upper lip, which her curt talk moistened.

Coming from the storage room, one could now hear the honey-toned yet urgent growl in English of the sailor who was with Mémé:

"*Come on, sweet maid! Sit on my knee, dearie!*"

And then an infernal chorus, with stools dragged along the floor:

> *Hence Burgundy, Claret, and Port,*
> *Away with old Hock and Madeira!*
>
> ....
> *My bowl is the sky,*
> *And I drink at my eye....*

Suddenly, the sound of someone being slapped, followed by a woman's scream:

192

"Bitch? *Bitch*? Your stinkin' daughter's the bitch, you prick!"
Shattered glasses. Stools flying.

Damião, unable to resist the temptation of the free-for-all, took off his coat, adjusted the cuffs on his shirt sleeves, and hurried to the storage room on the heels of a pale and frightened Mariquinhas Estragada's clogs. Espínola and João Garcia, fearing the arrival of the police (what would they think, if the officers saw them there?), watched through cracks on the partition and saw Diogo Dulmo laid out by a punch landed by the sailor, but still holding on to the hair of a woman who was struggling to free herself:

"Police! Police!"

....

From the street of houses with identical eaves under a row of stars, someone was heard opening and then closing a window and saying: "All we see nowadays are these shameless scenes... till all hours... shameless...!"

Chapter XVIII

"When Flowers Are in Bloom" [1]

By mid-April, Margarida was busy with preparations for the event which Manuel Bana's sister was going to organize in Capelo.

The Holy Ghost celebrations fill springtime on the islands with a fantastic excitement, as if men and women, in imitation of the fields, come into bloom then. The time between Easter and Pentecost and Holy Trinity comprises seven or eight weeks of rites–the "Mystery"–a kind of Christian floralia adapted to farm life, that of pastures covered with dew and clover in a soil of lava scoria. The Angra bishops, perhaps in remembrance of Brother Jorge de Santiago and of his erudite struggle for purity of the faith and worship in the Council of Trent, tried in vain to banish from the islands' religion these strange practices: the Paraclete among candles and young girls' impassioned eyes and the *Veni creator* intoned in a transept filled with light dresses. The very improper use of the *foliões,* or merrymakers donning jesters' attire and dancing to the sound of drums, right in the middle of the chancel, was abolished, though it took some doing. The islanders' souls are candid and tenacious: they want a living and cheerful God; they call upon Him to share the intimacy of their table and of their fertile fields. May God forgive them....

The Holy Ghost, in the form of a spread-winged silver dove surmounting a royal crown, connects the heavenly Father to his Azorean children, like the very bird that signaled, in the Majorcan and Venetian portolanos, these dead places: *Insula Columbi... Insula di Corvi Marini... Primaria sive Puellarum....*

---

[1] *No tempo da fror* is a phrase from a Portuguese medieval *cantiga* 'song.' –Trans.

... Isle of the Young Girls. A flock of them, in rows, sowing the streets with roses and honeysuckle, carry the emblem of the Holy Ghost to the homes of rich and poor alike. The standard-bearer unfurls the banner of a dream royalty, of a spiritual empire. Next come the emblem-bearers carrying their brotherhood poles, then the crown page invested with this special Kingdom's greatness, a child or beggar crowned by the priest. The village band and the lingering burning smell of the fireworks bring up the rear of the procession. "Emperor for the sixth week: Chico Bana!"–boom! boom!

New boots, rounds of ring-shaped sweet bread and brandy making their rounds on a tin tray, a throne burning with candles and roses in full bloom in the corner of a dirt-floor house. "Come on in, ladies and gentlemen! Let's all eat and drink!" And so it goes for seven days.

That "vow" made by the Banas, servants of the Dulmos, lent a tangible note to the peace of mind Margarida had been enjoying ever since she wrote the letter and to which her conversation with her uncle on the veranda of the quinta had affixed a seal of confirmation, a firm guarantee signed the London way. As she had read in St. Teresa (mere chance had placed *Las moradas* [2], kept in Uncle Mateus Dulmo's glass-enclosed bookcase, within her reach), the *dry spell* of the first few days, of Counselor Calapez's ball, of Holy Friday (and, of course, the cathedral's dark draperies, the day spent on bread and water... stupid excesses! had contributed their share) had been followed in her by a cheerfulness from head to toe, which reawakened in her the consciousness of childish playfulness when, in the walks of the quinta, the scabiosa stems were sweetly shaken by butterflies beating their white-powder wings, eluding her pincer-like grasps, despite the astuteness with which she approached

---

[2] *Las moradas* 'abodes' or *Castillo interior* 'inner castle' (1583) is one of St. Teresa of Avila's (1515-1582) mystical works. The work guides the reader through a series of *moradas* of the human soul to the innermost one wherein God dwells.–Trans.

195

the little green branches. It was like coming out of a bath in the Well and wrapping herself in a towel: "Heavenly!"

It had been decided that she would remain in Capelo from "steer Friday," when they slaughter the steer, until the Sunday of the Holy Ghost procession. The steer would be cut into portions to be distributed to the poor along with bread on earthen plates garnished with mint sprigs, laid out on improvised cloth-covered plank tables set up on the street. As the popular saying goes, the poor man who gives to the poor lends to God and saves his soul. These are days of plenty! Boiled and roasted meat dishes for friends and relatives are prepared in huge caldrons by the "master chef." Busy Sundays! For months, Margarida dreamed about arbors erected in the backyard, with tables set up underneath, lots of meat, large vases full of roses, and glasses filled with sparkling wine and showing the fennel-and-sugar comfits thrown by the brethren at the girls' bosoms. Live and covered with ribbons, dazed from the daisies and the powder of a myriad exploding fireworks, the steer, walking ahead of the bugle and violin playing the Azorean tune *Pèzinho*, smelled of matted hair, vetch, and of arum lilies growing in the islands' bottomless ravines. The steer had been brought here from the other side of the fog that fattens the pastures and veils the island soul. Still hot from the pitch pasting the paper rose between its horns, the beast was forced to kneel at the "emperor's" door, as if the Holy Ghost wished to remind the islanders that they are of the same dust that the cow breathed upon the Son of the humble Virgin. The Good Lord moves in mysterious ways....

Rosa Bana had gone to the end of the lane to wait for Margarida. Manuel Bana looked proud, filled with triumph. "I wouldn't dare expect the master to show up...." But convincing *Dona* Catarina to allow Bidinha to come, to have her in Capelo for three days, sleeping on the cornhusk mattress that when she turned in bed in the wee hours of the morning, made plain the presence of a tender body on the other side of the plank partition (it's always difficult to sleep in strange beds... "This is a poor man's home...")–all this exceeded "my father's son's" wildest expectations. And he was carrying in his hand his polished, canary-yellow staff with a new metal tip. Manuel Bana was riding high.

Besides, it was he who had helped his sister with the expenses; in fact, the vow was his. A poor widow did not have the organizational skills nor the financial wherewithal for these outlays. And he was preparing a surprise. "Nothing much.... Just something I've been thinking about...." It doesn't mean that a man, just because he cannot read, doesn't have a good head on his shoulders. "The little miss... The little miss...."

He had brought João Garcia's letter with ulterior motives. That relationship would go nowhere; the families had quarrelled with each other. The sublieutenant's shoe was not big enough for Bidinha's foot–nobility's prejudices. But Manuel Bana had a long-standing respect for Januário Garcia; he missed the good old days at the Granary, when they still owned the pastures in Flamengos and milk cows (he used to be given a calf every year). And his own inner voice told him that the family's comedown was a result of "my master's kicking out in the street" that first-rate bookkeeper, who was as sharp as coral. And then the little miss... no, she didn't fool him. That going back and forth in the walkways, that stopping to pick vine twigs, as if the cedar trunks impeded her walk. ("Look... She stopped!" Manuel Bana would take a quick rest by sticking his bare foot in a hole of a stone wall, and his shepherd's eye would discover a caped officer pounding the pavement at a distance.) Nay.... That was a love gone awry, a sad situation for his little angel....

On Saturday, there was a "round dance," with musicians solicited from Flamengos and Cedros. In the middle of the little house smelling of incense and pine boughs, six boys lined up in front of as many girls, moving right and left with the lassitude of a slowly receding tide. They danced the *Charamba*. Manuel Bana, leaning against the altar of the Holy Ghost, which was built in a series of illuminated steps rising to the crown niche, did not take his eyes off the door. His city guests would be arriving any moment now. They had promised to come. He had sent for Palmira Folarinha from Flamengos, offering to pay for

197

the taxi carriage. He wanted a woman singer who could match the voice of *Senhor* Damião Serpa and those tunes heard on the "dance floors" of Fayal, and Folarinha was a famed dancer who could improvise a beautiful eight-line song as in the olden days. Feijó from Cedros, master of the Spanish guitar, called the movements of the *Charamba* with a swaggering forwardness second to none on the island: "And again! And on back! A lady's turn.... Only one!" A crowd smell, rising from the roses and new woolen skirts, burned in everybody's faces and made Folarinha lower her roguish eyes as she replied to the song of a rival singer from Capelo.

At last the dance went into full swing, and here the guests had not arrived! Finally, carriage wheels were heard. Manuel pushed his way through the group of guests to the door as if he were rushing from a bar to break up a fight. But he returned a little downcast, followed by Damião Serpa and Lieutenant Espínola, who came in civilian clothes. João Garcia sent his regrets, but he was on duty. He had to pay back a day's service to Captain Soares.

Rosa Bana had gone to fetch Margarida, who was sitting on the chair next to the altar, the place of honor. Margarida shrugged an apology, her arms spread wide to indicate that she lacked the talent they were looking for; she alleged the beginning of a sore throat she had come down with the afternoon of the steer, when she had gone out after eating hot corn porridge.

"Come, Bidinha; don't play hard to get!"

That argument won her over; she pushed the chair back and took the place of Chico Bana's girlfriend in front of him. Damião Serpa had passed under the neck of the guitar to stand in for a boy from Funduras and right away improvised an appropriate and well-received song:

> *To all I bid a good evening,*
> *As my mother taught me to do;*
> *May our hostess enjoy a happy life,*
> *And these young ladies, too.*

Margarida, taking advantage of the break Feijó needed to tighten the guitar's pins, seized Manuel Bana, who, disheartened, had positioned himself by the wall with a hand on the plank partition. Amidst laughter, she had to almost drag him onto the dance floor and squeeze him into his nephew's place, causing the amused guests to break into applause and "*Vivas!*" Feijó yelled out "Encore," and Margarida sang:

> *In order to build a garden,*
> *I brought the soil, you see,*
> *To plant this carnation*
> *That's standing in front of me.*

Margarida's voice had a clear timbre in that ironic image of the "garden" and of the "carnation," which seemed to grow from Manuel Bana's moustache and bloom in his green eyes surrounded by knavish wrinkles. He was all smiles, shaking his head "no," and seemed as if he were looking for a way out of there.

"The things you come up with, miss! Putting me down like that.... An old man with only a few teeth left, and all broken at that!" And he spread his hand over his sunken cheeks, in his own crafty way.

But his penetrating yet affectionate look quizzed Margarida, whose head cocked a little toward one shoulder. Her hair a little dishevelled, she had a faraway, thoughtful expression on her face. Her eyes seemed to be following the progress of a cavalcade that disappeared in a cloud of dust as fields, trees and cliffs were left behind enveloped by night and the chirping of crickets.

Lieutenant Espínola's head emerged from behind Feijó's shoulder, and holding the latter's guitar-strumming hand, he moved to the center of the floor:

"Play another tune, master! Lady Margarida has won this round!"

Even if she lived a thousand years, Margarida would never forget that night of dancing amid the jackets of those boys from

Capelo and the wide skirts of Rosa Bana's neighbors. There, she felt like the plank tossed about in the high seas that finally finds a position that can support the seagulls, its fibers, and its holes for little shelled creatures and green algae to cling onto. True, those boys were loutish, coarse, and sweaty; following the patriarchal tradition, the old ladies insisted on segregating them into "men only" and "mere females" in their hearth-side get-togethers. But they were alive. They had been her people, who in the person of Manuel Bana had carried her in their arms. They trusted her palate in tasting the roast and her good taste in pinning greenbrier twigs on the loaves of bread (with one end shaped like a head) to be given to the poor. Besides all this, these two days and nights in Capelo were, above all, the countryside, the fields of corn already high and with banner-like tassels, the mill in Cabouco where she had spent an entire afternoon reading and from where she had spotted a dot against the horizon–a great sailboat impelled by the wind toward the Island of Flores.

Chapter XIX

"Cucumaria Abyssorum," Théel

The late-spring weather enveloped the island in a fog that hid São Jorge from view and cast a fantastic glow upon Pico and the charabancs moving along the Pasteleiro loaded with people coming to Horta to see the mobilized troops, priests defending sharecroppers' causes, and parents who had children in America. Now that her uncle's visits to the quinta were fewer, Margarida seldom went to the Granary.

Roberto had discovered, in the depths of the storage room behind the office, a little launch propped up by cedar planks and filled with old wicker baskets used during the orange harvest. A piece of grimy sail–behind which, and camouflaging it, lay a stack of sacks and utensils piled all the way up to the ceiling–hid the front half of the boat. Roberto, absorbed by his search of the storage room as if it were a mysterious dungeon filled with Jules Verne characters, raised the piece of sail and touched those timbers aged by time and darkness. The boat's prow was smashed. He took off his coat, piled up baskets, sacks, a reel with some thread. Something pricked his finger: a pair of wool cards. A spindle, with the tip of its rod broken, still spun like a top. Pulling out his flashlight, Roberto pointed the light beam at the ribs of the boat, now in full view to the edge of the keel. He admired its line, its benches with pieces of upholstery still remaining, the rope mat in the stern seemingly awaiting an unsure and furtive foot. Undoubtedly, it had been a little luxury vessel, one belonging to his father or to old *Senhor* Roberto, the *British subject*. And he wondered: how often must old Clark have had it beached in Guindaste at night, carrying Ana Silveira to spend a few days at a Vineyards hideaway. Regardless, he had made a find. Loading his pipe and unbolting the folding doors that let a little air and light into the storage room, he surveyed his treasure, measured in spans its curved board from the damaged prow to the rudder rivets, and thought that, with very little money, Resolve's boat-repair yard would make it seaworthy again. These operations were what kept him busy now and what accounted for his three-day absence from Santo Amaro do Pico.

With lateen sails fitted out like a whaleboat, the launch braved the channel close to the wind. Margarida, who had stood for half an hour in Well's turret with binoculars, saw it trace a wide S in the wind, with its border at the water's edge and two hands aboard. One of them had hauled down the sail on the port side. "Easy does it!"

With her foot resting on the rampart of the lava turret, she whistled. But the wind played with her skirt and blew away her whistle, her voice, and tousled her hair. The launch was already steering toward Well, with its sheets as sharp and perpendicular as studdingsails. Her uncle even offered her a hand so she could walk over the beach boulders, but the tide was receding. The boat, under bare poles, rocked like a nutshell.

The firm's "whaling officer," João da Cezilha, who had taken over for Roberto at the stern while Margarida tried to grab her uncle's hand, raised his hairy leg over the rim of the boat and, getting into the water, was determined to carry Margarida on his back. But no! She'd get all wet. The whaleman's arms, open wide to catch her, seemed thick and hard, as if they were already squeezing her tight, and she refused.

"Come down, Margaret! It's all right!"

"Tomorrow! Tomorrow!"

Roberto shrugged his shoulders; the sail rose and slowly swelled up. But from the veranda, with binoculars in hand, all afternoon Margarida was able to follow João da Cezilha's maneuvers and the figure of her uncle on the prow, throwing handfuls of bait into the channel waters.

For days and days, Roberto gave himself totally to sailing and angling. The weather was clear. When the sun came out, the extreme heat immobilized the sea all the way to the lilac strip of São Jorge and heated the cobblestones of Pasteleiro, whence rose a smell of lava and dry seaweed. The quinta apple blossoms were still; only a weak afternoon breeze displayed patches of white in the checkerboard orchards hedged with cedars, which remained dark and dense despite the devastation caused by the hurricane.

Margarida, now busy making a cover for the altar of Our Lady Mother of Man, surprised herself by being able to read while negotiating the raised and open work of her embroidery, which was like someone from very far away waking her up to full consciousness of herself. Uncle Roberto's sportive fury left her cold and indifferent. How could she, who had refused to be carried on João da Cezilha's back when she had spent many afternoons on the dock, now learn how to row in the Port Authority's boats with the harbormaster and his assistant, Maria da Paz, the Lemoses, Daisy Warren, a group of girls and the best of the boys from the Trans-Atlantic Cable Company?... To save money, she had made a white blouse and a blue percale tie herself. Since her mother did not enjoy regatta races and disliked the harbormaster's wife, she objected to lending her the seamstress who made sets of pillowcases and white gowns for Maria das Angústias, and so Margarida had decided to get half a dozen kerchiefs from the Funchal Embroidery Agency on Infante Square and embroider them for pay. She worked for days and days, with scissors and ball of thread on her lap; she trimmed everything in competition with Rosa Bana, in the sleep-inducing afternoons at the far end of the quinta, until she had earned enough money to be fully presentable when assuming her place on the regatta *équipe*. Poor Uncle Mateus, who had to make his way down the footpaths to go visit them! He called her "the lugger's captain."

But of the two crews in that amusing nautical club (a flash in the pan), Daisy was the one who by far rowed the best. Roberto, informed of the championship and feeling despondent about Margarida, had once succeeded in bringing the English girl with him. For that purpose, he had to convince Mr. Warren

–he of the Panama hat pushed down to his ears because of the strong breeze–who despite being very sporting, got a little seasick whenever the wind was blowing in an east-northeasterly direction. *"If we go on this tack, I'll be seasick."* The Lemoses even referred to him as *Sissique*.

At first, Margarida found solace in the company of her nautical comrades and tried to fight her own stupid inertia. But her uncle did not succeed in hiding his disappointment at not taking her with him also. He helped her look for her thimble amid the rocks of the orchard, to which they repaired on those rare occasions as of late when he visited; and as soon as she took up again the raised embroidery on the altar cover, he picked up a book in which, clenching his pipe between his teeth, he now immersed himself for hours.

The book had one of those red and golden leather covers with little engravings depicting shipboard scenes and bearded men with raised lanterns, as in adventure novels. The cover of the book read: *Albert I, Prince of Monaco*: *LA CARRIÉRE D'UN NAVIGATEUR.* On the title page, with wide spaces in between, the prince's hand had written the following words in a firm and slanted penmanship: *À Monsieur Matheus Dulmo, officier de l'Ordre du Roi Léopold,–en souvenir de notre croisière à bord du PRINCESSE ALICE. (a) Albert.*

Roberto had borrowed it from Mateus Dulmo to while away the time and especially because of the chapter "La mort d'un cachalot," which interested him greatly since both his discovery of the launch in the depths of the Granary's storage room and his sailing in it piloted by João da Cezilha had suggested to him the possibility of assuming control of the whale fishery, now under the tight grip of creditors. Margarida had felt enthusiastic about the idea, due to the prospect of better times for her family and because Dr. Marr's clinic would appear to her in a more positive light after an honorable settlement of the family debt, as if London were at the same latitude as Velas and could sail toward her on the prow of a Pico whaleboat. But when her uncle called her attention to the descriptions provided by the Prince of Monaco, Margarida forgot about the Avelars; even

Januário Garcia vanished from her mind, as if his belly were the cone of Pico lost in a fog covering the channel from one end to the other. What interested her was the whole drama of the *Hirondelle's* voyages of exploration, the prince's descent, with a rope tied around his waist, into the volcanic caverns of Graciosa; and the engravings that illustrated the chapter about the hurricane and reminded her of the risks Captain MacWhirr undertook as narrated in Conrad's *Typhoon*: the masts disabled by the crest of a tidal wave and the *Hirondelle* tilting until its cabin almost grazed the water, chairs overturned, cabinet doors slamming, couch pillows strewn about, and *Satan*, the ship's dog, tormented and whining among the debris:

> *Il est midi: le vent souffle avec une rage inconnue de nous tous. On se répète à chaque moment qu'il donne sa plus grande mesure, et pourtant, d'heure en heure, il augmente encore. Les nuages fondus par le vent remplissent l'atmosphère d'un brouillard cuivré; il fait une obscurité jaune. On ne saurait dire s'il pleut, mais une poussière d'eau salée vole en meurtrissant les visages; c'est la crête des lames, rasée par le vent, tandis que leur masse creusée en caverne violemment rabattue, jalonne de blancheurs fumantes le passage des rafales." "La goélette se cabre devant le choc des grandes vagues..." "parfoi tout semble perdus...."* [1]

Holding her breath, Margarida turned her eyes to the next page:

---

[1] "It's noon: the wind is blowing with a fury none of us has ever experienced before. We all keep repeating to ourselves that the worst is over; however, with each passing hour it keeps getting worse. The wind-blown clouds fill the air with a copper-colored mist, creating a yellow-tinged darkness. One couldn't tell whether it's raining, yet a salt-water spray brutally whips our faces; the huge swells violently carve deep troughs in the sea, the passing squalls leaving trails of foaming whiteness. The schooner prances under the impact of the big waves... at times everything seems hopelessly lost..."–Trans.

> *Chacun, sur le pont, se retient alors à tout ce que peu-*
> *vent saisir les bras crispés: bittes, claires-voies ou cor-*
> *dages.*[2]

And, finally, the scene with the dog:

> *Satan, le pauvre chien, d'habitude si joyeux sur le*
> *pont..." "cramponné, fléchissant quand le sol manque*
> *sous ses pieds...." "Son corps tremble, ses dents cla-*
> *quent...." "Il lui fallut deux jours pour retrouver son*
> *calme...".*[3]

Even the dogs fell prey to the typhoons!... Rolling between her
fingers the serpent ring that had lost an emerald, Margarida
thought that, despite never having experienced a hurricane
aboard a sailboat, it must be exactly as described.

But the prince's narrative went on, tempting her:

> *Nous courons alors devant la tempète, qui décline rapi-*
> *dement...." "Les oiseaux marins acourent de nou-*
> *veau...." "La lumière et la vie renaissent partout...." "Ce*
> *jour, ce lendemain...." "une étoile brilla dans la premi-*
> *ère éclaircie des nuages...."*[4]

Shutting the book, Margarida actually saw a lone star the color
of copper sulfate shining against the backdrop of the vertex of a
Pico overgrown with thick grapevines to its very shoreline.

Uncle Mateus used to tell her that the *Hirondelle* caught in
its knowing nets thousands of calcareous little stars from the

---

[2] "Everyone on the bridge grabs tightly onto whatever they can: bitts, portholes, cordage."–Trans.

[3] "Satan, the poor dog, usually so happy on the bridge... unable to move,
unsure-footed whenever he does not feel the ground under his feet... He's shaking all over, his teeth rattle... It took him two days to recover..."–Trans.

[4] "We try to stay ahead of the storm, which begins rapidly to subside... The
marine birds return to the sky... Light and life return to the sea... Today, the following day... a star shone through the first opening in the clouds."–Trans.

fathomless abyss. They bore legend-like names, *Asteria* "this" and "that"–Latin rubrics under which they were cast on lead placards bound for the great oceanography museum into which the Prince of Monaco was benevolently turning over the ivory chips of the gambling houses of his microscopic principality. There they remained, dried up, imprinted like underwater enigmas in a cemetery. And she had never forgotten those tiny creatures, *Cucumaria abyssorum*, found by the scientific crew of the *Hirondelle* in the gullies of the Azorean Atlantic and by the *Michael Star* at 45° 26' N. latitude and 25° 45' W. longitude, at depths varying between 2,870 and 3,120 meters. But the echinoderm's desperate appetite for solitude and depth achieved even greater vertiginous feats: sometimes it lived at a depth of more than 4,000 fathoms in salt water, below the track of the whales spouting water and blood into the sky and the wake of ocean liners illuminated from bow to stern and in whose most hidden corners of the deck, plunged in the darkness of a propitious shade, women coming from America receive the terrible embrace of the first men who happen to succeed in breaking down their resistance. Poor Cucumaria of the Abyss, stranded little star of the solitary depths....

The following day Margarida woke up feeling nauseous. She had no appetite. Towards the afternoon she was running a slight fever but was careful not to take too many aspirin. In the half-light of the little towers, with the shutters closed, the dark rings under her eyes moved Maria das Angústias, who was stirring the milk in a cup:

"Come, Bidinha! This time it hit you really hard...."

She smiled, wrapping the shawl tighter around herself. A feeling of self-pity, which that ailment always brought out in her, embarrassed her somewhat as she stood in the darkness of the room wherein one could see, strewn about, the clothes she had removed the night before, already under the effects of her light-headedness. Their shapes appeared to her to trace lands on a map whence something like a sail could emerge at any instant–a shadow that Maria das Angústias' skirt suddenly cast on the wall.

Waiting for Margarida to finish drinking her milk, the wet-nurse looked toward the door and said that *Senhor* Diogo Dulmo had shown interest in seeing her but did not know whether she felt rested enough to receive him.

"Do come in, Father! Why all this ceremony?"

The door to the little towers staircase made a creaking sound, followed by a pause necessary for two people passing each other in an awkward passageway. Diogo Dulmo's boots cautiously trod the floor. He kissed his daughter:

"Feeling better?"

"So-so.... Mother has seldom come upstairs. I find her worse... all swollen...."

"As you can hear.... Your grandfather is always calling her.... He can't get along without her." Diogo Dulmo, always a little enigmatic, stroked his full moustache. He opened the shutters. "The weather's getting hot. That swelling is also due to the weather."

Margarida quickly raised her hands to her eyes:

"Please close those shutters, Father! I can't stand this much light."

"I've got news to share with you." Diogo Dulmo paced the room back and forth. Always clumsy in the art of transitions, he tried to disguise his embarrassment by picking up objects lying on top of his daughter's dressing table and by pulling out an English-language book from the little bookcase. "At the office, things are not going as badly as they seem...."

To raise the issue of the firm was tantamount to setting Margarida's nerves on fire, especially if her father was the one doing it. She adjusted her body under her clothes and said in a slightly mechanical voice:

"Really? I'm glad...." But faced with her father's accommodating smile, she felt sorry for him: for his strong chin lowered to his tie, for his pacing the floor almost on tiptoe, to avoid shaking up the bed. "So you finally found a way to shut those people up?..." Venturing a mild censure, she asked him almost maternally:

"Are you behaving yourself a little more these days?"

Diogo Dulmo stopped and smiled with a certain melancholy:

"I don't want to see you sad.... You'll see that everything is going to turn out all right. Let me take care of a few details.... As the saying goes, it's a long lane that has no turning. One must bide one's time...." Hoping in vain that his daughter's curiosity might wrench from him the only important words he had to say (his *idée fixe*), he ended by informing her: "We've just bought a few hundred dollars' worth under favorable conditions.... José de Lemos has a keen eye for business; we stand to make almost one hundred per cent." Margarida kept quiet. The firm's exchange operations were particularly distasteful to her, even though she had always defended José de Lemos' contribution to the office, in order to protect her cousins' financial interests. But Diogo Dulmo, whose cunning did not stop short of cocking an ear to hear someone else's opinion, and who was especially attuned to his daughter's moods, did not hesitate: "Your uncle Roberto is very much interested in the fishery now.... He wants to revive it. The other day he even locked himself in the office with André Barreto to discuss the future of sperm whale fishing in the islands... given the oil shortage that is going to hit after the war.... the importance of the cosmetics industry, which usually follows a war... They turned the books inside out, rummaged through all the records! They even insisted on seeing the books as far back as the days of old man Roberto, all that paperwork...."

Margarida's first impulse was to show her rage against what she took to be another marriage-arrangement scheme or at least a half-step in that direction. But Diogo Dulmo showed such a blind faith in her uncle's fancies, born of those romantic readings of the Prince of Monaco's book, that she did not have the heart to recriminate or to disappoint him.

"I'm well aware of it.... The American whaleboat deal, the Shetland Islands motor...."

"Don't forget that the deal isn't as silly as it seems! With new capital... young blood in the firm capable of renewing confidence...." Margarida's silence was, more than a simple neutrality, an abstention. Diogo Dulmo noticed her familiar expression, one that was simultaneously apprehensive and somewhat softened by a dreamy faintness dissolving into a penetrating smile. "Ah!" she concluded with a clap of her hands, in one of those expansive moods, very rare in her, that constituted the burst of enthusiasm with which she transformed a boring evening party into a jovial get-together. "If that happened, it would be the happiest day of my life. My little angel!"

Sitting on her bed amid these conciliatory outpourings, Margarida allowed her father to kiss her. And while she did not join in with reassuring words or gestures, her shoulders yielded to Diogo Dulmo's affection, who was now adjusting the shawl around her and stroking her hair. Since the previous day, her illness had made her feel loving and almost detached from her physical self. Now that she was feeling better, she insisted on having the shutters overlooking the quinta thrown open. Catching a glimpse of the bluish sky, sensing the sea from its remote and everlasting resonance that was like the soul of the house, and hearing *Açor*'s furious barking in his doghouse, she thought that if she could be in touch with her true personality, she would not be in this place: she would instead be roaming somewhere, free and relieved, feeling as if she were tagging along in the wake of that very body of hers now reclining in bed.

This state of mind allowed her to accept her father's presence without misgivings, starting with his coming into the room on tiptoe, much like a pet dog already a little fat and heavy and with the bad habit of sniffing at one's groin but also preserving the sweetness characteristic of the species in the sharpness of his eyes and in the intelligence and humility of his head held high. She even detected a secret affinity between that misguided energy, betrayed by the red moustache and the abrasions left by the punch, and her own flights of fancy–or what her mother referred to as her "little moods"–her ability to make unwise retreats from life and to engage in small and sudden acts of violence.

The peace between father and daughter having been more or less made, Diogo Dulmo sat by her bed and, holding the open book and glancing at the English sentences in an attempt to crack their meanings, he read random passages, with his torso bent over his knees:

"The fruit trees need systematic and timely pruning. To keep the market regularly and constantly supplied, it is necessary to combine types and varieties of fruits whose ripening seasons lend themselves to alternate and productive harvesting, so that when the early-plum season is over, the first pears and apples, being more resistant and comprising a broader variety of types, may afford the farmer a stable and profitable source of income from his orchards." Diogo Dulmo stopped; then he read a passage to himself. Afterward, leafing leisurely through the book, he marked the top of a page with his finger; he went back and, nodding his head, raised his voice once again: "There is no spectacle more beautiful than a fruit orchard in bloom. The pear trees seem bent over as if... as if a snow shower had fallen upon them. The apple trees are like brides in their gowns. (*"During the spring, nature around us seems to sleep"*)...." He started to shut the volume.

"It's funny! I was not familiar with this... *The Compleat Farmer*. You must loan me this book...."

But noticing that Margarida was still and breathing tranquilly with her eyes half-closed, he got up on tiptoe, tucked her in, and started down the stairs gently and a little sideways, lest he wake her up and let that image of his daughter vanish from his sight.

Chapter XX

The Spiders Closed their Webs

João Garcia was enjoying a leave from his duties at Uncle Jacinto's home in Praia do Almoxarife. As he strolled along the seashore or whiled away the time playing bingo in the courtyard of the Honórios' estate (*Villa Laura*), he tried to sort out the recent weeks of his life, which seemed to him apportioned by lots, as if he had a winning lottery ticket but had only gotten a trifling prize. Would he have spent a whole month in his uncle's company had it not been for that unexpected letter from him (who was also his godfather) invoking the icy reconciliation with his brother Januário, one which until very recently remained unattainable because of old grudges? Or had it not been for his father's insistence that he enjoy the sea air and take in the relaxing countryside, in addition to the charitable gesture of spending some time with his uncle, who felt touched by the amicable resolution of that family drama? No. It had not been solely for those reasons, but also because of an inner lassitude, an ill-defined weariness of everything, as when he had suffered, during vacation while a junior at Coimbra, those gastric fevers which made him lose so much weight but also afforded him a long period of convalescence. In Figueira, he had stayed in the home of a retired judge and former prosecutor in Horta, who had been hand-in-glove with his father. Then he had managed to almost forget Margarida; or rather, he had been content with giving himself over to a sweet dreaminess about her, which allowed him to remember, as he lounged until late at night with a forgotten book on top of the cool, turned-down sheet, the amenable world of his childhood.

As for Laura, he could not deny being captivated by her. Perhaps she had caught him at a vulnerable time because of the disillusionment caused by Margarida's reply to the letter he had sent from the barracks, an inner peace akin to that of his convalescence in Figueira. As he jumped over the stone walls dividing the fields by the high escarpment and followed along the deserted road of the island's mountainous coast, whose autumnal marasmus was only broken by an occasional bullock cart loaded with corn or squash, João Garcia could see in his mind's eye Laura's little teeth glinting with malice, her angelic brow sheltering her silken eyelashes, her eyes focused on her hand of cards. An evening-party sweetness had prevailed at the games of quadrille at *Dona* Carolina Amélia's, just as it now descended upon the bingo cards in the Honórios' courtyard, whose inlaid stone floor was cluttered with canvas chairs. Holding a flickering lamp, Uncle Jacinto moved with heavy steps along the walkway leading from the front gate to the gaming table, dislodging some of the courtyard stones. The ebb tide smoothly brushed the shore boulders.

João Garcia had also felt his old sadness dissipating in the atmosphere of the pharmacy, in the company of that uncle and godfather of his who acted like a brother or father toward all of his clients; who drained the abscesses of those who went barefoot and always had a witty remark to cushion a groan of pain, who filled prescriptions for free, who prepared tartaric-acid sodas to quench João's thirst.

The approaching winter meant some mornings were already chilly. João Garcia had stayed in bed until late. Water dripped from a fig tree branch outside his window, fallen from a dirty sky opaque as a cotton swab. But when he opened the courtyard door, a break in the rain brought him the acrid smell of a dampened and comforted earth, and a patch of lilac sky promised good weather. He walked into the pharmacy. His uncle was putting a bandage on a child's head:

"It doesn't hurt at all.... Not even a little bit! Do you want me to show you the little puppet?"

From the bottom of a drawer there appeared a marionette that danced to the sound of a little harmonica which Jacinto comically ran under his moustache.

"ALABAMA, U. S. A. That's the way they play in America...."

The customers waiting for their bottles of medicine laughed, resigned to the delay. Outside, heavy sheets of water fell again, striking the panes noisily and clouding them with raindrops. The wheels of a fast-moving horse carriage slashed through the mud; from the driver's seat, where the coachman sat wrapped in his overcoat, came the sound of a loud voice:

"The laxative for the priest, *Senhor* Jacinto!"

But the weather generally lifted in the afternoon, and João Garcia accompanied his uncle on his house calls to check on patients who lived far away; Jacinto steadied himself with a walking stick. They went to Boiões, to Caldeira, to Mangas Street. The miller who worked for Manuel Homem had a carbuncle. Jacinto placed a package of cotton swabs on top of a spare millstone, opened the bottle of permanganate, squeezed the contents onto the purple and pus-encrusted inflammation. The miller, covered with flour, moaned and grinded his teeth:

"When are you going to squeeze the core out, *Senhor* Jacintinho?"

"Tomorrow.... Tomorrow.... But, for God's sake, don't you touch it yourself!"

On Mangas Street, there was an old lady who had been suffering from a stubborn fever for three days. Jacinto had no aptitude as a healer and felt awful about performing that illegal service. But the public-assistance doctor came to Praia only once a week and had asked him to keep an eye on the chronically ill patients and to take care of the minor needs. It was especially necessary to prevent a local healer, the master tailor Timóteo, from contributing his clientele to the population of the parish cemetery. A silent rivalry had thus sprung up between the pharmacist and the "artist"; but Jacinto was so conscientious and sincere regarding the limits of his therapeutic abilities, learned in thirty years of filling prescriptions, that master Timóteo, who also was assailed by scruples and feared the doctor's wrath, had decided to ground his practice on the pharmacist's advice.

"I don't like the looks of this patient's scabious tongue and this stubborn little fever...." (Master Timóteo was very well read and had an easy bedside manner; he was a great friend of Ângelo's). "I checked his pulse yesterday afternoon.... Not bad... not bad.... This morning I checked his temperature: 37 1/2° C. He stays within that range! 37 1/2 in the morning... 38 1/2 in the afternoon... I don't like it...." And he twitched his albino-rabbit nose.

Jacinto bit his nails and looked steely, like one of those children who do not pout like the others but who hide in a corner protecting with both hands their disputed toy: "Well, let's call the doctor... the sooner the better...!"

"What if we gave him some pyrimidine? I don't like antipyrine very much.... Antipyrine will not produce the results I want. What do you think, *Senhor* Jacinto?"

"Let's call the doctor! The sooner the better!"

His "country-doctor's" visits continued, on foot, to deserted lanes carpeted with dry cow manure. The flickering candles in Manuel Homem's mill beckoned in the distance. The church bell awoke the world from its torpor with its midday chimes. He still had yet to visit an old man who could not urinate without a catheter and a young tubercular girl, a coachman's daughter, at whose house Jacinto sometimes left, under a cracked saucer, a little silver coin bearing the picture of King Manuel II, called a "twelve-and-a-half." They ran into a young boy herding four sheep. Jacinto talked to his nephew about his dream of offering him a woolen winter suit–a nice outfit (like the ones the inhabitants of Pico wear), reeking of tannin and tallow and which could almost stand when Jacinto hung it on the back of the chair. Sometimes, if it was the season for them, a field of chick-peas with their reproductive flowers would form rows of blue along the stone fences. Jacinto invited his nephew to walk across the field with him; with half-a-dozen deft caresses, he carded the shaggy coat of a grazing goat tied to a stake: "Poor old fellow! Easy now!... Easy now!..." And patting the front of its horns, he enjoyed cushioning the goat's tentative charge, as if it were a well-executed and pre-established move between two players. Fearing he would elicit an expression of irony from his surprised nephew, Jacinto fled from the goat, striking the gutted path with his walking stick, his nervous laughter gradually abating, as if he had left it leaning against the stone fences. "*Senhor* Trovão, now that his catheter has been changed, will be all right for a while! I'm something else!... Something else, I'm telling you!"

It was during one of these emergency clinical sorties that Jacinto Garcia mustered the courage to broach the subjects of family and romance with his nephew. He did not like to see such a young man so given to an obsession that prevented him from really enjoying anything in life.... It was high time to be thinking of marriage. What difference did it make whether or not he got the desired appointment for general secretary, in view of the brilliant curriculum he had been able to present? Besides, the vacancy in Horta was still unfilled; and public officials from the mainland, his competitors, never stayed in the Azores for very long. His father's solicitor general's office was doing very well; it never failed to attract some of the best customers on the two islands: there was plenty for him to do until he was appointed and remained in the military service. What more could he want?

But Jacinto did not know how to disguise a rehearsed speech. Looking askance at João, who walked in silence (something which did not help Jacinto much), he sensed his nephew's innocence even in the fact that he wore his cap backwards over his brush-cut hair.

"Aren't you going to say something, boy?"

"What do you want me to say, Godfather? Is there a woman you want to set me up with?"

"No, not I.... There are so many pretty girls in Fayal!"

"Well, then; let's cast lots. Tonight, before bingo, let's match up numbers with names. You shake up the numbers, Godfather.... And I'll draw...."

"You'll come up with Laurinha, you'll see.... And I'm not going to cheat!"

Having said this, Jacinto could breathe a sigh of relief. But he still kept mum about the big mission with which Januário had entrusted him. João Garcia seemed to go along with everything, and Jacinto felt his naïve conscience being spied upon by none other than his own eyes, so accustomed to deciphering doctors' prescriptions.

They spent the holidays this way, without Jacinto having said a single word about his big plan. Januário had everything set up, all his pawns on the chessboard. Having sent his mother and João to Praia do Almoxarife in order to mend the severed relationship as the old lady had begged of Saint Rita, whose image she kept in the oratory with lots of flowers arranged by Ângelo and with a wick lit at nightfall, he had left Ângelo and a former maid to keep Aunt Secundina company, and alone with Henriqueta, had locked himself up in Fern Lane, with long and mysterious stays in the Flamengos Creek house. Fat and suspended like a spider in its iridescent web, he listened to the song of the blackbirds in the darkness of the orange orchards.

At last! At last! *Dona* Carolina Amélia was an old crone and a little suspicious, but he was no dummy himself, and the Coicão fortune would soon be his. Unless.... But no! João was naïve, all given to literary pursuits and hidden passions. Still, he had a good character and was amenable to his father's advice. Everything depended on how things were done, on not forcibly confronting affairs of honor and the heart. One does not poke the belly of a stuffed mule. (Januário liked to put things in down-to-earth language.) And, after all, wasn't it stupid of João to linger in the vicinity of Pasteleiro, stubbornly pursuing a girl who, on the one hand, encouraged him, but on the other, slammed the shutters in his face? Margarida Dulmo had actually become for Januário a small hope for getting even, but no! For that to come to pass, João would have to be a different man, one who knew how to take advantage of the darkness provided by the cedars of the quinta; one who could, as the saying goes, sample the wares–in fact, one who could flee with her to Pico and cause a scandal all over Horta. That, he must admit... On those nights of plotting by the safe, or in the silence of Flamengos Creek, hearing the rain hammering against the windowpanes and the wind wailing among the orange trees, which were as dry as when he had planted them, all kinds of thoughts came into Januário's head... and lingered there.... That elegant, polished young lady, daddy's little girl from Ocean Street, appearing from one day to the next in maternity clothes and with her belly almost to her chin, and with the typical morning sickness, causing her to be sick in the nightpot... People in the Yankee House, in Alexandrino's pharmacy, at Badela's, even at Mariquinhas Estragada's would then spread rumors in secret: "Dulmo's daughter is pregnant. Rumor has it that the father is Januário's boy." There...! Or else the kidnapping: at night, by way of Guindaste, in a motorboat from Porto Pim with its engine muffled and, ta-tahn, ta-tahn... all along the channel, João and Margarida heading straight to a house in Criação Velha, one of those that the owners had abandoned and which had lost all its windowpanes one by one until its shutters had to be nailed shut in that deserted area of Pico filled with burned lava, a good place to have a man killed or for some gross unspeakable act. And on the following day, the coming to terms. Januário and Diogo Dulmo secretly meeting in some out-of-the-way house, and all the chips on the table! all pretenses unmasked: "My dear sir: if my son cracked the door open, it was because the lock was not very secure. He who would preserve his daughter's honor should restrain her!" "And now?" "Now there's only one thing to be done: marry them. I'll get the firm out of the main jams (the creditors, I'll take care of), and you, my dear sir, provide a dowry for your daughter, consisting of a generous portion of the wealth which I am going to deliver from the creditors' claws. I'm not bitter, but we must agree on something: a fair share... As for me, I am going to draft a deed of the Flamengos Creek house for them." Diogo Dulmo (whom he knew like the back of his hand) would sulk, assuming he wasn't already what's called loaded. And then Januário, like one who aims for the head in a night assault, would impose his last condition, his old wound, one which for years he had kept bound up in the dignity of his rehabilitation and of silence. "But wait.... There's still the question of the office, the firm. Your cousin José de Lemos must be kicked out; you, my dear sir, will stay home taking care of the old man, and I will be reinstated in the position that was unjustly taken away from me. Needless to say... as main partner and director of CLARK & SONS, HEIRS. And we'll let bygones be bygones. Let's charter a ferry at once to take us to Madalena. ... my daughter! My darling daughter! May the blessing of the Lord protect you!"

Such divagations were sometimes so vivid that Januário was surprised to realize that his face was bathed in tears as he leaned his head on the desk or buried it in the sunken pillow, like an actor of the company of the great Pedro Cabral. Profound and theatrical sighs shook his mammoth frame. But he could sort out and weigh things; he was not like his foolish son, who was always ready to cave in to the first nightmare. And now that everything had cleared up, that the Beef had surprised everybody by returning, that the girl was cozying up to the Baron da Urzelina's son and to her uncle (God knows what had already transpired! he must have at least fondled her...), now that Ângelo, all involved with Pedrinho Dulmo's pals and buddy-buddy with him, had used his fag's gift of gab to pry some secrets, things were shaping up; retract what was said–and on with the business at hand!

That's how he should proceed.... Actually, only in the theater and with music could there be a proper denouement to that drama begun in the early days of his life! For a long time now he had felt something, like a span-length worm, gnawing at him, blinding him, making him unable to hit upon the solution regarding *Dona* Carolina Amélia's business affairs, regarding that nice little chunk of property which he protected for a mere pittance and which someone, God only knew who, would end up inheriting.... As procurator and close friend of the family, he could not expect to get more than a miserly bequest, not to mention the tidbits apportioned to this and that person in the will of that gullible devotee of many saints. He still had open to him the possibility of some sort of manipulating in the selling of properties producing hard-to-collect income; in the settling of accounts in different banks, which always yielded something; and in addition, the fee legally allowed a solicitor-at-law who, after all, is not expected to work for nothing. But what did all this amount to in comparison with the power to collect income on rented lands, interest on loaned monies, on leased houses and stores in the choicest sites in the city, on the stretch of pastures in Castelo Branco, and on the dining-room silverware? Yes! The solution was to get all this down on paper legally: two reliable witnesses and an "indisputable" will. (Where was that nice Roquete's *Dictionary* that Ângelo had snatched from him?)

Father Joaquim Maria cleansed him of these and similar professional vexations every month while sitting in front of his place setting at Januário's dinner table and, on special days, with *Dona* Carolina Amélia seated to his right. Maybe there were things that the finger of God touched, providential chances.... God could read in his contrite sinner's heart. "I, a sinner.... Almighty... *mea maxima culpa.... Ideo precor...*" Ta-ran, ta-ran....

The mass celebrated in *Dona* Carolina Amélia's private chapel had, it seemed, a second virtue: that of brushing the dust off one's knees, as one made one's way to the table on the silent side of the house, close to the backyard and in the midst of the sweet smell of the first June plums casting a purple glow upon the dining-room server. Januário finally saw the light. Of course! The solution was to persuade the old lady to leave everything to her godchild, that pretty little face under the golden bun in the picture brightening the table and providing a truce, a breathe of fresh air to those three beings attacking their steaks and stuffing their faces with scrambled eggs: Father Calhordas, the wretched widow, and him.

The news that Ângelo, who was as sharp as a razor, brought him was the "necessary element" in the execution of Januário's plans. Without what might be termed a verbal agreement between the two, Ângelo could guess the most secret intentions buried in Januário's pallor and exhaustion and seemingly inexplicable sighs at the office. All Ângelo needed was a single word from his brother, a mere "Oh."

"Have you seen any of the Honórios?"

"No."

Ângelo allowed his probing its full effect by pretending to be busy with his papers and with his shiny little moustache.

"And what about the girl? Does she still visit much with *Dona* Carolina Amélia?"

Then, as if the pieces for a secret plot had mysteriously appeared on top of a game table equipped with a hidden spring compartment, Ângelo made available half-a-dozen precious clues, without raising his eyes from the sheet of ruled paper.

"She does... she does.... And our João is not being so coy anymore. And Laurinha has been laying a trap for him."

"Well." (Pause.) The wind kept blowing the plantain tree leaves around the cathedral, now empty and massive-looking with its heavy ashlar masonry. "Haven't you heard anything from those people in the Granary?"

"Some rumblings.... And there's no doubt they're plotting to marry off the girl. It seems that the Beef and Barreto are both competing for her. I predict that Barreto is going to catch her.... In no time at all, *he* will have been caught."

"You're wrong about that! Diogo isn't going to give up on getting some property-exchange deal with his brother-in-law; he'll throw his daughter at him."

"He's her uncle, after all.... They have their blood relationship standing between them."

"You'll see...." And, suddenly clear and pale as a sheet:

"Don't lose sight of our boy! Keep an eye on those evening parties at Carrasca Well, on the girl's disposition...."

"Come now...! Do you take me for some blithering idiot? You act as if *Dona* Carolina hadn't already made known to me what her last requests are...."

"And what are they? Spit it out!"

Ângelo, with self-importance written all over his well-known grimace of nausea and disdain, which was his weapon, attenuated his expression by converting it into a mime of generous solicitude. He felt avenged for all the humiliations he suffered at the office, for all the putdowns that his brother inflicted on him in front of everybody.

"The old lady told me a few days ago that she's going to leave all she owns to her Laurinha: Castelo Branco's property, her house, and her money. And to you she is going to leave...."

"What?"

"Come now! Don't play dumb.... The Cedros house and the fruit orchard... ten acres of land."

"Some inheritance!"

"Of course, the income from leasing Lombega will be left to the altar of Our Lady of Peaceful Death."

"Oh! That João, that jackass! That idiot...."

"The young lady will entrap him, you'll see.... And leave the rest up to me! There's no longer any great danger coming from the Pasteleiro people; João has stuck his nose elsewhere."

"Who says?"

"A little bird told me..."

"I bet it was Bana's nephew, Chico. You have no scruples whatsoever!... I have already told you that I don't want you hanging around with scrubby young boys."

"What, did you want me to become pals with the priest magistrate or something?... He who wants reliable intelligence doesn't make unreasonable demands."

In Praia do Almoxarife, the rains of an early autumn were followed by beautiful days. The bullock carts loaded with the last vats of grapes made their way, squeaking, toward the wine cellars. The boulders closing the circle formed by the sand strip turned golden at nightfall, and all the lava in the vine fields remained denuded underneath a straw-colored ground cover to which the vine leaves, crinkled and falling one by one, lent a sanguine hue. João Garcia would return from his grand strolls, alone or accompanied by his godfather. One day they passed by the overflowing public water troughs, which the cows, their heads topped by impressive horns, beslavered as they slowly drank. In the distance, the men then made out a short skirt coming toward them: it was shy Carlota, all dressed in black, and following her, the elder Honório, who strode along supporting himself on his long staff. Laura broke into a run towards João, picked up a corn husk fallen from a bullock cart and, shredding it with her teeth, bought time until all had gathered together:

"Are you coming to bingo today? Please do...."

Her ulterior motive, underscored by the proximity of her lips and by her quick speech, stung João's soul like a raindrop giving a false augury of a downpour or like the insidious tiny prick of a misplaced pin.

From time to time, Ângelo showed up in Praia, having hitched a ride or in the *charrette* of the *Americano* from Ribeirinha, which creaked to the trot of a sorrel horse, handsome in its reddish-brown coat. He arrived at nightfall. The bingo game was interrupted and the ladies gathered in a snug little circle, hungering for the latest gossip which he, feigning his comic disgust, dished out little by little in sync to the numbers being pulled out of the green bag amid pointed bits of levity: "22, José do Nascimento's legs; 19, the canning jar; 90, the idiot... I'm out of luck!"

This is how he skillfully wove an intrigue that raised suspicions about Margarida Dulmo's reputation in Horta, now that she was staying at the Clark Vineyards house somewhere in Pico alone with Roberto, the caretaker Manuel Bana, and Mariana Caçoa, who was so old and broken-down that she could hardly keep her balance while handling the cooking pots in the kitchen. Rumor had it that they already were making wedding plans, but that someone had sworn to having seen Barreto kissing Margarida during a picnic organized by Mr. Warren on top of Mount Guia. Besides, it was absolutely certain that Roberto had received a letter from a lover he had left in London, the widow of some lord. He was living off her. And it seemed that the widow was now threatening to come to Fayal, should he stay too long.

Shy and annoyed, Jacinto begged his brother to shut up. It wasn't becoming to them to be badmouthing a family like that just because both had had their problems in the past.

"You are a humble do-gooder, my dear, and you judge others with the yardstick of your own shortcomings...."

Dona Rosa, whose bad temper had always been the great barrier preventing any reconciliation among the Garcia siblings, sided with her husband against her brother-in-law, an inveterate gossipmonger.

"Jacinto is absolutely right! You always had a mean tongue!" And turning to Honório's wife: "Aren't they slandering the poor girl, Mariquinhas? Because she is so pretty and outgoing, so pleasant with everybody. They're eaten away by envy and are just wagging their tongues."

"Oh, sure, she's so innocent...." said Ângelo.

"I grant you that she's no saint, *Dona* Rosa! Do you remember what she did to my Laura? They're childhood friends, practically raised together in Elvira Moules' embroidery classes, but now she gives her the cold shoulder everywhere, at the balls and on the dock lawn! Does she think she's better than my daughter? If she has any claim to blue blood, it could only come from the Dulmos.... As for the Clarks, everybody is familiar with their genealogy: a sack of tea on the back of a whale.... I know her weak spot!" And feigning exaggerated care in making sure that João Garcia was out of hearing range and speaking with Jacinto, Mariquinhas squeezed the elbow of her right arm, which zealously guarded the bingo cards: "Here, *Dona* Rosa! here...."

Laura, pretending to remain indifferent and beyond those disputes over honor, went out to the courtyard and put her arm around Jacinto's patient shoulder. The house had a stone courtyard overlooking the road with a little bougainvillea bower that caught head-on the breeze blown in from the sea. João Garcia had sat on the stone bench under the bluish glow of the exceptionally bright night full of deep scattered stars. Jacinto, more scared than moved by Januário's instigations–whose meddling and matchmaking attempts he detested, even though they awakened his paternal tenderness toward that sweet and friendly girl–started walking away along the wall, whistling and with his hands behind his back, secretly overcome by the soft and complicitous air of the starry darkness.

"Beautiful night!" said João Garcia when he realized that Laura and he were alone.

"True.... Too bad you are not in Pico!"

"What do you mean? Why in Pico?..."

"You know! You'd probably have a better time there... in more pleasant company...."

"I don't know what you are driving at...."

"I'm referring to the new whaleboat that Roberto went to buy at the auction in Flores.... A big American whaleboat...."

"You know very well that I no longer have anything to do with Margarida's life.... In fact, who knows if I ever had...!"

Laura looked at him slowly. Her smile, slow in coming, lent her eyes a fleeting spark, a flash both of censure and regret that was unknown to João and which perturbed him.

"Everything is over and done with between us."

"Seriously?"

"Does it matter that much to you?"

"I don't know. The future isn't for us to tell...."

"Laura! can you still like me, knowing everything you know?..." She blushed deeply, kicking the loose stones from the bower floor with the tip of her little shoe. "And if I told you that I love you!... that I never cared for anyone but you?"

"Come on in, you love birds; we've missed you at the game...," said Ângelo, sticking his head under the cold bougainvillea caught between the strips of wood. "*Dona* Maria won. And on the fifth play!"

Chapter XXI

A Pigeon Shooting

From Jacinto Garcia's house above the pharmacy one could see Honório's vineyard, Villa Laura's dining-room window, the kitchen and the cistern, next to which stood a pyre of rotting bridal broom. It was an island custom: to let time consume that cartload of firewood stacked pyramid-fashion on the wedding day and left out in the sun and rain to measure the erosion of life. Laura was about nineteen, Honório and *Dona* Maria having gotten married twenty years earlier. Dark cevadilla plants, dotted with little red flowers, had sprung up in the sun-baked lava vine fields. At the far end of the vineyard, which jutted out like a prow between a lane and the main road, there flew, at certain hours of the day, a red flag attached to a bamboo stick. From the window of the Garcias' patriarchal home (now sporting the signboard with the emblematic serpent of the pharmacy) João Garcia could make out that lively banner with the help of his binoculars. His godfather teased him:

"A lugger within sight of the port, sublieutenant?"

And in fact for a week now, one could see a little sail cutting the choppy waters at the inlet to the channel. The little flag was a sign of clear passage. Honório had taken the little carriage used to transport back and forth the three or four summer vacationers employed in Horta. *Dona* Maria, her kerchief tied around her neck, beat rugs or supervised lunch. Appearing on the road by the cattle watering troughs, João could see Laura's white blouse as she arranged her golden hair under the bougainvillea bower.

Their courtship had reached a semiofficial status. Jacinto had found it wise to hold fewer bingo parties until his nephew gave at least some kind of hint to the family. Honório had become slightly distant; but *Dona* Maria, allowing Laura time to make her movements in the veranda appear natural and speaking toward the road as if João had stopped to greet her, came down the walkway, excused herself for being in her apron, and asked after *Dona* Rosa. An admonition on Ângelo's part had discouraged Januário from repairing to the faya and orange groves of Fern Lane and Flamengos Creek. He would linger there in seclusion, squeezing the late-season pears and leaning his huge frame over the tree-lined stone fences. It was the beginning of the hunting season; and once in a while an amateur hunter from Flamengos, thick-necked and wearing heavy boots, would open fire within a few meters of his shelter–that of "*a man who was standing on his own property.*"

("One of these days they're going to blast my head off.... Call out the dogs!")

Mónica hitched the pair of mules to the victoria; Januário and Henriqueta went to spend the day in Praia do Almoxarife. Since the day to celebrate Our Lady of the Estrela was approaching, the festivities to be held up there on the summit of Zimbreiro, Ângelo had left the city house under Pretextato's care and set out a few days ahead of time. He was going to decorate the chapel. A nice-looking, strapping lad from the Fandulhos do Almoxarife fishing crew carried boughs of incense as well as dahlias and pine needles to the tiny church-yard perched on the cliff. Laura and Carlota cleaned the deposits from the flower vases, and once in a while, Ângelo, setting the ladder aside, went to throw the contents out in the rubbish pile, burying his nose in his pin-encrusted lapel.

It must have been two in the afternoon when the caravan of Honórios and Garcias headed out toward Zimbreiro, making their way with difficulty up the steep incline leading to the rocky heights. Januário, heavy and ill, had gone on ahead of the others; and resting on some boulder or on a sheltered ridge, he turned his eyes toward the little Praia do Almoxarife houses nestled around the church like a flock of gulls lazing on a wave. What he was at the beginning of his life lay covered by one of those tiny roofs, underneath which his brother Jacinto had patiently set up his pestle. Not he. He was of a different temperament. He couldn't stay put. An inner frenzy had forced him to flee the Angra Seminary for a notary's office in Horta and had stuck him in that maze of streets within streets (a ship coming in, a ship going out...). A man should remain active to his dying day. He didn't subscribe to the idea that the poor were destined to a life of toil, waiting for the rich to stroll idly through the countryside to further grind their heels on them! There lay the acre of land covering the bones of the notary Severinino, his father, under a pointed cypress. Not even a decent railing around his grave... or a sharp-edged flower vase... Jacinto's carelessness! As for him, he already had taken precautionary measures. He had a huge marble stone off the main walkway of the Horta cemetery awaiting the vault, ordered from Oporto, with a crying angel and a figure underneath holding a scale:

THE FINAL RESTING PLACE OF THE FAMILY OF
JANUÁRIO JOSÉ GARCIA
PAX. LEX.

And a great ceremony would be held when the mortal remains were transferred.

The sound of Honório's walking stick, pounding the ground rhythmically with every other step he took, came to interrupt Januário's deep thoughts:

"The girls are almost here. Are you tired? This kind of work really takes its toll on you...."

"Thank God I can still manage it! The worst is this belly of mine."

There was some bitterness in Januário's voice, one which the sour sarcasm innate in the Garcias could not totally hide. He spoke of his memories of himself as a young man, his life's worries; and continuing up the cart path leading all the way to the pinnacle of Zimbreiro, with an attentive and fit-as-a-fiddle Honório by his side, Januário motioned toward the entire area with an appraiser's gesture, appearing to emphasize the difficulties of an existence made up of his picking up from the hard ground, a thousand times, the same heavy load. Honório shortened his steps and, trying not to hurry, fearfully reached for his arm. But Januário offered the resistance of his massive frame, stopping and addressing him reticently:

"You have no idea what it's been like to keep the boat on an even keel! Without a wife, with everything falling only on me, fighting off a whole gang hell-bent on destroying me... having to change my profession in my thirties, after working like a slave for the Beef and his bon vivant brother-in-law! I made of the Granary what you very well know, the top firm in Horta, after the Bensaúde Company. Even FAYAL COAL had to reckon with me when it came to supplying their product. If the Clark coal storehouse went bust, it did so after my departure. That's a fact! If they had left me in peace, the business would have gone far...."

"That's what everybody is saying now. Just the other day I heard Fragoso say the same thing at the Porto da Horta office: 'Had Januário continued at the head of the Granary, the dock would have expanded by now. He had everything well planned: coal supplies, oils weighed, sufficient tonnage capacity to export whale products far and wide like the people of São Miguel did with pineapples, and even found a Portuguese cable company, with Azorean capital.' To put an end once and for all to the caravan of foreigners, who are only good for leading other people's daughters astray and to make life more difficult for the locals...."

"That was my dream, Honório!... But they spoiled it all for me.... They floored me. That jackass Dulmo!"

"Of course, you, with that little solicitor-at-law signboard of yours, didn't exactly fare badly...."

"That's true!... They didn't do me in totally.... That I must admit!"

"Especially since you became a registered solicitor and the Avelars and my daughter's godmother from Carrasca Well made you their procurator...."

Januário, exhausted from the climb, again stopped and acknowledged the hint:

"You're right.... My administering the commander's affairs has helped me to keep myself on a steady course. The seas can get rather treacherous around our islands, Honório.... Our channel can betray us... But... (just so you see how people can be mistaken!): everybody says that I really have it good, that I was born with a silver spoon in my mouth... but everything I've earned has been by the sweat of my brow. The Avelars, before they hired me, couldn't handle their own affairs. Chico Avelar is a fine young man, but his father is a tightwad, a gutless wonder...! He's afraid of his own shadow; he's a doormat for certain city gentlemen. As for *Dona* Carolina Amélia's fortune, you are the one who is her godchild's father and you're well aware of the state it was in: scattered capital, rents in arrears, dilapidated buildings.... Tell me if you can recognize Lombega now? I had all the walls repaired.... I rechanneled the creek.... I straightened out the tenants at Bishop Alexandre Square. Can you put a price on that kind of work?... Tell me!"

"No way. It's only too bad that...."

"Too bad that what?"

"That the whole thing is going to be inherited by some nephews of hers, people who are stinking rich.... Just imagine! living in Barra Mansa, God knows where in Brazil, without her having ever laid eyes on them...."

"Relax...." said Januário with an enigmatic air, running his thumb through the ornamental chain pulled from his vest.

"I, for one, don't really care, if you know what I mean.... It's just that..., only a fool looks a gift horse in the mouth, however little it may be. It's stupid to be too proud when you're poor! My daughter Laura is her godchild; she's always treated her like her own daughter..... If the old lady leaves her a little something, it's nothing to marvel at."

"She'll leave her everything, I tell you!" said Januário. He stopped short, evened the tips of his boots, which were fastened with hooks to the ends of his black trousers, whose fabric looked as if it had been peeled off an elephant. "And now that you've brought up the subject, I've something to tell you. I don't want you to go making rash judgments, but life does present us with some of the darnedest coincidences...."

From where they stood to Our Lady of Estrela was still a pretty good stretch; but they could already see the pinnacle of Zimbreiro with its sheer cliff dotted with basalt peaks spreading a blotch of color against the sea. At a turn in the roadway, a tamarisk, roughened from its wind-swept existence, acted as signpost to a lava grotto. The area smelled badly, both from the waste left by the passersby and from the rue. But beckoned by the shade and by the warmth of the conversation, the two men sat on a boulder.

"Look, Honório, I like to be very frank. I jealously guard what's mine; yes... I don't let anyone in on what's mine. And as for the procurator's business, I act on the assumption that those who seek out a solicitor-at-law can't handle their own affairs and I claim what I have coming to me. No..., I don't do charity work. I make an exception whenever I can; I protect people's interests as if they were mine; but business is business.... What's more, *Dona* Carolina Amélia needs no special considerations from me."

"Of course not! And you owe me no explanations. Everybody knows how much that lady owes you...."

"I'm not finished.... Listen to me. You know that she had scruples about cutting her nephews in Brazil out of her will, out of respect for her husband's memory. (We used to have our disagreements. I've been like family for twenty years.) 'You, madam, are not under any obligation to people whom you never saw and who, to be absolutely honest, never gave you a second thought after the commander's death, may God rest his soul. Not even a couple of lines of condolence... or a Christmas card.... Not to mention a visit to the land of their elders to pay their respects. And here they could afford it better than anybody else! And then you must remember that you have Honório's daughter, your baptismal godchild, granddaughter to Claudino Honório Dutra, who was the commander's right-hand man in the political life of this island. The young lady feels a devotion and respect toward you that are very rare these days. When you encounter any serious problem, you work through it with me, that's true.... But when you want to go to church, she is the one who takes care of you. When it comes to any culinary worry, any prolonged illness, to whom can you turn, except to the Honório family, to Laurinha's companionship?'"

"You've always been a friend."

"Oh, just listen to you...! I just did my duty. I, and Father Joaquim Maria, who is kind enough to hear me out and to sit at my dinner table. He's the pro-synodal examiner for the Bishop of Angra! That's no small thing."

"And what did she say?"

"I drove home my point so long and hard, and she listened so well, that she ended up agreeing with me. She made a will a week ago, leaving most of her fortune–to your daughter."

Januário dropped the last phrase as if he were folding a newspaper after reading, in a country with well-guarded neutrality, the news of surrender of the fortress he had ordered sieged. Honório himself restrained his enthusiasm, saying almost in a whisper:

"If my daughter ever inherits anything, she'll owe it all to you, Januário! I won't forget this."

"Wait... not so fast! There's a matter of conscience here...."

"Where? I don't see it...."

"I like to lay my cards on the table... make things very clear.... Ângelo came to me with some story.... It seems that my boy has fallen for your daughter. I grant you that, given a choice between that witch of Pasteleiro and your daughter Laura, a father's choice is an open-and-shut case. I say it in confidence. Otherwise it might seem like an outrageous remark. But the truth is that I don't like to stick my nose in my son's affairs of the heart. It's their business. Marriage and death are decided in Heaven. What I don't want is for you to think I had ulterior motives in getting involved in all this. They're young.... They've got their whole lives ahead of them." He stood up heavily and contemplated the continuing road amid the dried manure and the rough branches of the stinking rue. "One can at least hope not to get bogged down in this filth, and may God take care of the rest!" He rubbed a shoe on the weeds: "Jeez! What a stench!"

232

A harsh voice was heard:

"Father! Father!"

"That's exactly what I think," replied Honório. "But I'm telling you I'm very happy, and should I ever become João's father-in-law, I'll feel honored." And striking with his walking stick the wheel ruts of the Zimbreiro road: "If that's in the cards... so be it!"

"Where have you been, Father? I'm hoarse from calling you!"

"I walked on ahead to meet up with Januário. Did your mother stay behind?"

Laura, who was out of breath, allowed Januário to greet her with a caress. But she was in a hurry, a little rough-mannered, and set out by herself along the narrow ribbon of road, spitting out chewed bits of a flower she was holding in her hand.

"What do you think you're doing? Did you leave Carlota alone?" asked her father, hurrying along.

"She's way back there with her brother. She's a slowpoke!"

"There's some fine manners for you!" And noticing in the distance the rear of the caravan swerving around a straw thicket, Honório raised his fingers to his mouth and let out a whistle.

When the celebration of Our Lady of the Estrela had ended, the Honórios and the Garcias sat down for their picnics in the churchyard. But the afternoon passed in silence, and joylessly. Nervous, Laura's heel extracted a perfume of crushed stalks from the mat of white mallow that Ângelo had ordered laid out on the ground. Despite Henriqueta's and *Dona* Maria's protests, João Garcia had distanced himself from the little chapel with Jacinto and Carlota. They were going down to the Zimbreiro fountain to drink the water cascading down the rocks. Laura, despite *Dona* Rosa Garcia's insistence, claimed she had a caul on her foot and remained sitting in a corner of the little sacristy listening to the funny stories that Ângelo was telling Father Joaquim Maria, who had handed him a pinch of snuff from his silver box.

The day before, João Garcia had arrived at the bower wall half an hour late. Laura was embroidering at the family room window, sitting in front of her mother. It was a calculated act, so that João Garcia could see very well that, just to punish him, she was not going to come down. On the morning of the celebration, noticing that she was bitter and standoffish, Ângelo had understood everything: they were having a lover's quarrel! Honório's little girl was like that: very pretty, very blond, but a stubborn and touchy little mule. A shift in the wind was enough to set her off. Ângelo, who had invested much care in his annual Our Lady of the Estrela celebration and who enjoyed seeing the families together and the young mingling, ended up having that nose of his, which pricked at the smell of fireworks, put out of joint.

Not even the walk down to the fountain... nothing at all! The maidenhair plants growing in the depression that time had carved in the rocks waved against the pantile spout. The young people would fill their earthen jugs and drink large draughts of that gushing, pure water, which flowed through the bowels of the island until it reached the crack into which the winter sea cast its spray.

"I'm on my way."

"Wait, João! Hold tight to the wall on your way down..."

Jacinto, who looked almost rotund in his crude woolen outfit, was helping Carlota down. But João kept on descending; one could already see his hat at the bottom of the steep walkway.

Having cleared the passageway carved with explosives and pickax in the forbidden cliffs crumbled by the winter and onto which no one dared venture without saying a *Credo*, he stopped on a level area choked with ferns and low-lying grasses, where the occasional drawing oxen left hoofprints as they strove to avoid the sting of the goad on their rumps. He looked toward the chapel. A trail of skirts and green branches seemed to point in the direction of the ringing little bell hung from iron supports. The patron saint's little blue star brightened the façade, whitewashed for the celebration. His father, his uncles and aunt, Honório and his wife, and Laura were all there. His present circle of human interests did not extend beyond them. He had more than enough worries with jockeying for position in the civil government, one which would bind his future to the windows of the former Jesuit school building and to the doorstep of his father's office, at whose entry the renters from Castelo Branco left their dripping umbrellas. Who was he to aspire to that rare flower in the little towers of the Dulmos' quinta, a flower like that kind of unscented magnolia found in the Fayal mornings when sports were played, with soccer players running all over the dock lawn, and a mare moving along a tree-lined alley at an English trot, and the faded, yellow-washed Granary fallen out of its preference for dark tea and for half an hour of violin music heard on Ocean Street? And Laura's quarrel seemed to him a cat-and-mouse fight, a blind man's buff in which the only real thing was their island overhung with clouds and gulls.

... somber weather, a lingering sultriness, and a complacency of soul. His thirty days of leave almost over.... Not even that semi-literary dalliance into the lectures in the barracks, nor the articles on local history published in and clipped from the *Insulano* succeeded in filling the void he felt in Praia do Almoxarife. All he was left with were Uncle Jacinto with his charming kindness, the tin *Alabama* harmonica, and the ancient Garcia house smelling of medicine and mildew. His uncle was the spitting image of his grandmother Maria Florinda, her brooched and spick-and-span shawl transformed into a whitish coat that looked like cloth turned inside out to guarantee a presentable appearance. But at the same time that he gave in to this sadness and as he lost himself on the summit of Zimbreiro, getting farther and farther away from the chapel and the fountain, and as the breath of the gray afternoon scorched his face and hair, João Garcia felt, in his dejection, absolutely certain about one thing: a blind serpent had coiled itself around his youth, and there was a precious stone missing from his destiny, a stone without which that perverse and enchanted creature would not break its spell. And in that vipers' nest–like the red, fresh-looking apple in the serpent's mouth in the sign at his uncle's pharmacy–Margarida seemed to be nestled, in the same fashion that the women of Fayal sit on piled-up ears of corn in the barnyard

235

and shuck, shuck all night long.... Her sweet and enigmatic face kept watch over his destiny, hid his future, as if each of his mistakes or obsessions was a particular straw or a fragile twig reserved for the remote warmth of a fire extracted from the ashes of a burning bush. And that night, as long as a lifetime, seemed destined to put to the test the Foolish Virgins and the Wise Virgins from the parable. Laura had gone out into the wind with her loveless lamp; Margarida harbored the old flame in her mysterious aloofness.

João Garcia had reached the spot in Zimbreiro from where one could see the channel stretching between the depression of Horta and the dark cone of Pico, which at the time was wreathed by a lilac-colored cloud. The cliff did not allow for the growth of anything green on that site; only a sparse brushwood tuft, picked nearly clean out of the burnt rock by daring peasants to make brushes for whitewashing houses. Once in a while, a flock of wild pigeons covered the sky, their sudden fluttering takeoff resounding against the lava cliff that rose straight up from the sea.

A crack in the lava rock caught João Garcia's attention. It was located on the land side, sheltered by what remained of the wall of a former wheat field now overspread with gram grass and dry-podded sweet sedge. A mat of feather and straw lined the hole. In the harsh Zimbreiro environment, there between the darkened late-afternoon sea and the precipitous black cliff, those nest fragments seemed like a last appeal to life, a hope that had survived the summer's severity and heat. João Garcia grabbed hold of the crags protecting the lined fissure and, clambering up with perilous agility, holding his breath in the expectation of finding a live creature, checked the hidden shelter. A startled pigeon took to the air, leaving a handful of feathers at the den's entrance. A shot was heard. The bullet whistled by, a short distance from João, who, hitting the dirt, yelled:

"Eh, you!..."

But another shot rang out, and the wounded pigeon, suddenly flightless due to a broken wing, dropped in the sedge. Crawling in that direction, João Garcia saw the form of a hunter who, appearing mysteriously from the craggy side of the cliff, had leaped another section of the fallen wall:

"You, Barreto!..."

The latter ran and, seeing a pale-looking João Garcia still crouching in the sedge, asked:

"Are you hurt?... Oh, my God!"

"No problem. But, really, you almost shot my ear off.... Where did you come from? Scaling cliffs after wild pigeons is just plain foolish, especially for a hunter. Are you coming from the Marraxo fishing spot?"

"For God's sake, Garcia, please forgive me! I never thought I'd find anyone in this wasteland. What a close call!..."

André Barreto picked up the pigeon by its feet and, like all keen hunters, examined the effects of the buckshot, as if he were weighing the possible consequences of which he now felt relieved. João Garcia was fighting to overcome his jitters.

"But listen! How did you manage to descend the cliff to the Marraxo ledge, a pathway that few fishermen have the nerve to take? Unless you came by boat...."

"I came with Roberto in his new boat. Can't you see it?..." André could not let go of the bleeding bird: "What a wonderful pigeon! And it belongs to a rare species... a shore-dwelling wood pigeon: *trocaza laurivora*, according to Pretextato at the Weather Station. They are both easily frightened and fastidious: they only eat laurel seeds."

João Garcia, shading his eyes with his hand, looked out to sea, but saw neither mast nor sail:

"The boat? Where is it?"

André then pointed to the light on the prow of a boat very near the cliff, and João Garcia could make out Roberto's pipe glowing and fading next to a light-colored dress:

"Oh...."

"Come with us. We'll dock in Madalena. The boat is big and resistant enough. Come on!"

"Who, me?"

"Yes, you! Are you afraid you're going to get seasick?"

"No, not really."

They heard a woman's voice yelling out:

"Ih... ah!..."

"Hear that?... Somebody's calling you! Come on... come on... And don't give what happened a second thought."

"But you're really shaking all over.... Do you want me to go down with you?"

"What, because of such a little incident like that? Hear that...? There's that voice again. It sounds like a password. It must really be fun to be out hunting on an evening like this, with such a glassy sea... The boat is very nice looking. Don't stay too long. And make sure you don't fall on your way down...."

"Good night, then...."

"Good night."

João heard the sound of André's nail-studded boots on the steps dug into the cliff and saw his indistinct figure, with his gun astride his chest, vanish vertically into the darkness.

João Garcia did not stop until he was very near the chapel. Uncle Jacinto, feeling uneasy, had come out looking for him. João smiled to make him feel better.

"We heard some shots.... Just think what a scare it gave us! These clay-pigeon shooters just flail around firing at random."

"I was out of range of their guns.... Relax."

But his pallor betrayed him. His eyes reflected the wild scene of the disturbed nest, the frightened pigeon taking off like a dart, then the stupid shot that broke its wing, and André Barreto's fingernails smoothing its blood-soaked crop feathers. The family caravan was already heading down the mountain toward the house. Under some broom bushes and standing next to Honório's walking stick, he caught a glimpse of his father's huge frame. Uncle Jacinto, distractedly whistling a sad tune, walked in front. And his memory of that female voice arising from where the little light shone on the boat fired in his tightened chest, blazed in the sea breeze that roughened his fingers, burned in the fire ash of the cigarette he obsessively puffed on, hiding in a cloud of smoke his tear-filled eyes.

238

Chapter XXII

Fourth Nocturne
(Lento)

"And so?" asked Roberto as he paced the dining room floor with large strides. A little English clock ticked on a console table.

"I see motionless lights.... They must be fishermen."

Margarida, leaning against the windowpanes and holding her head in her hands, watched for the minutest pulsation in the dark-enveloped channel. The lights of Horta and the broadly starlit sky were mirrored in the voluminous waters crossing the tide paths. Roberto concluded his counted steps up to the wall with the clock, then took as many steps in the opposite direction, stopping near the window. Margarida moved the hood formed by her hands and head over to another pane. They both looked out intently.

"Something is moving there.... And it's a prow light."

"It's fishermen from Porto Pim, Uncle!" she insisted, wiping another pane with the folded hem of her gown. "Can't you see? It's moving forward very slowly...."

"Dr. Nunes sometimes requisitions the health department's boat, and in that case, they row. There have been cases of the plague among the motorboat personnel."

Margarida went out of the window.

"What a bind we're in! Should the wet-nurse become ill here, dear God! You, Uncle, were ill-advised in insisting that she come.... As a chaperon, it was enough to have Mariana from Pico. Can't you hear her?"

From an interior little room, located between the dining room and the wine cellar, there came, through the door left ajar, a deep breathing, to which the lips of a toothless mouth lent a wheeze like that of a torn bellows. Margarida entered the room

239

on tiptoe and lightly lifted the bed covers. A low-burning kerosene lamp cast a shadow on her maternal smile, which she bestowed first on the old lady and then lifted to Roberto's eyes.

"She looks like a little bird...."

"Huhh?..." The old lady opened her eyes, smiling also. "It's you? I'll get up."

"You bad girl!... Don't you make a sound! Let's get back to sleep now...."

What was left of the old lady's smile went on shining in one of the two or three teeth that pinned up her gums; and when the door had been closed behind the hushed steps of her "little ones," she went back to sleep.

The tide, swollen but slowed down by a cross wind, lapped from time to time against the cliffs of Guindaste. A rounded bar of foam crowned with white the matching pebbles of the launching ramp, and a muffled sound made the wharf timbers vibrate. But the house, despite being buffeted by the ebb and flow of the majestic sea assailing the coast of Pico, maintained its unshakable dignity in the silence and roughness of the lava. With its doors and windows shut against the deserted vineyards and the night, it seemed like a seal, a discoverer's *padrão*[1]. In the backyard, a rooster crowed.

"The doctor is most definitely not coming...," said Roberto, sitting on a convent bench and crossing his legs. The worm-eaten back of the bench dimmed by contrast the brightness of the whitewashed wall. "And what are we going to do about our man with such a high fever and a tumor?"

"Do you think it's gotten bigger since a little while ago?"

"He's got a big tumor, no doubt about it! And in that area, no less..."

"It looked the size of a plum."

Roberto stared at Margarida for some time. He bent his head down and felt in his pockets for his pipe, tobacco pouch, and matches.

---

[1] The *padrão* is a stone monument placed by the Portuguese on lands they discovered.–Trans.

"The size of a plum, you say?"

"Maybe I'm exaggerating.... The blanket is thick; Manuel is in so much pain, poor guy! And he didn't want me to check on his private parts."

In the semidarkness of the room, Roberto's anxiety was easy to detect by the click of his tongue against his chewed-up pipe stem:

"And your mother worrying herself sick.... Your grandfather insisting on his armchair being brought to the window, with his crazy idea that from Pasteleiro you can easily see the Vineyards house; that you can even see people standing behind the windowpanes...."

"And it's true!" Margarida went to the window again: "Look! I saw a light in the quinta just now. It looked like someone going down the veranda staircase to the courtyard. And in the window of the little towers... a brighter light, can't you see it? The light going on and off...? It must be in the wet-nurse's room. The other light was yellower. It must have been the lantern."

"That's very strange!"

With the thick shadow of the channel drawing their attention once again, they remained at the window, looking out. The silence of everything–of the house and of the night–seemed to win them over to something profound and recessive, which diminished, little by little, the vivacity and meaning of their conversation and put an end to their shared expectations, as if they were two surviving members of a polar expedition surrounded by and forced to capitulate to the snow. Roberto again took up his pacing back and forth over the old floor, puffed on his unlit pipe, and then disappeared toward his room. By the light of the American lamp, Margarida measured with the prick of her needle on her embroidery the rhythm of the burning kerosene's flickering shadow. A filature dove had its schematic body, with a little branch on its beak, repeated along a strip of cloth stenciled with carbon paper.

A clock struck midnight... Then one o'clock... Roberto's steps traced the entire length and breadth of the deserted house; a distant sigh of pain compelled Margarida to stifle the rustle of the silk paper she held in her fingers and to train her ear intently: Manuel Bana was waking up. Margarida went through Mariana's room and took the stairs leading to the cellar.

The Clarks' residence, known as the Donkey's Stone and situated in the locality of Campo Raso, was typical of Pico's scorched vineyards. A high floor, with a turret at the corner, flanked the low-lying cellar, which was fully inside the house. Along one end of the cellar, there was, as a rule, a kitchen with bare stone walls. But (without altering the genuine Picoese architecture) old *Senhor* Roberto, the *British subject*, had built on three sides of the cellar the rooms and nooks required by the size of his increasing family and his love of comfort. The whole ensemble resulted in a kind of polypary, as if a ship's captain had been retained indefinitely in a foreign port by suspicious custom-house officials and had decided to reinforce the crew's sleeping cabins and rearrange the cargo. The cellar, with its deep press tank, its immense joist, the stone weight soldered to the slender, threaded shaft reaching up to the ceiling, and the vast fixed stands with casks of decreasing size, was the ship's hold. At night, Margarida always walked through the musty-smelling ark, experiencing a mysterious sensation. The staircase was weak and seemed to emerge off a gangplank. She would grab her skirt with one hand while holding a candle in the other. Her furtive steps startled the rats in the unfinished partitions of the building. And the shadows of the casks and the old beams danced on a wall bearing hash marks from counting thousands of jugs of wine, imbibed by time as if by an invisible sponge.

"And so, Manuel.... Are you feeling any better?"

Two red and sunken eyes were the answer to Margarida's question. Roberto turned up the lamplight. Restless and burning with fever, Manuel Bana sighed. He complained about his head and his "loins"; he wanted to walk. Lowering his arm over the pile of blankets, he stopped his hand in fear:

"The worst is the lump...." And turning to Roberto, taking advantage of a distraction that Margarida feigned in the direction of the railed loft overlooking the cellar, he whispered: "Right here, master, almost on my privates."

Margarida removed the warmer from the teapot lying on a small wooden tub, held the pot high while pouring and, with Roberto sustaining Manuel by the shoulders, helped him to drink. Manuel Bana was shaking badly. It seemed that his fever had skin and, like an invisible annelid, had coiled itself around his tendons, his chest, his whole body. Above his Adam's apple, which bobbed like a piston, the edge of his moustache moistened his parched lips with strong tea.

"When the doctor shows up, miss, you pick up your clothes and get out of here with him. Have you sent word to my sister in Capelo, as I asked you to? She's the one who needs to be here taking care of me. This kind of illness is really bad."

"Not at all!" said Roberto. "You caught yourself a cold, that's all.... Climbing to Pico summit on a morning like that.... What did you expect? Had *Senhor* Diogo not insisted that you have the cow rested to be milked in the morning, nothing like this would have happened...."

"I've got the plague, master!..."

"The plague? What are you talking about?"

"I know... I'm dying...."

A childish sigh syncopated Manuel Bana's voice. Margarida, unobtrusively moving her head away from the poor man's breath, softly placed her hand on his dry mop of hair:

"Come now.... A big strong man like you saying such silly things!..."

"Go away, Bidinha! Pack up your belongings and leave!..."

"No use insisting; I'm not leaving you. And now you listen to me! And *look* at me! Do you think I'd remain here if I thought you had the plague?"

Manuel Bana, with the eyes of a cornered animal, searched Margarida's eyes, as if he wanted to extract from them a clearer truth than he perceived in her voice. But her tender hand was caressing his forehead and seemed to cover his mouth; from her healthy and, for him, sacred body rose the certainty that his life had a guardian angel, had a sponsor. His eyes slowly began to close. His eyelashes, accustomed to the flies in the stables and to the awn and dust of the threshing floors, widened the dark spots around his drowsy eyelids, which covered eyes that looked as sunken as the birds' eggs at the bottom of the well-wrought nests which he used to bring to his miss when she was a child. Margarida watched his swarthy neck, marking the beats of his old heart–"the heart of a horse," as her father called it. Manuel was no spring chicken. (And all his gestures, his predictable and annoying speech, came back to Margarida in the silence of that room above the wine cellar, a silence cut by the presence of her uncle, who stood like a statue at the foot of the bed: "I'm no kid anymore, master.")

The plague! That's all her unfortunate family needed now, a family delivered into the hands of evil spirits seemingly bent on wrecking, in the dead of the night, their communal nest and shared fate! At fifty, Manuel Bana was old. He had not spared himself any work. In the good times when they owned the pastures, he would milk early, returning to the city with his lungs full of the April mists cloaking the Flamengos Creek, as though in an enchanted forest; he would brush the mare, hitch her, pack heavy loads to carry to the Granary. He even beat the mattresses and sometimes served at the table.... His body bore the trace of the Dulmos' full decadence. As her father dismissed the quinta personnel and the farmhands, Manuel himself assumed the responsibilities of shepherd, coachman, domestic servant, and even the masons. The hems of his cotton-cloth trousers were reduced to threads, and the crown of his wide-brimmed hat was all torn. But not he. Strong and wiry, he confronted his employers' and his own misfortunes with his endless prattling sayings, his cunning hidden behind his moustache, now drooping from the fever, and with his paw-like hands: "As the saying goes, a worthless pot never breaks...." "Whatever I lay my hands on, is mine!"

"He's sleeping soundly...," said Roberto. Tucking in her servant's bedclothes, Margarida placed a finger over her lips.

They had returned to the dining room. It was two o'clock in the morning. Over the revolving, moonlit earth, sheltered from mankind, the roosters seemed to have taken the island of Pico, which looked like a huge, dark and massive battleship in the middle of the deserted sea. Roberto wound the clock. The doctor, of course, had not braved the channel, perhaps because he had no boat or because he had not gotten the news in Pasteleiro. And perhaps because *Dona* Catarina could not dispense with Maria das Angústias' services to fetch him.

"What now?" thought Roberto. They were all alone in that place, without a doctor, Margarida taking care of a plague-stricken man in that condition—without even having a servant to at least help her in the kitchen and with the laundry, except for Mariana, who was in such sad mental shape....

Despite being sure that no one would show up before morning and that Manuel Bana would sleep comfortably the rest of the night, Roberto and Margarida seemed in no hurry to go to sleep. Roberto had gone to his room to fetch his things so that he could sleep next to the patient; but when he was returning to the dining room, he heard the noise made by the corn-husk mattress and decided to take a look at the ship's ladder leading down to the cellar:

"Margaret...."

"Shh!..."

"Come down! You're not going to stay there."

"Not so loud! I'm coming...."

By changing the buttons on a nightgown and sewing a collar and pocket on it, Margarida had improvised a perfect gown. A strip of unembroidered cloth adroitly wound around her head was used as a cap. Roberto remained at his watch post, saw that white figure come down past the railing, go around the casks overrun by mice, and then come up the gangplank ladder holding a candle in her hand. He employed all his logic in trying to alert her of the danger—and even the indiscretion—of remaining in that nook by the side of a servant with a burning fever and who, from one moment to the next, might even need to use the chamber pot, or require the assistance of someone strong enough to help him turn over in bed. But Margarida argued that on the loft there was room for two beds, one next to the other. They could both stay there or else watch the patient in shifts; she promised to call her uncle in case Manuel became delirious or needed to go to the potty like a little child. Not knowing exactly how, when his niece brought the earthenware teapot used in the Vineyards, all steaming and covered, Roberto felt he had to accept these wartime measures and embrace that mystery woven by the patient and shared by the two of them.

"We can't even escape the plague!" said Margarida. "Do you see, Uncle? You come all the way from London to see your old papa, and then all these tragedies strike...."

Roberto felt half-a-dozen words surging up in his spirit like a spring gushing from an artesian well; but his hesitation ended up allowing him to vanish into the soil of the Anglicized being he was, like a sudden shower soaked up by the parched earth. He intended to say: "Blessed be the hour, Margaret, that...." But what he wound up saying was:

"Quite right, the islands don't seem to be riding a wave of good fortune.... It's serious.... The plague!"

The word hovered in the air for a while, like a forgotten plume of smoke rising from a snuffed-out candle. Gazing off into the distance, Margarida went on stirring her tea:

"Did you get a letter from London?"

"No."

"I thought that...."

"Marr is in Switzerland."

"What about Mary? She used to write so often...."

"It's not surprising that she doesn't now. Her work with both the exchange of prisoners and correspondence keeps her very busy; the Red Cross is much more important than an old and faraway friend.... Besides, sea communications with Holland have become very difficult; the Allies search the neutral ships and sometimes detain them for weeks in the military ports...."

"And where is she?"

"In Scheveningen, close to The Hague. Bankastraat."

"Would you mind showing me her picture?"

Roberto slowly pulled out his wallet and handed her a picture showing a figure in a somewhat stark pose, revealing an almost sharp contrast between the creases around her mouth and her hair. Margarida, holding the steaming cup in one hand and the picture in the other, shook her head between two lingering sips of tea. It must feel good for a man to be able to count on such unconditional dedication–more than camaraderie, less than love–was she right?... Roberto, keeping his wallet open on the table, arranged his escudo bank-notes, a check from the Anglo-Spanish Bank, his calling cards printed in cursive. Afterward, slowly emerging from that operation like one who is doing a puzzle and doesn't lose sight of any possible combinations, he merely said in English:

"*Two good companions.... Two fellow-sufferers, indeed....*"

Margarida, pushing the cup aside and returning Mary's picture, after passing it under her nose as one does with a chocolate, said with a childish air:

"It smells so good.... *Old England. Thank you!*"

Roberto found it difficult,... *very* difficult to repress his innocent and compact smile, which seemed protected and made almost impenetrable by his pipe, by his brick-colored handkerchief which he took out and put back into his pocket, by his modest and somewhat worn pigskin wallet. Roberto lived imprisoned by his monosyllables and by his tics, like the enchanted prince in the body of the Blue Bull. [2]

Margarida lay in bed with her clothes on and slept badly, buried in the corn-husk mattress and ready to get up at the first summons. As for Roberto, he insisted on lying on a mattress on the loft at the entrance to the patient's room. The structure was a kind of platform or high loft supported by triangular trusses built above the casks, one of those English architectural caprices. It must have been used by old *Senhor* Roberto, for example, as an observation post from which to watch the steward handling wine containers on days of harvest and decantation. Roberto's mattress, laid perpendicular to Margarida's bunk-like bed, lent the site the appearance of a sailing ship that unexpectedly stops at a small port to install supplementary bunks and

---

[2] The story of *Toiro Azul* or Blue Bull is an Azorean adaptation of the fairy tale *Cinderella*. –Trans.

where the inhabitants, waiting to embark, have no preference whatsoever as to ship or captain.

Restless, Manuel Bana woke up towards first light. He absolutely insisted on walking, despite the dizziness and cold shivers that ran over his rough skin. Like a drunkard, he staggered at every step; and when he found the chamber pot that Roberto charitably pushed towards him, the room was filled with a dry and fetid noise. The edges of his eyelids were red and swollen; his eyes could not stand the light. In a strained and lisping voice, he addressed Roberto:

"Is Bidinha still here? Please, master, tell her to leave! Tell her, for God's sake!"

In order not to distress him, Margarida remained propped up in bed, trying to decipher her uncle's movements around the patient by watching the play of shadows on the cellar wall. Manuel Bana ended up by falling into a torpid indifference and finally into a deep sleep.

Margarida then dreamt she was aboard a big liner, like those the Fabre Line advertised in posters all over Fayal and Pico. But she was not sailing to America or London or anywhere in particular..., nor was the ship anything but a cavernous hold full of pitch. There was no first class, sleeping cabins, nor any table whatever, and the unseen piano, where Debussy was being tortured, seemed like a miracle or a mockery. Cousin José de Lemos, who had come on board with her, had promised he would introduce her to the ship's captain; she then had grabbed the lapels of his coat and both had walked from deck to deck, each of which was strewn with piles of boxes and bags, like in the game in which a bunch of jolly children surround "Mr. Thief" and then run through all the rooms in the house until they reach the kitchen. Uncle Roberto was supposed to have come on board also, but where was he? A black man in jeans was ringing a large bell. Then a column of foul-smelling smoke filled the ship. On the bridge, a steersman with an unkempt beard was pulling the chain that controlled the furnace valve: three plaintive roars resounded in the air, like those made by the *Funchal* on leaving the dock.

Cousin José de Lemos had vanished; Margarida had lost her way behind a stack of bales. She wanted to scream but could not. A gull flew by and plucked a lock of her hair. She stumbled over other bales: *Cotton Checks*. At that moment a nun, disentangling herself from a roll of cable, began staring compassionately at Margarida. From under her starched *cornette*, flapping like a nightingale's wings in the breeze, she yelled: "Flee, young woman! flee! Look at those rats!" "Where are we headed, sister?" "I don't know! We're coming from Java...."

Then grabbing onto the nun's skirt and following her down an endless hallway smelling of rope and of staleness, Margarida was able to hide in a kind of cell on port side where she found a crucifix, a little lamp, and a first-aid kit on the floor.

The sister had forced her to sit down and was telling her a mysterious tale, which told of Saint Louis, King of France amidst lepers in Tunis, and an orphaned young man, who was about to get married when his fiancée took the veil. She then saw a human trunk, a naked torso dotted with blood-rimmed holes and half an arrow still buried in the flesh... the quills... the vibrations still perceptible on the bare skin. The mutilated body was bound to an orange-tree trunk, and Margarida could detect, near the fresh cut made by the saw, a bunch of perfectly-drawn leaves with a tiny white bud sprouting in the center, like a candle teardrop. Beyond the figure itself, there were myriad imagined things, sprung from her sensation-laden, mournful, and indistinct thoughts. An effeminate individual wearing a derby was announcing holy stamps for sale: "The venerable image of St. Sebastian, patron of the plague-stricken!" It was Ângelo. *The rosy light of dawn....*

The voice of Uncle Roberto humming that tune woke up Margarida. Maria das Angústias was primping the sheets around her:

"What's happened here, Bidinha?"

The sun, coming in through the cellar dormer windows, cast a golden glow upon the doctor's glasses as he stood stroking his downy beard.

Chapter XXIII

Fire!

The Vineyards house was still under quarantine by order of the secretary of public health when Marr's letter arrived. But Manuel Bana, despite feeling very weak, could already sit for a few hours in front of the window, having gently been brought there by Roberto and Margarida to celebrate his release from that long confinement so very near the edge of death. To avoid having him climb the stairs, they had moved his bed to Mariana's little room; she now slept on the dining room floor with Maria das Angústias. And since Manuel Bana, his old trousers dangling from his beanpole legs, still could not walk, Roberto and Margarida carried him on an improvised chair formed by their clasped hands. Amused, the wet nurse remarked: "Looks like the sacred knot.... The only things missing are the priest and the stole!" They all laughed, happy in their unexpected sense of security, like passengers on a ship that has cleared the brunt of the typhoon and keeps on sailing on the still-rough seas, despite some broken portholes and loose cables. At the window, the patient was enjoying the broad view of the channel and the telegraphic gestures made by passersby inquiring after his health.

Dr. Marr had sent encouraging news regarding Roberto's inquiries about a possible position for Margarida in England. A Scottish couple who had just returned from Rio, where they had received a windfall inheritance from an engineer relative of theirs, was looking for an educated Portuguese young woman from a good family who could teach them the language and introduce the lady to the literatures and customs of Portugal and Brazil. In addition to room and board, they would pay half a pound a day. As for office jobs, they were a little more difficult to come by, but Dr. Marr kept hope alive. He prescribed patience: *wait and see*!

Roberto had quickly skimmed Marr's letter, and as soon as he read the news, he went to share it with his niece, who was dissolving sublimate in a large basin at the entrance to Manuel Bana's room.

Margarida dried her hands on her gown and threw her arms around his neck. The hot smoke from Roberto's pipe stung her flushed face.

"Will you take me with you, Uncle?..."

"*Wait a bit, please....*"

Suddenly changing her at once sweet and brusque manner and switching to English, with which she did not feel very comfortable, she said, with a gleam in her eyes:

"*I feel so happy.... Let me go with you!*"

The following day, after the authorities lifted the quarantine hanging over the Vineyards house, it was announced that the family was coming to visit. Her father and brother soon arrived. Diogo Dulmo, finding that his daughter had changed, remarked: "You look prettier!" He then chastised her for her imprudent refusal to leave the patient: the demands placed upon her, in the midst of a serious epidemic like that, were beyond a young girl's capacity to meet them. But the results of her imprudence seemed reflected in the brightness of the house, that clear day of blue seas bathing Horta and leaving the burnt Pico stones dark and calm, and finally, in Manuel Bana's dull eyes, as he sat at the window with as week's beard and the air of a happy invalid. Diogo Dulmo paced the rooms at length, went down to the cellar and pounded the tops of the casks with a mallet, as if he expected some sort of reply from the wine inside. As *Dona* Catarina had stayed alone with Cecília to take care of her father, who was always grumpy, they left early.

Uncle Mateus Dulmo arrived later, adjusting his rubber band around the stretchers of his umbrella.

"Are you going to scold me, too?..." asked Margarida, placing her hands on his shoulders and leaning her head backward in a gesture of both approach and retreat.

"Me..., scold you? Come, little one, give me a kiss! Now *you*'re what I call a real woman."

What looked like tears shone in the old man's eyes. Margarida held him tight in her arms, then dusted off a chair for him.

"And what about Horta? And your harmonium?... Any news from Cousin Corina?"

"I rarely see her these days. Cousin Francisca doesn't let her go out, for fear of contagion. You can't walk into the house with all that eucalyptus and lavender smoke.... They look like confectioners, with their wood-burning ovens always going! I ran into André Barreto this morning! He was coming from the cathedral with his sister. They want to come and see you, and they send Roberto their regards." Mateus Dulmo took a white handkerchief out of his pocket and wiped his glasses. "Yes, sir.... In the city, it's all they talk about. You and Roberto have saved the day...." But upon hearing Manuel Bana clearing his throat next to him, he slowly got up and said: "Let's take a good look at our man here."

"You spoiled brat, you! Almost as good as new.... You're ready for another." He squeezed Manuel's knee. "But you're all bones, my boy!"

"Ah, master! If it hadn't been for *Senhor* Robertinho and Bidinha, I'd be a goner.... What they did for me was charity work!"

Margarida erupted with genuine laughter. She spoke about how difficult it had been to make him down a glass of milk, take a bite of toast:

"That's Manuel for you, Uncle. A real macho! Always saying he was never going to see his sister again and always obsessed with the pasture rent: 'Our Lady of Mercy, how am I going to pay the rent to *Senhor* Matesinho!'"

"Silly man!..."

"But today he already had visitors from Capelo; they brought him this huge sweet bread... two chickens... everything but the shirt off their backs..."

Manuel Bana had happiness written all over his face: the

beatitude of simple souls who seem to dwell in a purely animal body, which is their salvation. Roberto accompanied Uncle Mateus Dulmo out to the courtyard to see the perennial rose-bushes spreading buds all over the wall; the sun cast a round, dim reflection upon the sea. Although in no real hurry, Mateus Dulmo wanted to catch the eight o'clock ferry in Madalena. But the house was but a stone's throw from the village, and so he still had some time to chat. He would ride back in the carriage, that old clunker belonging to Bica from Criação Velha.

Because the house had been cleaned up and because Maria das Angústias was in the kitchen attending to supper and Mariana was nestled on a bench saying the rosary, Margarida very happily met her uncles as they returned from the courtyard and then joined them in the dining room. It seemed that the old man's visit was what had been missing for a proper denouement to that drama of the plague: the secluded house with communications cut off; the doctor coming in, once in a while, like a relief ship sailing into port of a desert island; the sorting on the cellar table of the amount of sublimate to last through the quarantine. And now that Uncle Mateus was a tangible reality, now that she could touch the golden down of his nobleman's hands and hear his sober and ironic voice and see his closed Malaca-cane umbrella, she felt that the action she had taken, daring or banal, levelled the playing field for everybody and everything. It was almost like having received Holy Communion in the church of Angústias for the well-being of someone special.

Mateus Dulmo reacted positively, although a bit listlessly, to the news in Dr. Marr's letter. He was presently the only other person in the family aware of the plans and announced his approval of his niece's resolution. Horta was a place of good and decent people; they all had been born there, like the chicks hatched in the cellar of the Granary. And woe to those who forsake their nests! The Dulmos had been native birds of Fayal for over four centuries, like the buzzards and the shearwaters. They were of Flemish origin, to be sure, but hatched in the warmth of the islands. He himself, although he had spent the better part of his life abroad, hoped to die in his little niche, near his begonias and the Peters' chestnut tree. But Margarida was also a Clark–almost as much a Clark as she was a Dulmo–and so he could understand why she felt attracted to England, besides her own private, family-related reasons for wanting to leave.

"Go, little one! You should.... If your uncle didn't live there, I wouldn't recommend London. Those are self-indulgent lands.... Babylons! But this place here also has its problems... Small places, people who keep to themselves.... And then there are those of our caste, who are even worse! A bird with a rich repertoire is never comfortable locked up in a cage. Go.... Try it out!"

On hearing the words of the old man, who seemed to personify her real, unmistakable destiny that lay before her, Margarida was overcome by sadness. Uncle Mateus Dulmo was like the root of her being; his white hair was the flower of experience blooming, bearing the miraculous fruit of Pico on the Piedade side, watered by the winter rains and ripened by the heated lava. Margarida felt as if she were already on board heading for London or already in some park in England in the company of strangers, talking and listening, like a tree putting on and dropping its leaves. And Uncle Roberto himself, whose life she had imbibed during those days of the plague, as the soil soaks up the rain, now seemed less close and less necessary to her life, as if he had been brought near her like a once-floating plank that now lies as driftwood on some beach and has been lost as a crossbeam for some anonymous roof or even actually floats out to the sea again. No, she did not feel sad, but she did feel disillusioned. It was time for tea.

While the tea leaves opened up in the pot, Mateus Dulmo wanted to take a look at the cellar and at Margarida's bedroom, which was actually her grandfather's and grandmother Margarida Terra's room and commanded a view of the fruit orchards. He touched the old myrtle bed and seemed to push aside some unpleasant thought. Poor Ana Silveira, Roberto's mother, had also slept there for many months. And the thought of that unscrupulous act on Charles Clark's part–allowing an innocent and irresponsible lover to lie in his own marriage bed–dissolved in a look that encompassed Roberto and his niece, joining them in the quick miscalculated sum of two numbers.

"Is this picture of grandmother's the one that resembles me the most?" asked Margarida, picking up an old framed daguerreotype from the dresser.

"Maybe...," said Mateus Dulmo. "Corina gets sort of carried away. When it comes to resemblances, it's like matching up of gifts with her: she likes to pair them.... But make no mistake: you do bear some likeness to her.... More in the mannerisms than the features."

Roberto reminded them of the tea. There were crackers and scones that Margarida threw together, and butter from Candelária. The cheese was a little rancid. Mateus Dulmo, unfolding his napkin, inquired of Roberto about the whaleboats, the deal with André Barreto. Was the money advanced for the new boat fitted out American style a guaranteed loan or was it, as rumor had it, his partnership contribution to the new firm?

Roberto answered that the subject was under discussion. His first impulse, besides rescuing the firm and helping his brother-in-law, was to stay in Horta and handle the business himself. But, come to think of it, it was not prudent to leave the Anglo-Spanish Bank and precipitously jump into a business deal with the Baron da Urzelina's son, since he, Roberto, could not come up with the necessary capital, not by a long shot. André Barreto was a jewel of a young man, but business is business. André was the son of a rich São Jorge landowner, used to always getting his way and to seeing the poor goatherders of Topo, who address their masters with cap in hand, bending to his will. He could not be expected to adapt easily to a modicum of *fair play* demanded by the firm, a type of whist played at a table in Praça, requirements almost as mystical, for a man raised in the city, as the quest for the Holy Grail or the court of King Arthur. And Roberto feared the loss of the freedom he was used to as an office worker and was afraid he would miss the London fog, a fog more comforting and sooty than the hot ashes from a smoking pipe. He wanted to avoid some of those boring afternoons at the Royal Club of Fayal... and that feeling of malaise that afflicts the city....

Mateus Dulmo gave Roberto an intelligent and understanding look; Margarida started to put the cups on the tray.

"I asked the question," said the old man, "because the deadline agreed to by Diogo and the Avelars for paying the debt is here, and I have serious misgivings about that crook Januário. There is a certain uneasiness at the Granary, some warning signs... It would be a good idea to resolve the issue of the whaleboats, if nothing else."

"At this point the situation is as follows," said Roberto. "André, perceiving my interest in João da Cezilha's boat crew and subtly hinting at the Granary's financial difficulties, insisted on going to Flores with me to buy that American whaleboat that we've heard so much about. And he said money was no object since the baron had a long-standing financial plan in mind for hunting the old cetaceans in Velas. If the Clark firm should be unable to live up to its financial end of the deal, he alone would assume sole responsibility for the boat. Perhaps he could even free Diogo from the Avelars' and Januário's claws...."

Mateus Dulmo smiled with ironic melancholy:

"He's a generous young man, no doubt!..." And turning to Margarida, who repeatedly walked to the balcony window overlooking the channel and who seemed uneasy: "Pumpkin, pack up your things and head for London with your uncle! From here to Lisbon, and to keep up appearances, there will be plenty of people who can keep you company.... And from Lisbon to London... Now what's the matter with you? You look like you've just seen a ghost.... What is in the channel that could possibly hold your interest that much?"

"It's nothing, Uncle...." Filled with anxiety, Margarida's eyes turned inquiringly toward Roberto, who sat silently on the convent bench wondering what decisions he should make. "It looks like a fire in Horta!"

"A fire?!"

And seeing her old uncle getting up, she anxiously rushed forward ahead of him, dragging Roberto by the arm:

"It's probably nothing.... I'm probably seeing things."

"No, it's really a fire...!" said Mateus Dulmo, making sure. "And it's in the area where I live.... How do you like that!"

Indeed, an undulating ball of fire rose above a row of houses in Horta, from the end of a street. A sooty mass was rising toward the sky, topped by a thick plume of smoke.

"Oh, God, what a disaster!"

"It must not be very far from Infante Square," said Roberto, trying to divert attention from a thought that he himself could not confront. "Perhaps it's the Fayal Coal... some bunkhouse near the dock..."

"No, no," said Mateus Dulmo with a serenity that was also an attempt to overcome his worst fears. He had become pale, stunned. "It's much farther up than that. Perhaps it's my house...." And stroking the hair of Margarida, who was on the verge of tears: "Don't be frightened, little one! If that's the case.... May God's will be done!"

Roberto went to his room to fetch his overcoat and soon came back with his scarf wrapped across his chest, making sure he had his pipe and matches in his pockets:

"Let's go, Uncle Mateus. I'm going with you." He drew close to the window once again: "It's more likely some bunkhouse near the dock; maybe it's the Cable Company drums on fire.... Mount Guia blocks the view of Angústias and of the ball of fire. It's really rising up to the sky, though...."

"What a terrible fire!" said Margarida, getting a hold of herself.

"I'm coming, too. Nurse!... Mariana!..."

"Yes, miss!..."

"Bring my dark coat.... I'm going with *Senhor* Mateus Dulmo."

"No! You're not going anywhere. Don't forget that I'm an old man who still knows what courage is. And right now, the site of the fire is mere conjecture. Maybe luck is on my side. From here to the city, there's still a long time to ascertain where the fire really is. In Madalena, they probably already know. The worst is my chatelaine. Poor Rosária.... You can just imagine what a nightmare this must be for her!"

Even Manuel Bana tried to put on his coat. He could already imagine himself with a pickax in hand, the one he had used to knock down half the roof of a shack on Old Street to save some prostitutes' home next to the haystack of a burning stable. But Mateus Dulmo gave him a stern look. Manuel Bana, feeling like a child caught misbehaving, let up.

Maria das Angústias was ready to swear that she heard the church bells sounding the alarm. If they could only count the number of tolls.... Angústias, 4; Cathedral, 6; Conceição, 8.... But, maybe not! It was probably only her imagination, an indistinct sound, and far away, that blood-red ball of fire filling the sky and the sea.

"Good-bye!"

Both the shadow and the voice of the old man vanished down the road. Roberto had stayed back thinking that he had, with two English monosyllables, convinced Margarida to stay put. He looked back, suspicious. But Margarida was resting her elbows on the windowsill, pale and immobile, unaware of anyone else's presence or absence. She had descended to the most forlorn and deserted depths of her own being, like a stone that falls in a sleepy cistern and leaves on the surface a ripple, and another and another, leaving a trail of bubbles.

"May St. Martial deliver us from punishment by fire!" exclaimed Mariana from Pico, whose idiocy was deepening with each passing day.

"And may St. Sebastian protect us from the plague! Our Father who art in heaven...."

The old woman's voice summoned Margarida back to reality. How wonderful to pray! To be able to exchange this unquenchable thirst for life and the misery of the flesh for that nameless water of the God of the afflicted and plague-ridden–fresh and potent water like the torrent that she, while in bed, heard rushing over Pico's loose stones washed by the winter and the night.

Chapter XXIV

Smoldering Debris

Sullen-faced, Januário got out of the victoria in front of the door of his office, causing the carriage springs to creak. That sight, which the neighborhood residents had observed so many times in the last twenty years, lent the street the sudden look of a jungle clearing a passage for a heavy and sovereign elephant. Ângelo, who had been entrusted with summoning the Avelars, looked like a bailiff standing guard over vicious criminals.

"Gentlemen, let's get it over and done with."

Januário threw his overcoat on a rocking chair, brushed the edge of the desk with his dress coat, then opened the safe:

"If you want to recover your money, there's no time to waste! Everything has been arranged. I succeeded in expediting the requisition and having the Pico judge order the seizure of the whaleboats in São Mateus this very day. From now on, the boat house is as good as sealed. No one will be able to touch it."

"But, *Senhor* Januário...," hazarded the old man.

"There are no ifs, ands or buts! I had enough trouble getting things ready on the sly and not without having had to apply some extraordinary measures. My usual business tricks...." He had a fake smile and was as white as a sheet. "When you made me your procurator, you agreed to everything. And I actually kept Chico abreast of all developments, except trade secrets. My solicitor's investiture and the lawyer's signature will provide cover for any slight bending of the evidence required under Article 364 and following articles of the Civil Code. As for claims that Leal is a con man and brings shame to the legal profession in Horta, I say 'Baloney!' If that is the case, they shouldn't have given him his license.... Anything goes when the ends are noble, like this one: to squash that scoundrel Dulmo, who nearly put you in the poorhouse! The double-crosser thought that all he had to do was dangle his daughter under Barreto's nose or sit her on her uncle's knee–we don't even know which one of the two is the partner in crime in that filthy deal! Partners in the girl and in the whale fishery, that's just too much! He's going to pay!..." And, making like he was going to leave and had forgotten his scarf on the umbrella stand: "Oh! And don't you gentlemen forget that you signed a document assuming responsibility for losses and damages...! That is to say: you are responsible for everything, in case of nullification of seizure! Art. 364 of the Civil Code, applicable to commercial matters." (Januário, in his eagerness to expedite the "conservatory measure," had spared his customers this minor detail.) "As they say, if you don't want to be a wolf, don't put on its clothes! But don't worry.... The case is as good as won! We have the last word! It's on this teensy-weensy probability that I bank my judicial credibility..., Leal and I!" And halting his pacing, he pounded a pile of deeds with his open hand, as if he had just been dealt an ace of trumps in a card game.

"But it's going to cause a scandal all over Horta!" insisted the elder Avelar.

Chico Avelar, as if hypnotized by Januário's eloquence, shrugged his shoulders:

"Let hell itself turn inside out! We aren't going to change a thing!"

"Do you hear what your son just said? You are a weak soul, a goody-goody.... and I have to protect your daughter's interests, who is a widow, and your grandchildren's.... I swore it by the Sacred Host!" Januário's voice rang with a terrible conviction, one which lent gravity and purpose to his monstrous words. He was standing by the desk, shuffling papers. "Justice is on its way to Madalena with two gun-toting policemen, because Dulmo is tricky and has his tried-and-true supporters. The entire coast of Pico, from São Mateus to Madalena, will rise up to defend him."

Trembling, the old man signed the paper that Ângelo handed him, then passed the pen to his son. The office took on the dense atmosphere of a full spittoon and of irrevocable decisions. The elder Avelar sat in an armchair and hung his head.

"And what of the fire in your home?" asked the younger Avelar. "What a terrible loss!"

Noisily opening his desk drawer, Januário pulled out a portfolio, flipped it open, and with a frozen smile on his flame-colored face, said softly:

"The insurance policy is right here! The Universo Company agent has already telegraphed the headquarters. There will be a just compensation for the house, furniture, and all the valuables! Only for old Aunt Secundina there's nothing to be done. Poor woman!" And a genuine tear clouded his eyes.

"The worst was the safe not withstanding the heat! They say it was because of the soldering in the safe bolt: solder and cast iron blend together. I can just imagine the devastation you must feel! Private documents... possessions that we all have and want to keep out of the hands of just anybody. I can only put myself in your shoes!"

Januário turned even more pale; but as Avelar's son was about to elaborate, he interrupted him by yelling:

"Zé Mónica! You'll ride with *Senhor* Ângelo wherever he's going, and then come back here. Don't spare the mules! And you... (no, never mind... I'll go there myself!)."

He put away the papers and locked the safe. Ângelo held his wide-sleeve overcoat as if he were unfolding a shroud:

"Are you sure? I can get to the scribe's in a heartbeat. Unless you don't trust me..."

"No, no... I'll go myself! Make sure to lock the doors!"

On the very morning following the blaze and after having sent off his mother, his sister and Carlota to Fern Lane (João was going to sleep in the barracks), Januário reserved a room with two beds at the Delmas inn for his brother and himself. He had sent word to Flamengos Creek to have the spare suits he kept there brought to him. The city of Horta watched him go by in his carriage, climb the stairs of Universo Company, and personally go to the undertaker's to order Aunt Secundina's casket. And except for some intimate friends, such as Pretextato,

Honório, and Father Joaquim Maria (*Dona* Carolina Amélia had already gone by toward the inn in a closed carriage), almost no one dared to offer condolences for the fire or for the horror of Aunt Secundina's body reduced to ashes. They kept watching him, hurrying by in his overcoat and striped trousers, leaving in his wake a sense of mystery and bustle, that the whip on the mules' back served to intensify. Locked in his office, his diabetic's face was bent over documents all night long.

His visit to the ruins, where great puddles of water from the fire hoses still swamped the rubble, had been short and courageous: only long enough for him to check the ashes inside the wide-open safe and stir with the tip of his cane the powdery remains of Aunt Secundina's bones. Summoned hastily from the house of Flamengos Creek, Januário had watched, from a distance, the horrendous' fire spread; and through the window openings, he had seen the burning girders come crashing down. Half the people of Horta had rushed to Jesus Street and adjacent streets; the balconies were filled with women making the sign of the cross and gesticulating, horrified. A great many sirens wailed, and the ostentatious sound of a bugle arose to interrupt the prolonged crackling noises of the burning timber.

João, who was on daytime duty, arrived from the barracks wrapped in his cape and was comforted by Espínola and Damião Serpa. Father and son embraced without a word; a single sob from Januário died on João's shoulder, dampening the stripe on his collar. Ângelo went to console his sister and niece, who had just arrived from Fern Lane and were at the Honórios'; he was the one who had encouraged his brother to approach the fire. Only he expressed his pain:

"My beautiful oratory! My poor aunt!"

Aided by a fireman and on behalf of the Garcia family, Pretextato assumed the painful duty of searching for Aunt Secundina's body among the rubble. She was unrecognizable, charred, reduced to a formless smoldering mass with a few pieces of coal still glowing. The fireman insisted that a scorched filament of skin from her chin, a hair-like thread, had escaped the flames. Once in a while, a little spark rose from the remain-

262

ing half of a Child Jesus lying on a chair thrown on the sidewalk among the few items they had managed to salvage.

Different opinions about the origin of the fire made the rounds in Horta. The house had been practically shut up for over a month, with the shutters of the balcony window facing the dark street sealed up tight. Old Secundina occupied her den up in the attic toward the back of the house, under the watch of an old married servant from Flamengos, expressly hired to take care of her. With the family in the countryside and João staying at Jacinto's in Praia do Almoxarife, Ângelo, who remained in the city once in a while, started sleeping in his nephew's room close to the entry so that he could come and go more freely. Some were of the opinion that the servant, a heavy sleeper, had dozed off and a curtain next to a kerosene lamp had caught on fire. But the fact is that when the firemen went to find her, she was in bed, snoring soundly. They used a Magyrus ladder to lower her to safety. Others said that Ângelo had brought a group of friends home that afternoon. There had been a lot of eating and drinking; people heard a lot of merrymaking and foot dragging in a mock dance. The fire was blamed on a drunken individual, who supposedly had started it to hide the evidence that he had robbed Januário's safe. And people superstitiously established a parallel between the way the safe had been acquired (for it had belonged to the public treasury) and the curious fate of that family, which had become rich through the wheelings and dealings of its paterfamilias.

To get João Garcia away from the atmosphere of the city and spare him the grim spectacle of the burned house surrounded by makeshift fences, Espínola had arranged with the battalion commander to get the high council to grant him a special leave and then had accompanied him to Praia do Almoxarife in the barracks' car.

But only at night when his aunt brought him tea and cookies in bed did João Garcia fully realize the monumental catastrophe that had befallen them the previous day. His uncle's home had had an especially soothing effect on him. Going into the pharmacy, seeing the clock in its place, the ripe apple in the mouth of the fork-tongued serpent, the lined-up bottles with labels carefully handwritten by Jacinto—everything, from the cat to the toxins, induced in João Garcia a tranquilizing peace. He measured the astronomical distance separating this home, cradle of his family, from that lugubrious and now burnt-down house where his mother had expiated her sins, real or imagined; where Aunt Henriqueta despotically ruled over half the world; where Carlota tortured the piano, while Uncle Ângelo cut papillotes; where his father came in to have lunch and dinner and afterward hid in that mysterious office of his; where Aunt Secundina moaned between obscenities and her display of tenderness towards her Child Jesus; and where grandmother Maria Florinda's shawl constituted the only suggestion of winged purity.

She, too, had lost her best clothes in the fire, as well as her chestnut chest, from whose secret drawers, when João was a child, had sprung wondrous objects: hard candy, donuts, and handmade sachets filled with glass and wooden buttons for João's "button game." Her gold filigree rosary, which had been wrapped around her mother's wrists in her death throes, also burned; and the chisel her father had used the day before he had his stroke; and the little morocco portfolio engraved with golden flowers where the notary Severinino kept the records of his children's birthdays and the names of his friends who took them to the baptismal font. Everything lost... everything reduced to ashes amid the banners of flame that had filled the Horta skies. And what had not been turned into rubble or ashes became a thick muck under the nozzles of the fire hoses.

But perhaps only the loss of her precious oratory was a dagger in the nice old lady's heart of gold: the seven swords of the Virgin melted or twisted, and especially the statue of St. Rita of Cassia, patroness of the impossible: "Grant me, dear Lady, that my son Ângelo be as normal and proud a boy as any other!"

It was all over.... Resting her chin on her clasped hands and fixing her eyes on one spot, which forced her to straighten out her hump a little, grandmother Maria Florinda could only say: "Praised be Our Lord Jesus Christ! May it all be for the blessed name of God!"

Jacinto knocked lightly on the door; his obese and sluggish figure leaned against the footboard of his nephew's bed:

"Do you want a book to read? I brought you *The Lives of the Saints* and *Lisbon in Shirtsleeves*. It's good... for whiling away the time. Even I sometimes laugh at these silly stories."

"Thanks, Uncle!"

"But try to get some sleep; what's past is past.... Our family has always had bad luck. It seems that someone cast an evil spell on us! Perhaps ever since your father left the Angra Seminary for Meireles' notary office... No: The bad luck comes from his insisting that he take Henriqueta and my mother to go live in the city. And then, it was one thing after another: your mother thrown out on the street... he, fired from the Granary...." Noticing how sad and silent João had become, Jacinto scratched his head; then he took a few fearful steps towards the headboard and clumsily straightened the sheet fold: "Sleep, my boy! And don't forget to turn off the light...."

"You're a saint, Uncle!" said João Garcia, deeply moved.

"Oh, let's not get carried away...! We're all made of Adam's clay. The world is a sad place..."

"Maybe so.... But there are those who seem destined to bring misfortune upon themselves and others. And hatred, Uncle! deadly hatred! And for what?..."

"Your father has his mean streak, no doubt about it.... But, deep down, he's a loving person and a mover and a shaker! He's good to his family; I'll never forget all he's done for me.... If it weren't for his help, today I would still be preparing linseed poultices in Rilha-Rolhas' apothecary!"

As cautiously as he moved around the large table with test tubes, Jacinto tactfully avoided discussing the problem to which João had alluded.

"True enough...," said João. "Very good to his family but always trying to bend us to his will." And in a violent outburst, one which was very unlike him and seemed to arise from the pain of an open wound, he added: "He destroyed my life! He always opposed my true vocation. He did all he could to tie me down to that hideous office of his, where no one ever knows what goes on between him and his clients. All so hush-hush... shady deals!" And raising his voice: "The contemptible atmosphere you breathe there... all those mysterious exchanges with *Dona* Carolina Amélia's tenants... Uncle Ângelo's habits...!" He quickly lit a cigarette and pulled out the chamber pot to use as an ashtray. "Listen, Uncle Jacinto! For the soul of my departed mother, let me get this off my chest right now! And I promise you that I'll never breathe another word of this again...."

"I forgive my father for the misfortune he brought upon us and for blackening my poor mother's reputation: hers, my sister's, and mine. Carlota became a dejected soul, deprived of her youth, glued to Aunt Henriqueta's skirts and to that stupid piano.... As for me, I go on swallowing the shame of noticing my friends motion to one another when the subject of women of ill-repute comes up!..." He choked back a sob. "She died without my seeing her one last time! without her being able to kiss my sister... left to die like a dog! But what can be done.... Nothing. He was convinced that mother had cheated on him; Aunt Henriqueta is a bitter woman and not on the up-and-up... He thought he was exercising his husband's rights by throwing her out of the house." And harsh, white with anger, he proceeded: "But to persecute that family, and so hatefully! deprive them of the last crumb of property... to get me embroiled in the same hatred they feel toward him and to render our lives this ugly, horrible mess in that lair that yesterday went up in smoke all because of Uncle Ângelo's indecencies!..."

"You're being offensive to God, João!..."

"Yes, yes! It's my father who's stealing her from me! And she's the one I care about! I love *her*...."

Jacinto, his face contorted by pain, put his hand on João's head:

"Let's get some sleep, my boy.... Remember he's your *father*! Come now!... We have to bear the blows life deals us...."

And his plump, still shadow blanketed the body of João Garcia, who had already become quiet under the sheets.

Chapter XXV

A Whalemen's Tavern

"That's game!" said Espadinha, after his docile blue eyes glanced for a few seconds at his cards, displayed in his hand like the pierced blades of a rattler used to scare birds from the vineyards.

"A three and a six!" replied João da Cezilha, spitting on his fingers to separate his own cards.

An old, tall slim seaman, whose skin was as lusterless and wrinkled as a prune, haughtily raised his head and, arching the four of clubs like a roof tile, said in a soft voice that despite its firmness seemed to belie his daring claim:

"A three and a nine!"

João da Cezilha stared at him a little suspiciously; but imparting a jerking movement to his body, by means of which he seemed to pledge life and property, he cried out:

"A three and a twelve!"

"Let's see your cards."

"Huhh?... You've cleaned the table, Uncle Amaro. Of course, with a hand like that, even I could have done it...," said the young man whose only eye was blue. Where his left eye should have been, there was only a lid resembling the cap of a jellyfish, quivering once in a while in its empty, bony socket.

Without saying a word, the old man shot him a contemptuous look typical of those who have the Gospel truth in their souls and enough brute force in their hands with which to back it up. João da Cezilha, separating the kernels of corn used to keep score, agreed with Espadinha:

"Yes..., it's not what I'd call a 'harpooneer's hit.'"

After quietly staring at them for a while, the old man broke his silence:

"Harpooning whale calves like you is a piece of cake. The line won't even foul...."

And looking at João da Cezilha, who as whaling officer was responsible for feeding and maintaining the tension on the line at the bow: "Is it true or not, João, that you cannot be hunted and at the same time keep an eye on the line-tub?"

Despite what might be expected in a game dispute, the losers kept their composure. In the semidarkness of Josèzinho da *Dona* Ana's tavern, the only one on the Campo Raso and São Mateus roadway, their calm and weather-beaten faces reflected their good-natured dispositions. Only the round right earring that Uncle Amaro wore in the American way, scintillated. His curly, fan-like beard, shaped like a load of shot aimed at a flock of sparrows, revealed a few untrimmed bristles.

Silence fell. Moving away from the table, the players sat on a row of boxes lined up in the tavern and yellowed with age and from the rubbing of trousers.

"A lot of fish, Joaquim?" João da Cezilha asked a burly fellow, who had just come in with a jug in his hand.

"What are you talking about! Not a scrap! We cast the net twice.... It came up almost empty, just like a coffee filter that's been cleaned and only a few grounds remain." And switching to his Pico accent, with his *r*'s on the tip of his tongue, Joaquim added: "My boy kept pointing to the empty net: 'Nothing but *prrumbetas* [1], Dad!' But not even that! Just a handful of sticklebacks. A sorry lot to show for the work!"

"There are no more big catches...," exclaimed Uncle Amaro, crestfallen. "That thief of a dredging machine has done away with the fish eggs!"

"And what about the lookout stations? It's been a long time since I've heard a rocket going off or a blast on a conch shell in these parts!" said Josèzinho da *Dona* Ana, shaking the funnel after filling Joaquim's jug with kerosene.

"Either there aren't any whales left in the São Jorge Channel or else Januário has secretly put ground glass in the tube of our

---

[1] *Prombetas* are butterfish.–Trans.

268

station's telescope. That darn bastard does nothing but hide in his warren! Like a scared rabbit...."

"I wouldn't put it past him!" said Espadinha. "Well, Uncle Amaro.... What you'd like to see is a whale like Januário under the tip of your harpoon! That's what I'd call a big catch.... A hundred and twenty barrels–or even more!"

They laughed peacefully, the palms of their hands resting on the boxes. Then the teacher, who had been the last to come into the tavern and was absorbed in reading the ads in the *Insulano*, folded the paper and said:

"Have you heard the court's ordered the seizure of the whale-boats in the boat house? They can't be touched anymore...."

There was a moment of stunned silence. Uncle Amaro clenched his jaw behind his beard, pushed back his wide-rimmed hat, yellowed and gnawed by the sea breezes, and stood in sepulchral silence.

"Don't even say a thing like that, *Senhor* Silveirinha! Seize what! We'll go there right now! We'll break the door down!" And heading for the tavern door, Espadinha grabbed a club that Josèzinho da *Dona* Ana kept on top of a wine cask. "Let's go get them, boys!"

"Wait just a minute!" said Uncle Amaro stepping out to the square and dragging Espadinha back by the arm. "Nobody sets foot outside this place! I'm the oldest harpooneer on this stretch of coast and I've got my pride. A court decision is like a royal decree! They'll dishonor this beard over my dead body!"

"What are we going to do, then?" asked João da Cezilha, slamming the counter top shut. "Are we supposed to let Januário impound our employer's whaleboats and just take it on the chin like fools? I've got six mouths to feed, Uncle Amaro!"

"And I'm responsible for the five children of my invalid son.... I say: nobody leaves this place!"

"Get out of the way, Uncle Amaro!"

On witnessing his officer João da Cezilha's attitude, Espadinha, who for a moment had been deflated by the old man's patriarchal gesture, swelled with courage:

"Let's go, Uncle João! We'll break the door down. Justice, in Pico, is a well-aimed oarlash!"

Defenseless but for his bare, open arms, the old man blocked the main door of the tavern. The wall-lamp reflector cast a glow upon his snow-white beard; his bony figure, notable for that eye-catching feminine earring contrasting sharply with his prominent nose, seemed to be that of Abraham pointing out the chosen path to the scattered people of Israel.

The tavern was full of fishermen arriving from *Dona* Ana's Square, some attracted by the dispute between the old man and Espadinha, others brought there by the news the teacher had spread, and still others by the secret laws that bring beasts and men together when they are faced with a common peril. Then, a heavyset and unfriendly-looking whaleman, who had been observing the scene while leaning, cross-legged and nervous, against a sack of carob pods, walked toward the group of seamen cowering in front of Uncle Amaro, shoved him aside and addressed the undecided company, hollering:

"Real men would pay no attention to a senile fool like this!"

"Out of the way, you scum!"

Gently but firmly pushing *Senhor* Silveirinha aside, who despite his frailty had gotten between him and his adversary, Uncle Amaro grabbed the stocky whaleman by the vest, causing him to do a quick turnabout by the door, almost suspended in mid-air. But the old man was pale, almost out of breath and, feeling tears of anger and wounded pride streaming down to his beard, let go.

There was almost an all-out melee when Roberto Clark, coming from home, appeared at *Dona* Ana's Square.

"Watch out, boys! The English gentleman is coming this way! You ought to be ashamed of yourselves!"

"*Lord*! What's going on?" demanded Roberto.

"You just try hitting the old man, Intavante! I dare you!"

"Be quiet! Get a hold of yourselves...."

Holding his straw hat in his hand, João da Cezilha tried to explain to Roberto what all the commotion was all about. But because he stuttered a little and was interrupted by other fishermen gathered in a circle around them, he only could produce, amid grimaces caused by his efforts, fragments of sentences. "The whaleboats! because of Januário.... What right?"

"To raise a hand against his own skipper! The oldest harpooneer in the entire region!..."

"He was pretty darn near blown away from the deck of the *Alabama* just to come to my father's rescue!"

"All up and down this coast he's respected!... He lost his son at sea when that nursing whale fluke-wagged her calf to death, capsizing the boat, and almost by himself, he brought the crew to safety, rowing, rowing all the way to the landing ramp. And his own son drowned at sea.... Is this any way to treat a man like that?"

Roberto, holding his empty pipe tight in his left hand, made repeated pleas for silence. He insisted that the seizure of the whaleboats and of the contents of the boat house was legally unfounded. Januário had taken advantage of the judge's good faith, forcing Leal to make false allegations and coercing the Avelars to come up with forged declarations and dates having no factual bases whatsoever. As legitimate owner of the whale fishery, the CLARK & SONS firm had retained Dr. Luís da Rosa as its counsel. They were going to win the case. Just because of a few weeks, perhaps days, it was not worth risking the freedom and livelihood of those families by intervening violently.

"If that's the case, it's okay by me," said João da Cezilha. "Your word, boss, is good enough for me."

"*Y-e-s*!..." groaned Intavante.

"I'm gonna smack you one, if you don't shut that trap!"

"What's stopping you?..."

But the atmosphere at the square was not encouraging to troublemakers. Some of the more peaceful fishermen began to break up the circle. Two or three courageous women, who had come near and thereby broken one of Pico's household commandments–the one that says that women should stick to the needle and the loom–continued on their way toward the church. A limping old man wearing sandals went by, carrying a wooden bucket of water on his head. Roberto, acting like a referee after a hotly-contested match between rival teams, lit his pipe and said:

"You should go to your homes now. The boat house will be open in a short while. Trust me."

"The least you could do is let us harpoon Januário, *Senhor* Robertinho, while we wait for the whale-alarm to sound.... We'd be having some fun...."

(Laughter.)

"Leave the man alone!"

"That cheat!"

Before all of them had dispersed, Roberto signaled to João da Cezilha and Uncle Amaro de Mirateca to stay; and also inviting *Senhor* Silveirinha, they entered the empty tavern.

"Gin, Josèzinho!"

"Not for me, thank you. I don't drink hard liquor," said the teacher.

"Why don't you have some wine, then... or beer?"

"Come, *Senhor* Silveirinha...." said João da Cezilha, the white of his eyes moistened with tears, "a drop of gin is good for the stomach!"

"Thanks all the same! But I don't want to drink."

"Bring only three glasses, then," said Roberto.

They sat at the table where the fishermen had been playing cards. In that cozy atmosphere, Roberto repeated and reiterated his reasons for insisting on calm. Besides, for a period of a few days nobody was going to miss the whaleboats. As for whales, the channel was as uneventful as a morgue. For months now, no one had seen a sperm whale spanning his wide-arched spout across the ashen sky; schools of them must be swimming the Gulf Stream right now, with long-tentacled squid clenched in their jaws. And looking beyond the faces of those simple seamen, who testified to the danger of the hunt in Cezilha's round eyes and on Uncle Amaro's scarred thumb, which resembled the head of a blind gull, Roberto was revisited time and again by the Prince of Monaco's words: "'*Lepidoteuthis Grinaldii*'... One hundred kilos of pelagic cephalopoda in the stomach of a cachalot!"

João da Cezilha nodded. *Senhor* Silveirinha had unfolded a newspaper. The old man, his chin buried in his chest, kept quiet. Josèzinho da *Dona* Ana went to get a rocket, cordage, and a grain-sample case and then locked the door behind him.

After a long pause and a discreet draw on his pipe, Roberto asked:

"What kinds of things were kept in the boat house?"

"Four whaleboats, not counting the American one, *Senhor* Robertinho." And counting on his fingers, he enumerated: "Four whaleboats, besides a lot of whalecraft. Twenty main- and four steering-oars... twenty small paddles... four hooks... twelve lances... eight line-tubs... four irons (You've got yours at home, don't you, Uncle Amaro?)."

"And it won't get out of the house.... From now on I'm no longer a harpooneer."

Roberto looked at him with a doleful, almost imploring, expression:

"Come now, what are you saying? What do you mean you're no longer a harpooneer?"

"Just what I said!" Taking his hat off, the old man stood up. "I mean no disrespect toward Your Excellency or the friendship your father always honored me with, nor toward all the Dulmo family.... I remember the day the little girl was born! A family worthy of respect. On my word.... They're nobility; that says it all. Captain Dulmo, *Senhor* Matesinho's father, was the kind of man who could still send a man to the gallows! But Amaro de Mirateca, I don't go back on my word, and these seafaring scoundrels really did it to me. They soiled my beard, and in front of women and children, to top it off. To me, a man who sailed the waters of the Arctic Ocean for a year, those of the Western Ground for three, and the seas of Japan for two years!... I'm one of those men who have a pierced ear!"

"Come on, take it easy!..."

"Uncle Amaro!" said João da Cezilha, bending over the table with the expression of a shipwrecked person, which instantly choked up the old man, his vow notwithstanding: "Tell me something: if the whole crew goes to your house and asks you for forgiveness, won't you reconsider? Will you or won't you? Come on, tell me, for the sake of your invalid son!"

The old man's eyes filled with tears, but he remained unmovable and intransigent. He put his hands in his trouser pockets, stroked his beard and sat down:

"No use trying to butter me up...."

"Leave it to me," said Roberto. "No, not in his home, but right here in the square; you'll ask for his forgiveness right here in public.... I take it upon myself to speak on behalf of all of you."

"In the early evening, *Senhor* Robertinho! That's when the crew gathers together," corrected João da Cezilha. "And if Your Excellency does not mind, I'm the one who'll ask for forgiveness!"

The old man stood up and went to look out the door.

"Did you say... four irons...?"

"Yes, sir, and four spades... four knives... four blinking lanterns...."

"What do you mean 'blinking' lanterns?"

"The type where the light is covered up, you know what I mean? And four compasses... four drogues... four flags for signals... [surprise on Robert's part] yes, sir... the boat-crew's signal... those little flags you stick in the blubber of the harpooned whale when you have no choice but to cut the line...."

"What's your estimation of the value of all that?"

"Some thirty years back," said Uncle Amaro, who, little by little, drew nearer and nearer the table, "a whaleboat was worth ninety milreis; the rest of the equipment, eighty. That's 175 milreis... for a total of 700 milreis.... These days, I don't know. I can't handle the business of the new and old currency; I'm a holdover from the days of the old *patacas*. One dollar equals one pataca...."

"*That's strange!*" exclaimed Roberto in English, as though talking to himself. And looking alternately at the two seated whalemen, he said: "But that's right. The Granary figures are correct."

"Everything has got to be written in the books, unless Januário pulled one of his fast ones.... We are poor souls.... I, for one, can only figure in my head."

"Well, you'll see how everything is going to work out," said Roberto, getting up and paying for the gin. "This is just a little blustering; a little rough weather.... It'll soon be over."

"May God hear you, boss!" said João da Cezilha.

"The sea is our lifeblood.... If we stay on land for long, we can manage a little corn for bread.... I've got a hoe leaning against the wall, next to the fishing pole I use for catching sea bream. But what about cash for soap... for kerosene...? Isn't that right, *Senhor* Josèzinho?"

The owner of the tavern let the three men out, bolted the door, and smiled in the darkness of the square:

"You know that your credit's good here."

"As far as that goes.... Even if I had to sell the shirt off my back!" said João da Cezilha, as he tucked in his pea jacket with his leathery hand.

Someone half-opened the window on the floor above the tavern. A woman's voice sweetly asked:

"Are you bringing sugar, Josèzinho? I'm keeping your tea warm...."

"I've got it right here, Mother!"

Roberto slowly walked away from the square, followed by the two whalemen, who walked a little behind him adjusting the coats hanging from their shoulders.

"It's gotten cold...."

"The wind's blowing this way," said João da Cezilha, turning his thumb like a helm. "It's a northeasterly."

In front of the public fountain, whose spout whistled slightly under the breath of the north wind, the old man bid his colleagues good night and vanished down the lane leading to the launching ramp.

"Good night, Uncle Amaro! I'll see you tomorrow morning in Pedra, okay? And remember we're out of bait...."

But the old man, with his head bent down, continued to walk quietly. Only the sound of his leather-strapped sandals broke the silence of the night.

When he arrived home, Roberto found out from Maria das Angústias that Margarida had gone to bed earlier than usual. She was not sick, only tired:

"'I'm in one of my little moods...!'" (That was *Dona* Catarina's way of putting it.) "And there she is, burning the midnight oil, reading a book...."

Roberto went to his room, started putting loose leaves of paper in his portfolio and straightening out the drawers. A great sadness slowed his movements, and his eyes seemed distant. There was no doubt about it. It was urgent that he accept André Barreto's proposal to allow him to join the firm. That was sure to please his brother-in-law. Only that way could they rapidly counteract the seizure of the whaleboats and restore their credit. Hanging in the balance were his sister's and niece's futures, as well as his paralytic father's peace of mind for whatever little time he had remaining. Besides, the whalemen's very livelihood was also at risk.

But the order which he suddenly discovered in the things he mechanically kept putting in the suitcase as if he were packing to leave–his mountaineering gear, which he had brought from Horta to climb Pico with Margarida (then both of them got stuck there because of Manuel Bana's illness), the clothes and documents he had ordered brought from the Granary–gave him an absurd and vague consciousness of himself. He experienced the particularly strange sensation of realizing he was taking stock of himself, as if his life had become a sailboat that suddenly veers about and which a passenger on a liner, within hearing distance and with binoculars in hand, cannot resist interrogating. It was an impression at once soothing and painful, one which soon turned into the need to put yet something else into the open suitcase, like a beloved book, a jacket....

Looking around the room, Roberto discovered a little volume covered with a dust cloth. Ah! He almost forgot: he needed to return the fiddle to Pedro Folião, who had insisted on leaving it to see whether Roberto could do something about improving its sound. Picking up the screeching tobacco-colored instrument, checking its slack bow and grimy neck, Roberto lightly stroked its strings until he stirred those four notes customarily used by violinists for tuning and from which emerge, like two apples from the same branch, both the art of a Kreisler and the cacophonous strumming of a Folião.

Timidly, he plucked the two sharp chords and then extracted a deep chord. Despite his lack of intention to play anything, a vague and quiet melody began to take shape under his fingers. With some difficulty, he recognized it as some strains from Handel. These were followed by vague, quivering tones which, meandering and unconnected, were destined to go nowhere, like his very thoughts. Then, smiling and softening the tones, he played the *Charamba*, the *Pèzinho*, the *Fayal Chamarrita*, the beginning of a movement from.... No! It wasn't that. He set the fiddle down and thought: "Tomorrow at nine o'clock, when Folião comes by on his mule on his way to the shore, I must return his fiddle."

He cased up the fiddle carefully and again straightened the ends of the flower-patterned cloth that Margarida used to dust the furniture at the Vineyards house. He then put out the lamp and, loading his pipe, sat down to smoke in a darkness broken only by the dim light of the channel.

Upstairs, lying awake in bed and listening, Margarida felt those furtive tunes vanishing into the distance. She put out her candle and soon fell asleep.

Chapter XXVI

An Embroidered Tablecloth

For no apparent reason, Margarida had prolonged her stay in the Campo Raso Vineyards house, although it was true that Manuel Bana still felt weak and seldom ventured out. His overgrown beard took the hard edge off his crafty eyes, and now he wore those sparse whiskers ("my bush," he called them) to occupy his fingers and to underscore his cautious hesitation before trivial tasks: "I'll take care of it...." "Of course." He had lost his healthful color, his self-assurance and his appetite. His sister had offered to take him to Capelo until he recovered. But in the state he was in, the best place for him would be the kitchen in Pasteleiro–helping with the dishes and the rest of the time sitting on the little wooden stool exchanging gossip with Chica. Still, no matter how well the Clarks and Dulmos treated him, a servant is always a servant.

But various circumstances had come together to compel Margarida (who in her soul was more of a convalescent than Manuel Bana was in his body) to allow time to move slowly at the Vineyards house–now almost submerged under a perpetual fog, which rarely made it possible for her to see the hull of any vessel crossing the channel. The sails, soaked and rendered useless, became a blurring outline against the humid and misty mass of that hooded cloak made up of Fayal and Pico, visible from time to time during the year.

Now that the delicate situation holding him there had disappeared, Roberto, citing his ongoing negotiations with the Baron da Urzelina's son about the whaleboats, picked up his suitcase and pipe and departed for the Granary. At *Dona* Catarina's request, Maria das Angústias was in the *charrette* on the pier waiting for the first ferry to arrive from Madalena; she would be picked up by Chico Bana, who had been filling in for his uncle at the quinta. Besides, since Roberto had already left, there was no need for her to remain at the Vineyards as a chaperon. Margarida would be fine staying with Manuel Bana, who was already permitted to chop some firewood in the kitchen or, if dressed very warmly, to go to Josèzinho da *Dona* Ana's tavern to buy candles and sugar as needed. Pedro, who was working in the Granary office as an apprentice clerk of CLARK & SONS, had gotten a few days off from Cousin José de Lemos to go have a little fun in Pico. The curlews were starting to contemplate the marshes with melancholy, their beaks hidden under their brilliant wet feathers. Pedro had oiled and checked the gunlock on the stupendous Winchester that Uncle Roberto had brought him as a present. And despite her deteriorating mental state, Mariana was doing a good job of tending the fire.

One of Margarida's secret joys was assuming sole responsibility for the care of a house. She tied a striped apron over her skirt, put on an old blouse and, in her short sleeves, chopped the collard greens, beat egg yokes to try out a simple recipe, and stirred the slices of wild onions in the frying pan. At other times, tired of tending the fire and cooking, she would send for Espadinha's wife and stay in her room all day, reading and embroidering; or when the fog lifted a little, she would walk along the mountain and seaside footpaths, very often not returning home until night, with strands of her hair blowing in the wind. And if Pedro challenged her, she would go hunting with him, burying her feet in the galingale patches and helping him to suspend from his belt (though so little accustomed to such things) the sad, limp carcasses of dead snipes.

These solitary days and nights probably would not last much longer. With a somewhat brisk northeast wind, the thick fog was beginning to separate into smaller, looser, and progressively higher and more fleeting patches above the burnt rocks and the round sea. The clouds looked like fantastic birds flocking together and enticed into migration by fate. When the sun managed to break through, it revealed, between the ring of Mount Guia and the ridge of Espalamaca, the houses and portions of the streets of Horta. At night, a lively and unreal moon whitewashed the Candelária church tower with a kind of a nun's veil, and the tower seemed set in motion by the eternal cloud patches over the islands' dark-blue skies, as if it were starting to wander with tortured arms over the checkerboard vineyard fields.

The good weather had brought about the promised visit of André Barreto and his sister. As soon as he found out that Manuel Bana was well enough to be at the window, André had rushed to Campo Raso in the hope of seeing Margarida. But the house was still strictly under quarantine, and the conversation between them, like that of boatmen throwing lines from one vessel to another, had not gone beyond the exchange of vague gestures filtered by the tiny windowpanes. By calling attention to himself, even the presence of the poor patient at the window interfered. At times André had to shout, only to have his words swallowed by the fierce wind.

This time, André was accompanied by Clarinha, whose words and face instilled calm. But a little incident in Madalena had marred the joyous excitement of this visit, which had been prepared like a delicate torch-light fishing outing. Bica's little carriage–the "old clunker"–was not waiting for them at the pier as usual: it had left for Campo Raso with Roberto and Diogo Dulmo. André and Clarinha had to wait until it returned and had to accept the invitation to drop in for a brief rest at Father Ávila's home. The priest's niece had brought them sweet ring-bread and vintage Pico wine.

"'Sweet-scented Pico,' in the words of our great poet Almeida Garrett. Did you know that his father was from Fayal?" André showed a tepid interest in that historical note. "Well, he was. The name of Bishop Alexandre Square is an Horta tribute to his uncle, the bishop. And the poet, who was raised in Terceira, where he wrote some of his early poetry, actually preached a sermon at Santa Cruz Cathedral in Graciosa. Devilishly smart! What an honor for the priesthood, had he taken holy orders!..." The priest pulled out his pocket watch: "I'm really surprised! Bica's mule is pretty fast.... Perhaps the delay is because Bidinha decided to take advantage of the carriage and went for a ride with *Senhor* Roberto Clark. It's a pleasure to see them together! They're like two children... They don't even seem to be uncle and niece!"

Disappointed, André kept going to the window to check if they were coming. Finally, Bica showed up, still in time for them to spend a few daylight hours at the Vineyards house.

André found Margarida different. She seemed whiter to him, sweeter and almost ethereal. The sporting affability with which she used to handle any situation between them, for example, one calling for her accepting certain very clear words or some direct or gradual challenges bearing signs of his love for her, had disappeared and been replaced by a solicitous kindness, as if she were still exercising her nurse's role and saw in everything an appeal and a need to help the sick. Margarida asked them about news from Urzelina and whether they had heard from their parents. She asked him to tell again the story of the marriage of *Senhor* Constantino Barreto, heir of Urzelina, to *Dona* Petronilha Teixeira Borges Acompanhado, heiress of Norte Grande.

André Barreto agreed straightaway. But, since Roberto and Diogo Dulmo had gone out to the orchard and Margarida was eager to have her uncle hear the story, she quickened her preparations for tea, lovingly straightened the corners of the tablecloth, and asked Clarinha to help her set up the plates of scones and raisins.

"Let's wait for them, André! Father has already heard the story, but Uncle Roberto hasn't. He's going to enjoy it a lot... He has to hear it. He shouldn't miss it!"

André had assumed the sweet and happy air of a man who makes every effort to please and knows how to wait for something, however long it takes. Moreover, his face acquired the self-gratified joy of those who know they are as indispensable to others as places of repose, those blessed sites from which a fountain suddenly springs. A little suspicious, he looked at Margarida and then at his sister in a childish and almost ironic way.

"My, what a beautiful tablecloth you have, Margarida!" said Clarinha, touching it. "I never saw it in Pasteleiro before...."

"Nor could you have. I embroidered it here at the Vineyards while Manuel Bana was ill. That's what I occupied myself with during those long nights and frightening days!... You can't imagine what it was like!"

"I *can* imagine, dear!... How courageous you were! Even Mr. Warren wrote a long letter to England, singing your praises. He says that, if you want to, we could open a chapter of the Salvation Army right here in Horta.... But what a fine embroidery design that tablecloth has... very unusual. It must be a very difficult stitch to do. But it's a little stained..."

"It's from the disinfectant. I don't even want to talk about it! For a whole day and night we sealed everything in here and the fumigators went on and on... spraying everything so thoroughly that I even thought they were spraying sulphate on the vineyards! I had to go sleep in Josèzinho's house in *Dona* Ana's Square.... But do you know that Uncle Roberto actually played a part in embroidering this tablecloth?..."

"How funny!..."

"Let her talk, Clarinha!" said Roberto, walking slowly into the dining room, followed by Diogo Dulmo. "What I did was select floss silk of different colors for her to make the dove's beak and the branch, which have to be done with the exact same featherstitch, that's all...."

They were leaning over an end of the tablecloth which covered Clarinha's hand. Looking over Diogo's shoulder with some difficulty, but relaxed and with both hands in his pockets, André examined the embroidery work.

"He didn't put in much!..." said Clarinha.

"And what about his taking the carbon paper with those nails of his–they're as delicate as tweezers–what do you say to that?" intervened Margarida, looking over Roberto's strong shoulder with a gleam in her eyes. "You can't imagine what patience and flair he has for these things! Even in Pasteleiro, in the summer, he was the one who always helped me with my knitting. He was my skein-winder... For hours on end... standing on the veranda, without moving his arms! Isn't that true?" And with two fingers Margarida squeezed Roberto's very serious chin, so used to the heat from his pipe.

In silence, and taking advantage of the breakup of the circle, André raised an end of the tablecloth and began to examine the detail on that filoselle dove holding the little branch in its half-opened beak as if startled.

Finally, they pulled out chairs and sat down. Clarinha, in front of her brother, was seated to Roberto's left; Diogo Dulmo, installed at the head of the table, was to Clarinha's left. Pedro sat on the far side of the table–wearing his hunting boots and with his shirt unbuttoned.

"Would you happen to have anything 'substantial' to eat... like a nice piece of pork sausage?..."

"Oh, just listen to you! It's going to spoil your appetite for dinner."

"Come on, I'm so hungry...!"

Margarida opened the cupboard door and checked the shelves. Her movements betrayed her complete happiness; her black skirt swayed to the beating of the lock ring against the cupboard door. Leaning against the kitchen door, Manuel Bana followed her with his eyes. His recent close-cropped haircut and shave made his head look even more cadaverous. He felt a little like the householder hosting his masters.

Placing a plate of cold cuts in front of her brother, Margarida sat to André's left and in front of the cup of tea that Clarinha, making herself at home, had poured for her; then, turning in her chair toward André, she said at once, with that air of a floral games enthusiast that Uncle Mateus Dulmo so admired in her:

"Come on, André! Tell us how it came to pass that your grandfather decided to marry your grandmother!" Speaking very matter-of-factly and fixing her eyes on her uncle, who sat in front of her, she added: "Prepare yourself to listen... (none of it is made up!) how well people in the old days handled something so serious, on which one's whole life depends!"

"No wonder!..." said Diogo Dulmo. "They were sensible... they didn't chase will-o'-the-wisps!..."

"It was really very simple," began André Barreto, who, as a mediate and perfect product of such a union, delighted in his privileged position as a rich heir: "My grandfather Constantino was the second son of the heir José Urbano da Urzelina, 'Captain Urbanino,' as he was referred to. The first son was my Uncle Caetano, who was an invalid.... On Sundays, he rode a donkey to church, and after helping him to dismount, two people had to hold him up by the arms... Despite the fact that there was no hope for a cure (it was a spinal infirmity) and that José Urbano was already eyeing his second son as the possible heir, my grandfather Constantino, who had finished his humanities requirements with a friar in Velas, insisted on going to the seminary...."

"Pardon the interruption, Barreto; but I've already noticed that here in the islands a lot of people go to the seminary," said Roberto, reflecting his English prejudices.

"Used to go at one time...," corrected Diogo Dulmo. "By my day not many young men who went to Angra returned with tonsures, except for Pires, who became curate of Salão; and Chico Goulart and a few others. There are, on the other hand, dozens of defrocked priests. And all of them are perfect scoundrels, I might add. Take Reis, for example..., or that rascal Leal, who's still a nuisance.... Not to mention that bum Januário, *the greaseball!"*

"*Please*, Father...!"

"In Pico, it's quite different; there, we can speak of true vocations. Some even went on to become bishops! Our own João Paulino, for example. Or we may just cite, as another case in point, his brother Father Xavier, who was ordained after he'd become a widower with a houseful of children. Once at the auditor's home, when the bishop was visiting the western Azores islands, Father Xavier is said to have told him: 'And now, Lord Bishop, allow me to introduce my children!' And he presented to the bishop grown men with moustaches... and adult, married women.... And the bishop, despite being abreast of the situation, started, a little self-consciously, playing with the cross on his chest.... It was a pretty sight!..."

"Regarding that..., I don't think my grandfather Constantino had any vocation whatsoever," said André, a little impatient with the digression. "It was probably a way out of São Jorge... to get a change of scenery... At that time, there weren't that many other excuses to leave."

"What do you mean?... What about a little trip to Italy, as you yourself took last year?... What would the old man have said about that?... He could well have afforded it...," said Diogo.

Looking up at the ceiling, André wore a smile of superiority:

"As I was saying... the fact is my grandfather Constantino did go to the seminary. He actually made a name for himself as a theologian and received his first tonsure from Friar Estêvão de Jesus Maria (as he always called him, rising a little from his chair)." André vertically raised a match to light his cigarette and, elegantly blowing it out, returned to the story: "Well. When my grandfather came to Urzelina on vacation, everything seemed to point toward his soon singing the Epistle at the celebration of Our Lady of Victory. There were even rumors about Uncle Caetano, the first born, getting married. (The story gets a little crude at this point; but that's how my grandfather used to tell it, even in the presence of ladies, and no one was more of a gentleman than he! I can just see him, with that thin white moustache... sitting at the storage-room window): 'I'm only an invalid from the waist up,' he would say...."

"Please, André, for God's sake...," exclaimed Clarinha, blushing.

"*Shocking... Shocking!*..." said Roberto in English, forcing a smile.

Margarida, to whom André had omitted the invalid's smutty remark when he first told her the story, made a strong effort not to break out laughing and started to nibble on a handful of raisins.

"As for the identity of the invalid's intended sacrificial lamb, I haven't the foggiest idea. There was no shortage of good family girls on the islands, ready to be used by their parents as piggy banks...."

Margarida seemed fascinated with the unexpected turn that André's story was taking. She admired his casualness: that somewhat morose, albeit fresh and spontaneous, gracefulness that made him such a nice young man. That conclusion, however, like a wise and discreet moral inscribed at the end of a fable, awoke a strange feeling in her–something like the absurd attraction experienced by a hunted creature who suddenly finds relief in receiving the hunter's blast. And it was in this spiritual frame of mind that she, leaning a little toward him, listened to the rest of the story:

"It's even possible that there was no bride at all. Be that as it may, a more rigorous winter saw the passing of Uncle Caetano. And now we have our friend Constantino Augusto Romeiro de Matos Barreto, almost 'Father Barreto,' called to my great-grandfather in the oratory to assume his rights and responsibilities as heir to two majorats. And since his vocation for the priesthood had never been strong and since he enjoyed branding and corn-husking parties, he resigned himself to removing his frock. And now? Get married? He kept dragging out the issue. Captain José Urbanino, seeing his property in good hands, died in peace. My grandfather, then, as if he were seeking advice on buying a piece of long-lasting fabric to make a fine-fitting pair of pants, called the Vicar of Urzelina to him and spelled it out to him in no uncertain terms: he was getting on in years and had to ensure the continuation of the bloodline. Accustomed to living alone since his seminary days, and now that he was totally giving himself to taking care of his cattle and his properties, he stated that he didn't care whether he married a Rosa or a Maria, provided she was from a good family and well-heeled. Did the Vicar know anyone who met those qualifications?..."

Diogo Dulmo, pushing aside his empty cup, leaned back in his chair, enraptured with the story. It even caught Roberto's attention, who was not much given to listening to tales or anecdotes not his own. Holding the pipe in his hand, he kept puffing it and inspecting the singed mouthpiece.

"It was then," continued André, "that someone brought up the name of the heiress of Campo Grande, *Dona* Petronilha Teixeira Borges Acompanhado. She was still a rather youngish widow but apparently quite ugly. They say I look a little like her.... Of course, I don't remember her. Title and property, all belonged to the nice lady, since her first husband, a former navy officer and member of a family of lieutenants of the militia in Topo, was a kind of prince-consort who didn't leave an heir to the throne. My grandfather accepted forthwith the suggestion as a good one, then (and here is where the story gets a little spicy) sent her a bunch of "head-loaves" of bread (the type of loaf with one end shaped like a head, traditional local fare during the Holy Ghost celebrations); and, just a little later, in December, he sent her another present: a basket of camellias and a pair of breeding hogs. It should be said that they had never laid eyes on each other, despite the fact that their properties abutted each other somewhere along Mount Hope: he kept to Urzelina, except when he went shooting wild pigeons at Point Cabreira (a vice I inherited from him...), and she kept busy churning butter in Norte Grande..., a place that is a few hours up those gutted roads that cross the island between two rows of hydrangeas. In sum: some weeks after Christmas, the heiress *Dona* Petronilha sent her regards to the heir *Senhor* Constantino; and, as for that hump on the mule, it was as big around as two cheeses like this..., round ones, the kind they don't make any more!"

Leaning over the table, they all laughed heartily. André, trying to prolong the effect he had created, raised his voice a little in preparation for the grand climax of the story:

"A few months later, they met for the first time at the Holy Ghost celebration in Fajã, like a king and princess meet at the border of her father's realm; and a few days later, they tied that sacred knot without which I wouldn't be here drinking tea right now...."

Another burst of laughter.

"... at least," concluded André, triumphantly, "with this face of mine and with the healthy-minded disposition that God bestowed on me..."

Diogo Dulmo solemnly stood up and embraced him:

"André, with your knack for telling stories, you could make even the dead laugh. I'm telling you!..."

The moral of the story had gotten lost in the colorful details regarding the hogs and in André's tracing a circle in the air with his finger to suggest the shape of the cheeses. Clarinha smiled a little insincerely, feeling somewhat uneasy on account of the possible blow dealt by her brother against the family's reputation, especially in this gathering of Fayalese, who were excellent hosts but also very arrogant about their own genealogy. Margarida was the only one who, looking over Roberto's head at the sea framed by the window, was rapt in sorting out the details of the story, like an ostrich tucking odds and ends under its feathers in preparation for a long trip.

"So what's the story with the whale fishery?" André asked Diogo Dulmo. At Clarinha's request, she and Margarida went out to see the orchard. André's sister did not feel like listening to a business discussion in such a relaxed family atmosphere.

Diogo Dulmo, after a long look at Roberto who, whistling softly, had put an arm around Pedro's shoulders, finally said:

"Since Roberto no longer has any interest in the firm, we accept you as managing partner." And after a momentary frown: "Whenever you want to, we can draw up the papers."

Chapter XXVII

Peopled Solitude

With Margarida's absence and Manuel Bana's departure, the Pasteleiro house sank ever deeper into the solitude of its cedars and its roof shaded by the immense araucaria, which rose like a scaffold between the street lamppost and the rollicking tides. *Dona* Catarina, sitting next to him in her armchair, kept watch over her father. The old man's state of health had stagnated like a small dirty pool hidden in the galingale of his fluffy, downy beard; only once in a while did he take a sip of whiskey and hold the trembling page of a months-old issue of the *Times* in front of his lackluster eyes.

When Pedro arrived with the news that his father, because his son was going home, had decided to stay at the Vineyards house that night, Mateus Dulmo was trying to unstiffen his legs in preparation for leaving.

"Father says that he's decided to make the best of Uncle Roberto's presence at the Vineyards and go speak to Amaro, the harpooneer, and to João da Cezilha about whales and what have you."

"And you, my boy, why don't you take full advantage of your vacation?" asked Diogo Dulmo. "Not enough game?..."

"No, it's not too bad.... I managed to shoot a few turnstones. The woodcocks seem to be in the nesting season right now.... There aren't any around. I had some problems and not enough shot left...."

"Your sister, of course... isn't even talking about returning home," said *Dona* Catarina. "Just to come to the city and see me after that great tragedy, I practically had to go down on my knees and beg her! Her excuse, that she needed many days to leave everything disinfected and in order, is not very convincing...." But her protests were very lukewarm: "Well.... she already turned twenty-one and wants to leave us... who's going to stop her? As they say, she who makes a good bed will lie in it! (Son! please go take those boots off and put on a tie. You look like a wildman!)"

She hid her crossed hands under her shawl and, during the silent moments, lightly swung her small feet, which looked crumpled inside her tight shoes. Old Clark extended his fingers and the fringes of his quilt as he muttered a good-bye to Mateus Dulmo, who shook his hand after having picked up the umbrella to leave.

"Did you see, Catarina, how your father agreed with me?... It's like I say: if Margarida wants to go with her uncle, you should let her. She is a big girl and, as Manuel Bana says, she can take good care of herself.... England is not China. It's a prosperous, civilized land! Here in Fayal, it's what we all know.... Besides, given your financial circumstances.... Let's say that she had a boyfriend, good marriage prospects... well, something tying her to this place.... But, despite some silly rumors, there's nothing at all! On the contrary, it seems that there are no possibilities for her, unless she sets sail and leaves the Point Baixio Grande behind her...."

Dona Catarina kept combing the fringes of her shawl. After going to see her uncle off, she returned to her armchair. The greenish light cast by the lamp on top of her father's nightstand, and her eyes fixed on the small window frames and window-panes gnawed by the sea breezes, said it all. A resignation not strong enough to sap her will was carved into her aged face, on that swollen body that still bore vestiges of elegance, and on her choice of loose-fitting dresses and kerchief brooches made of outdated coins.

Uncle Mateus' visit had been his second or third, each carried out with the same clever purpose in mind. To try to convince *Dona* Catarina, the old man relied little on his arguments; instead, he seemed to draw inspiration from the night, as he stood by the window listening to the sea's murmur which, invisibly circular and blown by a light southwest breeze, beat against the shores of Pico's Point Espartel.

Her desire for tranquility and ostentation had made her want very much to marry Margarida to the Baron da Urzelina's son; but now *Dona* Catarina felt undecided, paralyzed. London? Perhaps.... She had heard so much about the city that she felt as if it was located right next to Horta, on the other side of the channel. In her childhood days, the name of the English capital was often on her father's lips and, whenever a ship arrived, on the tip of his busy pen. Her daughter's princess-like air since she was fifteen, coupled with her brusque peasant ways, flattered *Dona* Catarina's maternal pride. Margarida was as capable of enlivening a corn-husking party in a barnyard as she was of reigning over the festivities on the deck of a destroyer, inspiring half-a-dozen foreign officers to find the most ingratiating ways to show her the ship or to ask her for a dance. And then *Dona* Catarina thought of *Dona* Angélica, the Baroness da Urzelina, who had such strange manners, always said "much obliged," and wore those fanciful hats made by the *Senhorinha* from Velas. Caetano Barreto had been given the purely nominal title of "Baron da Urzelina" on the occasion of the king's visit, in recognition of his important electioneering work in São Jorge. And *Dona* Catarina mentally compared the weak Caetano Barreto, the owner of an entailed estate with a hand still grasping the tail of a plough, with the elegant Uncle Mateus, who had refused ("No... No! That will ruin my signature!") the title of Viscount de Flamengos, a title which was, at least, not ridiculous. (After all, hadn't the majorat of Ribeira been in the Dulmo family back to their fourteenth paternal grandfather? And weren't they full-blooded nobles, descendants of the Flemish captain Fernão Dulmo, "discoverer of a hypothetical island north of Terceira"?)

She recalled the anecdote told about Caetano Barreto, who upon arriving home with the news of his title, had said to his wife: "Attire yourself properly, Angélica! Now you are a *she-baron*...." She then thought of her daughter confining herself to her room for hours and hours after Diogo's long conversations with Roberto and José de Lemos, her daughter who came down from the little towers to receive Uncle Mateus and to give her opinions about the anxiety in the marketplace and also the rumors concerning the pressure Januário was applying on the Avelars and that old cockatoo in Carrasca Well Square. To speak to her of André Barreto apropos of the Granary and the whaleboats was tantamount to forcing her to take piano lessons, something she had always detested. She would then offer irrefutable arguments to try to prove that when the war was over the price of spermaceti would go up and the firm would recover. She proposed numerous schemes to counter their well-founded fears that the whaleboats were immobilized and that the Granary was on the brink of bankruptcy. Regarding her at length, Roberto carefully went on wrapping his pipe tobacco in tinfoil to keep it fresh. Paradoxically, when her uncle expressed his desire to establish closer ties with the firm and advised family cooperation in order to save it, Margarida's spirits would sink immediately, and would somehow work out, with simple arithmetic, that a bankruptcy, no matter how tumultuous, would be the best solution. They would still have full ownership of the Campo Raso vineyards; Uncle Mateus would be able to enjoy a restful old age, and with his fortune intact, he might even be able to help them. For sure, that young lady was a walking enigma! Her "little moods" were a secret and irresistible force.

The possibility of her daughter going to London and working in Dr. Marr's clinic pleased *Dona* Catarina, whose imagination was seduced by the vaguely utopian nature of the project. How chic it would be to know that her daughter was at the center of some European intrigue, with convalescing *ladies*, modern cameras clicking in some park, and, in a matter of a couple of weeks, the impression that all this would make on gatherings at an evening in Horta or in the *garden-parties* in Pilar! But, all of a sudden, she seemed impelled to her feet by a hidden spring in the armchair in which she sat in a state of torpor watching over her paralytic father. A rebellious whisker stuck out from the old man's beard; his scrutinizing eyes were

292

riveted to his daughter. Oh, no!... The blood of sin, never!...
And the image of Ana Silveira, cut off from the world in the
Vineyards house like a plague victim, and that of her mother,
so pretty and unhappy in the somber portrait hanging in the
Granary, sufficed to bring back to her another image of her
absent daughter. All this, however, which was made worse by
Margarida's forced sojourn in Pico on account of Manuel
Bana's illness (a young girl, all alone with a young uncle and a
demented old lady and having to play nurse to a servant!), all
this, which would seem to make her all the more in need to
tighten the apron strings around her daughter, who had been
her right arm in caring for her own father and her moral support on those nights when her husband returned home late and
drunk, now left her somewhat alienated, almost with a feeling
of sublime indifference. And she felt that way because
Margarida, even when she was absent, always rubbed off on
people and brought them out of themselves, just as the proper
balance of wind and calm creates the right atmosphere for life
to genuinely thrive in.

Night had fallen. In the shadow-filled living room of the
quinta, the silhouettes of father and daughter seemed to hover in
the air. As on the night of the storm, a gust shook the girders and
then mysteriously abated. In the distance, a weak moon lit the
Pico crater, whose congealed lava extended down to sea level.
Down the deserted hallways came the sound of Pedro cleaning his
Manchester in the kitchen. *Açor*, old and suffering from whoop-
ing cough, barked in desperation, trying to drag his doghouse.
Installed on the little table in front of the pier glass, stood a
bronze Venus. *Dona* Catarina, benumbed in the folds of her
shawl and in the depths of her armchair, found herself experiencing this strange feeling ("How silly of me, dear God!"): knowing she was there alone with her father but, in the meantime,
abandoning herself to silence as if there were a light in the little
towers and Margarida were about to come down for tea!
"Someone must be coming down the stairs.... Maybe it's the wood-
en steps–they're all worm-eaten and sometimes they creak...."
And raising the backs of her hands to her semi-closed eyes:

"Did you call me, Father?" "No, he's sound asleep... snoring away.... Oh, my legs are killing me!"

"The moonlight is covering the Vineyards all the way to Campo Raso and beyond. The channel is as clear as glass! She'll probably soon be sailing through it... Perhaps never to return...!"

"But I can't bear it.... I just can't! All alone in this desert! Buried alive within these four walls...!"

Chapter XXVIII

Arctic Ocean
(In the Portuguese of Pico: *Ariôche*)

At that very moment Margarida was heading down the cellar stairs at the Vineyards house holding a lit candle stub in her hand. Her father, leaning against a vat, was listening to the story that Amaro the harpooneer was telling, while Roberto, seated on a cask, cleverly kept the old whaleman talking.

"Your Excellency knows what I mean, don't you? Hookers... young men.... I was still wet behind my ears.... Oh, I don't know... I guess I must've been about fifteen. But I got the better of the infection...." And on seeing Margarida, who came down the last steps backward, like a sailor, Uncle Amaro leaned toward Roberto and whispered in his ear: "(Our midshipman, Bob, from *Nantaque,*[1] is the one who administered the medications, which was so charitable of him....). Well, my shiny pearl! You are coming to hear the old man's tales too? Well then... I was telling your uncle and your father here that I started whaling way before going to the physical for the service.... I still played with tops once in a while. If only I had a *pataca* for each time my father caught me playing with my top as I tried to hide from him, I'd be as rich as *Senhor Altre*[2] Bensaúde! Those were the good old days! And we showed respect for our elders...! If you belonged to a whaling crew, you asked the captain or skipper for his blessing, as you do today only to your father and mother... if at all!

"The authorities had just seized a French brig that was trying to catch whales and chowder fish on our coast. I can still see the

---

[1] From the English *Nantucket.*–Author.

[2] *Walter.*–Author.

boat: squat, high in the prow; *Denis* [3] was the name. The guard said: 'I'll hand it to the highest bidder!' And a bearded man who was there kept upping and upping his bid. The others kept trying, but he always offered more. Then the guard counted to three and handed it to him. The man seemed to be rich; he wore nice clothes. But it was the kind of fancy boat that not everybody could afford. That's why a group of men from Horta and Flores formed a society and then hired a boat crew.

"I went to see my father at the launching ramp and told him: 'The brig is going to set sail tomorrow morning for the coast of America and the captain asked me to go. Will you let me?' 'I won't stop you. But you know the guards are always on the lookout for young men who try to escape, and there's still a long time before you get called up for service... If you get caught, I'm gonna give you the beating of your life!' I ran home as fast as I could and told my mother to pack my clothes and throw in some food for the trip. 'What are you going to do, you scamp?'

"My father was waiting for me out at the point of the pebbly beach and handed me a *pataca*: 'That's for the trip.' And he pulled out a relic that he always carried sewed to the hem of his shirt and put it around my neck." Uncle Amaro leaned forward a little and showed a little brass cross, all bent and dirty: "It's still here.... And I told him: 'Give me your blessing, Father!' 'May God be with you, my boy!' And, scuttling by way of the shore cliffs so they wouldn't see me from the pier, I headed for the brig!"

Margarida had glued the candle to the top of a wine cask and, with her arms crossed and her head leaning forward, listened... and listened... now looking at her father, now at her uncle, her chest rising and falling.

"The brig must have been the *City of Horta*," said Roberto, who knew almost by heart all the old books in the Granary since the time of his grandfather, old Roberto. "A seized brig was registered under that name in 1857. The French captain was tried in February; the new owners ordered repairs made and sent

---

[3] *Adonis.*–Author.

the ship to America to be fitted out as a whaler. Judging from your words, Uncle Amaro, you were part of its crew.... The *City of Horta* started whaling in July."

The old man, stunned, kept nodding:

"Your Excellency really knows his stuff! Things that happened some sixty years ago!..." Margarida looked at her uncle with a sweet expression in her eyes. Diogo Dulmo, always silent, gave the cask spigot a turn to fill two glasses with wine. The old man returned to his interrupted story: "And then those things that I was telling your uncle and father about happened to me... do you understand, miss? I suffered a lot... went through hell! Misfortunes...!" Margarida thought of asking Uncle Amaro to repeat "those things" for her; but she felt far away, as if enchanted, and her dreamy smile penetrated the old man's eyes with the precision and effect of a bee pollinating a flower. Uncle Amaro, holding the glass and inhaling the wine's fragrance, resumed his story: "You suffer a lot at sea, but you learn more than you do in school! I'd always gone around in rags, and my mother had a hard time finding any clothes for me to take. Clothes?... What am I saying!... Rags! It's true that I spent more than a year feeding firewood into the trywork by the foremast. Each one of those trypots took 36 gallons of oil! The stench of the whale blubber almost made you throw up.... It stank like rotten pork! But I got used to it.... One day the captain called me to the quarter-deck and said: 'You, Portagee! I need a man to work at the line-tub, *charape!* [4] I want you to do it....' Then I worked for a while here in Fayal aboard a schooner called the *Witch of the Seas* (and the damn boat really seemed bewitched!), and it was then that I harpooned my first whale, a cachalot that produced some ninety barrels, so big you couldn't move it on dry land.

"The *Gazelle* then showed up at our island and there I was already married with a mess of kids and with my mother to support (the schooner had caught very few whales... it must've been bad luck because of its name!), so I decided to get a job

---

[4] From the English *shut up*.–Author.

that paid more. Now that was a good job! Good food! Beautiful schooner! With all its sails unfurled, it looked like a royal brig!..."

A direct breeze coming in through the cellar cracks bent the candle flame; the old man's unkempt beard, seen through the transparent glass which he held by its ends and covered with his trembling hand, had a fiery glow.

"I drink to you gentlemen's health and that of the miss! Her eyes are exactly like those of her grandmother, the daughter-in-law of old *Senhor* Roberto, may God keep her soul.... She had the prettiest face on the whole island!"

Margarida, remaining very still, smiled. Roberto, putting his hands in his trouser pockets, rhythmically tapped the floor with the tips of his heavy boots.

Then Diogo Dulmo, who was getting tired of Amaro de Mirateca's seafaring tales, posed some questions to him, in hopes of filling certain lacunae in the Granary record books:

"Listen, Uncle Amaro: didn't the *Gazelle* also fish for cod?"

"Yes, sir, it did. I, too, sailed the Bank, right outside St. John's of Newfoundland. And Greenland, too, more than ten degrees to the north, almost in the region of the ice floes... It was nearly always at night, but with a little moonlight... like a reflection from a clay oven full of wheat bread.... Six months of *Ariôche* are like twenty years here. It even surprises me that my hair didn't turn greyer than all that falling snow!"

"I remember seeing the *Gazelle* whalehunting right outside Point Espartel," said Diogo. "I was about to get married. I guess it was the only whaler still sailing the channel. But Uncle Mateus, he still remembers the *Alabama* chasing other American whalemen."

"Me, too! Very close to land. Those bastards tore at you like wild dogs, armed to the teeth! Yeah, but I did one of them in. I lay in wait for him behind a hatchway, and when he was about to grab José Pequeno from Lajes, I cracked his skull open with my *chipeira*.[5] The captain entered the incident in his logbook,

---

[5] From the English *cutting-spade*.–Author.

just like Josèzinho da *Dona* Ana enters the names of his debtors, even though the comparison isn't that good.... And it was no big deed on my part. Was I just going to stand there and let him kill José Pequeno? That's when they tied my hands and feet and whipped me right on the deck. *Alabama*...! Just at the sound of the name we all started to shake... frozen with fear!"

"Those whalers you worked in were the last of their kind, weren't they, Uncle Amaro?"

"Practically... The seas were empty of whalers for a long time... The *Argo*, the *Gribalde*,[6] the brigs, the schooners... all of them sunk or just doing easy jobs! The *Júlia*, for example, ended up transporting oranges from São Miguel to England...."

"I know! My father-in-law's father was one of the co-owners of the *Júlia*. Her captain even brought him tea from Southampton. All that is recorded in the Granary record books...."

"Just imagine, *Senhor* Dioguinho, what it all came to! Deep-sea schooners, almost *south-seaman*, carrying oranges like a train of stupid donkeys from Graciosa. The wreckage of some of them even washed ashore, a pitiful sight!..."

Roberto paced back and forth the full length of the cellar, stopped in front of all the casks, and lightly tapping them with his knuckles, extracted a kind of carillon-like sound from those not completely full. Now that he had given up on the crazy idea of becoming a co-owner of the whale fishery, those whaling yarns had the impact of an adventure novel, of a kind of magical music played offstage.

"Not bad.... Not bad.... The *Gazelle* continued to sail," said Diogo, starting to hum.

"Yeah, the boats did what they could.... Still, they had to be made worthy to sail in the high seas. The rest were all lateen-rigged whaleboats between 30 and 37 feet.... The first that came from America was bought by José Constantino from Flores–still from the time of my Uncle Raivinha, who got whale-hunting into my blood. He used to tell me about his adven-

---

[6] *Garibaldi.*–Author.

tures, sitting on the shank of a beached boat anchor, paralyzed with rheumatism.... My mother always blamed him: 'If it hadn't been for your Uncle João Raivinha, that big bag of wind, you wouldn't have had the misfortune of going to the high seas!... Look at your father! That man, he was an incurable sea dog, but he never abandoned me....'

"Let her talk!... But the other seamen knew nothing, so to speak... not even how to hoist a sail, except for my father, and others like him. What am I saying! Begging your pardon, miss, those who never sat their asses on a bench beside an oarlock lined with a bunch of dry grass used for matting and never had to dip a fifteen-foot oar into the water while a whale floats by like a plank and the men with their hearts in their throats don't know what whaling is all about. We are the ones who taught the art of whaling to that rabble from Lajes and Calheta de Nesquim, who before had done nothing but catch sticklebacks and easy fry..."

"And were there many whaleboats in Fayal by then?" asked Roberto, still pacing back and forth, like an infant who nods off, wakes up, and falls asleep again.

"Maybe fifty of them," said Amaro. "Let's see, master... *Senhor* Manuel *Dabne*[7] owned one in Porto Pim, two in Ribeirinha, two right here in São João..., three in Cais. *Senhor Altre* Bensaúde owned one in Porto Pim and eight in Cais. But what you're interested in are the ones from Fayal, right? Well, *Manel* da Costa Nunes owned two in Varadoiro and two in Salão; João Silveira, two in Cedros. Here in Pico, it's really impossible to count... there were so many. The owners included the Maciéis in São João... José *Anriques* in Ribeiras... Anselmo and João Machado in Calheta de Nesquim.... In Santo Amaro, there was the Santo Amaro Society of Whalemen. But most of the boats were in Lajes: *Manel* Faustino, Lauriano, *Manel* Brum and several others.... All of them on shares. Fifteen whaleboats aground and all lined up next to each other made a beautiful sight!... But now, everything's changed!... The goddamn kero-

---

[7] *Dabney*.–Author.

sene or petrol, or whatever you call it, ruined us... did everything in! And I ask you, gentlemen, if the whale-oil lamps didn't stink a lot less than the ones today and weren't more delicate. For the poor, the oil was a fortune. It was as plentiful as water in the earthen pot: all you had to do was pour it into the lamp! My poor mother earned a pretty penny making thread wicks. They lasted longer.... Now?... You can't even make enough to buy groceries in the *marqueta*!" [8]

"What about the lays?" asked Roberto. "Did all the boats follow the same practice?"

"It all depended. In Flores and Corvo, after they took out the owner's half, they divided the rest into equal parts with two shares for the harpooneer. In Fayal, three shares for the officer, two shares for the harponeer, and one for each oarsman. We in Pico counted everything in barrels: out of every fifteen barrels, the officer got one, we got half, and the oarsmen each got one of every fifty. As far as the shares for the Holy Ghost and St. Peter, both got as much as the oarsmen: a barrel for every fifty. Miss, haven't you ever heard the priest say, 'Peter! cast your net to the sea and leave the fish up to me....' Well!... What he meant by that was that, in the end, faith is what saves us!"

"You're right, Uncle Amaro! Faith... and Hope!" When she spoke with the common people, Margarida, almost unconsciously, found herself imitating their way of talking: "Have you ever seen those framed pictures you hang on the wall showing three girls with straight hair hanging down to their shoulders, each wearing a different colored robe...?" The old man kept gravely shaking his head.

"At the bottom of the picture there is a heart, an anchor, and a cross. The cross represents Faith; the anchor, Hope... the picture belongs to the Sea Brotherhood... Uncle Amaro, why don't you give me a boat anchor as a gift?..."

Diogo Dulmo's face was filled with childlike surprise; Roberto, with his head lowered, looked somber. The old man, turning his beard to the moonlight, looked like Father Time.

---

[8] From the English *market*.–Author.

"A boat anchor? And why not! You're very young, miss, but you say very wise things that really leave me dumbstruck."

"You're right, Uncle Amaro... I'm kind of crazy. A boat anchor is much too big, but bring it, anyway!... If you promise me you won't miss it, please bring it!... It's for my schooner, the *Witch of the Seas*.... It's to ward off the evil eye. How many grandchildren have you got, Uncle Amaro?"

"Six born to my daughter Maria and five belonging to my invalid son. It's very hard to earn one's daily bread to feed all those mouths! You know, that's all they've got to eat–a piece of bread in one hand and another piece in the other, poor things! Around Christmas, when he saw me going out to sea, my grandson Lauriano asked me: 'What's the Child Jesus gonna bring me this year?' 'Shut up, boy!...,' says his father, lying in his bed (who, thank God, knows how to discipline his son): 'You're always bugging your grandfather!' My son was feeling ashamed in front of me; he's not gotten out of that bed in ten years... his legs look as skinny as dried sticklebacks... not being able to earn a dime, poor son!... I left the room 'cause I thought my heart was gonna break.... Christmas Eve arrived. Since my son hasn't left his room in ten years and because ever since my better half died I don't enjoy anything, I didn't even go to midnight Mass.... I just sat down on the *tabranaclo*,[9] and started to think... and think.... I'd bought a few yards of striped calico at Josèzinho da *Dona* Ana's (on credit, of course) to make handkerchiefs, a gift for the grandchildren.... I called my grandson Lauriano and sat him right here on my knees, holding in my hand the handkerchief I was gonna give him: 'Here, my boy! So you won't go around with a runny nose....' 'Look here, Grandfather! See what the Child Jesus brought me!...' And he pulled from under his arm a toy whaleboat made of boxwood, with its keel, its rigging, and everything! His father had made it with his penknife.... He'd kept it hidden under his bed covers for

---

[9] *Tabernáculo* or *estrado* is a wooden platform built in the window opening of the main room of the poor houses, the room itself being called "middle of the house."–Author.

weeks and weeks!... He didn't want his little daughter to see it! It looked like a real whaleboat sailing out of the channel under a good wind!"

Uncle Amaro's eyes filled with tears.

"Bring Lauriano here!" said Margarida, tucking in her blouse and picking up the little that was left of the candle stub. "But bring him tomorrow, without fail! I want to give him some hand-me-downs from Pedro. The pants will probably look a little baggy on him...."

"That doesn't matter...."

"... Pedro had a big backside.... And he's going to be upset when I tell him! But I can handle him...."

Deeply moved, the old man tried to kiss her hand, the one not holding the candle. But Margarida was already hurrying up the gangway stairs as if it were an endless stairway leading to some tower, and soon vanished into the interior of the house. Diogo, Roberto, and the whaleman, taking advantage of the moonlight that came in through the cellar lucarnes and lit up the shaft and joist of the winepress, blazed a trail through the casks out of the wine cellar.

Chapter XXIX

Barcarole

Diogo Dulmo gulped down his cup of tea to try to catch the first morning ferry from Madalena to Fayal. Margarida had been insisting that her father eat something: bread and butter, or sausage and eggs, his usual breakfast. She bantered with Mariana, who was having trouble lighting a damp match to start the heather fire. Margarida blew on the fire until her cheeks turned red, trying to melt the lard in the frying pan before her father was ready to leave. But Diogo Dulmo only ate a few left-over scones and, after fastening his watch chain, left. Roberto also had gotten up early and had gone for a walk down to *Dona* Ana's Square. He was going to return to Horta in the afternoon, perhaps on the ferry or, if there was a breeze, in his launch.

It was an uneventful morning, both around the house and in the skies. Toward dawn the southeast wind had died down, and the sea, a little choppy along the shoaled coast, now stretched out its calm, gray waters to the north of the channel.

Margarida was leafing through a knitting catalog that Daisy had loaned her when she heard a blast echoing from the direction of Candelária. She thought aloud: "It's a rocket." But upon reflection, she said to herself: "It *can't* be a rocket. The whale-boats were seized; no one can enter the boat house. And most likely the lookout men used the time off to go and visit their families.... They spend so little time at home...." But another strong powder blast was heard, followed two or three seconds later by the loud and clear explosion of a rocket from the direction of Espalamaca. Margarida ran to the window in time to see the plume of smoke vanishing in the cottony sky.

Could it be?... Opening the window, she looked over the parish's little houses for some kind of confirmation. The smoke from the pots cooking collard greens rose from the chimneys. The clock in the tower of the Candelária Church struck the first hour of noon. There was no one on the streets or in the lanes, except for two barefoot children squatting down looking for black leeches in the mud. But suddenly a door half opened, and then another, and another, and in the twinkling of an eye men and women poured out of their houses and crowded the footpaths and lanes.

"Look over there! *Baleia*! *Baleia*!... "

"*Blós*! *Blós*!" [1]

"Mariquinhas! Have you seen my man?...."

There was no doubt now: it was the century-old signal, the lookout man's rocket and the bonfire on top of Pico do Calado. Soon the pebbly beach would be filled with people–the humble but determined poor people of Areia Larga and São Mateus, simple little offshoots of the three main towns comprising Pico, just like Judea, Galilee, and Samaria, the main branches of the villages trod by the Nazarene. Courageous and simple people, mild of speech and manners, oblivious to everything and everyone save the cry of "*Blós*! *Blós*!"

Fast as lightning, Tromba whizzed by sounding his trumpet. From far away came the piercing sound of a conch shell.

"Look, Bidinha, look! See that? An *espalmo* [2]... toward Point João Dias," said Espadinha's wife.

Margarida looked in vain, then hurried home and quickly returned with Roberto's binoculars. Holding between her teeth an end of the little red kerchief she had wrapped around her neck, she adjusted the focus.

"Not that way!... A little closer to land, more to leeward.... A really high spout. What a huge sperm whale! It's two!... Two!... They're blowing off steam! They're feeling threatened; it's a school. They must've passed right in front of the Salão lookout station.... Maybe the Cais whalemen are already on their trail!

---

[1] From the English *Blows*! Among Azorean whalemen, the term alternates with *Baleia*! (Whale) when a cetacean is raised.–Trans.

[2] From the English *spout*.--Author.

We really could do without them, those greedy bastards! I hope our men get there first!... Where's my man?"

"Are you crazy? Don't you know the judge ordered the whale-boats seized, and they can't be taken out of the boat house?"

"And you think we're gonna let a good chance like this slip by?... It's been months since my husband harpooned a whale! And there's no chowder fish on the coast, either... If he hadn't sold boatloads of firewood and worked in the fig distillery, we'd have starved to death!"

"Please be patient... It'll just be a few more days. The judge promised *Senhor* Mateus Dulmo that he was going to reverse his decision. We've enough to pay our debts, thank God! But until the judge gives his permission, nobody can come close to the door of the boat house. These are serious matters! Do you want to get in trouble with the law?"

A man went running by:

"Hurry up, Piedade! Bring down to the ramp a bag with some bread and my *froca*.[3] We're putting out to sea."

Espadinha's wife had already started off, her sandals raising clouds of dust a distance down the road.

"Where are you people going?" cried Margarida, running home to get a coat and then hurrying after Espadinha's wife: "Piedade! Piedade! Wait for me!..." The wind blew her red ker-chief and a lock of her hair; her quick steps were like springs on the dark and rain-soaked road. "Piedade! (Oh, my God, the woman is crazy!) Wait for me, woman!..." And seeing a group of boys coming from the direction of *Dona* Ana's Square, she asked them: "Did you see the English gentleman? Please, one of you go call him at Josèzinho's tavern! (These people have lost their minds!...)"

But Roberto had already gone by on his way to the boat house. With Intavante leading the pack, the fishermen had rammed with their shoulders the wide double door. At the third try, it gave way as easily as an orange peel yields under the pressure of two fingers. And in the twinkling of an eye and despite

---

[3] From the English *frock*, but meaning 'shirt.'–Trans.

the commotion and shouting, boats and crews were ready and at their posts.

The boat house was a wide, low building with bare stone walls, a triangular façade, and a glass lucarne right on top of the door supported by almagra-stained jambs. Tufts of grayish lichen grew between the stones of the end walls, and a kind of leprosy or yellow rust spread over the pure lava arrises. Not all the whale fisheries could afford storing their boats in a dry and protected building; but old Clark, who had been to Nantucket and was not to be outdone by the fine tradition started by Samuel Dabney, had built that huge stone box resembling, at once, a life-saving station and a Noah's ark run aground. The better to move the boats, cement keelgutters had been built from the doorway down to the launching ramp.

Of the four whaleboats owned by the fishery, one had cracked floor timbers and most of its support beams missing. Despite having its cracks caulked and pitched, it still took in water. As João da Cezilha put it, you could see the sky through the holes... Another, an older model, also had a leak in the bow. With its stern post broken, it was also missing two beams and some wooden plugs. And so, besides the little launch bought in Flores with André Barreto's money, which awaited, tied in the dock, the final permission signature at the office of the new corporate office, there was the whaleboat built by the Santo Amaro boatyard (this one in excellent shape and, according to the whalemen, "as smooth as a top"), and another whaleboat, much weather-beaten by the high seas but still swift and solid, with its rim half an inch above the water, all in pitch pine and susceptible to taking in a lot of water.

The crew of the two damaged whaleboats attempted to launch them. Feeling sorry for the others, Intavante, the officer of the still-usable one, tried to solve the problem by plugging the cracks with chunks of cork and pieces of oilcloth; but given the size of the holes and the urgency of the situation, he gave up. Demoralized, with the sterns of their sorry-looking whaleboats already in the water, the crewmen let their arms fall in a gesture of defeat.

"Rot in hell, you blasted boat!" And using the grip of a steering oar, he struck a hard blow against another oar.

When Roberto arrived in front of the boat house, the two whaleboats and their crews were already braving the swells. The whalemen's foolish bravado, the cries of *Baleia! Baleia!*, and the clacking of the women's wooden clogs had combined to send Roberto into a mild fit. As he ran, his cap blew off. Hurrying to the very edge of the water and spitting oaths much like those of Uncle Amaro de Mirateca's, he yelled out:

"*Come back, John!* Return to shore right now! You s. o. b.! You scoundrel.... Do you want to ruin your lives?"

Standing on the stern of the last boat, João da Cezilha gestured, his arm signaling:

"It's two sperm whales!..." and he raised his right hand in a V-sign. "Two big *espalmos*... Moving towards the northeast!..."

His voice was drowned out by the wind blowing towards Point Espartel, the same direction in which the boats progressively moved, impelled by strong oarstrokes to the chant of "*Pulaiéte! Pulaiéte!* [4]"

"Let them go, *Senhor* Robertinho!" said an idle fisherman, one of those who preferred shellfishing and remaining in the taverns drinking while the others were out deep-sea fishing. "The men won't even have to leave the channel. The whales won't go very far.... I saw the first one sounding before I heard the rocket, close to Point Ribeirinha... at a distance of three hundred fathoms...."

"Just my luck!" murmured Roberto, staring at the whaleboat's wake and ignoring the seaman's words.

"What they're doing is preventing the boats from being seized by taking them to Velas...." said the limping old man who earlier had been seen carrying the bucket of water, as he adjusted the thong of his rawhide-sandal. "And I don't blame them one bit!... They shouldn't let those thieves rob them of the bread they've earned with the sweat of their brow! Dirty thieves!"

---

[4] From the English *pull ahead.*–Author.

308

Roberto gave the old man a look of disapproval and surprise. As there was no time to lose and noticing the Granary's launch tied with a girthline to a half-buried cannon, with a killick suspended from the stern reel cable, he quickly gained the small dock, untied the line, and jumped into the little vessel, which lurched to one side like a nutshell. He then cranked the reserve engine and started off after the fugitives.

Meanwhile, Margarida arrived from the direction of Campo Raso, all wrapped up in her knit coat, and leaping from boulder to boulder, she yelled out, trying to make herself heard by her uncle:

"Robert! Robert!... Uncle, wait for me! (Oh, my God! Everybody's taken leave of their senses....)"

"Calm down, miss! You'll slip and fall... The English gentleman shouldn't bother at all.... They aren't gonna get very far."

"Bite your tongue! We've got to bring them back, no matter what! Get me a boat! I'm going to get them.... I'm sure I'll bring them back! João da Cezilha won't disobey me.... He was driven to do this.... Robert! Robert!..."

Standing on a boulder with her skirt billowed by the wind, Margarida surveyed the channel. The launch was heading straight for the whaleboat in front. But its engine began to falter, robbing the small vessel of its usual projectile-like momentum. In turn, the whaleboat had hoisted its heretofore hidden sail in order to catch a favorable wind and started veering in the direction of Areia Larga and then maneuvering towards the mouth of the channel on the way to Ribeirinha. The second whaleboat, João da Cezilha's, had fallen behind, and first backwatering and then tracing a wide circle with its stern, returned to port, heading straight to the boulders where Margarida had stopped. João da Cezilha began waving his arms.

Margarida still tried to make out what he meant and pointed towards the boat house at the end of the mooring area, where the tide, slowly and indifferently, kept emptying its lapfuls of water. Finally, she realized that João da Cezilha's gestures were meant for someone standing behind her. Turning around, she saw Uncle Amaro de Mirateca walking at a hurried clip. In a moment, the old man was standing next to her on the boulder.

"Help me, Uncle Amaro! See if you can bring them back...."

But nearly out of breath, Uncle Amaro could not utter a single word. His rapid, labored breathing made his beard move the way a rough sea causes a vessel to rock, and his large ingenuous eyes scanned the horizon.

At that moment, João da Cezilha's whaleboat was almost touching the boulders that formed an ideal little bay resembling the pincers of a spider crab.

"Come aboard, Uncle Amaro!" said João da Cezilha. "We can't let a school like that get away...."

"You're really doing a fine job!..." answered the old man, stern and enigmatic. "Let's see how it's all going to end up...! You can't say I didn't warn you... But you just couldn't stop yourselves, could you? Now... it's in God's hands!"

"Give me your hand, Uncle Amaro!" said Margarida decidedly, as she rolled up her skirt.

"Where do you want to go? Please forgive me, miss! But you're out of your mind!..."

"You're the one who is out of your mind, João! It's not my fault.... Since you don't want to do what I tell you, I want to go and join my uncle! I'll get into the boat... and we'll head for Porto Pim! At least from Pasteleiro you can't see the jail bars, which is where the harbor master's assistant will soon be taking you, like smugglers, and you'll be forbidden to dock at any port! That's what's going to happen! Come on! Give me your hand!"

As soon as the whaleboat drew near, the old man grasped the gunwale and, as much as his position allowed, turned to face Margarida with wounded surprise and the air of one who is under the spell of a siren's song. He let himself slip into the water, trousers rolled above his knees, grabbed the young woman by the waist, and a little bent by exertion, placed her in João da Cezilha's arms like a trophy. Then he himself climbed aboard. The maneuver, despite the security afforded by the little rock-bordered bay, had to be executed in a hurry to take full advantage of the swells. But the old man, full of resolve and vigor despite his almost eighty years, performed his feat as easily as a youth. Lithely, Margarida gained the stern and positioned herself behind the boatmaster. Laying hold of their oars, the whalemen took their first powerful stroke.

Sailing close to the wind and aiming towards the open sea, the first whaleboat left behind the long sandbank known in the charts as Chapman's Rock, or "the Rock." Roberto's launch, in hot pursuit of the whalemen, had started drifting towards the shore and was now moving within the shadow of Pico off the coast of Pé do Monte. The little engine must not be working well, for a few moments after the boat yawed, one could make out Roberto's silhouette hunched over the steering wheel and then his brusque movements in an abortive attempt to restart it. Anxiously, Margarida watched him stand with his hands on his waist and his arms arched out like wings. Concentrating her full, undivided attention in that direction, she could almost hear him sighing with exhaustion and cursing in English.

"Row more towards the coast!" yelled Margarida. "The launch isn't moving! The engine must be stalling...."

But the whalemen, their eyes fixed on the other whaleboat, which had already rounded Point João Dias, rowed on and on like desperados. João da Cezilha, pounding the mast to disentangle the halyards, already had a large bundle of cloth in his arms, which prompted one of the whalemen to joke:

"Eh, João, is that a baby you're carrying?"

Now the launch's engine seemed to have restarted, and Roberto was traveling, a little against the current, in the direction of the whaleboat carrying Margarida, whom he had just spotted. The wind had picked up considerably; and the waves, growing taller and faster, seemed to be testing the solidity of the dock's thick walls, like a railwayman inspecting the wheels and couplings of an express train about to leave the station and then proceeding toward the tunnel with the flag rolled under his arm. High on Espalamaca, the weather watchman had already hoisted the sign for rough weather: a kind of large funnel with its spout facing downward. But the southeast-northeast winds, fierce up to now, seemed ready to give way to a milder southeast wind. The weather watchman's pole stood dry and bare against the sky.

"Lower that sail, João! Uncle Roberto can't catch up with us... Oh, my God!"

Uncle Amaro, his foot resting on the *lagaiéte*[5] and his forehead showing wrinkles caused by the cry of *Whale in sight!*, turned his head and said:

"Can't you hear what Miss Margarida is saying, João? Wouldn't it be better to throw out a cable and tow the boat in our wake?"

But João da Cezilha, excited about the maneuver, continued on almost at full sail; the launch, even though falling farther and farther behind, seemed to be holding its own. Margarida, lulled by the exhilaration of wind, sails, and water and by the prospect of seeing a whale, was carried away in the moment. Certain maneuvers caused the whaleboat to heel, its rim skirting the fresh, live waters of the sea. The Azorean clouds, at first hanging in pairs–

> *Clouds, copper-colored and still*
> *harbingers of an approaching storm–*

now broke up into light, fleeting wisps, as if Pico were a basket of feathers blown by the wind. From the land came a pungent smell of fig tree and a whiff of hot lava.

Towards São Jorge, as a beautiful rainbow emblazoned the horizon, João da Cezilha, turning toward Margarida with the expression of a child caught red-handed, slyly remarked:

"Ahn, miss? Look at the Old Lady's Arc[6]... It means you're very lucky on your first whale hunt!

> *With an early rainbow, it's hard to remain afloat;*
> *with a late one, you'll fill your boat.*

And don't you be scared!... *Senhor* Robertinho is almost within hearing distance.... And you're very safe here with us."

---

[5] From the English *loggerhead*.–Author.

[6] *Arco da Velha* or 'Old Lady's Arc' is a popular expression for 'rainbow.'–Trans.

A voice resounded over the beautiful green sea that seemed like her own backyard, and reached her ears in the whaleboat bought with family money. Coming from that gigantic, hairy man, a man as docile as a child or a Tiberias fisherman, that voice seemed to issue from another world, from the depths of memory and life, as if Maria das Angústias or Mariana do Pico were singing lullabies to her. And Uncle Roberto, lost aboard the slow little launch that could not even be seen anymore, seemed a throwback to the time when a letter from London, stamped with the likeness of George V, brought the family news of his arrival. Sitting on the skipper's bench of a Pico whaleboat, her back turned to Campo Raso, Margarida had the impression that she was sailing on the ship of Captain Fernão Dulmo, her Flemish forebear, heading toward the ghost of a hypothetical land all enveloped in hot mist and lying in the proximity of the Fortunate Islands.... Far behind and smoking his pipe, Uncle Roberto sailed on another ship from the Dulmo fleet.

The first whaleboat blindly followed the invisible school of whales. João da Cezilha's crew, with Uncle Amaro at the bow poised like a discus thrower, doubled the efficiency of the sails by rowing like galley slaves. As if in a film, the night of the hurricane projected itself upon Margarida's mind, and in her mind's eye she saw her father in his overcoat walking along the wall of the quinta; her father reading the letter from England by the light of the old kerosene lamp, laying plans for Uncle Roberto's arrival; then, her project to rearrange the furniture and knick-knacks in the Granary to accommodate their guest... the bell ringing downstairs... the torrential rain pouring on Jewel's ears as he waited outside... nobody... then her father and the *Typhoon's* ship almost went down in the China seas....

They probably could already see the roof of the Granary, make out its windows.... Margarida, returning a little to reality, remembered the points of reference for that crossing, so familiar to her since childhood that she felt almost capable of attempting the crossing by herself, either swimming or in a canoe: "From Horta to Madalena, the Church of Praia do Almoxarife in view. Sailing in front of Espalamaca, half the channel crossed; from

Madalena to Horta: the Church of Praia do Almoxarife hidden by Espalamaca astarboard... half the channel still ahead."

But peering at the horizon from the stern and seeing the rocky shore of Ribeirinha and Parede bluish and bare in the distance, Margarida leaped from her bench and abruptly turned her head to look back. Roberto's launch had stopped in the middle of the channel. Its little engine, which had been in use since Grandmother Ana Terra's time, when the boat had been adapted as a recreational vessel, was now stalled for good.

Noticing a huge sperm whale spouting a short distance away, João da Cezilha quickly lowered the sail and mast and grabbed hold of the steering oar. The whalemen, shipping and laying their long oars on the bottom of the boat, prepared the six paddles. And with their hearts in their throats and holding their breath, like a group of gangsters about to launch a furious raid, they approached the leviathan.

Chapter XXX

Fifth Nocturne
(In a Cavern)

What now?... Soaked to the bones, wearing nothing over her shoulders except for that little knitted coat that barely covered her chest, trying to conceal the pea jacket that an oarsman had lent her to prevent her from freezing to death in the boat, she sat on a boulder in that short São Jorge strip of beach between Point Ruiva and Velas among whalemen, boulders, and two huge beached sperm whales lying belly-up like frogs....

What would become of her?... What would the family think? Would the city be alarmed, perhaps scandalized?... Would ten... twenty binoculars be peering over the São Jorge Channel at her from the back doors of Ocean Street and from the hills of Horta?...

Sitting on the boulder, resting her face on her clenched left fist–for her, the sign of the little mood–Margarida took pathological delight in anticipating the triumphant gestures of the "attic" busybodies, that entire Horta scandal-mongering system springing into action at its northeastern maritime observation sector! And she derived a sick pleasure from imagining the kinds of comments they would make: "Oh, dear! Who could ever believe that Bida Dulmo would go off the deep end! Just think of her in a boat, alone with all those men, hunting whales!..."

These thoughts, besides filling Margarida with pride, amused her. But then she started to notice the darkness enveloping that tiny strip of land strewn with loose boulders and pebbles, reducing it to a single beach and footpath that, through lava folds and clay-pits, wound its way to the interior of the island; she watched the hulks of those two whaleboats beached in that solitude and the men already intoxicated by those fetid monsters, climbing up and down the carcasses by steps dug into the blubber and preparing in their immense flanks the future paths for the cutting-spades and mincing-knives.

A lingering patch of daylight had turned the sea into an immense sheet of denim, as if a giant had put on a pair of overalls and lay down to sleep–with one leg stretched towards the São Jorge Channel and the other towards the Fayal Channel.... The lighthouse at Point Ribeirinha had already signaled the end of day. If not for its plunging the channel in darkness, one would have been able to see the lights of Horta from Mount of the Maidens and the Pilar mansion to the poorest shacks of Cano and Old Streets.

But what about Uncle Roberto? He was alone in the drifting launch, already past the Madalena course, and no one to come to his aid!... How could she have allowed herself to be drawn into that madness, not realizing that at that distance there was no possibility that he could ever catch up with the whaleboats!

Margarida was then seized with a kind of secret terror and had the impression of having been left to fend for herself in the depths of her subconscious–that realm of images, sensations, and thoughts in which her sense of wholeness could not assemble the aching fragments of her shattered self. And upon thinking that she herself had been party to the absurd flight, indeed had helped to mastermind it with a devilish cunning, she was overcome with an almost physical horror of herself: her ability to charm the servants, fishermen, and colorful old people; her ability to withstand privations; her courting danger; even the fact that she never got seasick....

But could the engine really have stalled?... Or had Uncle Roberto, disappointed and offended by her part in the boat's flight, given up and decided to steer for Horta, moor the launch to some dock buoy, perhaps store it in the depths of the Granary from which he had taken it, fold his clothes, pack his suitcases in a hurry, and throw his violin and books into a trunk, determined to return to England on the first available ship?

The Island of Pico projected into the darkness the immense lava mass that daylight was wont to tenderly tinge with blue and lilac. On the coast and hillsides, a few scattered lights now marked the location of a slumbering inlet, the door of a tavern, the window of some ailing fisherman, or the home of some *Senhor* Laurianino of Terra Alta or of Santo Amaro, sitting at his patriarchal table after rolling back the tablecloth, busy with the bookkeeping for his wine, fruit, and firewood businesses. Pico was exactly this: a Holy Land pointed toward the southeast, with vineyards, pastures, and fishing boats amidst whitish whale spouts and piles of whale blubber, with poor people whose legs were their only means of locomotion, with mothers still strong and beautiful after bearing their eighth child, with long-bearded old men and young men equally ready to hold a boat tiller or a bishop's closier in the Patronage of the Orient, and who would be happy with either fate. And all this was contained under the 3000 meters of that "mystery"[1] called Pico, crowned by a needle of snow. In front of the broad curve that the coast of the sacred island began to trace off Point Cabrita and that extended beyond Espartel on the quasi-peninsula where São Mateus lay, Fayal appeared relatively flat and dark, punctuated by the lighthouses and by the traffic lights of its cosmopolitan city, but also filled with its poor and patient humanity, maintaining its peculiar pronunciation and archaic expressions. All this in the midst of the coal piles, the warehouses of the Fayal Coal & Supply Company, the Bensaúde Company's Coaling Station, and the trilingual codes of the Trans-Atlantic Cable. The brighter lights, in the windows of the houses of Santo António do Pico, brought to Margarida's mind the Hughes apparatus and the little blue ribbons that made inter-island communication possible. And why not send her father a telegram?... "*Diogo Dulmo–Horta–Came ashore Point Ruiva after unfortunate incident whaleboats going hotel Velas awaiting instructions....*"

What about money for the hotel?... She needed some. And where was her father going to get money? He was always short and now in an even tighter bind because of the awful seizure of the boats... Would he borrow it from André Barreto? That,

---

[1] In the Azores, *mistério* 'mystery' refers to an old lava bed.–Trans.

never! Margarida then rethought the text of the telegram, addressing it to Uncle Mateus Dulmo: "*Came ashore Point Ruiva*".... ("*Came ashore*," no! As if she were a plank... or a bottle!...) "*Arrived Point Ruiva after unfortunate incident whaleboats unhurt going hotel Velas please telegraph money put Mother at ease don't blame whalemen explain later*"....

No, it was ambiguous: it gave the impression that the sole purpose for the telegraph was to put her mother at ease; she added an "and" before *please send money*.... (Poor Uncle Mateus!...) *a little money*. And then she cut *telegraph money*. There was no other way for her family to help her now.... But what about Uncle Roberto? Two or three more words would not add much to the cost of the telegram, and she would rest more assured. She would add: "*request news Uncle Roberto*" or even: "*anxious request news Uncle Roberto*"....

She had memorized that long SOS, almost imprinted it on her mind, and now counted its words one by one: 28! What about cutting *anxious*? It added nothing. (It was also superfluous to include her name.) But it still contained 26 words! Where was she going to get money to send a telegram of 26 words? She had some passing acquaintances in Velas... She had it now! Why not contact André Barreto's father, the Baron da Urzelina? But Urzelina was far from here, on the road to Calheta. She knew no one else from whom she could get help without dying of embarrassment. The effort she expended in drafting that laborious message made her recall the common saying the people of Pico used to express mental anguish or their reaction to some public disaster: "Tremendous sorrows...." What a marvelous phrase in the mouths of those simple people! It was as if the whalemen were entirely conversant with the language of Camoens' sonnets, which use the same phrase–"*Mágoas tamanhas...*"!

As night fell upon the strange beach where the seamen had been cast, they determined to postpone until the following day the cutting up of the sperm whales. Getting the jump on the other men, João da Cezilha, dark lantern in hand, approached Margarida:

318

"Miss Bidinha! Now that your clothes have dried somewhat, I'm gonna see you to Velas. I don't know the way very well.... but ask and you'll know!"

"You're crazy, João!" cried out Uncle Amaro de Mirateca, who stood behind him, covered by and bent under the weight of a sail. "You don't know what you'd be getting yourself into! From here to Velas is a good stretch! And there's nothing but goat paths and lava beds!... There's scarcely a house along the entire coast.... And to arrive at the town at this hour, with the young lady..., poor fishermen like us... without any decent clothes! Those people in Velas would speak ill of us. They're all a bunch of snobs... I say 'no.'" And with a top-to-bottom glance at the legs of the boots that Margarida had put on while still in the boat, as if he were trying to exhume her real feet, he added: "And with those delicate feet of yours, miss, you'd never make it! Only if you put on strong sandals with cord soles like ours.... What we should do is go see if we can find a house nearby for you to stay at until tomorrow morning...."

That romantic albeit wise suggestion, which would relieve her from having to find the money to send her long telegram, prompted Margarida to succumb to the inevitable, asking:

"And what about you?"

"Who, us? No problem! We'll manage as we always do when we go whaling close to shore... no matter if it's Terceira, São Miguel... anywhere. Don't you know how we do it? If the weather is good, we bring the boats ashore, place them board to board, and then huddle together under the benches the best we can! If it's only one boat, we sometimes turn it upside down with one rim raised up and sleep under it. But that can damage the whaleboat, which is a very delicate vessel.... Each one of its parts costs the owners a fortune! And we are accountable for all damages...."

Intavante drew near, carrying a big *baila*[2] of salt water in his hand:

---

[2] From the English *handle-bailer*.–Author.

"The sea is rough, Uncle Amaro... All those speckles of foam look like flocks of sheep." With his trousers rolled up above his knees, the whitish and shiny reflections on the soles of Intavante's feet showed that he had been treading all over whale blubber. "Some distance north of here, there is a cavern, a nice place to sleep. Do you want to check it out, Uncle Amaro? It's like these two big cracks in the ground, nice and cozy...."

"How did you discover it?" asked Margarida.

"It was my little boy.... He's crazy for taro; he went along the coast looking for ravines, where taro plants grow well. He came back empty-handed.... But he found a big cavern... a good shelter. The ground on our islands, thank goodness, has holes all over it! It's good for the pigeons, the rats, the rabbits of Pico, and for us.... Each hole is a warren.... Right, Uncle Amaro?..."

Ever since the scene in Josèzinho da *Dona* Ana's tavern, Intavante treated Uncle Amaro de Mirateca with kid gloves. Despite the public reparation which had turned the plaza into a Jerusalem Sanhedrin, Intavante felt eaten away by remorse and, as João da Cezilha put it, tried as hard as possible to "butter up" the old man.

"You're the one who turned out to be a smart rabbit.... Let's go check that big discovery. But this young lady cannot stay here alone. Somebody's got to protect her, João! You go right along and see if you can find her some shelter...."

"No, Uncle Amaro, no! It's getting late... and you're all very tired," said Margarida. She raised her head and, for conscience's sake, visually searched the barren cliff and the deserted mountain for a roof or hovel. In the distance, high up on the steep southwestern slope of São Jorge, she caught sight of a little flickering light. It was probably a house, or the hut of one of those shepherds who spend their time throwing stones at their goats and carving little flutes out of the green cane-reeds that the wind bends and tests. Margarida wished she could take refuge under that roof, spend the night on the dry cot of the wife of one of those goatherders who justify the Arcadian names of certain hamlets in São Jorge: Mistério das Vacas...

320

Fajã dos Bodes[3]... How wonderful it must be to sleep under their coarse blankets amidst the smell of their sour curds and hard bread. But the little light flickered and went out. Determined, Margarida declared:

"This late, everybody is already asleep up there. There's no use trying to find a place... I'm going to stay with you."

It had grown completely dark by now. The land, all furrowed, rose almost vertically above that accessible little strip of deserted rocky beach. Glimpsed as if through a mirage, the sun revealed a country untouched or still undiscovered. Only from the side of the sea did a pale aquatic and starlit glow assist those sixteen men stranded there with a woman and two whaleboats towed by the pelagic force of two cetaceans who belonged to a period predating animal life upon all the islands of the West.

The whalemen built lichen and reed bonfires at the entrance to the cavern. The latter consisted of a single opening in the cliff which, as one advanced toward the interior, became progressively narrower and filled with superimposed trachytic strata held in place by creeping vegetation, forming a natural staircase. At the center, a cave-in had formed a kind of partition riddled with holes, crevices, and a pile of lava debris–making it all look like the cellar of a fantastic house or of some troglodytic dwelling with a clay-oven ceiling. The floor was strewn with fallen chunks of rock, fragments of whale skeleton, shearwater feathers, and wisps of delicate maidenhair shining in the faint light coming in off the sea.

The oarsmen, instinctively gathering around their fellow crewmen, squatted, removed their wide-brimmed hats and opened the bags of bread they had brought in the boats. Some got up to go fetch more firewood. Uncle Amaro de Mirateca, João da Cezilha and Intavante kept an eye on the bonfires. Trousers and pea jackets soaked with seawater were hung out to dry on a cane-reed.

"Have you got anything to go with our bread, Uncle João?" asked a young man from Pico, nicknamed "Red" because of the color of the hair covering his legs and chest.

---

[3] Literally "Cows' Lava Bed" and "Billy Goats' Flatland"–Trans.

With his chin, João da Cezilha motioned toward the small net that one-eyed Espadilha had placed close to one of the bonfires and was now opening to take out its silvery contents:

"Are you blind, or what? Fishermen always catch something, thank God! Even if it's only sticklebacks...."

From the net, heavy with sand, jumped three little fish that bore all the colors of the rainbow:

"Here! *Verdugos*[4]!"

"Let's grill them for Miss Margarida," said Uncle Amaro. "Don't you like *verdugos*? They're the quail of the sea...."

"Of course I do!" And picking up the net and rubbing the blind serpent of her ring against a bloody, shiny gill, she added:

"Let me have all the fish! I'm the one who is going to grill them! Look at these flapping tails!... There aren't many..., but there's at least one apiece... at least enough for everybody."

"No, don't you fuss with it!..."

"Yes, I will. Am I not the only woman here? Do you want me to just stand here with my arms crossed like a princess while you grill the fish?"

"Why not? We're used to it... No use your getting your hands dirty!"

"What do you think, Uncle João? Where did you ever hear of Pico whalemen being cast upon a São Jorge shore with a cook like this... and a lady from Fayal at that?" said a stocky and swarthy oarsman from São Mateus, his amazed eyes fixed on Margarida's face, who was leaning over the *verdugos* and whose hair had streaks of light from the fire.

"This is the kind of story, Uncle Amaro, that you never could recount from your adventures in the polar seas...," said another whaleman.

"And to top it off we have beached two 140-barrel cachalots, larger than the Isles of Madalena."

Squatting in a circle around the fire, the men then began to relive the strong emotions experienced during that hunt on the high seas:

---

[4] Parrot fish.–Trans.

"That was some harpoon stroke, Intavante! You buried it to the hitches at the first dart! All I kept saying was: 'St. Amaro, he isn't even going to graze that mountain of blubber with the barb of his iron!' Given the distance, you know... and a big animal like that, lifting its huge flukes higher than the tower of the Church of Lajes!"

"And it took such a deep sounding that it made the bottom of the channel quake! By golly, for a while I thought that the boat was going to plunge snout first to the bottom with the whale and the line and everything.... The stern was raised way up in the air and squeaked like those wicker baskets they used for building roads! And those waves were as high as mountains! And that sea full of blood!... Something like a dart hit me so hard in the pit of the stomach that my rib cage is still aching!"

Despite the heat from the bonfires and the stimulating smell of grilled fish, it was starting to get cold. Margarida, still in her high boots, was squatting in front of and tending the fire, her face reddened from the heat. But because she seemed, nevertheless, to be feeling cold, shoulders hunched towards her chest, Uncle Amaro slowly got up, walked around the circle of men nestled by the fire and placed his oilcloth raincoat over her shoulders.

"Thank you, Uncle Amaro! Now I feel nice and toasty...."

They all sat down to eat and to finish drying up their clothes; they all risked a word now and then. But, even though all of them spoke, a religious and fitting silence reigned primarily, interrupted only by the intermittent humming of the sea and the sizzling of fish over the fire.

When a more talkative whaleman tried to strike up a conversation, his neighbor confined himself to a dignified silence, as if in observance of some mystery rite, and answered him in a grave and curt tone:

"No talking!..."

Finally, they all got up one by one and began looking for a place to retire for the night.

Without consulting her, Uncle Amaro spread out a bunch of dry grass and leaves on a step of the stair-like formation on the side of the cavern and said to Margarida:

"It's not very comfortable here... not an ideal place to sleep, but, for only one night, it's okay! You can pretend that a witch came in through the roof of the Vineyards house and delivered you to some werewolves."

"What do you mean, a witch? Unless it was your own *Witch of the Seas*... And what about the little anchor you gave me as a present? Doesn't it ward off evil anymore?"

"You're right, miss... while there's life, there's hope! Tomorrow morning, you can rest in a bed at the Velas' inn."

"Don't worry, Uncle Amaro!" said Margarida, cracking a big smile, which lit her face to her shining eyes. She held a golden grilled *verdugo* on her fingertips. "Never have I prayed to my Guardian Angel with such joy as I have here in this cavern with you!" An earring sparkled above the beard of the old *Ariôche* harpooneer. "But, tell me! Am I supposed to take up this whole side of the cavern by myself, while the rest of you sleep on the other side like sardines? Sixteen men... exhausted from a hunt like that... sleeping practically on top of one another?"

From the other side of the cavern, which Uncle Amaro de Mirateca had reserved for the boat crews, came the sounds of the men settling in to sleep. Through the cracks in the fallen lava debris one could see some of them lying on their backs, their knees raised, the heads of some resting on handfuls of pine needles, while others held their crossed hands under the napes of their necks.

Uncle Amaro went to fetch his dark lantern, which he had left behind a rock, lit it, and placed it on the edge of the lava bench where Margarida sat:

"If you're afraid to sleep here by yourself, I can lie down right at the mouth of the cave.... All you have to do is holler for me.... I'm leaving you this lantern full of oil, and here are some matches...."

"I'm not afraid, Uncle Amaro! But do stay here! Sleep next to me, in this corner. Bring more straw!"

Margarida removed her hairpins one by one, placed them on the top of the lantern, and then straightened her hair. Afterward she removed the boots that covered her shoes and stockings to her knees.

Within a few moments, the two crews were sound asleep. While Uncle Amaro de Mirateca went out to look for more straw, Margarida lay down on her dry mat, snuggled under the oilcloth overcoat, and with an ironic coquettishness, arranged the folds of the sail she was using as sheet and blanket; then she began to stare out the entrance of the cavern at the glimmer of the São Jorge Channel which, at turns phosphorescent and dark, stretched the full length of the specter of Pico.

Her family, Horta, Campo Raso, the Vineyards house, all lay beyond that death-like silence that had quickly descended upon the whaleboat and beyond that cry of encouragement whispered to the six men: *Pulaiéte! Pulaiéte!*–which was immediately followed by the appearance of that slippery, shining mountain of flesh crowned by an intermittent spout, much like the breathing of a huge volcano, alive and fulminating. "Good job, good job, wolves of Pico! Now!... Take your aim and thrust your iron!"

The thrashing of the monstrous flukes had caused a great splash, and the fantastic body of the cachalot had sunk like a torpedoed cruiser. Then, curled up at the bottom of the boat and cowering, covering her ears with her hands as if preparing to witness a naval battle, Margarida saw only a little puff of golden smoke caused by the whale-line leaping through the chocks after passing through Uncle Amaro's sailor's palm. Layers of Flemish-coiled line, resembling a São Jorge cheese or a Holy Ghost ring-bread, were quickly vanishing from the line-tub.

The men struggled, pouring buckets of water over the coils of running line to prevent it from catching on fire. Wielding a big knife, an oarsman prepared himself to sever that umbilical lifeline, should it kink, loop, or be pulled down to the end by the agonizing monster. Elegant and streamlined, its paddles suspended in the air like a hovering wasp, the whaleboat drifted under a great shower of spray, its bow almost sky-high.

It was this way that Margarida, numbed with fear, crossed more than half the width of the São Jorge Channel, watching off starboard as the last clear images of known sites disappeared: Merato pier... port of Cachorro... Point Cabrita... Point Queimada.... On larboard and almost in the opposite direction emerged the contours of that nonnative island, which a whale-man pointed out with a movement of his chin: Point Rosais... Rosalina... Point Trigo.... And finally–that great lake of blood staining the water and spreading to everything: hands, men, boat, monster and sea, even penetrating her eyes as if the heart of everything she loved in the world had suddenly exploded.

From there the seamen had hauled that huge carcass over the water by hand to the little port of Point Ruiva. Schools of sharks, mouths gaping, followed the boat, while a few noisy, agile gulls circled in the darkening sky. Sea and setting sun cast one final bloody reflection before night fell.

Uncle Amaro de Mirateca, after having discreetly set his bundle of straw in a corner of the cavern, had lain down and fallen asleep, his chin and beard turned toward the sky. The waves outside were the only sound punctuating the silence.... Then, the whalemen's snoring was interrupted by a dry, loud sound coming from the other side of the cavern.

"Who farted?"

"All right, have a little class, you animals! Show some respect for the young lady!..."

Only then did Margarida realize she was lying in the cavern of an island that seemed deserted, wrapped in a sailcloth, in the company of men for whom sleep and exhaustion had restored the instinctive, brutal ardor of nature. She evoked images of other men she knew: Álvaro Bettencourt... Cerejo, midshipman on the training tall ship *Sagres*... Dr. António Lopes who, in the Royal Club of Fayal, almost lifted her off the floor during the cotillion... and, finally, João Garcia, who had kissed the serpent on her ring, and André Barreto, who had told her once by the moonlit Caldeira road: "I don't like to see you so sad...." So many... so many knights-errant had traversed her youth, now wrapped in the shroud of a sail!...

But upon seeing, right next to her, Uncle Amaro de Mirateca's heaving beard softly blown by the breeze coming in off the sea, Margarida was filled with confidence and soon fell asleep.

Chapter XXXI

The Ballad of the Living Dead

"No, baroness. This one fits me just fine. Look how nice it looks on me! Around the chest, and the back... even the length of the sleeves seems to have been made just for me! They are just the right length."

Seated on the bed, Margarida was trying on a large nightshirt that the Baroness da Urzelina had dug out of a chest.

"You decide... I also have others that I've never worn. They were part of my trousseau; of course, when I got married I was a lot thinner.... But you know how it is–they aren't very fashionable now! Tastes are very different these days... Here in São Jorge we couldn't afford to be very choosy. It even was difficult to get a hold of a pattern magazine. At our house in Velas, we were lucky to have *Senhorinha*, who received the *Veldons Ladies Journal* with the arrival of every other ship. And when it came to intimate apparel, the situation was even worse. One of the most common ornaments of the day was the cross stitch. And I must say that some of those open cross stitches were actually very beautiful!..."

Her chin resting on her chest, Margarida examined the lace on the nightshirt's discreet décolletage, her soft curly hair bouncing on the sides of her head:

"This embroidery is beautiful, baroness! What fine trim.... The time and patience it must have taken!..."

"It's a shame Clarinha's nightgowns don't fit you. They're a little more in style...." Margarida had actually tried on some of them; forced by the baroness, one had split up the back, with one of those dry tearing sounds that seems a cry of revolt from one skin crammed inside another. "But there's no question about it! You are, thank goodness, a robust and well-built girl. As for

my daughter Clara, she's tried to become like a bamboo shoot....
She eats like a bird! Her father keeps telling her, 'Dear, you
don't eat... you *peck!*' She and her brother are very much alike;
but when it comes to eating, they're very different. And you,
also. Look how well-fed you look! I can still see you sitting on
Senhor Mateus Dulmo's knees, with those cascading curls.... It
seems like yesterday! It was back when we lived in Horta. Your
Uncle Saavedra was the captain of the *Açor*; he was courting
Teresinha. It was the time when the English fleet came to Horta,
and there were many regattas. I had never seen so many sailors
in one place! Every night there were balls... picnics in Pico... tea
parties on board.... Your Uncle Saavedra held a reception aboard
the gunboat *Açor*; and I must say that, despite being a small
vessel, it was well equipped, with its two big shiny guns and its
crew lined up on deck. The captain's cabin, which was just a little larger than our study, was all decorated with flowers and
maidenhair. Your mother and Aunt Teresinha had arranged the
table.... Even the *Açor*'s big guns smelled of daffodils! What a
wonderful time I had!... But, after that, Fayal changed a lot. I
don't know if the fault lay with this wretched war, or whether
it's because all the girls from my time are almost all grand-
mothers now.... As for the girls of today... but no, you are an
exception; you are so full of life and verve! But Clara and her
cousins from Horta are all such sad girls... always sulking! In
your mother's and my time, it wasn't like that at all; and the boys
also had better manners.... They were more friendly. Almost all
the boys from these western Azores islands married young. And
how handsome some of them were! Did you ever hear about a
man by the name of Diogo Paim, from Terceira, a grandson of
Count da Praia Sr.? Now there was a handsome specimen! and
so refined in his treatment of the ladies, whether they were
attractive or homely.... He displayed the same cordiality toward
all.... You could tell he was a gentleman, accustomed to dealing
with those noblewomen at the king's palace and in the São
Carlos Theater...." The baroness smiled. Her little eyes, the
color of soapy water, stared at the trailing hem of her dark skirt.
"And there were many other boys like that.... Your father, too,

was very handsome, with that red moustache and that air of a foreigner. He looked just like a German! He was one of those who married early, and how well he married!... I always tell my son André: 'Be very, very careful; don't go marrying some flirty scatterbrain!...' Because, you know, I'm very wary of these foreign women who smoke.... They get you coming and going, *they* will!... I'm talking about the type of woman you see in fashion magazines wearing knickers. And André often travels abroad and likes these modern get-ups a lot.... You know, even as recently as last year we spent five thousand reis on their trip to Italy. Think about that: five thousand! Who could ever have convinced my father, Captain José Urbanino, and others from his time like him, to spend five thousand reis on travel and hotel expenses alone! And, heaven forbid, we don't begrudge our two children the expense! We're very happy they went... Money isn't just for earning interest. Long gone are the times when people stuffed their money under the mattress.... Avarice is a great sin... a mortal sin! And they really enjoyed themselves! They saw the gondolas in Venice, went to the sanctuary of Our Lady of Lourdes... kissed the Holy Father's slipper... and they thought of us, their old parents, while preparing the consecration of our house to the Sacred Heart of Jesus, with the Holy Father's blessing. All in all, André and Clarinha had the time of their lives!"

Since Margarida had kept quiet during this whole monologue, her eyes fixed on the hinges of the shutters, which the wind shook intermittently, the baroness put an end to her reminiscences about the good old days. And caressing Margarida's hair with a bony hand that displayed her wedding ring, she said:

"Don't be sad, Bidinha! Now it's just a matter of waiting a few more days until the *Funchal* arrives. You stay here with Caetano and me. Maybe you won't believe this and perhaps you'll think that I'm confiding too much, but I already am as fond of you as if we had been in close contact since you were a child. And, what's more, we're not even related! What can I say?... I either like certain people or I don't. And I make no bones about it. I just show my true feelings. I don't like to be rude, but I don't like to fake it either! Come on, now. Why are those shining eyes so sad? Do you miss Horta? Is it because you can't get used to sleeping in a strange bed?..."

Margarida, feeling as if she were waking up from the effects of some narcotic, ran her hand briskly over her hair and got up from the bed, straightening the pillow upon which she had been leaning:

"Not by a long shot, baroness! How could I not get used to such a soft bed?..."

"It ought to be soft.... I just changed the moss in the mattress, three new bags of it from the woods, less than a month ago. And I used the fluffiest kind."

"I couldn't possibly feel more comfortable here, with all the things you've done to spoil me. But you understand, baroness... What happened was something awful, something that you only think happens in romances! Just try to imagine what people are thinking and saying in Horta right now!..."

"What of it! It wasn't your fault. The whalemen are the ones who should be taught a good lesson! Sailing the channel just like that and with a lady on board, practically against her will!..."

"Poor guys! They didn't mean to do it; they were caught up in all the excitement of giving chase to a whale.... I am the one who shouldn't have gotten into the boat, knowing how they are. They are all very attentive and very respectful; but, when they hear the rocket exploding, there's no reasoning with them. All I wanted was to catch up with Uncle Roberto... make sure that he didn't do anything foolish. He is a very sensible man, but, if you push him, he becomes determined, rash. And I wanted to use the whaleboat to then transfer to his launch when the two got close enough... How could I foresee that the launch was going to stall and the whale was going to show up like that and drive the whalemen into a frenzy? But it's all over now.... And your son's telegram was really reassuring. I'll sleep easier now."

"Get some sleep! Get some sleep! And if you need anything, don't hesitate to call. The hallway is long, but I'll be able to hear you very well on the other end of the house. Domitília's room is right next to this one, and she's a light sleeper. I'll leave this bell here. It's not a fancy one, but that's all we have. This is a farmer's house...."

A large cowbell, with a fine greenish-blue patina, lay on the nightstand next to a crystal glass and the pot of tea. The clapper, a big wooden tongue worn out from use, prevented it from resting flat on the table. Margarida tried ringing it a little. Two pastoral notes roused the shadows in the room.

"How wonderful! It has a fuller sound than a gong...."

"Did you call, Angélica?"

A small face appeared at the door, with a pointed and shiny head covered by a few strands of grey hair. It was the Baron da Urzelina, Caetano Urbano Romeiro Acompanhado Barreto.

"It was Bidinha trying out her bell. Now it's the latest thing to use bells to summon the servants: a cowbell. It may seem funny to you, but that's what we have...."

The baron's smile shook his thin white moustache. As much as he wanted to draw near, he felt self-conscious upon seeing that young woman in bed, buried in one of his wife's nightshirts, having unexpectedly arrived in São Jorge aboard a Pico whaleboat with an urgent telegram from his son ordering them to receive and shelter her like they would their own daughter. Margarida covered better the one shoulder that proved to be more rebellious against the São Jorge linen and said, completely at ease and with a broad, friendly smile:

"Come right in, Baron! I'm already feeling much better, thanks to the nice warm tea."

"That's what I wanted to hear. After what you went through! What a close call that was! Those men harpooning a whale right in the middle of the channel, with a young lady on board, and the boat could have tipped over and everything!..."

Husband and wife looked at each other. They still had not recovered from having that scandalous stone thrown into the depths of the lake of their peaceful life. Their faces were congealed by over sixty years of silence and morning meals of bread soaked in milk, and from staring at the volcanic profiles of the Islands of Pico and Fayal. After having exchanged a cautious look, they slowly turned their eyes toward Margarida for some kind of confirmation or denial. But their suspicions were finally put to rest. And, deep down, they felt flattered and rewarded by that unforeseen presence, as if their pastures had sprung magnificently into bloom as a result of a rare kind of seed brought to them from afar by a generous proprietress.

The baron then pulled out a crumpled telegram, apologizing for not having delivered it earlier. But he had wanted Margarida to make herself at home, to take off those boots and that coarse and foul-smelling fisherman's sweater. And after André's message, this telegram could not possibly bring any news that was more alarming.

Margarida popped open the perforated seal. It was a telegram from her father: "*Whale fishery deal resolved our favor André signed contract stop await ship thank Baron kind hospitality greetings Baroness regards from Uncle Mateus Roberto and us–Diogo.*"

"Didn't I tell you?... See how everything is turning out all right?" intervened the baroness, assuming, from Margarida's deep, happy breathing, that the news was good.

"It's turning out okay...." Margarida read the telegram aloud. "The only bad things are the ship's delay and my imposition on you..."

The baroness, fixing her wide skirt, assured Margarida she was nothing of the kind. Then the baron spoke:

"Well, the bed, as you can see, is probably not to your liking.... Here we are used to our country mattresses stuffed with moss.... But it's a large bed; the sheets are new and recently bleached. And no one has ever slept in them. We have dozens and dozen of sheets, thank goodness. I've always said, 'The room next to the granary is not for visitors; we have lots of other rooms for that!' Since Uncle Caetano's passing, only one guest has slept here, as far as I can remember.... Do you want to guess who that was?..." Margarida waited for the baron's answer. But he drew out the riddle's solution.... "Guess... it was none other than the Bishop of Nilopolis himself; and there, in that corner, slept Canon Ferreira in an iron bed. None other!... Bishop Francisco Maria de Sousa do Prado e Lacerda, coadjutor and future successor to the Bishop of Angra.... And now it's you, Dona Margarida da Terra Clark Dulmo, illustrious great-granddaughter of Captain Fernão Dulmo, nobleman of the house of Prince Henry the Navigator, Lord of all these islands.... I'm telling you this for you to know in what high regard we already hold you! We are reserving this room for my son André, when he gets married."

Margarida brusquely interrupted the Baron da Urzelina's hospitable effusions:

"My parents [and she assumed an old-fashioned phraseology, modeled upon that of her quaint, cheese-making hosts from that 'neighboring island of São Jorge']... my parents remain very grateful for the hospitality you've shown us. They, too, hold Your Excellencies in the highest esteem...."

As she said this, she felt as if she were in the salon of the Granary or in their Pasteleiro house parlor, in charge of receiving guests with whom her mother did not wish to spend much time, but toward whom, for the sake of etiquette befitting a person of their social standing, it was necessary to show a discreet affability.

The baroness, who was a little taken aback by Margarida's hesitancy, started to straighten the bedclothes as if they were the pleats of a long ball dress; then, with her slightly enigmatic and distant look fixed on the dark applewood ceiling from which the gusts of wind wrought creaking sounds, she walked away from the bed, forcing the baron to step in front of her:

"Let's go, Caetano.... This young lady has to get some sleep!"

"No, I'm not sleepy! I even took the liberty of picking up this book from your desk, baron, to keep myself occupied a while. I didn't even bother to ask your permission... I can never fall asleep without reading something."

That unexpected familiar tone cheered up the old hosts. The baron said:

"No need to ask permission. Read whatever books you want. Make yourself totally at home... But remember that reading at night isn't good for your eyes. And please be careful with the lamp... I'm very much afraid of fires!"

333

"Rest assured that I won't forget to put out the lamp."

"Good night, then!"

"And tomorrow morning you'll be served your milk in bed...," said the baroness. "Do you eat bread and butter, or do you prefer cookies?"

"Everything homemade, mind you. We don't eat anything but homemade butter, churned by hand," declared the baron. "The batches made in the mechanical churn are all to export. Tomorrow you show her how it's done, Angélica! You'll enjoy seeing our facilities. Hasn't André told you that a Dutchman has just brought us new equipment and materials... machines, coagulants, a secret-formula ferment to replace the whey, a whole range of new stuff! Van Dam is an expert in the milk-processing industry! He was a gold-medal winner at an exhibition in Copenhagen."

"Yes... yes... I seem to recall...."

"Well, you are going to see all of that. It's a shame that André isn't here to show you the machinery... to explain it all to you... all those technical terms van Dam uses.... Sleep well, now!"

"A little bread and butter, or cookies?" the baroness asked again, from the doorway.

Margarida hesitated, picking up the book on the nightstand. Her face, having an aura of fatigue and showing signs of sleepiness or inattention, seemed to be saying, "whatever you wish to bring... whatever...."

"Bring her both," said the baron, looking over his wife's shoulder, his hand holding on to the somber door. "And let her rest now!"

"Good night..."

"Good night!"

Margarida opened the book to a yellowed page with effaced print. It was a single issue of the *Azorean Archives*. It contained a series of documents, relative to the 16th century, on earthquakes and volcanic eruptions: an excerpt from Gaspar Frutuoso on the Vila Franca quake, the passage from Garcia de Resende's *Miscellany* on the same catastrophe, and finally, the "Ballad

Written on the Occasion of the Suffering and Damages Brought About by the 1522 Earthquake in Vila Franca do Campo."

At first, Margarida could not find in that interminable, tedious narrative anything but a pretext to while away a few moments, perhaps a vehicle that might transport her far away from the Baron and Baroness da Urzelina and from the private prison of her own memories of those last two days, a time so full of strange and strong sensations:

> *On October the twenty-second,*
> *When the moon was on the wane;*
> *A Wednesday it was:*
> *A day of sorrow and of pain....*

But then the lines started to make more sense and to break away from the tedious recitative-like narrative:

> *Though the season was of gales,*
> *The wind held its breath;*
> *The trees in silent stillness,*
> *In the heavens stars like sand....*

The earth, in the ballad, started to quake "like waves out on the ocean." In the lines penned to their monotonous vocalic rhyme, one began to hear the screams of the poor people of Vila Franca and to feel the houses tumbling down, burying the inhabitants alive under the rubble. Friar Afonso de Toledo, after lighting the torch in the dog's mouth on the statue of St. Dominic, addressed the people:

> *Ere your lives are whisked away,*
> *Brethren, your sins confess!*
> *Pray to Mary, one and all:*
> *You're staring in the jaws of death....*

Nobles, burghers, and commoners all began carrying stones to build a makeshift chapel to the greater glory of God, the God who lorded over all calamities and ruins. Captain Rui Gonçalves da Câmara (undoubtedly an ancestor of *Senhor* Manuel da Câmara, who was tax collector in Horta and who wrote in such a picturesque way and who was so open-heartedly expansive...) ordered his horse saddled and rode around Vila Franca, only to discover that his own palace had been destroyed and that one son and two daughters had been crushed under two beams:

> *And also a bastard son,*
> *Free of bastardy's stain;*
> *And also a beloved sister:*
> *Melícia was her name....*

(Alas! Uncle Roberto was not the only bastard in the world... The powerful gentlemen of the Azores had always done what they very well pleased. There were scuffles in the homes... many girls behind the latticed balconies or soaping up clothes in the washing places along streams.... "Good afternoon, washer-woman!" "Good afternoon, huntsman!...").

Then Captain Rui Gonçalves ordered people to dig on the spot where the altar with the Holy Sacrament had been, where the living Jesus lay dead once again for men's sins. But finding the tabernacle empty, those present then saw a distant cloud surrounded by angels transporting the Host to the throne of the Eucharistic Lamb. The clamoring of the people resounded through the devastated village.

After the survivors of the catastrophe had dug for nine whole days and brought out those still alive under the debris, they heard a mysterious voice ordering them to dig even deeper in that holy site. They then realized that there were people still buried alive there and saw three men emerge from under a beam, giving thanks to Heaven for having escaped that darkness that had engulfed them. A cock crowing heralded the new morning to them; they, passengers in Charon's boat, had survived by eating hardtack, the type the sailors ate during their sea voyages. Now, risen Lazaruses,

> *To those who met their death,*
> *Fate has indeed been kind;*
> *They now mourn the real victims:*
> *Those who were left behind...*

Finally (what a long and strange ballad this was!), the living dead all went to the chapel of St. Catherine and fell to their knees in gratitude for this miracle, and the narrator persisted with his monotonous rhyme scheme until the very end of the ballad, which ended right after the following passage alluding to the few survivors:

> *After being buried alive,*
> *To farms some did repair;*
> *While others fled to villages*
> *The Lord had chosen to spare....*

Shutting the issue of the *Azorean Archives*, which she had opened to escape dwelling on her own worrisome troubles, Margarida now felt, sadly, that all things in life, no matter how seemingly unrelated, end up by appealing or responding to our deepest feelings that are undying in us, like trickles of water running all night from the lead spout of some public fountain. That macabre scene of the dust cloud after the quake, the empty tabernacle and the three men buried alive under the rubble, all vividly brought to her mind the tragic fire she saw from the window of the Vineyards house. Then, she had supposed that it was devouring Uncle Mateus Dulmo's house and harmonium, even as he stood dumbfounded next to her. But, as it would turn out, it was actually melting the safe containing Januário's shame, like a fire in a wheat field consuming the snares set up for catching fleeing birds. Old Secundina had burned like a witch taken in a one-hundred-year procession to the pyres of an auto-da-fé. João Garcia's possessions had also been reduced to rubble and ash. And somewhere among the charred remains of his books, his *sticks*, and his portrait of Antero, lay the letter that Margarida had written to him under the shade of the araucaria in the silence of the afternoon broken by Manuel Bana's approaching steps. The words she had written in that letter now appeared to Margarida to have been alien to her will, dictated by the waters of the channel, by the purple clouds surrounding Pico, by the perfume of the gillyflowers her uncle Roberto picked in the garden, by the anxieties of her mother, who spied on her, to the point of trying to guess whether or not she had gone to *Dona* Carolina Amélia's to allay the lady's fears regarding her father's financial obligations to her. Thank God, she now thought, the flames had licked those absurd words, written by the hand of a sleepwalker and which, as she now lay in that room at the end of the Baron da Urzelina's house, seared her mind and her flesh like a branding iron! *I'm going to be married*! But to whom?... This time there was no mistake about it! The answer had been carved into the sea by the prow of a Pico whaleboat and by the blind choice of a harpooned whale.... She was going to be André Barreto's wife! The daughter-in-law of the Baron da Urzelina!

Chapter XXXII

Pastoral

The first few days of Margarida's stay in Urzelina went rather smoothly. Captain José Urbanino's house–as it was still known–stood at some distance from the center of the village. Its long, low roof, as well as its threshing floor and creamery, pointed towards the "Serra"–that vague and markedly sloping São Jorge mountain range, mother to thousands of lowing cows and to millions of calves buried in its bosom of fire, virgin meat for the gourmet's palate.

Built on slightly undulating terrain, the baron's residence overlooked the so-called Old Tower and the erstwhile rectory house–remaining relics of the human presence that the lava of the 1808 eruption had buried.

Margarida recalled having one day found in the Granary, among the papers that had belonged to old Grandfather Roberto, a yellowed issue of the *New York Philosophical Transactions* from 1815, in which the American consul in Fayal, John Bass Dabney, reported to President Madison on the damage caused by the cataclysm. Leafing through a pile of documents, which had been brought by *Dona* Petronilha Teixeira Borges Acompanhado, heiress of Norte Grande, when she married Captain José Urbanino, the baron had shown Margarida the report sent by the island's military governor at the time, José de Bettencourt de Sousa e Silveira, to the Captain General of the Azores, who, in turn, sent it from Angra to the Supreme Government in Rio.[1] But the manuscript of Urzelina,

---

[1] Before the first of three Napoleonic invasions of Portugal (1807-1811), the Portuguese royal family took refuge in Brazil. Rio de Janeiro became the seat of the Portuguese Government until 1821.–Trans.

traced upon the very crust of the island with an ink of fire and sulphur, lay there before one's eyes more clear and eloquent than any possible or imaginable report.

On the west side lay the denuded, dark earth piled around the huge hole that had suddenly opened in the middle of the island–the "Queimada," or Burnt Land. Impressed by the appearance of these lava beds, common to all the islands and which resemble the cowls of penitents expiating monstrous crimes, the people refer to them as *mistérios*, given as they are to that tellurian sense of fate that neither Cain and Abel had. Vegetation, however, was beginning to win the century-old duel between the dark fiery surface and the vital forces hidden underneath; lichen rocella, pine, the madder that yields dyes for cheeses and skirts, and incense trees with waxy little flowers and sticky berries, were already clothing that spellbound solitude in leaves and birds.

On the east side, the boldness of burned Cybele went much farther, making the orange trees blossom and filling the chestnut-tree groves with burs. Extending north were the cultivated fields and, past the poorer grazing lands, the sleepy pastures that supplied cheese to Prata Street. On the south, and offering a change of scenery, lay the Casteletes' vineyards with their denuded vines, reduced, at that time of the year, to stems of dormant sap grappling with the volcanic soil.

The older people in the area still remembered the pain and suffering unleashed in the aftermath of the cataclysm. Goatherders coming down from the mountain had been buried in the lava flow, along with half-a-dozen of their animals. Some, their clothes on fire, had managed to escape with burns all over their bodies. A rockslide had demolished a house, burying an elderly man and his wife under their own roof, binding even in death those whom life had brought together....

One of the baron's elderly sharecroppers told Margarida that his father, a boy of ten at the time, vividly remembered the great tragedy, as if the eruption were a panel of Purgatory, with a view of Hell and a depiction of its principal torments in the background. A cloud of brimstone rose from the cracked earth,

340

like vapor rising from a wet sheet being starched. Through the open crevices on the ground one could hear a distant thunder-like roar, which the sea, almost level with the cliffs, caused to echo nearby. And the thick burning lava slowly gurgled like a river of slime kept in the bowels of the Atlantic as a reminder of the biblical Flood.

It was this infernal plasma that, now congealed, formed the rocky soil of the baron's justifiably famous vineyards, which Margarida loved to look at after hiking on the more elevated areas covered with volcanic slag and pumice. Exhibiting twisted shapes and sharp points, these rocks, porous and dark at the base, turned progressively purplish and reddish toward the edges. Whenever one broke, an odor of fire and sulphur hung in the air. Once during a stroll in the Pasteleiro backyard, Margarida, stone in hand and sitting on a rock wall, absent-mindedly chipped away a piece from one of these rocks, as if she meant to use it in some fanciful construction project. She recognized that volcanic emanation as the same one as the slightly acrid smell she had noticed a few days earlier in her white linen and undergarments. That odor arose from her having left the clothes bleaching outside the night before, spread over the vineyard rocks.

In the public pantry of the Holy Ghost Brotherhood, they had shown her some of the poles used by former celebration organizers, which were "tipped" by a ring of dark lava. During the eruption, the bolder men followed the stream of lava that threatened to engulf Urzelina, and dipping the tips of walking sticks, as well as those of the canopy poles (under which the priest carries the Blessed Sacrament in the Holy Ghost proces-sions), they rendered the ends hardier with that hard, grayish volcanic paste. Other people lit their candles in the lava flames. Margarida, who was given to superstitions and symbology, con-trived to have a celebration organizer recently offer her one of those lava-tipped poles to use as a magic wand.

But the sap of the earth little by little had transformed that scene of horrors into the Queimada. It seemed that Pluto had charged Ceres and some friendly dryads with the duty of erasing, as much as possible, all vestiges of ancient divine grudges. The breeze from the Atlantic softly stirred the branches of the pine grove. When the baron surveyed them with his sharp little eyes, it always occurred to him to chop down the pines. The cultivated fields pushed the *mistério* toward the Old Tower; and vast vegetable gardens, well manured and using hardy seeds, seemed to be savoring the very verdure of the collard greens and cabbages that grew there irrigated by the autumn rains. An immense fruit orchard extended almost to the stream's edge, along which grew patches of wicker and clumps of hydrangea bushes. On the side of Manadas, this stream had served to baptize, with its generic appellation, a true baron who had resided there: the Baron of the Stream. Every time he thought of that unfair competition on the part of his former neighbor, our baron was pleased with himself. The part was absorbed by the whole: Urzelina was, after all, much more than the Stream....

From the well-irrigated hollows emerged that sea of wide, velvety, and dark-green leaves of plants that no one notices when they appear in any botanical or private garden on the mainland, where they are mere curiosities. In the islands, however, the taro plants enjoy the privileges of humidity, their floury tubers thickening in the basaltic soil. The plants' abundance in São Jorge (they thrive especially in the stream-crossed fields of the northern part of the island, around Calheta) gave origin to the humorous name by which the inhabitants of the pastoral island of São Jorge are known among their fellow islanders: "taro rooters."

During her solitary hikes through the orchards and fields, Margarida sometimes picked a taro leaf and, funneling it in her hand and raising it to her mouth, swallowed big draughts of that sweet and heavy liquid accumulated on the velvety container, shining like drops of silver or mercury. The oranges had already grown full and golden upon the trees. Bunches of early blossoms alternated with branches bent under the weight of the fruit growing and ripening under the rays of a fast-fading sun. Tiptoeing around the orange trees, Margarida inspected those beautiful and ardent blossoms on that grayish morning, counting the oranges miraculously supported by a single branch, sometimes using a fingernail to flick away a caterpillar–as if she were reading, critiquing the pages of that Urzelina orange grove, that sort of patronless green library.

Sometimes, startled Azorean chaffinches and blackcaps flew from branch to branch, shaking the orange blossoms when they took off. Holding her breath, Margarida kept watching them–and, on tiptoe, treading that thick dark humus of São Jorge fed by clover and basil, she kept waiting... waiting until another little bird came to brave another blossom, as gently as if it were landing on a thorn. The chaffinch, or whatever it was, flew away again; Margarida then ran toward the cornfields and the orchards, where the camellias (or "roses of Japan," as they are known in some of the Azorean islands) opened their veils of white or bloodred icy flowers.

All she had to do now was wait until the ship's arrival. Her father's telegram indicated that that wicked whaleboat matter was closed and that the whale fishery financial situation had been solved with the inclusion of André Barreto as a main partner in the firm. Uncle Roberto had not been able to assume that responsibility for lack of funds. Too bad... Even she, who had thought that her uncle's extended stay in Horta would be the panacea for all ills, had finally subscribed to his cautious views: he missed England and his old English ways too much....

And then there was Mary. After all, wasn't he entitled to harbor a strong interest in life? He was almost forty; all he had ever done was work, chained to his desk at the Anglo-Spanish Bank, under that London fog pierced by evening lights, amidst the hustle and bustle of commuter trains and the epic tolling of Big Ben. And Margarida's London (seen through Dickens' Christmas stories), deploying London's octopus tentacles, came to her mind: the two banks of a Thames as large as the channel and crowned with lighted bridges quaking under the heavy traffic.

But the die had been cast.... And it seemed to be for the best. Her father would clear his debts; and her mother, even though she was getting more and more neurasthenic, nestled in her big house next to her invalid grandfather, would be better off where she was. Wasn't it even possible that she... (her grandfather, bless his heart, wasn't going to live forever...) could go spend a few months in Lisbon at Uncle Saavedra's? (Her mother and Aunt Teresa got along so well that they didn't even seem to be sisters-in-law....) Cecília's attendance at the private school–paid for by her Lisbon uncle and aunt, who did not have children of their own and who loved her very much–was a magnificent pretext. For a few months, her father and brother would be under Maria das Angústias' care and benefitting from Uncle Mateus Dulmo's counsel.

Thanks to these plans, so easy to make in Urzelina, in the humid silence of the fields and of the island-encrusted sea, Margarida could feel free to put into practice the only wish that recently had taken root in her vagabond soul, of late assailed by winds bent on upheaving her: to join Dr. Marr's clinic, to don a nurse's white uniform and cap, accompany the convalescing patients on a stroll to the park, draped in a dark blue cape–in short, become a sort of nun who had not taken vows, save money to rent an apartment of her own, buy her own purses, be able to afford a trip to the Mediterranean or a visit to the islands, but the latter only after a long, long time....

Once, while sitting at the table, a little warmed by the Casteletes wine scintillating in the glasses and casting topaz reflections upon the tablecloth, her vanity a little spurred by the way the baron related a trip that André had forced him to take to Paris under the pretext of a simple pilgrimage to Lourdes, Margarida spoke at length about London, about the Anglophile traditions of old Uncle Roberto's time, about the portrait of Ralph Clark, who had crossed paths with Lord Byron in Lisbon in 1809 and who had been a friend of Lord Stuart of Rothesay, English Ambassador in Rio in the court of João VI, and who also had been bearer of the Constitutional Charter and Marquis de Angra.

The baron and the baroness listened to her in rapt attention. Margarida spoke of these matters with much ease, as if she had witnessed them firsthand, without the least pride. Her conception of England came naturally from magazines, learned from novels and memoirs. But the baron, who did not know any better, was dazzled by those different customs and raiment, those strange names, those alien foods, those evocations of social life in a distant country, as if in Margarida's mouth and eyes scintillated the flame of a magic lantern–the colorful images of the *Life of Jesus*, whose staging was shared between the Velas Incentive Society and the little Velas theater.

"Wouldn't you agree, Caetano, that it's a pleasure to hear this young lady speak about great foreign lands?"–asked the baroness, her countenance bathed in a sincere tenderness of the type that older people are wont to display on special occasions around a pretty girl all dressed up for her wedding or her Communion. "And to think that she's never traveled beyond Lisbon! But how well informed she is!... Come to think of it," she said, looking at Margarida and nodding her head as if she wished to correct some unfortunate hazard that had befallen her, "you're the one who ought be in my shoes when André starts putting notions in my head to go with him and his sister on his big tours!... Not even the Virgin of Lourdes or the Blessed Bernadette succeeded in persuading me to visit the miraculous grotto! And God knows how great a devotion I feel towards Our Lady... the canon went to great lengths to take us on the great pilgrimage for the Holy Year Jubilee, eighteen years ago. I keep a book by Canon Ferreira that explains everything: all those people kneeling in the grotto... bishops from all nations... those pilgrimages to holy sites in Rome, and the kissing of the Holy Father's slipper... If you want, I can show you the book." The baroness brought the book, put on her glasses, and read: "'*The banner is made of white satin, with a border of blue satin all around, and on it, flowers embroidered in gold....*' All of this embroidery was done by women from the islands, with special help from a woman named Cota, from Terceira, a very pious lady! Look here.... The words *São Jorge* were embroidered by a friend of mine. It's all written there....." The baroness handed the book to Margarida, who, skimming through a page, read this passage aloud:

"'*The motifs on the banner, the gilding on the staff, the cross and the lily are the work of the famous painter and gilder from Braga,* Senhor *José da Cunha, who, for years, has been living*

345

and working in the islands, and is much esteemed for his artistry.' Yes, sir.... How beautiful it must have looked!... That was a wonderful idea!" The baroness again picked up the book, opened it to the prologue and marked with her nail a passage she wanted Margarida to read.

"*'Due to the examples of divine grace bestowed there, to the miracles observed and which constitute proof of the existence of the Supernatural, Lourdes is a little corner of Heaven on earth. It is impossible to express the immense consolations dispensed there, and the devotees of the Mother of God can truly say: 'See Lourdes... and then die and go to Heaven.'"*

"Just imagine what I missed by not going!...." said the baroness. "But I did receive a great consolation! They brought me a beautiful statue of the Virgin, blessed by José, Bishop of Angra during the Mass he celebrated on the holy altar of the grotto for the Azorean pilgrims. I keep it in the oratory room. It's almost life-size, with those eyes full of peace and mercy!" Margarida's attentive expression and clasped hands indicated pleasant expectation, the surprise of listening to that rustic lady talk about the Virgin and the shepherdess of Pau with such candor. She always felt so close to her two statues during those nights that she said the rosary by the light of a candle and of the first stars shining far above the sea and perhaps for their very distance, unable to take her from that simple life of hers, that stagnant peace. "I know it's silly of me...," concluded the baroness. "But I just can't bring myself to leave my corner of the world. I've gotten used to this inactivity...."

"Angélica has never been much given to traveling about...," remarked the baron. "Even when she was single, she rarely ventured out to see a procession or attend a food distribution for the poor during the Holy Ghost festival season... other than in Velas."

"That's why I say: 'Bidinha is the one who should take my place! If only I could, I'd gladly give it up to her!...'"

The baron caressed his little white moustache maliciously:

"Dear, you talk as if you wanted to marry me off to this young lady!... An old goat like me!... Though I refuse to believe you want to take advantage of the divorce laws, despite the fact

346

I'm sometimes a little hardheaded with you.... No! Spare us the horrors of divorce! I vote for Afonso Costa because he's the one in the Ministry of Justice, but my man has always been Hintze Ribeiro. Not even Jacinto Cândido managed to get my votes after he split to found the Nacionalist Party. And this despite the fact that he was an Azorean and a friend almost since childhood. I did subscribe to the *Word*, but betray Hintze–never!"

"You know very well what I mean...," interrupted the baroness. "There are many ways of doing things.... We have two children. Bida and our Clarinha get along very well, I think.... It's perfectly natural the two of them should plan a trip together...."

Margarida managed a smile that harbored a word of gratitude and reserved courtesy. Both the situation and the wine had made her feel a little giddy. And therefore, not to spoil the friendly tone of the conversation, but at the same time, not to leave herself open to hasty intimacies, she spoke about her work plans in England, Dr. Marr's reputation, and about the English family who was looking for a lady's companion willing to go to Brazil with them....

"What! Don't you feel bad about leaving the Azores at the drop of a hat? With a family as united as yours and with kin on all the islands...?" asked the baroness.

As for the baron, what confused him somewhat was the fact that Margarida should wish to exchange her status of privileged young lady from the most prestigious family in Horta, at an age when she could marry or have herself some fun, for a subordinate position at a clinic of postoperative convalescents or with a foreign family. No! It was a very risky step–"begging your pardon, an idiotic decision!"

Later, on the courtyard that extended along the imposing facade of the house (although, with its eight front windows and lengthy roof, the building resembled a barracks), Margarida again alluded to Dr. Marr's European reputation, to the blood ties between the surgeon and the Clarks, to the naturalness with which, in England, even the wealthy and fashionable girls donned work clothes and war uniforms.

Days and evenings were whiled away in these exchanges punctuated by frequent teas. Margarida was always served her milk when she woke up—when it wasn't tea and crescent rolls. Tea was served at ten, after a small repast.... And, again, tea at two, after the heavy soup, the boiled or roasted meat.... Another little tea came later in the afternoon, this time with slices of toasted sweet bread that had been stored in big tall canisters.... And, once again, tea was served at supper right before bedtime.... Tea... tea... tea.... The baroness, almost transparent in her wrinkled skin and wearing very tight clothes, always had two cups. The baron generally preferred milk ("Tea isn't my cup of tea..."). At eleven, he would crumble half a loaf of corn bread into a white bowl and then fill it with thick, sweet-smelling unskimmed milk with the foam still bubbling hot.

The weather determined Margarida's activities during those days of idly sitting by and waiting. An unstable sky, with scattered clouds ever changing in brightness and shape, seemed to reflect the protean aspects of the sea, now green and somewhat stormy on the edge of the rocky shore, now blue and almost dark and foamy from its rough, resonant thrashings against the boulders from points Topo to Rosais. If there was no break in the clouds to allow Margarida to wander through the golden darkness of the orange grove or the dense freshness of the vegetable gardens, she stayed at home conversing with the baroness or else went to the kitchen to chat with Domitília.

Van Dam, the cheese-making Dutchman, sometimes was bold enough to come smoke his pipe in the dining room. He was a short, rosy-cheeked, block-headed man, who spoke broken Portuguese. Taking advantage of his being there, Margarida trotted out the few random German words she had learned from Fräulein Wartel:

"*Trinken Sie Kaffee und Milch gern? Der Riesenkäse* [2]!"

"*Ja, juffrouw* [3]... *Sie sind viel zu gross* [4]!"

In order to sound more fluent, she would wait for the morning greeting, which she used when van Dam came out of the

---

[2] German for "Do you take your coffee with milk? What a large cheese!"–Author.

[3] Dutch for "Yes, miss."–Author.

[4] German for "It's too big."–Author.

creamery with his blue woolen cap and his cheeks red from the loquat rum and the cold:

"*Haben Sie gut geschlafen, Herr van Dam* [5]? Or, varying the past participles to suit the occasions: ... *gegessen;* ... *getrunken;* ... *gekommen* [6]?

The Dutchman, instinctively reverting to his native tongue, invariably replied:

"*Ja, juffrouw... Danke schön* [7]!

Enchanted with the scene, the baron and baroness were reminded of the Paraclete bestowing upon the chosen apostles the gift of tongues. Under the prideful eyes of the baron and baroness, who relished the honor of being the employers of such a worker and the hosts of such a guest, poor van Dam felt, as he touched the Dutch velvet of his suit and the leather of his thick boots, as if he was caressing the fur and paws of a pure-bred pet bought out of mere caprice.

The baron's cultivated lands extended through Manadas, along the mountaintops; vast and varied, these ploughed fields, under the warm, ashen island skies, seemed adaptable to any kind of weather–as receptive to the sun that scorched the furrows as to the rain and fog that forced passersby to seek shelter in the creamery or in the barns.

Van Dam, thanks to Margarida's knowledge of a few words of German and to her ability to communicate through gestures, turned out to be a good substitute for André Barreto in showing her the creamery. His pipe reminded her of Roberto's, although it had a shorter bowl and an ugly metal ring. One day, when she was in a particularly good mood, Margarida confided, in the baron's presence, her opinion of the Dutch technician: "He's a really nice man!..." Feeling somewhat self-conscious, the baron went to show her the Jersey stud and four pregnant cows. Tied to their stanchions and with their flanks stretched out, the four cows' monstrous udders almost brushed against the barn floor.

---

[5] German for "Did you sleep well, Mr. van Dam?"–Author.
[6] German for "eaten... drunk... arrived..."–Author.
[7] "Yes, miss, thank you."–Author.

349

Their engorged teats seemed to illustrate an absurd and brutal symbolism. One of the them, while scratching herself, had clumsily rubbed against one of her teats, and a kind of precocious milk, a bloody presage, inadvertently squirted out all over those emblems of maternal dignity.

Quite often Margarida went into the barn by herself and, getting between the stanchion wall and the cows, pushed against them and patted their hind quarters. The straw and stable beams reeked of a crèche, the lingering strong smell of a recently cleaned barn. A warm, golden jet of urine fell between the heifer's legs. Margarida missed Manuel Bana, and she would stand at the barn door looking at Santo Amaro do Pico's little houses and at Fayal, that ash-gray stain in the distance. A ray of sun made the Pico snowcap scintillate. Margarida rested her elbows on a stone wall, picked a little snapdragon growing in a rock crevice, and put a little twig between her teeth. The *Funchal* should be arriving at Ponta Delgada about now; sometimes it took more than a day to unload and reload the ship.... How slowly time passed!

But, in general, the delay caused Margarida to fall in a pleasant reverie, one of those pleasant dreams one has in the morning while dozing off in bed, at those moments when the mass of the brain itself seems to acquire the shape of the traversed dreamlands and becomes as malleable as paste for cartography in relief. The beauty and simplicity of it! The manorial house up on the hill, with its imposing facade; the roofs of the bunkhouses; the mule with blinders pacing the floor of the treadmill with tiny, uninterrupted steps, as if being taught a lesson in patience...; the edges of the two wells crowned by flowerpots holding carnations and the lemon-verbena plant... (*Lúcia-lima*, it's called...; Margarida, in her waking dream, thought of Lúcia Lima, a friend of hers living in London...). Up top, near the ridge, the baron's pastures stretched farther than the eye could see, fat with grasses fertilized by a wayward humidity, as if the masses of clouds had built above an island of fire a celestial isle with roots sunk in the sea.

At the end of those days of somewhat enervating and prolonged calm, the family got together at nightfall to say the rosary. The baroness' oratory was decorated with palm leaves, festoons, and little chains; the smell of lavender and linseed permeated the house. André's and Clarinha's rooms, located at the far end of the dwelling, constituted a kind of civilized oasis. Clarinha's contained a cheval glass, a rosewood armoire and lots of knickknacks. André's had lots of hunting outfits, cartridge belts hanging from pegs, a small desk with books on agriculture and on milk-skimming methods, *La Hacienda*, and pictures of friends, snapshots taken on board or next to famous monuments: Clarinha in Saint Marcus Square with a pigeon perched on her shoulder; André in front of the Lions' Gate at the Coliseum in Rome; on the Promenade des Anglais, in Nice; on the deck of the *Baloeren*, in Rotterdam harbor. An immense picture of Vesuvius hung over the four-poster bed meticulously covered with a damask bedspread that rendered the pillow underneath all but imperceptible.

Margarida had entered that room only once, listening absent-mindedly to the information supplied by the baroness, droning seer of her children's secrets. She preferred the attic, despite the tubs and grain-measuring containers piled behind the door. She plunged her hands and eyes into the chestnut trunks whence the baroness brought out homespun linens and other fabrics, at least a century old, as well as an assortment of discolored bedspreads from India and splendid lacy purses.

One afternoon, following a line of association occasioned by her remembrance of Manuel Bana's illness and her embroidering the tablecloth in the dining room at the Vineyards, Margarida decided to use her fractured German to ask the Dutchman whether he knew Scheveningen:

"*Waren Sie schon in Scheveningen, Herr van Dam?*"

"*Ja, juffrouw... Scheveningen ligtl vlak bif's Gravenhage*; close to The Hague.... A fishing beach.... *Sehr hübsch!* very pretty... *Nederland is een herlijke land*! My country.... A lot of water.... *Kanal...* tulips.... *En de Zuider-zee* all *blauw*! blue... blue.... *Sehr hübsch!*

Van Dam hailed from the village of Maassluis, Vlaardingen's rival in the herring industry, which lies by the railroad leading from Rotterdam through Delft and on to The Hague, Leiden, and Haarlem. But now he lived with his wife in Bennebroek, on the dunes of the North Sea, surrounded by fields of tulips and hyacinths. One afternoon, as Margarida was about to ask him to explain his particular method of cheese-making, the master technician disappeared for a while, returning a little later with a snapshot of his little house built by the roadside, fresh curtains on the windows, manicured bushes, Vrouw van Dam leaning on her bicycle with a baby in the bike basket. Margarida praised the photo to the skies; and, since the noise from the motor of the milk-skimmer was nearly drowning out her voice and van Dam was a little hard of hearing, she leaned toward him, practically shouting in his ear:

"*Welch schönes haus!* "*Welch schönes baby!* This is your grandson?!

"*Ja, juffrouw....*"

Van Dam smiled, absorbed by the seam of the endless driving belt, which, every second, reappeared on top of the motor's little flywheel. Then, he took the picture back to his room, returning afterward with a little sweetmeat box of Delft porcelain, which he handed to Margarida, his face becoming redder than before:

"*Is voor U, juffrouw....* It isn't much, I regret...."

"Not at all! Not at all!" Margarida put her arms around van Dam's strong shoulders and then ran toward her room.

Little did it matter that the master technician had not been able to describe Bankastraat in Scheveningen! Except for the pipe, he really, really resembled Uncle Roberto! Since she had no purse or place wherein to store her treasure, Margarida thought of the whaleman's jacket that had protected her from the cold in the whaleboat and had met with the baron's strong disapproval. She carefully unfolded and wrapped it around the little box, after having proudly verified the name of its manufacturer: JOOST-THOOFT & LABOUCHRE, OOSTEIND.

As usual, Margarida felt like reading a little before going to sleep; not having anything else, she opened Canon António Maria Ferreira's *Recollections of My Pilgrimage to Rome and*

Lourdes on the Occasion of the Jubilee Holy Year of 1900, the book that the baroness had been so taken with. After having passed a lazy finger over the chapter on the canonizations of St. Jean-Baptiste of La Salle and St. Rita of Cassia, patron saint of lost causes, she fixed her attention upon an article, quoted in full by the canon, inviting pilgrims to journey to Rome:

> "*To ROME, Portuguese Catholics, to ROME! with no discrimination by social position or hierarchies....*
>
> *Let us go kneel at the feet of Leo XIII, that incomparable elder man who has astounded and filled the whole world with admiration....*
>
> *Let us go listen, perhaps for the last time, to the words of everlasting life that pour like sweet manna from his sacred lips....*
>
> *To ROME, that world full of wonders....*
>
> *To ROME, that land of martyrs, that cradle of Christian heroes, who, by sheer dint of sublime virtue, succeeded in erecting the Cross of Redemption above the Capitol!*
>
> *Oh! how at home the Catholic heart feels in that place....*
>
> *The Coliseum, where countless thousands of Christians were fed to the wild beasts for the amusement of a people who called themselves the most civilized in the world and their masters, sets before our eyes the immense good to be derived from Christianity, even in this world...*
>
> *There we will see all the temples used in ancient times for the worship of idols....*
>
> *There we will see, consecrated to the Virgin Queen of Angels, the famous Pantheon where the nefarious pagan gods were worshipped in olden times!*
>
> *There we will see with our own eyes the holiest of Relics of Jesus Christ and of the Blessed Virgin: the nails that pierced the most sacred hands of the Divine Martyr; the lance that pierced His most sacred Breast; the sponge*

353

soaked in vinegar; the Effigy of His Divine Face stamped upon the cloth with which St. Veronica wiped away the sweat from his brow; the Table upon which he held the Last Supper with his disciples and upon which he instituted the Holy Sacrament out of His love for mankind; there we will climb on our knees the same stairs of Pilate's palace that the divine Convict ascended and descended; we will see the Column where he was flogged and so many other most sacred objects that rouse our faith, piety, and love.

There we will venerate the sacred ashes of Peter and Paul...

There we will visit the Cells of so many Saints, still adorned with utensils they used when alive and where so many mysteries of love took place, mysteries to which only the Angels were privy.

There we will contemplate, full of faith and wonder, the most beautiful temples in the world.... (This passage and the next one were long and contrasted with the naive unction of the other paragraphs.)

Let us, therefore, journey to ROME; let us go and contemplate the new Jerusalem....

There, before so many wonders both divine and human, the soul feels as if it is detaching from the earth....

There the eyes see what nowhere else on earth can be seen...

There faith is ennobled and redoubled.
There everything is grand, majestic, sublime.

....

Therefore, let there be no second thoughts.
TO ROME, TO ROME....

The canon added the following comment: *"So beautiful and pressing was this invitation! There was, therefore, no need to think twice! One needed only to pack one's bags at once and depart!"*

Margarida, overcome by sleep, her ears still ringing with that incessant "To Rome! To Rome!," her face buried in the sheets, really had the impression that she was about to set out for parts unknown–Horta, Lisbon, London, ROME! ROME!–in an immense caravan that included bishops, shepherds, whalemen, the baroness (finally determined to sail away), the baron, Clarinha, van Dam, Daisy Warren, João Garcia, and even his Uncle Ângelo, the queer one... all of them spurred on by an untiring sperm whale tied to the end of an endless line, whose million knots Margarida was in charge of counting one by one.

Chapter XXXIII

Lullaby

The baron planned to accompany Margarida to Velas that morning so she could get away from the torpor of the house and farm and visit the municipal capital. In his heart of hearts, he felt very proud walking around town with his new guest, introducing her to the judge's family, to the archpriest, to Dr. Trajano, having the secretary of Misericórdia show her the Consistory hall, with its portrait in crayon, maps, abacus, and glass case containing solids and other implements of the metric system that, months earlier, André had donated to the two primary schools in town, as he also had done to the primary school in Urzelina. Clarinha, in turn, had opened a cafeteria and donated embroidery hoops for the girls' school. And the baron had offered the club a collection of books chosen by one of the local literati, who wished to continue in the tradition initiated by old Soares de Albergaria, the retired colonel of the Liberation Army. After he had spent years and years in the bunkers around Elvas, the colonel had settled in Urzelina, entertaining the leisured adolescents of Velas and environs with evening talks on history, rational and moral philosophy, latinity, and on the so-called "ultimate" Portuguese. He knew Napoleon's life by heart and was acquainted with every single detail on the Catiline Conspiracy. He thus guided the older youths away from the dangers of bar life and the entanglements of bastardy. In a humanitarian gesture, the baron ensured the project would stay afloat by supplying books by Oncken, Herculano, and a set of volumes on the Dreyfus Affair.

Margarida took advantage of the early hours of the morning to go for a hike in the mountains, accompanied by van Dam, who had promised to show her the latest hygienic methods of milking cows into closed metal jugs, the way it was done in Holland. Antonico Massinha, the baron's dairy foreman, supervised the two milkers, who wore special caps, white frocks, and a kind of loose-fitting homespun apron slit up the sides, like those still worn in Terceira.

They rose early. The morning was cool, but the dawn slowly began to reveal the curves of the mountains and the contours of the sea cliffs. Despite the choppy seas and a little veil of fog hovering over the mountain, the day looked promising. The checkerboard pastures were dark and damp, hedged on all sides by dark green hydrangeas; and though they lacked those myriad dream-blue water droplets also typical of a recently sulphur-sprayed vineyard, which Margarida had so often seen along the Caldeira roadsides, the puffs of torn clouds in the whitish sky were like great deflowered inflorescences.

Margarida admired the big, full udders of the purebred cows. Antonico Massinha lifted the cow's tail, coiling it against the hindquarters, after having separated the recently born calf by tying it to one of the mother's front legs. Then, washing the teats under the watchful eye of van Dam, who squatted near him smoking his pipe, he passed his hand around the cow's engorged udder and spilled two or three squirts of milk on the ground to prime her, after which one could hear the rhythmic spattering of warm milk inside the can. The cow let out a seemingly melancholy moo, closed her eyes, raised her cold wet muzzle, and scratched her back with one of her horns. Other cows, grazing a little farther away, bent over until they could lick their bellies with their tongues. Here and there, a cowbell sounded in the cold silence of the morning. Margarida drank milk warm from the cow and ate a little sweet bread that the baroness had packed for her in a little patchwork bag, and after hiking down the mountain and leaving van Dam working in the creamery office, she continued down through the fields until she reached the first houses of Urzelina.

Stopping in the middle of a little dead-end street and counting the silent doors between the still-closed little windows, she felt as if lost in a foreign town, like one looking for an address.

Then, walking resolutely toward a grimy shack and stepping on a stone slab that provided a kind of bridge over the paved gutter, she knocked on a door. A woman, still half asleep and with her hair all disheveled, answered:

"Oh, my dear young lady! My house is in no condition to receive guests.... It's a pigsty! I got my bread out of the oven past midnight. I bake and wash for pay.... I still have a mountain of clothes right there, waiting to be bleached and scrubbed. But please do come in! Make yourself right at home...."

Her name was Cândia Furoa.[1] Margarida had met her at the clothes-washing sites along the creek, and they had talked. She was not yet thirty but looked forty: thin and bony, her ankles swollen from walking barefoot; her body deformed from carrying big baskets of laundry on her hips; and her hands chapped from the cold water and the potash in the soap. Her hair tended toward blond and, despite the hard life, her face was still full. Work, a miscarriage, and four consecutive deliveries had sapped her healthful color, which a simple smile still managed to revive; her breasts, once firm under her spic-and-span blouse, now sagged a little and were much bigger. Only the gleam in her lively eyes, as well as her hair twisted into a bun in back, bespoke a persistent if wasted youth.

"Nighty-night, little beastie!" Using the edge of her hastily donned skirt to clean off the rickety chair she offered Margarida, Cândia Furoa rocked a little cradle blackened from the smoke of cooking, where a six-month-old baby tossed his tiny head and sucked desperately on a wet rag dipped in sugar. Margarida pushed back the chair and, seated on the bench built on the window opening, leaned over the cradle. The young woman, noticing her guest's interest in her baby, showed Margarida his magnificent teeth, despite the one missing in the front: "Thank God, he's developing very well.... At night, I don't even know he's there. He wakes up only once to nurse and then goes right back to sleep, the little pumpkin!"

---

[1] Literally, "Ferret."–Trans.

"What a beautiful baby!" said Margarida. Sliding her hands under the infant's arms and clutching him gingerly in his little diapers, as if she were removing a necklace recently arrived from a jewelry store, she cast a forlorn glance at the shack's bare walls: "And where do your other children sleep?"

"My oldest daughter is in the Girls' Orphanage, in Terceira. It was because of the baroness' kindness that she was accepted...."

"And what's her name?"

"Liberdade.[2]"

Margarida, upon hearing the ridiculously contradictory name, could not help but remark:

"'Liberdade'? What a name!"

Cândia Furoa, her head leaning towards her shoulder and with an ear-to-ear smile that showed she was now game for anything, explained:

"What can I say?... Her father was set on it.... And men are so stubborn. He always said: 'If it's a girl, her name is going to be Liberdade; if it's a boy, Miguel Bumbarda.[3]' He was a free-mason, you know. Priests, he just couldn't stand them!"

"Miguel would've been prettier...."

"I would've preferred a little boy, too.... It was my first baby.... But when I was young, I was very naive, didn't know what was what.... But now it's different.... I better not even start talking about it!"

"And where is your children's father? Does he help you at all?"

"Their father...?" Cândia Furoa, feeling suddenly apprehensive, as if Margarida had climbed a figtree and she, holding a basket up in the air to catch the figs, had been seized by the fear the young lady might fall, replied: "Please forgive me, but it's getting quite late... And I know that the baron likes to eat his lunch on time...."

"I've got all the time in the world.... Don't worry! So, tell me, doesn't their father put in anything toward their support? Does he live in America?"

---

[2] "Liberty."–Trans.

[3] Literally, "Cannon."–Trans.

"In America? Yep, that's where the low-life who ditched me is! And he didn't leave me a single penny! Just a kid! Yeah, he ruined my life.... And then he just took off... all stuck-up because he was the son of Soares das Manadas, 'Brelinde'..... Rich farmers. My mother, God rest her soul, was a poor widow who made a living by gathering lichen.... How I wish I had had a brother to break that sorry bastard's shameless face when he went back on his word and just slunk off to America on me! But I shouldn't even be telling you these lousy things...."

"Not at all!... Misfortunes.... Please, don't torture yourself!"

The baby, pushing his little feet against Margarida's breasts, broke into a scream.

"Oh, dear, he's got you all dirty! You just couldn't control yourself, could you, you messy little brat?"

Cândia Furoa's eyes were brimming with tears. Using a rag, she cleaned the blouse and skirt of Margarida, who, touched by the gesture, stroked her hair.

But when she had finished telling the details of that first love, which seemed to linger in the depths of the young woman's consciousness like a live coal buried in ashes, it was almost with pride that Cândia Furoa went into the story behind her four children, as well as her social status in Urzelina and Velas. Liberdade was the daughter of a tax collector, a braggart who had come from the mainland and subsequently been driven from the island for denigrating religion and non-payment of his bills. She was eight years old and had been in the orphanage for two. Had it not been for the baron's influence and the baroness' charity, the orphanage would not have accepted a girl that old.

After Liberdade came Simão, Dr. Feraústo's son. Now *he* was a gentleman. He worked at the Civil Registry and treated her very well. Those wagging tongues in Velas used to say, "He not only makes his own kids, he registers them!" But such remarks were to be expected.... He had set her up in a house in Fajãzinha and provided her with everything she could possibly want. As soon as the best printed calico arrived on the ship, he would tell the store owner *Senhor* Francisquinho: "Cut me a piece of fabric to make Cândia a dress!" And a pair of Cordovan shoes.... A merino wool shawl.... But, unfortunately, he was transferred, his father having been sent to prison in the African colonies for murdering a brother-in-law:

"The murder was because of fights over inheritance.... But I tell you: despite it all, he still managed to send me twenty milreis once! He addressed it to: 'The Illustrious Dr. *Óscre* Feraústo, Distinguished Officer of the Civil Registry, Paredes de Coira.' But he never wrote to me again! For so many people life is such a heartbreak...."

And then there was Vitória, who was standing at the door, in her little nightie, her nose running. This one was Father Picanço's daughter, a servant of Christ from abroad, whom the dean had sent away, lest he bring shame upon the older and more serious island priests. Out of pity for him, though, it seems they never barred him from saying Mass.... Vitória was the godchild of Domitília, the baron's respectful maid. And the little one, the baby, was named Joaquim. He was the son of a member of the Coast Guard.

"The backbiters even hinted that *Senhor* Andrèzinho was the father..... What a slanderous accusation! The baron's son!... Heaven forbid that such a thing should have happened!"

Domitília's head appeared at the door:

"Oh, I didn't know you were here, Miss Margarida...."

Vitória ran toward the old lady:

"Godmother, your blessing!"

"May God bless you! Let's get going, Miss Bidinha! The baron and baroness are waiting for you to eat. The baron has ordered the team of mares hitched and the coupé ready to go for a fun ride to Velas."

"Then I must say good-bye, Joaquim!" said Margarida, leaning towards the cradle. "Here, this is a gift for you to buy a little coat...."

Margarida caressed the baby's chin with her finger. The infant opened his mouth into a smile that wrinkled the skin around his little eyes. Cândia Furoa kissed her own hand:

"A kiss for your dearly departed, ma'am!"

At the baron's, lunch was silent and uneventful, as was to be expected, given the baron's opinion that Margarida's visit to Cândia Furoa had been inappropriate. Holding his pocketwatch in his hand and pacing around the table while Margarida had gone to her room to change and freshen up, the baron said to his wife:

"The very idea! Visiting Furoa's house at the break of dawn! This young lady has a pleasant character, but she can be quite set in her ways...."

"That's how they do things in Horta...," said the baroness, excusing Margarida.

"It's because she is always around English people. Here in the town, those habits call attention to themselves...."

"You're probably right... Her father is a bon vivant himself and doesn't apply the proper restraints! As the saying goes, to raise the sapling right, it must feel the farmer's might!"

That unspoken tension hovered until they finished lunch; it seemed to whirl on the plates and fall with the wine as it was poured into the glasses. The coupé waited out on the courtyard. The baron put on his overcoat.

That varnished big "chest" mounted over the wheel springs was the means of transport one would least expect from a dwelling that sat up on a hill. The road coming down to Urzelina was a goat trail, and despite the fact that the baron had had it regravelled out of his own pocket, one could still see, imprinted on the bare rock, the ruts left by the bullock carts from the time of Captain José Urbanino. Belladonna and ferns grew all over the middle of the roadway. To cover a distance of a little more than two kilometers between the town and Velas–and, what's more, down a Calvary-like incline–it was not worth keeping a livery like that driven by a uniformed coachman and two round-crouped mares that, except when ridden by André or Clarinha in her riding outfit, rarely exchanged the tranquility of the mangers for the harnesses. The trips to Calheta, by way of a road that was often impassable, were rare. The baron and baroness went there only when a relative or close friend died or when they had to catch the *Funchal*, which did not stop in Velas. And they always planned for these trips as if preparing to travel across Siberia by stage-coach. But the baron had lived in Ponta Delgada and in Angra and did not want to fail to keep up with the Marquis de Jácome and with the Count de Sieuve.... The amount of his budget earmarked for such endeavors permitted him a crown and the initials B.U. painted on the door of the coupé. André had always maintained that the family had a right to the ermine and the blond hair of the maiden on the Barretos' coat of arms (after all, wasn't Clarinha herself a blonde?). Those heraldic emblems stemmed, albeit by devious ways, from *Dom* Arnaldo de Baião, father of *Dom* Guido Araldes, grandfather of *Dom* Soeiro Guedes, 4th grandfather of Nuno Soares, husband of Maria Pires Perna, daughter of *Dom* Pedro Escacha... "Very well...," the baron used to say, "let's leave out the *Perna de Escacha*[4]... but, by all means, let's use the initials B.U. That's the logo that all the wine casks will bear."

The baroness, who was always indisposed, would not accompany them to town this time. With much use of the brakes, the coupé descended the hill, causing the Urzelina house-wives to appear at their doors. Then it rolled solemnly through the peaceful streets of Velas. Margarida and the baron paid a visit to Club Aliança and then went to the main church to view the statues of the saints and admire the wooden horse, used in the procession of St. George, which was operated by an urchin hiding inside. The curate always showed the "factory book," in which were recorded the donations offered for the legs of the equestrian statue. Margarida took a long time praying. The baron dropped a couple of coins in the poorbox. Afterwards, in the company of two available civil officers, they stopped at the assembly room of the Municipal Chamber to inspect the portrait alterations. Hintze's portrait, which used to hang on the back wall, had been replaced by the plastron and bicolored sash of Manuel de Arriaga ("The Azoreans are first in everything!" explained the Treasurer of the Exchequer); the place of the blue and white flag, which the baron had taken home and discreetly

---

[4] Literally, "Bowlegs."–Trans.

stored behind Clarinha's piano, was now occupied by the much-discussed colors of the Republic. In the Hall of Misericórdia, the baron, modestly moving away from his own likeness, pointed out to his guest the portrait of a full-figured, pleasant-looking elderly lady. Margarida read the inscription aloud:

TO THE BLESSED DONA MARIA JOSEFA DE ÁVILA,
FOUNDER OF THE INSULAR HOME FOR BOTH SEXES:
FROM THE PEOPLE OF THE MUNICIPALITIES
OF SÃO JORGE AND THE ANCIENT TOWN OF TOPO

Intrigued, the baron put on his spectacles:

"'Blessed'? 'Blessed,' no! 'Benefactor'.... 'Benefactor!'"

Margarida blushed visibly and, suppressing a strong desire to laugh, said:

"Pardon me, baron! But those little round letters are so funny...."

Trying to lighten his indiscretion, the baron then explained that it did not surprise him at all that *Dona* Maria Josefa de Ávila had ended up being counted among the blessed. She was an exceedingly good woman. Almost a millionaire, she had led a pauper's life in Lisbon, had made a pilgrimage to Sameiro on foot, and had left all her wealth to the poor. It had not been easy to carry out her last will and testament. In her will, *Dona* Maria Josefa had ordered a large refuge built in São Jorge to house invalids of both sexes, at a rate of nine men and nine women per island. Nine plus nine equals eighteen; eighteen times nine is one hundred and sixty-two. With eighteen more (for São Jorge, the benefactor's island, had been allowed double the number), there were a total of one hundred and eighty. More exactly, one hundred and eighty-two elderly persons: one hundred and eighty-two beds... one hundred and eighty-two bowls... one hundred and eighty-two spoons... plus replacements for broken ones. And blankets... and linen for all of those old folks....

It just so happened, though, that this kind of apportionment led to an injustice. For Corvo, with fewer than seven hundred souls and more than one sheep per capita, not to mention the flow of dollars coming from America, along with the Gulf Stream that warms up the inhabitants, would be represented in the Home by eighteen poor people. Whereas São Miguel, with a population of nearly one hundred and fifty thousand people, its system of large, landed properties, and economic crises which frequently forced the impoverished inhabitants to migrate to the western islands ready to do any work in order to survive (wayward dregs who could only get jobs as porters and grave-diggers...), had been granted the same eighteen old men and women. But still, except for that strange particular (the will had been recorded by an exotic *monsignor*, a Pythagorean preacher), it was a great document! It was a fortune of hundreds and hundreds of contos clearly earmarked for the common good and likely to stimulate the Azorean economy. At night, the fifteen large windows of *Dona* Maria Josefa de Ávila's Home, lit high up on the mountain, gave the island all the seeming of a liner anchored in a safe harbor.

Despite being almost moved by the little old lady's portrait in crayon, which filled the dark hall with an air of kindness and dreams, Margarida stifled an absurd urge to laugh. She had to bite her handkerchief to prevent the tears of laughter from welling up in her eyes. To hide her embarrassment, she kept coughing: "*Blessed*!... The *Blessed Dona* Maria Josefa de Ávila! That's a good one!..."

As they were leaving the Misericórdia, the mailman, hat in hand, approached them:

"I've got a telegram for Your Excellency."

It was addressed to Margarida, care of the baron. Nervously, she opened it: "*Uncle ill stop if yacht available take it*." "Uncle ill." Which uncle? Uncle Mateus Dulmo?... Uncle Roberto?...

"Oh, God! That's Father for you; always doing things half-way! Either way, I need to leave at once! 'Uncle ill...' Perhaps it's Uncle Mateus who is gravely ill... Could he be dying?"

"Don't you go worrying like that, all right? Things do happen. And it's probably nothing to worry about. Then again, I don't mean to suggest it's good news. You just don't send a telegram like that if there's nothing wrong... But, God willing, it won't be a matter of life and death, either..."

"And if it turns out to be Uncle Roberto?" said Margarida with a shudder, as though talking to herself. "He probably caught a cold in the launch; the channel wind can be treacherous! There have been so many cases of the plague in Fayal! As if the scare Manuel Bana has already given us weren't enough!"

"I know..... You're referring to your servant. But it's more likely to be *Senhor* Mateus Dulmo. At his age, it's to be expected..... Probably a case of pneumonia. But Horta has good doctors. And *Senhor* Mateus Dulmo is a resilient old gentleman. Let's not abandon ship just yet!"

"If my father sends a telegram and asks me to catch the next yacht [5], it has to be something serious! Do you think there's a Pico boat departing for Fayal soon?"

They had climbed aboard the carriage. The coupé rolled slowly within sight of the Velas pier. The little port had sufficient capacity for cruisers and liners. But, except for the regular ship that came in once a month, rare were the boats that came to ply its waters; and only at great intervals did its bottom receive the anchor of a cargo ship loaded with salt or the shadow of the old keel of the *Insulano* with a cargo of limestone for the kilns and drums of carbide... On this day, the port, with its slow, swollen waves, was shallow and deserted.

"What about Calheta?" asked Margarida eagerly, looking attentively at the channel spread out before the immense compact mass of Pico. "Maybe some yacht has come into port there..."

"No chance! They're rare this time of year," said the baron, sunk into the seat of the coupé. His shrewd, malicious face reflected a sincere sadness. "Dr. Martins told me that a week ago the *Santo Amaro* arrived at Calheta with a cargo of dishes and piglets from Terceira. It loaded cheese and lumber for Fayal. But I think that the *Ribeirense* went to Graciosa to pick

---

[5] In the Pico of the first decades of the century, the term "yacht" referred to a rather modest type of boat.–Trans.

up some casks of wine. Maybe it'll stop over at Calheta on the way back.... I'm going to find out right this minute."

The trip from the town to Urzelina, though short, seemed to Margarida, as they rode up to the Queimada, to take an eternity. During the afternoon a southeast wind had risen and once in a while lifted swirling clouds of dark dust from the road. The incense trees lining the two sides of the road, their leaves crisp and their drupes cracked, shook and bent. Margarida, curled up at the bottom of the coupé, her eyes wide and staring off into space with the air of a madwoman, bit her nails.

Fearing the steep incline up the roadway to the house, as well as the hard springs of the carriage, the baron was in the habit of stepping off the coupé when he passed the last houses in Urzelina; Margarida, still lost in thought, mechanically did likewise, and started sprinting toward the house. The baroness was already walking towards the carriage to meet them:

"What's the matter, Bidinha? Did something happen to Caetano? You look really distraught!"

"Please order a lunch packed for me to take, baroness. I beg you, please.... One of my uncles is dying!"

"What! Oh, dear Lord!"

Chapter XXXIV

Sixth Nocturne
(Full Moon)

All efforts the baron and baroness made to dissuade Margarida from going to Calheta were in vain. The town being so far away, why not send a messenger on foot to find out whether any yacht had come in or if one was expected any day soon? At a brisk pace, it would only take four or five hours on foot. "Wait a minute...." The baron remembered that he could actually send Antonico Massinha with the freight cart or rent one of those carryalls that could be found even in Urzelina. Maybe they already had heard something in Ribeira Larga; farther on, from the summit of Biscoitos, one could clearly make out the bare masts of little anchored boats rocking in the port for days and days.

But Margarida remained bound and determined and so packed her things: the borrowed clothes and the whaleman's jacket that served as wrapper for van Dam's gift, the sweetmeat box from Delft. As for the rubber boots she had worn aboard the whaleboat, she asked Domitília to make sure to return them to the whalemen.

"A trip to Calheta, down god-awful roads, this late in the day!..." observed the baroness despondently.

Margarida overcame her disquietude and the urge to cry by pacing all over the house and making herself useful. Her hand and head gestures and lively disposition lent the departure preparations, despite the tragic nature of the situation, a touch of lightness, as if she were preparing for a Holy Ghost celebration or a picnic.

"Since you insist on leaving, Caetano will accompany you... Chico went to feed and water the mares."

But Margarida did not want to impose anymore. The animals were tired from the trip to Velas and back. She suggested they rent one of the two victorias in town. She would be willing, though, to have one of the employees, Antonico Massinha or the coachman, fetch the victoria for her.

But the baron, walking into the room unexpectedly, was coming to exercise his authority as master of the house. He looked a little pale, was slightly hunched over, and once in a while clutched his hands to his abdomen.

"What's ailing you, Caetano?... Do you have a stomachache?"

The baron made a vague gesture with his hands, signaling to his wife to be quiet. The little hat he was in the habit of wearing around the house was pulled down over his brow, whose deep wrinkles betrayed considerable pain suffered in silence.

"I'm going with them. The weather doesn't look good, but the mares are fast. Of course, we'll be wasting our breath.... Yachts are very rare at this time of year. Besides, there seems to be no pressing need to take such an uncomfortable trip in an open boat! But I can understand Margarida's concern after receiving that telegram.... Plus the fact that she doesn't even know which one of her uncles is ill. Though I think it must be *Senhor* Mateus Dulmo.... But let's do what we can!..."

Weighing the disturbance caused by this incident upon the orderly lives of the two elderly people and reliving the slight discomfort that her stay there had made her feel despite their deferential treatment, Margarida pressed her idea of renting a carriage. It did not matter whether she had to take a victoria or a bullock cart or had to follow the shepherd on foot with lantern in hand and all wrapped in scarves–so long as she could reach a port as soon as possible and catch a boat for Fayal. If there was no boat leaving Pico, she was willing to take one of those big barges used to transport cattle to ships, get on a fishing boat, anything, even if she had to swim–provided she could get there in time to find her uncle still alive.

Darkness was fast descending upon Point Rosais, where the Dutch-style windmills, which so stirred van Dam's emotions,

369

were picking up speed. An east wind (coming from the point of Pico, which meant terror for seamen and mountain shepherds) spiked the slumbering fury of the channel. A splash of sunlight cloaked Pico with a golden, red-speckled splendor; and the rolling, fleecy waves seemed ready to quit the green watery pastures to transhume.

Domitília came to inform them that tea awaited them on the table; the baron had disappeared into his room. Taking long draughts of tea, Margarida, who was beginning to feel disarmed in the face of the baroness' insistence on ordering the coupé ready, reminded her that it was not necessary to inconvenience the baron, that she had no problem traveling alone.

"No, not alone! I couldn't allow a young lady like you to travel to Calheta unescorted!"

Margarida smiled; her eyes had an ironic and pained gleam:

"Come, baroness! Remember how I showed up here... all by myself! after crossing the channel on a whaleboat towed by a harpooned whale!" Her nervous laughter shook her steaming cup of tea. "Do you need any greater proof that I have nothing to fear from the Fates?"

"I can't deny that you are a courageous young lady!..."

"But you've got to admit, baroness, that I'm a little eccentric, right?"

The baroness smiled, lowered her eyes and dipped a biscuit in her tea. A muffled sigh was heard, coming from the far end of the house.

"Will you excuse me, Margarida? I think I heard Caetano. I suspected that he was suffering from his usual pain.... He's very patient. When the attack begins, he doesn't breathe a word.... He suffers in silence. He's a saint!"

Margarida got up and went to the door. The coachman was fastening the reins to the mares' bits; the cover of the coupé, polished and dripping water, shone in the twilight. Thank goodness that the baron's sudden attack freed her from two hours of his inopportune company, especially now that her heart felt darker than the luxurious carriage parked in the middle of that courtyard lined with chrysanthemums and squash. Her great desire was that they let her go by herself, buried in the coupé seat, alone with her unhappiness. Indeed, if the uncertainty of finding transportation to Horta did not weigh on her so, the prospects of riding for hours through the hills of São Jorge would have brought her a sense of welcome relief, one of those feelings of peace and liberation which absurdly overcome us when there is a corpse in the house waiting to be buried and the hour finally comes for one's body to finally reclaim its birthright.

Absorbed in these thoughts, like a sleepwalker, her arm resting against the doorjamb, Margarida was suddenly startled by approaching footsteps. It was the baroness, who had the habit of appearing out of nowhere, much like one of those insects that go round and round in circles and then, with a quick flap of the wings, reverse directions.

"I was right, after all.... Caetano has his usual pains! He suffers from enterocolitis, an inflammation of the intestines. Dr. Trajano used to recommend hot flannel compresses on his stomach; now it's ice that's supposed to help.... Fortunately, we can have it sent from Terceira. We have two boxes there, full of blocks of ice. They look like glass soap. They come wrapped in sawdust; the ice is then broken into pieces and placed in a rubber bag. But both Caetano and I are very wary of all that cold. The Sanitation Inspector is also a very good doctor... but that ice treatment couldn't possibly do much good.... The laudanum drops... now that's a good remedy. I always keep a bottle. But, my God, there's no proper person to accompany you now. Wouldn't it be better, then, to let Chico go alone?... Even if the yacht is already in Calheta, it's not going to sail this late in the day. Tomorrow, in daylight, you could then go by yourself...!"

"No, baroness. I'm very sorry to act against your wishes. But I'm leaving right now."

Wearing his peakless cap and his bombazine coat, van Dam unobtrusively appeared at the door. Having been informed of Margarida's impending departure, he had come to offer his help. Margarida actually thought that it would be a good idea to let the pleasant Dutchman accompany her, to have someone to talk to along the way. But, imagining that the baroness might be

371

unwilling to let anyone go with her except the baron, now laid up on account of his pain, and being already irritated by all the fuss, she stubbornly clung to her decision to go alone:

"*Danke schön, Herr van Dam!*"

"At your service, *juffrouw....*"

The baroness eyed her master technician enigmatically. Considering his age (fifty), his good judgment and good nature (dull and very calm), she seemed to find him fit to act as Margarida's page during the "voyage to Calheta"; she even thought that, if Margarida were a member of her family, she'd let him accompany her on a voyage to England, should it be necessary. But Margarida cut that indecision to the quick. The baroness' sorting out of protocol–should the Dutchman occupy the seat in the coupé next to the guest of honor, or should he sit in front like a lackey?–came to naught and soon vanished from her feeble brain.

The coachman loomed at the door, announcing that the carriage was ready. Margarida, adjusting the hat that Clarinha had loaned her, went to the master bedroom to say good-bye to the baron.

"Are you feeling a little better?"

The baron made a grimace to suppress a sharp attack from his rebellious intestines. He waved with his open hand:

"This time, the attack is not as strong, but it is enough to tie me down hand and foot, at the very moment when you insist on leaving. I've already given Angélica instructions for Antonico to get ready. He'll ride in the driver's seat. It's better that he accompany you to the pier and help you with all the last-minute preparations. It's still my opinion, though, that you won't find any yacht in Calheta. With seas like these.... I can feel them–even lying right here in bed!"

Margarida listened to all these arguments with the peculiar smile of a traveler who sees herself caught in the ritual of an endless farewell. Clarinha's gloves were a little too tight for her, forcing her to contract her palms as she tried to put them on.

"So I'll say good-bye, baron.... And much obliged for everything! When do you think we shall see one another again?

Since I don't know what awaits me in Calheta, this is a long good-bye. It's been such a long time since we have enjoyed your company in Fayal!... Why don't you take advantage of your children's delay in Horta and go meet them there?"

"Can't you see the condition I'm in?" said the baron, crossing his hands on the blanket. "Where would you want to take an invalid like me?" The baroness remarked:

"Now, it'll have to be when you decide to accept Clarinha and André's invitation to spend some time with us. You know how much we'd like that.... It may even happen that your stay in England may coincide with one of our children's pleasure trips. Though, deep down, I believe you'll change your mind about leaving.... It would amount to a kind of betrayal of all of us!"

Margarida smiled, and the movement of her hand caused the couple's bedsprings to creak. The baroness, breaking out of her silence, something which lent her the appearance of a statue quivering with animation and full of life, said, growing ever more talkative:

"Well, you want to know something? You were here only half-a-dozen days, but you really won yourself a place in our hearts. To think that you could be going so far away really ties me up in knots inside! The very islands will feel forsaken! Our home will feel so dark... so forlorn!" The baron requested more laudanum. "And, needless to say, you're always welcome here.... Our door is always open."

Margarida left the room a little regretfully and quite moved. When she climbed into the carriage, she could still feel in her hand the baron's silent, drawn-out handshake and the warmth of the baroness' face so close to hers, her eyes full of tears. Van Dam politely closed the door of the coupé; Antonico Massinha and the coachman took the driver's seat.

"Have a good trip, Bidinha! Have a good trip! Button up against the cold...."

"Good-bye, baroness! Good-bye!... And sorry for the imposition...."

When the coupé, already underway, traced a curve over the volcanic gravel and she could no longer see anyone, Margarida used the handkerchief with which she had waved good-bye to the baroness and to van Dam to wipe her moistened eyes. But, as the coupé rocked over the bumpy road, that moment of tenderness soon vanished.

She had telegraphed her father right away: *"Tell me which uncle fell ill will depart when possible."*

Now that the baron's team had just delivered her from the siege laid by the two elderly hosts and she was moving away from that environment of orchards and pastures where her mind had not dwelt on dark thoughts, or even on things she cared deeply about, the moment had come when the fear that she was going to find Uncle Roberto dead alternated with the painful possibility of losing Uncle Mateus Dulmo, who despite his advanced age, was the one whom she had loved and needed the most throughout the course of her sad life. For, at this moment, she had little doubt that it was Uncle Mateus who was gravely ill. That paragon of good health, that unassailable temperament could not last forever. He was almost eighty.... Despite the tranquility he enjoyed at home, and Rosário's care, and the harmonium played at night like a light turned on in the darkness of the desert, he was tired and spent. He had always lived a quiet and secluded life, but with no real attachments, without an affection strong enough to absorb the energy of that boundless heart, a heart of sweetness and humanity unmatched!

Having passed the small lava terrains of Casteletes, the coupé, slowly and sleepily, entered Manadas. To the right lay Terreiros, where Dr. João Teixeira Soares' mansion was. Uncle Mateus talked a lot about that old man, an Azorean patriarch, in his youth a model to his peers, a man of talent and learning who led a deliberately obscure life in that far-flung corner of São Jorge, gathering odd bits of historical information about the discovery of the islands, and about the assaults on the populations by Argelian corsair ships. Such must have been the terror spread by the pirates that the word *corsairo* still survived in the everyday language of the common people. *Corsairinho* was the term jokingly applied to children; a broken woman like Cândia Furoa was referred to as–*corsaira*! It was precisely this term heard in her childhood from the mouth of Uncle Mateus that made Margarida remember him as a smiling, lively, gentleman, with hair that was almost all grey, who sat her on his knees and, unwrapping chocolate candies for her, would say: *"Ah! corsairinha!"* All the ditties, ballads, and songs that Uncle Mateus sang for her were taken from a book published by Teófilo Braga, with information supplied by Dr. João Teixeira [1]....

A dimming full moon cast a golden glow upon the incense and faya trees along the edge of the road, piercing like a lance the door of the coupé, lighting the small bevelled mirror that André had ordered installed on the glass partition between the interior of the carriage and the driver's seat. Margarida watched the play of shadows projected by Antonico Massinha's cloak and battered hat and by the whip in Chico's hand, which was rendered quite unnecessary by the regular and brisk trot of the baron's mares. And since she had a good memory and a knack for languages, she remembered that the Spaniards called the driver's seat—*pescante* or 'fishing spot'! Come to think of it, both Chico and Antonico, so silent and bent over, seemed to be sitting on the Marraxo fishing ledge waiting for a bogue to bite...

Margarida rose a little from her seat to look in the mirror. Her cheeks looked hollow from the emotional upheavals and crying during that fateful day; her hair was stiff and unmanageable; and an air of weariness and her paleness made her almost unrecognizable to herself. Was this deathlike pallor what accounted for the resemblance she bore to Grandmother Margarida Terra? She recalled the portrait hanging in the Granary, her grandmother's enigmatic smile upon the parched and somber canvas. Cousin Corina used to say: "You're the spitting image of your grandmother Margarida! No doubt about it... from head to toe!" Uncle Mateus would say, in his turn: "Yes... there's a resemblance... More in the mannerisms than the features...."

---

[1] Azorean-born Teófilo Braga (1843-1924), besides being president of the Provisional Government of the Republic (1910-1911), was a writer and a prolific scholar. Nemésio is ironically alluding to what some consider to be Braga's not always scrupulous scholarly practices.–Trans.

Could it be because of her ball gown, because of that old-fashioned air that people used to notice in her under the lights of the chandeliers in the Royal Club of Fayal? All women with attractive faces and decent silk dresses looked more or less alike. And from these thoughts, there arose in Margarida's mind, like a silkworm butterfly emerging at the right moment from its cocoon, the suspicion that Uncle Mateus Dulmo might have been in love with Grandmother Margarida Terra. She remembered the letter that her uncle had consented to read to her one night on São Francisco Street. Between those perfectly handwritten lines one could read a complaint veiled in aristocratic reserve. The description of the inconsequential events of a reclusive and monotonous life; the pious request for the transfer of Francisco Brum's mortal remains lying forgotten in the Flemish cemetery in Oogenbom; the discreet allusion to Charles Clark's selfishness; and the strange attitude, reminding one of altars and martyrs, which she adapted in regard to her husband's affair with "poor Ana Silveira"—all bore the marks of a delicate femininity.

And what if Grandmother Margarida Terra really was Uncle Mateus' great love, if the poor old man had indeed held in the dead woman's heart a reluctant or impossible place?... And while the coupé lumbered up the steep and rocky incline, she imagined, lulled by the caracoling movements of the mares, charitably loaned by strangers, that at this precise moment she might not be Bidinha, daughter of *Senhor* Charles Clark's son-in-law, arrived in São Jorge in a whaleboat fleeing justice in Horta, but some other Bidinha. She might be the granddaughter of *Senhor* Mateus Dulmo, perhaps betrothed to the legitimate son of *Senhor* Charles Clark and *Dona* Ana Silveira, a young and pleasant young man employed in London—in short, a stranger, a good match—and for sure she would be feeling much more at peace right now and much less unhappy.

After passing the Church of Santa Barbara, where the baron had taken Margarida to view the famous porcelain tiles, they left behind the stone fences and the row of houses with their hearth fires burning and started climbing an endless, inhospitable hill. Planted fields extended out from both sides of the road, but one could see the stretches of volcanic terrain on that spread-out area of the island, to which the moon lent the odd appearance of burned-out, pale-green craters. They were the pastures for poor folk's livestock–the "communal pastures," abode of the winds convened at the center of the Azores and then charged with going the rounds of the whole archipelago, from the calcareous rocks in Santa Maria to the statue of Chactas in Corvo to the sargasso in the Gulf Stream.

Running in the opposite direction to the stone fences on either side of the road, the carriage rolled on. Every so often, a faya, dark and round, stood out, seemingly shrouded in moonlight. Sitting with her forehead pressed against the pane of a window she had raised, Margarida had the feeling that the mares were not only dragging along the coupé and her body, but her entire life as well–past, present, and future–much like those leaden clouds that encircle the thin neck of Pico.

She crossed Ribeira Larga with these thoughts, and rode by a large deserted public trough overflowing with water brought to it by an underground pipeline from the slopes of the northern part of the island. To the right rose the stretch of dilapidated stone wall guarding the precipice above Fajã Grande. Despite the distance between the curve and the abyss, Margarida, exhausted and dizzy, had fleeting glimpses of the coupé moving along the very edge of the cliff. As it negotiated a curve, and one of the wheels got accidentally caught in a rut, the carriage suddenly swerved. Looking through the pane and noticing Antonico Massinha's bovine, rough-hewn face, Margarida felt in the jolt the perfect consummation of a catastrophe–mares, coupé and passengers all plunging down right in the middle of Fajã.

Having reached the summit of Biscoitos, whence, down a long descent, one could see Calheta, Margarida tapped on the pane.

"Nothing to worry about, madam! The brakes are working well!"

"But, please, stop! Please!"

The coachman stepped down and half-opened the little door: "What's the problem?..."

"I want to get out! Let's check and see if there are any yachts in the port...."

But the little houses of Calheta, nestled close to one another, faced a deserted pier. Under the light of the full moon, the church tower overlooking the rooftops bathed in silence and in the light of a waning full moon, stood as fixed symbol of the wave-pounded land from the west-northeast all the way to Point Forcada.

The town was still stirring, though Margarida's lot improved not the least for it. They had stopped in front of a store that was about to close. A man in an overcoat informed Antonico Massinha that, at that hour, only at the Coast Guard office could she get any information. But....

"A boat from Pico? At this time of year? Only with divine intervention, madam...."

When they had reached the Pier Square, Margarida herself got out of the coupé and went to the Coast Guard–a huge building eroded by salty sea breezes. Two officials, still dressed in their linen uniforms, were playing checkers by the light given off by a stub of candle stuck in the neck of a bottle. They both stood up. The fatter one, informed of Margarida's emergency and state of anxiety, tossed his cap desolately on the checkerboard:

"I'm sorry to say, madam, that, as far as I know, no boat is scheduled to arrive...."

And essaying a smile in an attempt to brighten things up after the disappointment he had authored, he added: "When the summer is over, they all dry dock in their home ports...."

"And what about Azevedo?" suggested the other guard. "Perhaps Azevedo, the agent at Cais do Pico, has some news about other cargo vessels...."

"What do you mean, Azevedo? Do you think that just because he's an agent, he is more familiar with the sea traffic than we are?" And to let Margarida know that he was the local chief officer of the Coast Guard, he declared: "No boat comes in or goes out without my knowledge. Besides, Azevedo lives in Ribeira Seca.... By now, he's already in bed."

Margarida bowed her head.

"I'm sorry, madam...," said the slimmer guard, "... but there is now only *Funchal*, which arrives the day after tomorrow. Before sunrise, it'll round the point of Topo on its way in. And as soon as he sees our boat, the chief officer will order anchor cast. Commander Vidinha is always in a hurry...."

For a while, Margarida stood staring at the checkerboard, which was partially covered by the guard's cap. Then, making an effort to smile and thank the men, she climbed aboard the coupé, raised the windows all the way up and returned to the Baron and Baroness da Urzelina's by the same road that had just brought her, dazed but hopeful, to Calheta.

Chapter XXXV

New and Ancient Methods
of Rescuing the Shipwrecked

Having slept poorly, Margarida woke up startled and lit the lamp. The little gold clock that the baroness had placed by her bedside scintillated, suspended from a double oscillating chain.

One o'clock.... Two o'clock.... Three-thirty...

The hands of the clock seemed to suffer from a strange paralysis, as if the cogwheels, and time itself, turned in an oily dust. Through the half-opened seaward window came a beam of moonlight, obscured every so often by the passing clouds.

At quarter to five, she woke up to the sounds of a creaking door and furtive steps that the baroness, despite walking on tip-toe, could not avoid making. She had come to check whether Margarida had finally fallen asleep, because their young guest had been a little feverish at bedtime, even though she had not experienced chills or headaches. It was her nerves.

Close to midnight, the baron had started feeling worse; and Margarida, after having gotten out of the coupé (the coachman had pressed the mares, and the carriage seemed to fly along the gutted, deserted roads, like a sailboat propelled by frenzied oarsmen), had heard, from out on the driveway, his recurrent cries of bellowing pain.

It was almost seven when she woke up for good. A vague light brightened the windows. In the first mornings of her stay at the baron's, Margarida would get up early to arrive at the pastures in time to see Antonico Massinha separate the calves and milk the cows. But now, dawn meant nothing to her; indeed, it seemed to bring her a divine threat of more calamities and uncertainties. She heard the noise made by cans and milk pails rattling to the rhythm of someone's footsteps. But that sign of a full and normal life, far from calming her, heaped even more misery on her. Margarida checked her own pulse. She probably had no fever, but she felt excessively lucid and her emaciated face–which she saw by taking a quick peak in Clarinha's pocket mirror–worried her. Aggrieved and anxious, she got up, and half-opened the window overlooking the pine grove. The Old Tower rose from the bare gray "mystery." The rectory, still buried in lava, revealed two windows overgrown with nettles. She called out:

"Antonico! Antonico!..." The shepherd, who already was at some distance, came running back. "Do you know if a telegram for me has arrived?"

"It's still too early, ma'am! The post office doesn't open before nine. By the way... Senhor Fandango is getting ready to go to Velas."

Margarida suddenly closed the guillotine window.

No! No telegram would arrive, nothing would arrive!...

She had no father... no mother! And her brother was nothing but an overgrown child, unemployed, good only for hunting. Her father's consuming interests were Bishop Alexandre Square and the soirées at Mariquinhas Estragada's tavern. Only when the going got tough did he show any interest in the family problems. Her mother was totally lacking in initiative, standing by the side of her decrepit and senile father. In the face of adversity, she would raise her hands to her ears, much like monkeys who, when separated from their trees or bananas, let themselves drown. Maria das Angústias was her friend; still, she was only a servant. As for Manuel Bana, he was just an orphan in this world....

No doubt about it: she was all alone in this world! Alone... her youth under the watchful eye of only her God and, right now, the Baroness da Urzelina. Still, though she had no father or mother, she did have her uncles. But it was precisely her uncles whom she was about to lose–one of them, at any rate. However, since no one in Horta seemed to be kind enough to go to a post office and draft a telegram to at least tell her which one was ill, Margarida was beginning to suspect that she had lost both of them.

She had lain down again, hiding her head in her hands and her hands in the pillow. And if she should lose both of them (if Uncle Roberto was the one dying, Uncle Mateus, who was already so old, couldn't possibly survive him much longer...), what would become of her? Who would protect her? True, she was healthy and had "two strong arms," as Manuel Bana always remarked whenever he saw able-bodied young people who led a life of leisure. "They've got plenty of strength! What young men and women don't want to do nowadays is lift a finger!..." But obeying its stupid and presumptuous principles, the society of Horta could not suffer a young woman of her social standing to earn her own living. It was considered shameful to earn one's bread with the sweat of one's brow! On the other hand, to have no place to call one's own, to be forced to become, from one day to the next, the wife of a sought-after rich boy, the only son of a filthy-rich old man, or of one of those less fortunate idlers who have to share their wealth with siblings and live in the hope of inheriting from a tubercular or idiotic brother or from a sister who spinelessly follows her priest's advice, ends up in his arms, and later withers away in a convent–that, according to the prevailing Horta mores, was extremely smart! That was not shameful! How laughable!... What asinine double standards!... What a miserable farce!

Still leaning on the bed but raising her head from the crumpled pillow, Margarida sadly kept shaking her head. No, she would not send van Dam to Velas with the message; she herself would go, in person. An idea had just occurred to her: the whalemen! João da Cezilha, Uncle Amaro de Mirateca, still stuck on the little pebbly beach cutting up the whales, trying the blubber as best they could in caldrons charitably loaned to them, would not let her down now. One of the two whaleboats could very well take her to Fayal, under sail or manpower. In order not to tire out the men and to arrive sooner, they could aim for Santo António do Pico, and there she could rent some old carriage or car to whisk her off to Madalena.

She dressed hurriedly. And, without so much as a word to the baroness, to avoid raising any objections, she called Domitília and told her that it was urgent that she go to Velas. She'd ask van Dam to go with her and would be back in a flash.

At the post office she met with disappointment. "Margarida Clara who?..." "Clark! Clark Dulmo." No! There was no telegram addressed to that name. And the clerk showed her the apparatus' little wheel, still vibrating from imprinting the last characters on a ribbon addressed to the agent of the Insulana Company. There was nothing classified about it. It was a telegram from Terceira, informing him that the *Funchal* had departed for Graciosa at 2:00 a.m.

Margarida did not need to rent a carriage to drive her to Point Ruiva. She saw Intavante at the door of a pharmacy. A whaleman had hurt his foot with a cutting-spade and he had come to buy tincture of "odium" and cotton swabs. In answer to the question of whether they could spare a whaleboat to help her in that emergency, Intavante, holding the package under his arm, pointed toward the rough, green mass of the channel:

"Can't you see, miss?... The sea is *rofe*.[1] What oars could withstand a sea like that? As for using sails, no way at all! There's a headwind... blowing from the point of Pico!"

Everywhere obstacles!... Margarida still blamed the refusal on the ill will of Intavante, who always had a sour face, and wondered if she should go to the beach and try to convince João da Cezilha and Uncle Amaro. But on approaching the pier she saw huge sheets of foam covering the entire surface of the dark and pointed tiny seaport of Velas with a kind of canvas-like spray. Disheartened, she returned to town to look for van Dam.

Toward the afternoon the weather improved somewhat; it started to rain. From the wet lava rose a tepid steam, causing at once a sensation of freshness and of fire, its perfume heavenly. Domitília started to close the windows one by one; and in the

---

[1] From the English "rough."–Trans.

383

huge deserted house (with the baroness in the bedroom changing the still-ailing baron's compresses), Margarida stood quietly listening to the rain falling against the windows with the lightness and grace of little grains of salt sprinkled on glass.

She dined alone with the baroness, under a large lamp suspended from four chains and casting a somber light upon the nearly empty patriarchal table. Weighed down by that atmosphere of illness and suspense, they exchanged few words. Margarida complained bitterly about the lack of sea transportation between islands. The baroness–just to say something–reminded her that if Commander Saavedra was still in Horta and captain of the gunboat, he would not fail to come to the aid of his favorite niece at this time of dire straits.

"Do you really believe that?" asked Margarida. "That in order to help a family member... and without the Minister of the Navy's okay, they would allow a mothballed warship in Horta bay to weigh anchor? No chance!"

What did the country care about one person's misfortune! The sick could just die far from their loved ones.... If it were a question of going to Flores to pick up the results of the election of a governmental candidate, no expense would be spared–the *Açor* would be at the ready, its boilers running since the previous day. But a case of life-and-death, a true tragedy?... The baroness was being much too optimistic!... All she had to do was think of what happened during the plague, the terror sown in Madalena and Horta after the first fatal cases were reported. It had taken Uncle Mateus Dulmo, the Baron of Roches, *Senhor* Florêncio Terra, Commander Bulcão, the Goularts de Medeiros, Dr. Neves, Dr. Serpa, Father Osório... everybody who was anybody had had to send a telegram bearing all their signatures in order for the government to allow the *Açor* to awaken from its slumber by the dock and sail to São Miguel to get serum. And then it was forced to put into harbor in Terceira to repair one of its boilers. The vessel was nothing but a leaky bucket... Only Uncle Saavedra's dedication and courage and those of the other crewmen–namely the captain, the engineman, the first and second mate, the entire crew, really–were credited with making that worthless tub seaworthy and making sure that it didn't become a laughingstock to the crews of foreign fleets visiting Horta.

The baroness pointed out that it wasn't as bad as all that... True, our Navy did not have capable ships, but in know-how and courage it ranked among the best in the world. The Portuguese officers enjoyed a first-rate reputation. Navy captain Manuel de Azevedo Gomes, when he commanded the *Diu*, was much admired by the English and the French when he sailed among dozens of ships anchored several abreast in a roadstead in Hong Kong. Swept by a typhoon (Margarida immediately recalled Conrad's *Typhoon* and Captain MacWhirr), the boat entered the port of Shanghai while, from bungalows and bonded warehouses, the frightened harbor pilots watched the crest of the rising sea. An Englishman, the captain was on the Hong Kong-Sydney line. (Again Conrad!) The baroness, who loved adventure novels, could recite almost a whole feuilleton by heart. That English skipper was in the habit of shortening his route by navigating through a secret strait. To avoid competitors, he spread the rumor that only ships with powerful engines could hazard the way. But Captain Manuel Azevedo Gomes discovered the passage, and the *Diu* (a leaky bucket!...) crossed it. But there was more: In those stormy seas off Japan (what a pity that Uncle Amaro de Mirateca, who was old enough to have spun tops and played with toy boats with Manulinho do *Senhor* Antoniquinho Ávila Gomes, was not here to back up the veracity of the dangers of those "Jap waters" with his harpooneer's authority), caught in those whirlpools, a few feet away from those heathens who had beheaded an Azorean martyr and who, at this moment, were practically being instructed by Portuguese bishops, Captain Manuel de Azevedo Gomes had ventured across the legendary Strait of Simoneseki, in the dark, without a harbor pilot, standing on the bridge of his little riverboat-like vessel.... When the *Diu* dropped anchor at the port, heeling over so much that one of its sides clipped the water, the English admirals, accustomed to sailing on ships worthy of a Nelson, did not hesitate to clamber up those humble stairs to salute the captain. The excited crew screamed "hurrays" from atop the yards.

"Another example of those illustrious Azoreans, one of the last officers who mastered the art of sail maneuvering. His father was from Piedade; his mother, from Lajes: vintage wine from the craggy lava vineyards of Pico."

The baroness finally told a story that alluded to the sad situation in which Margarida found herself. A year earlier, in Santa Maria, a poor woman was just about to go into labor. Her life was in danger; the only doctor on the island was on leave in São Miguel. In a panic, the husband had radioed Ponta Delgada to see if they could send a tugboat with an accoucheur. The doctor of the *Adamastor* found out about the case from a telegrapher who had intercepted the SOS. He went to see the commander. On board, needless to say, there were no forceps; but he declared he was ready to assist the poor woman. He would do everything in his power.... What did the commander think ought to be done? The *Adamastor* changed direction and headed for Vila do Porto, and wouldn't you know it?–the ship's doctor succeeded in saving both mother and child! It was a little girl... They named her Maria Adamastor. Isn't that a beautiful story? It would make a good novel!

Margarida smiled; and after pushing in her chair and leaving the baroness to tend to her sick husband, she went to her room to think over her situation and while away some time before getting into bed.

Now she was firmly convinced, even though she could not explain why, that it was Uncle Mateus who was ill. "*Uncle ill...*! That abbreviated message, written by her father immediately after the address, at the moment when what had led him to telegraph his daughter had assumed the nature of unreflective thought, did not, could not, have any other meaning.

She pulled out the telegram from her bosom for the thousandth time, examined the characters on the little ribbon still shining from the glue, and read the printed words from beginning to end: (*On Hughes-system telegrams, the first number appearing after the name of the place of origin is the order*

*number; the second indicates the number of words; the rest of
the numbers designate the date and time the telegram was pos-
ted.*) "HORTA. 23. 17. 8. 12 H. 15 M. DONA MARGARIDA
DULMO. CARE OF MOST EXCELLENT BARON URZE-
LINA. VELAS. UNCLE ILL...." There was no doubt about it!
"Uncle"–meant the usual uncle, the one who lived on São
Francisco Street, the uncle par excellence, the one to whom she
had grown attached since childhood, while Roberto was
nothing but a kind of prince in an oft-told fairy tale, the
Lohengrin in an opera from which she had only heard excerpts
played on the Peters' piano–perhaps Meyerbeer's *Roberto the
Devil....*

And Margarida remembered a night when she and Uncle
Roberto–after a lively evening party at their Pasteleiro home,
and attended by the Lemos, Maria da Paz, Daisy Warren,
Cousin Corina, the entire Clark clan (as they were referred to
in Horta)–had danced a lot and, afterwards, all had played
mahjongg, up-down... even *berlinda*, a game of fines, of all
things!... "She is being penalized because she is a little vain....
She is being penalized because she craves the impossible in
life...." (Laughter. Margarida looked at Maria da Paz, a little
plump and good-natured, making those accusations as if she
were laying down some burden....) "She is being punished for
having taken a wild heifer by the horns...." (The origin of that
charge was well known: it came from Uncle Mateus.) "She is
being penalized because she wants to go and work as a nurse in
London.... She is being penalized.... she is being penalized...
(no, I'll hold my tongue...)" "Come on, let's hear it! That's not
how the game is played..." "She is being penalized for liking
Uncle Roberto too much." "Well, whoever claims that I like
Uncle Roberto too much has to come and change places with
me!" And Daisy Warren got up from her chair, red as the red-
dest bell pepper.

They danced more waltzes; her father had consented to dancing the lancers; Cousin Corina had insisted on a Chopin
mazurka. Pedro twirled his sister like a spinning top, sending
her colliding into Uncle Roberto, who danced with a serious

demeanor and stuck to Daisy like glue. They had their palms read; they drank claret cup and whisky. Then, Uncle Roberto had invited her to go out to the veranda overlooking the sea; he had pulled out a deck chair for her, then enigmatically lit his pipe. Pico was bathed in the moonlight just like during the trip the previous day. Never had they had that kind of intimate conversation, nor had they ever delved so deeply into each other's personalities and tastes.

It was the following day that Margarida spent a whole afternoon in Uncle Mateus' study poring through the *Encyclopedia Britannica*, copying everything that she found mysterious and attractive concerning the name "Robert." St. Robert de Champagne had founded the Cistercian Order and was buried in the Molesmes Monastery. Robert le Fort, Count of Anjou, father of Eudes and Robert, was the root of all the Capets. Robert II the Pious.... (How excited Margarida was as she delved into the fate of this Frankish prince who was tutored by a priest destined to be pope!... He had been married to Rozala or Suzanne, daughter of Béranger de Provence. Despite his being a God-fearing man, he had repudiated his first wife to unite his destiny to that of Berthe de Bourgogne, his first cousin. The Pope had excommunicated him: should he enter a church, he would be kicked out like a dog! He was not allowed to accompany a priest ministering the Last Sacrament to a dying person and could never be buried in hallowed ground! In a word, his status in the eyes of the Church had become lower than that of a pauper carried on the marble table of the dead of Misericórdia–for such men always had a coffin with a cross over the lid to protect them in the grave.)

Struck by this kind of union, which the unjust repudiation and the fatal blood ties rendered doubly sacrilegious, Margarida pondered the case for days–until one day, doing her utmost to assume a natural tone of voice, she spoke of it to Uncle Mateus. He showed her the reproduction of the painting by Jean-Paul Laurens, which he had brought, among other souvenirs, from his visit to the Luxembourg Museum. The Pope's legate, after having pronounced the anathema against Robert

the Pious, disappeared through a large dark door while supporting himself on his crosier and surrounded by dumbstruck
assistants–while Robert, defeated utterly, collapsed on his high
throne in front of a broken torch-holder, with the fallen torch
still burning and smoking on the floor, a terrified Berthe laying
her pale face upon her lover's breast....

And what if Uncle Roberto was the one dying, far away
from her?... What if he was already dead?...

Perhaps the warship that saved women in childbirth stranded on a deserted island might still come to rescue her.

Chapter XXXVI

Summer Farewells

At last, the telegram arrived to unravel the whole mystery: "*Uncle Roberto very ill hope almost lost–Mateus.*"

Margarida's premonitions, her silent plaints–that yellowed piece of folded paper confirmed them all. She would have no one left who really cared for her... who liked her for herself, independently of family obligations and conveniences: "See to it, daughter... that you don't leave me in this house all alone!" "If you were to go and talk it over with *Dona* Carolina Amélia.... "If only André took an interest in the firm...." "Be kind enough to agree to this little sacrifice!..."

All she had now was her old uncle, the shadow of an absurd and vanishing era, living holed up with an ignorant servant on São Francisco Street, with his fingers poised over a harmonium keyboard awaiting night and death.... What a misfortune was still reserved for her poor uncle: to watch die a young man who, though no relation of his, had endeared himself to all with his ingratiating ways? Forgetting his own youth, Roberto always kept in his pocket a salmon-colored handkerchief to make shadow-puppets or to turn a flower into a ring to delight a young child; he was always willing to tell a story to an elderly person or to some shy, unattractive woman hiding in the corner of the living room.

And then Roberto probably represented for Mateus Dulmo the incarnation of his own past, which cried out for justice and reparations. He was the fruit of that liaison between his grandfather Charles Clark and Ana Silveira, the ghost of a passing fancy that had locked his grandmother Margarida Terra in a tower, dead to social life, to a peaceful, loving, and happy home, to the love of self and others.... She looked so pure, so innocent in the somber portrait hanging in the Granary, that all she needed was the doe and the baby at her breast to be Geneviève de Brabant, the maiden exiled by Siegfried and left in the distant forest....

"Hope almost lost...." "Almost...." All but a little... strictly speaking, only half a hope, like the boat anchor she asked of Uncle Amaro de Mirateca during a night of "little moods" and desire for symbols–the anchor of Faith, with a broken bill. Margarida felt she no longer had enough strength left to hold on to that "almost," to repeat it, to breathe into it and impart to it what Uncle Mateus had wanted to convey when charitably he first wrote it: to furnish her with a floating piece of jetsam to which she could cling like a disaster victim during the few hours remaining for her to arrive in Horta and face reality: Uncle Roberto lying dead, his hands folded, more silent than ever before and separated from his pipe forever!

The day had dawned with patches of sunlight shining on floors and pasturelands and seeming to flow with milk-white light brightening everything: the humid Serra, the Old Tower, the rectory buried in lava, the scattered little white houses of Urzelina above the stark vineyards of Casteletes–and, finally, the cliff with the cave at the bottom echoing the lapping sounds of the calm tide. Now that the *Funchal* was due in Calheta, it offered, despite its limited tonnage (a little above that of a ferry-boat), guaranteed passage across the São Jorge Channel under any weather; now, when all was consummated and lost, was when the sky turned blue and white, the sea mockingly calm, with Pico turning lilac, the color of a bishop's vestments as he prepares to celebrate Mass!

The baroness soft-stepped through the granary to console Margarida, insisting all the while that she drink some citron tea. The baron, back to his old self, stood behind his wife, torturing his little white moustache and at a loss for words.

Domitília then came to announce that van Dam had just arrived from Velas. He had telegraphed Calheta to reserve a place for Margarida. But it was an unnecessary precaution. The trip to Horta would take only a few hours, even if the boat had to make a stop at Lajes; the *Funchal*, after leaving Terceira, had almost no passengers. But the baron, sympathetic to Margarida's plight and slave to his own conception of hospitality and decorum, which had led him to maintain coupé and uniformed coachman for outings in the towns and parishes, had thought it his duty to reserve a whole first-class cabin just for Margarida, and was determined to go and personally introduce her to Commander Vidinha, his personal friend. The previous September when the boat had stopped in São Jorge (something that both the commander and the baron remembered well, for it had been a celebration in Urzelina that had even extended to Santa Bárbara), the baron had given the commander a great dinner, one which almost the entire island had attended; afterwards, a long procession of friends personally escorted Commander Vidinha to his ship: the *Funchal*, with its lights on and little flags unfurled from bow to stern, blew its horn three, six times as it sailed past Casteletes, its lights on, nearly at water level.

Now, upon leaving Urzelina, Margarida said a real farewell, as if it were her last. Deeply moved by that young girl who cried like a widow for an infirm or dead uncle, the baroness left a trail of heavy tears behind the heavy coupé. The branches of the orange trees, bending under the weight of their fruit, cast bloody reflections upon the vehicle's heavy coat of lacquer.

In her cabin, Margarida found a huge bouquet of chrysanthemums that Commander Vidinha had ordered for her. He was a stocky and affable man who, since he had a habit of gazing out at the horizon or of spending hours on end leaning against the bulwark or a hatchway conversing with the ship's doctor and the first mate, mechanically kept one hand raised over his eyes like a visor or resting on his hip. He treated his passengers as a good host treats welcome guests at his home. Mateus Dulmo and Charles Clark were old friends of his. Diogo Dulmo and José de Lemos were in the habit of coming aboard the *Funchal* as soon as it cast anchor at the dock; and, when they did not have lunch or dinner with him (if, perhaps, doffing his cap and uniform, he had gone, foul-weather gear hanging over his arm, to some wedding or birthday party), the steward would offer them hors d'oeuvres while keeping them abreast of the latest gossip and scandals from the mainland.

Given that the personal touch was the norm for Vidinha, the Baron da Urzelina's recommendation was nothing more than simple protocol. The ship, with its hold rising above water and almost empty of passengers, traced the half-moon demanded by the southeastern point of Pico and headed for Lajes.

The commander, truly saddened by the state Margarida found herself in, did not leave her side for a moment. First, he spoke to her of the voyage under his command on which Roberto had come. He had known him for a long time. The *Funchal* had been to Southampton for repairs. The Bensaúde Company had a line of credit in the Anglo-Spanish Bank, that colossus; and Roberto had been charged by the management of Insulana Ship Line with accompanying Commander Brito do Rio, who had been sent to London to study the possibility of purchasing a ship. In every shipyard the *Funchal* entered there had been champagne and toasts. Roberto had spoken only a few words but expressed himself so well in that English which, nobody knows why, no foreigner, no matter how adept in languages, is able to handle: the kind of English that speaks to the minds and hearts of the English people. Yes, sir.... There was no doubt that, in England, Roberto enjoyed an enviable position and had a great future ahead of him.... What could be done now? Death singles out neither the young nor the old. Still, miracles do occur.... From Lisbon to Madeira, he had been sailing under stormy weather, but close to the Azores the ocean became a bed of roses.

Then, realizing that the turn the conversation was taking was a thorn in Margarida's heart, the commander spoke of the weather, which, despite its being a November day, had turned out to be very fine indeed. His arm, accustomed to our islands, called her attention to some minor sights along the coast of the approaching island: schools of dolphins, two or three gulls that never lost sight of the ship's topsail, and the successive summits of the Peaks Sibado, Lança, Cabras. "Look... look!" The gulls flew in a wedge-shaped formation, then shortened the triangle, increased their speed, their wings now forming quotation marks. Sometimes they brushed the water, looking for fish. They did this for miles and miles.... Incredible birds! With their innocent plumage and gracious flight, they were cruel and implacable, equipped for fighting and preying... ruthless predators! How calm the sea! For Vidinha, who had sailed both hemispheres, the sky over the Azores on a clear day was the most beautiful in the world! And that fantastic island of Pico just ahead.... Many foreigners likened it to Vesuvius. Its highest cloud-covered peak, as sharp as the tip of the thermometers that mountain climbers are known to gallantly leave on the summit of Saint-Gothard, rises five thousand feet above the massive portion of the mountain.

But Margarida, insensible to everything–to the most engaging conversation in the world, to the most charming and impressive scenery, to the biggest bouquet of chrysanthemums plucked from the craggy soil of São Jorge–could only fix her eyes on the topmost portion of the stone carcass of the new church of Lajes, a Cologne Cathedral without angels or spires, resembling a Jacob's ladder reaching endlessly up to Pico....

As soon as the boat touched land, the customs officer, a family friend, told her the whole truth: her Uncle Roberto had died of the plague that very morning in the Vineyards house. He had fallen ill five or six days earlier, with Manuel Bana and Maria das Angústias taking care of him. He had come to spend a night at the Vineyards and had contracted the disease he knew not where or how–perhaps from a rat in the Granary. In short, a fatal type of plague, with tumors under the arms and on the neck.

Margarida showed no reaction and shed not a single tear. She only asked the customs officer to help her get transportation to Campo Raso. She was ready to disembark; she wanted to depart as soon as possible. Her composure disconcerted the officer who, in spite of it, detected behind the simple and somewhat tight dress and the hat decorated with the wing of a bird, an irrevocable decision and mental confusion. Sitting near the gangway, Margarida had crossed her shapely legs, which were covered in sheer black stockings. The tip of one of her shoes visibly trembled a few inches above the deck.

To allow time to warn the family and thus avoid Margarida's solitary encounter with her uncle's fresh grave, the officer alluded to the difficulty of getting quick transportation to Candelária. In Lajes, there was but one taxi for hire; and it might now be out on service to Santo Amaro, Prainha, or Vila de São Jorge.... It frequently went to that side of the island; the doctor used it a lot, and so did people who had business there, or were building boats, or had to draw up a deed. While he tried to hunt down the taxi driver, Margarida could go to his house to rest. He wished to convey his wife's regrets she couldn't come aboard to meet her; it was time to breast-feed their baby; but he was honored to keep her company. The trip by boat had not been a long one; Calheta, São Jorge, was not as far as Lisbon or Providence.... Still, with all the commotion, she probably needed to rest..., right?

Margarida returned to her cabin; she had forgotten the flowers. Her heart felt heavy and all she wanted was to flee. But she did not want to hurt the commander's feelings; and she also remembered that, now, the bouquet had a providential application: that bunch of flowers was going to be her first tear shed upon the earth that covered Uncle Roberto, her summer farewell almost at the end of autumn–now that her springs, the real springs along the road to Caldeira and those of the afternoons spent on the Well terrace watching him sail close to the wind in the channel, had forever expired with his sublimate-corroded last breath in the mortuary atmosphere of the Vineyards house.

After leaving Margarida in his wife's care, the Lajes customs officer went to apprise the taxi driver of the situation; he knew very well that the taxi was available. And to make sure he did everything properly, he sent an emergency telegram to Mateus Dulmo, informing him of his niece's intentions. Margarida, who had been made aware on board of the difficulties of getting transportation, would not find the delay unusual; this way, there would be enough time for some member of her family to arrive in Candelária by the time she herself got there.

At last, the taxi took off and headed down the road to Candelária, leaving behind the rows of closely packed little houses of São Jorge and São Mateus. It was an old model-T Ford, a convertible with a canvas top, which was started with a crank kept stored under a rope mat on the driver's side. Margarida, a little dizzy from the smell of gasoline fumes, felt in the depths of herself that sense of "peace in war" that had begun to accrue in her spirit ever since the fatal news had put an end once and for all to her game of hide-and-seek. Now she did not have to wear that ambiguous mask–Uncle Roberto's lengthy silence and hesitations, of her plans for liberation in Dr. Marr's clinic in London, of the unspoken horror of the possibility of marriage to André, who circled his prey from above like a gull drawn to the smell of blood from a dying whale; of her insidious wish to see João Garcia again wrapped in his sublieutenant's cape, parading and disguising his lack of tact and courage along the walls of her quinta. From now on, she would rely only on herself: on that youthful skin caressed by the coat the baroness had practically forced her to wear, by that array of abstract notions, dreams, morbid sufferings made almost pleasant by her dwelling on and accepting them as a revolting inevitability, one to which Clarinha's little hat, topped by the dark bird with the invisible beak, added the weight of a hand pressing against a dormant muscle.

The resigned attitude with which she received the fateful telegram, notwithstanding Uncle Mateus's kind "almost," had prepared her to accept the customs officer's revelation in Lajes as the inevitable denouement of the entire drama–a drama which appeared to her like a miracle caused by that adventuresome whaleboat propelled by simple folk, whose relatives and friends she now could see along the road or working in the fields. That gesture of revolt against the laws and justice of men–although it was as sudden as a mob hit–was as natural to those humble seamen as the sailcloth woven by their wives and as the bundles of firewood or buckets of water carried by decrepit old men as unconscious legacies of patriarchy. But it was a miracle that seemed to spring especially from the lava and sky of the islands, from that porous, dark, dry soil–not to mention the clover, the Baron da Urzelina's cattle and even van Dam's cap!–which, instead of becoming a gushing fountain before the eyes of a shepherdess, as in the miracle of Lourdes that so moved the baroness, cascaded in foam down a cliff next to the cavern where she had spent a night in the company of whale-men exhausted from hauling the carcasses of two dead whales. To her, Uncle Roberto's death seemed the crown of the miracle, its ultimate mystical flower, grown in a vase hidden for months and months under a Yorkshire wool coat, secretly fertilized by the pure white ashes from his pipe, and finally blooming during a morning in Pico, its stem bending toward Fayal in her absence, as if the gardener feared that the more violent aspects of its color and perfume might upset her. "You have the head of a wagtail, you really do...." Uncle Mateus used to tease her, "but you are as precious as a flower!" Yes.... Perhaps, by his death, Uncle Roberto had changed her into a flower. He, so kind and so pure, was perfectly capable of transforming through his own death the harmless lie of someone his senior.

The automobile stopped at the edge of Campo Raso. From afar, Margarida had detected a group of people waiting patiently by the roadside. And right away she recognized, by his umbrella, the presence of Uncle Mateus Dulmo and made out his glasses and his white hair under the soft hat. But there were more people behind her uncle, seated on the improvised wooden benches used by the villagers as a platform. And Margarida's heart, which had remained absurdly still as she approached the place rendered sacred by her uncle's death, now beat much faster. What if André Barreto, prompted by his poorly timed solicitude, were there also? It's true that he probably had some right to act in that friendly manner.... Hadn't she just spent a week in his house, received by his parents like an imprudent wayfarer, with neither house nor home, flirting with expatriation? Wasn't she wearing a coat loaned by the old baroness? a winter hat of his sister's? Had she not used favorite mares that he rode? Had she not slept in a room reserved for him and his bride?... In the end, she was as much a prisoner of family relations as a besotted fly caught in an iridescent spider web! Instead of being the liberating removal of all her illusions, wasn't Uncle Roberto's death, instead, the death sentence of her identity, the bending to someone else's will and the succumbing to the claws of a merciless fate? Be that as it may, André's presence on that solemn occasion would be insufferable to her.

Fortunately, however, the identities of the men she had seen from afar became clear: first, she recognized her father, heavy and flushed from wine; then Manuel Bana's bare feet, kneecaps, and drooping moustache. Sitting at the end of the bench, minuscule and dressed in lilac, was *Dona* Corina Peters.

Margarida hugged and kissed them in silence. Her father, trying to avoid anything that might lead to an outburst of tears, which always reigned at funeral gatherings like dry thunder, asked his daughter about the trip... at what time the *Funchal* had left Calheta. But looking again at the face of Uncle Mateus, who was drying his tears and trying to suppress a sigh, Margarida could not contain herself any longer. She put her arms around him. One could only tell she was crying by the long shudder that shook her body and by her head buried in his shoulder.

Regaining her composure a little, she stared for a long time at what she was holding in her hand. But for a long while she could not see, did not notice anyone around her, did not sense her own presence. Finally, she realized she was holding flowers, and as everybody started on their way toward the Vineyards house, she declared that she would not enter the house without leaving the flowers in the cemetery. Diogo Dulmo explained that it had been their intention to take Uncle Roberto's body to Horta in a lead casket and place it in the family vault. After *Dona* Margarida Terra's death, no coffin had come to disturb the white indifferent Angel who guarded the sepulchral abode, much like a sea pilot who has given shelter to his small bark in the familiar port and then calmly crosses his arms while the chains drop the anchor to the bottom. But the day before he died, Roberto had told Manuel Bana that he wanted to be buried in a common grave in the Candelária cemetery.

Bringing up the rear of the cortege, Manuel Bana, choking back tears but keeping an ear on the conversation between father and daughter, quoted Roberto's last words:

"I want to rest in a grave next to the whalemen! Don't you forget that, Manuel...."

The dying man's words would be respected.

"Besides," declared Diogo Dulmo, after a brief silence, "Ana Silveira is not in the Clark family vault, either... there was no room. And Roberto was so respectful of his mother's memory...."

The ceremony at the cemetery was brief. The gravedigger pulled a huge key out of his pocket. With his hair cropped short, sleeveless duck vest and collar buttoned all the way up in the fashion of the peasants from that side of the island, he looked like a prisoner who, as reward for good behavior, had been placed in charge of the other inmates in a sort of penal colony garden. Manuel Bana, asked by Diogo Dulmo to relate the episode about which there were suspicions—even the certainty—that Roberto had contracted the plague, began:

"Well, the master here had told me the following: 'You go to the Granary and you ask Roberto if he wants you to help him get his suitcase from the storage room downstairs, anything heavy that needs to be carried anywhere.' Yes, because Robertinho—God rest his soul!—had gotten it into his head to leave for England.... I can still hear him, poor man! 'Make sure you don't say a word about this to Bidinha, you hear?... but, as soon as I can, I'm getting out of here....'"

"I went to the Granary right away, of course..... He was walking back and forth in his room, sticking mothballs in the sleeves of his suits, with suitcase racks scattered all over the chairs. The room looked like a kitchen when they're baking sweet bread.... I've never seen anybody with so many clothes! And for what, I ask? To die in five days with such tumors on his neck that he actually looked like the cripple from Lumbega, the one they call Sucker's Jaws.... He ordered me to carry a big pile of books downstairs to pack in the trunks. I had never thought that paper could be so heavy! Lordy me, it was a crushing load!... I took some time downstairs to put away all the old stuff, like the orange crates that had been stacked on top of the little launch. Upstairs, he kept playing and playing his fiddle (which was like his wine to him...). I was dragging the trunk with the intention of dusting it off when, all of a sudden, I see this thing, some kind of *boiling* creature, all covered with maggots!... Now, I'm not one of those who scares easy, but I dropped the trunk lid and jumped back as quickly as I could. It was a dead rat! a huge rat, one of those gray ones, and it reeked like hell!... I hurried upstairs to get a kerosene lamp (it was almost night and downstairs, even with the peephole open, you could hardly see an inch in front of your nose...). That's when he asked me: 'What's the matter, Manuel?' 'It's a rotten rat, master! all covered with boils... I'm gonna burn it.' For all I told him I could take care of it, he kept saying he was going with me. He's the one who wanted to soak it with kerosene and set it aflame. And then a bunch of little mice began scuttling all over the place, and he (I can still see him!), with his sleeves rolled up and holding the box of matches, leaning forward, started to move like he was going to waltz....'' And Manuel Bana, standing in the central walkway of the cemetery, bent his body and started to dance in front of Margarida. "He even told me: 'This one isn't going to be eating any more corn, Manuel....' As a matter of fact, there was such a burst of fire that I thought the whole Granary was going up in flames!"

"Who would ever believe that a goddamn flea, a thing that a man can crush between his nails, was going to kill a gentleman like that!... I'd rather have the darn plague *take me*! But, as they say, fate is blind... and a worthless vase never breaks. I had already had my share.... This time I was spared...."

"God has been kind enough to allow me to pay Roberto what he did for me when he took care of me in the Vineyards house... he and the miss...." Margarida, walking among the lavender and the graves, seemed both blind and deaf. "He died in my arms... with his dear head leaning on my shoulder.... He died right here!..." As he pounded the padding of his jacket with his calloused hands, the tears kept streaming down Manuel Bana's cheeks.

The group surrounded the little grave, whose soil was still fresh and ungroomed, and upon which stood a crude cross, a little crooked on top. The plot looked like a nursery in a botanical garden where a meticulous gardener, with a little knowledge of Latin, had disposed of a bunch of precious seeds resistant to a new climate. The root of a rosebush lay to one side with a piece of sod still clinging to it. Margarida bent before the cross and placed her chrysanthemums there. Then, making the sign of the cross, she paused in meditation. A blackbird flew from the cemetery wall and, hidden in the branch of a tree, started to rehearse one of those trills that, answered by an invisible chorus, fill with torpor and reverie the dawning day in the islands. The refrain was followed by multiple chirpings, and a swarming flock of blackbirds, led by the disputing pair, vanished toward the peak.

Dona Corina interrupted Mateus Dulmo's silence as he sat alone with his thoughts:

"This is depressing, Cousin... But Margarida looks so wonderful next to that cross, in this simple cemetery... everything is so peaceful.... It was too bad this had to happen! Before, I had thought that uncle and niece were so right for each other.... One looked at them and thought for sure they were lovers. This doesn't seem real...."

"Well, had it not been for this wretched death," remarked Diogo Dulmo to his daughter, already outside the cemetery, "you'd have had a triumphant arrival. I have already found out from André that you were treated like a princess in Urzelina.... They really went out of their way for you, eh? As I told you in my first telegram, everything is set, deeds have been signed, and our life has been straightened out. That scoundrel Januário set his trap very well, but he's paid through the nose! His schemes have come to nought. The rat got caught in his own trap! Even that horrible old woman, Canon Borges' lover, kicked the bucket!... (Poor old lady... I had forgotten we just got out of a holy place! Let's leave the dead in peace... But the truth of the matter is I just can't forget what that black-hearted demon did to our family!)"

There was a moment of silence. The sound of Diogo Dulmo's steps lingered on the road.

"Rumor has it his son is engaged to the daughter of that Honório fellow... another big swindler. When all is said and done, though... after the loss we've just experienced, nothing else matters very much.... Roberto was a jewel of a man! A little reserved, it's true, but still what I call a jewel! Don't be so sad, little one!... If our faith doesn't betray us, your uncle should be in a good place right now."

Margarida, wordless, walked on with her head down.

Chapter XXXVII

Epilogue
(*Andante*; *poi allegro, non troppo*)

I

Summer in the islands does not come with the dry, vibrant heat that, on the mainland, singes the fields and envelops the city in a golden halo of dog days. In Lisbon, the pubs fill up with crowds of bureaucrats feigning happiness as they suffer the torments of conventional woolen suits, the exception being an occasional light-colored blazer adding a clownish touch to what otherwise looks like a procession of penitents. It is in vain that the Weather Service of the Azores, proud of being the main European post in charge of the observation of hurricanes and trade winds, telegraphs on order the mean temperatures to the agencies responsible for the theoretical Azorean tourism. From the Azores one cannot, in fact, write (one is even tempted to say, as the novelist Camilo Castelo Branco used to, "*as the reader will remember from the preceding chapters...*")... One cannot write about the Azores what the Madeiran *BAEDECKER* reports: "*Temperate maritime climate, mild in winter, nice and cool in the summer.*" No one has ever seen an Englishman wearing white in December in the quiet streets of Horta or eating ice cream in a Ponta Delgada or Furnas hotel, as has already happened on the Mount in Funchal on New Year's Eve, while ocean liners' sirens blow a salute to the new year and the clusters of fireworks transfigure a Cytherean sky.

> (Hello, my dear Veloso! Has the Mount
> Proven easier to descend than to climb?) [1]

---

[1] My translation of lines 4-5, Canto V, of the national epic poem *The Lusiads*, by Luís de Camões (1524?-1580).–Trans.

Murky, cottony clouds hang heavily over the nine-island archipelago; haze and humidity distort the contours of land and sea, soften the pastures–to the detriment of farmers and shepherds–dilute and sap human vitality, instill in men and objects a kind of spiritual languor to which the English, medical specialists in well-being, put a label, acting like explorers who found a new species of plant in this old parched world: *Azorean torpor*.

That's how the morning of August 15, 1919 had begun in Terceira. The bay of Angra stretched, gray and somnolent, from the shadows of Mount Brasil to the pier of Porto de Pipas. Immobile, as if under the weight of lead, overflown by an arrow-shaped flock of fat, pensive gulls, the bay prolonged the sluggish sunrise to the southeast as far as the two hillocks crowned with rock samphire and sheep–the Islets of Cabras, or "Goats"–whose shapes resemble a loaf of bread with a hunk broken off. Farther away, as if delimiting with ellipses the boundaries of that dream-wrought seascape, rose the prominent rocks known as *Fradinhos*, or "Little Friars," to which land and sky lent an at once cartographic and unreal aspect, reminiscent of the island supposedly discovered by Fernão Dulmo. A legend associated with a man once banished to the islet holds that these rocks represent a petrified vision of the moment when one comes to the realization of the good or evil life one has led.

The city of Angra extends into the interior curve of the bay and is enclosed by a belt of the powerful system of fortifications accumulated by the Spaniards during the Occupation.[2]

The barrier of Canta Galo, topped by a chapel erected to St. Pedro Gonçalves in memory of fishermen lost at sea, adds to the landscape a note of aesthetic discordance. But serene and sprawling, Angra looks like a white-cropped, open-winged bird–the beautiful and elegant long-legged bird known locally as *joão-cardoso*. The streets are broad and well cobbled, with spacious sidewalks. Imposing noble buildings are everywhere to be seen, with fashionable stores on the ground floors filled with smartly dressed salespeople.

---

[2] Spain ruled Portugal between 1580 and 1640.–Trans.

Praça Velha or Old Square is the site of the Palace of the Municipal Chamber with its impressive ceremonial hall–"*the largest municipal hall in the country and one of the foremost on the Peninsula*"–as if the Cantos Manor, which today houses an orphanage, were still the Purveyor's Office of the India Fleet and as if Angra itself, its face turned to the North Atlantic, still felt in its body the nuptial thrill of Venice at the edge of the Adriatic.

From its massive roofs covered with drying ears of corn, there emerges, here and there, a tower. The Church of Our Lady of Guia houses the remains of Paulo da Gama and those of the sea captains who discovered Labrador. The Church of Colégio, in whose tower the Weather Station is housed, includes, besides its giltwood altars and precious confessionals, the statue of its own son martyred in Japan–the beatified João Baptista Machado. ("Màcàdô...? Màcàdô...?" asked a Bolandist in Holland of a curious man from Terceira. "*C'est bien possible. Mais vous comprenez, Monsieur.... Nous autres, jésuites, nous avons tant de martyres!...*")

The Church of St. Gonçalo is still filled with the shadows of nuns fresh out of the pages of Count Ségur's *Memoires* and Almeida Garrett's *Travels in My Country*[3]. The churches of Conceição and Santa Luzia, yielding their latest curates to the miters of Meliapor and Cochim, have thus added three more bishops to the Azorean ecclesiastical component of the Portuguese Patronage in the Orient... And then there is Angra Cathedral, with its pointed towers overlaid with porcelain tiles in the *mudéjar* style, with its surviving echoes of Father António Vieira's[4] voice, the memory of Almeida Garrett in his surplice of apprenticeship to the priesthood, and the recollection

---

[3] Almeida Garrett (1799-1854) is a Portuguese Romantic poet, novelist, and playwright. *Viagens na minha terra* (Travels in My Country; 1846), is a narrative admittedly inspired by Sterne's *A Sentimental Journey*. Garrett's complex narrative, notable among other things for its innovative style, includes a sentimental novelette.–Trans.

[4] António Vieira (1608-1697) is a Portuguese-born Brazilian writer, especially known for his sermons and letters.–Trans.

of that chorus of canons who, at eleven in the morning, walked down from the churchyard, whence they commanded a full view of downtown Angra and, warmly wrapped up, lingered on the staircase while comforting their female parishioners. Their faces covered by hoods, filled with new life as a result of their confidences, these lady parishioners then headed for the farmer's market to buy a melon or a cabbage and then scattered throughout the city like those caterpillars that the children of Terceira forcibly uncoil, asking: "Bug, bug, pray thee tell–which way to São Miguel?... Little bug, little bug, despite your size–can you tell me which way Fayal lies?..."

The prow of the *San Miguel*, which at two in the afternoon rounded the point of Mount Brasil, indicated that Fayal lay to the west. The ship had left Horta the previous day; on that same day it had stopped in Cais do Pico, and later dropped anchor in the port of Velas, where it spent the night until about three in the morning, arriving at Santa Cruz da Graciosa at dawn, just as one hundred years ago Captain Dujardin's boat from Saint Malo had done, transporting to Baltimore the Superior from the Seminary of Saint Sulpice, in the company of a group of seminarians. It also transported–urged by Byron's cry, "again to sea!"–the magnificent, melancholy Chateaubriand, who whiled away the time by strolling on deck with both Tulloch, the musician, painter and polyglot, and Villeneuve, the second mate, who stood on the prow chewing tobacco and sharing his reminiscences of Bretagne.

"*Il y a quelque chose de magique voir s'élever la terre du fond de la mer*"–exclaimed the Viscount, recalling the vision he had had at 6:00 a.m. on May 6, 1791, when standing before the volcano of Pico. In Graciosa, the sea was raging and the boat lost an anchor while Chateaubriand enjoyed "*une odeur fromentacé agréable, particulière aux moissons des Açores.*" But this time the *San Miguel* entered a perfectly calm little port, and in less than four hours, the cranes loaded the casks of ruby wine that would probably arrive in Angra in time to enliven the bullfight.

"... A great bullfight in the São João Bullring, featuring 9-PUREBRED BULLS-9, "especially selected" from the best breeders on the island, 5 horsemen for the "courtesies" or opening ceremonies, two for fighting the bull, the Spanish *cuadrilla* of Moyanito, "who has been fighting bulls in the most prestigious rings of the Peninsula," some novice *banderilleros* and the customary *bregas* or footmen, as well as a "group of fearless bull tacklers," led by the famous *Dom* Tancredo. The *espada* or swordsman himself will work with cape and red cloak the bulls of his choice. All police regulations will be in force in the arena. The doors open at 3:00, and the public is welcome to attend the *embolamento* or padding of the bull's horns. The esteemed public is hereby notified that there are no special-discount tickets available. *Olé! Olé!* Bring on the matadors!...."

This program, despite the warning that it was "subject to changes due to unforeseen circumstances," had brought the entire island to the city. Through the gates of São Pedro, through Carreirinha, through Vinha Brava and coming from all over the *monte*, or rural areas, of the island rode the charabancs loaded with farmers and pretty country girls; coaches with people from Praia; *Americanos* in their *charrettes* of creaking, shining leather; and carriages with revellers who, from the landowner to the teacher and sometimes to the priest–who might feel a little self-conscious about his gray dustcoat or his singed cigarette holder–hold in their hands the fate of the milk-producing cooperatives and the Holy Ghost brotherhoods of their parishes. The horses and mules, shaking their bell collars, sometimes stopped to drink in the lavish public troughs of the city; the clatter of wheels and whip handles, purposely held to the spokes, shook the city's cobbled streets.

"Eh, you there.... Watch out!"

"Out of the way, little lady, I'm coming through!..."

"May I rot in hell, if today I don't get my mother a daughter-in-law!"

On Cavalos Street, an elderly woman brought from Seville by Anillo, an old and retired banderillero who now ran the restaurant La Giralda in hopes of giving a little culinary flavor to the city, served macaroni, rice with pimientos, and *malacuetos*. And the cafés on Esperança, Santo Espírito, and Frigideiras

Streets could not handle the crowds' demand for fried linguiça and blood sausage.

The passengers who had arrived from the western islands had almost all disembarked behind the Board of Health's boat. Groups of people gathered in the courtyard of the customs building, others in the Duke da Terceira city park; a family from São Jorge climbed up to Memória. Standing next to its trite and yellow obelisk, known as "Skypiercer," one commands a view of the entire city, encompassing, and even extending beyond, the woods and lands of the Cortes-Reais, discoverers of Newfoundland; the garden and palace of the Captains-General of the Azores, where King Pedro IV played billiards and whence he set out, after a night of dancing, on his amorous escapades; the "castle" of São João Baptista with its citadel, its church with its perpetually slow clock, the Tower of Mosquitos; and the battery "Fidelidade," which salutes the warships. Sweeping the binoculars the full arc of the panorama, one is overcome by a sensation of majesty and green, gray, and white calm, from Count da Praia da Vitória's manor house, now in ruins, to the church of Our Lady da Penha de França, nestled in Pico da Urze, to the towers of the Fishermen's Basilica in São Mateus, which point toward the oblong and hazy form that is the island of São Jorge, with the tip of Pico peering through lilac clouds behind it. If Angra ever discards half of its superfluous name "of Heroism," it is there–in the foundation of the walls of the Castle of Moinhos, built to protect against the corsairs–that it must solemnly bury it.

The weather, usually overcast, had cleared towards afternoon. Some scattered clouds lingered on the Serra da Ribeirinha and on Serra de Santa Barbara–for the latter seems to use an immense straw to drink from the sea (from Christmas to the time of the Holy Ghost celebrations, Terceira is a regular sauna, for the rains never let up...). Mount Brasil, looking like a triple-humped dromedary against an oceanic Sahara, was still covered by a sizable blanket of mist, broken little by little by the tips of its pine trees–the same pines that had provided shade for a womanless kraal for the exiled African kinglet

Gungunhana and recently had become the rabbit-hunting grounds for another exiled native African ruler, the charming Matibejana, kinglet of Zichacha.

José Frederico Zichacha! This was the bartender's name by which he was known now. He had been given sergeant stripes to allow him to get his food and sustenance–he who had provided the likes of Mouzinho and Paiva Couceiro da Távola-Redonda de António Enes [5] with the pretext for the sound and fury of the last cavalry strike in the solitary and anxiety-ridden nights of Ponta Vermelha...

Wearing a little derby and rope sandals, with bellicose ardor still visible in his piercing Vatua eyes and in his graying hair, Zichacha came down to Tanque de Azeite with a group of sergeants and musicians in civilian clothes. He was going to the bullfight. Although the bullfight was not due to start until 4:00 p.m., at 3:30 the streets of Angra were almost deserted. Only a few old ladies from Corpo Santo and São Pedro could be seen at the windows of their little houses, melancholically watering little wooden window boxes of China asters. An elderly aficionado, whose small pension did not afford him the luxury of a ticket to attend the bullfight, rekindled his old resentment as partisan of Joseíto against that "daisy-trampler" and hack, Pechuga. (The old rivalry between the fans of the two bullfighters had split the city into two rival camps, a kind of War of *Two* Roses.) Faithful to the Espírito Santo bullring, which fire had reduced to a humble cornfield, the old bullring habitué played cards with his pro-Pechuga rival in the Garden of Alto das Covas in hopes of being able to enjoy, by the intensity of the applause and by the half-a-dozen measures of music with which a couple of *banderillas* are celebrated, the perfection with which a *pase* is executed, as well as the heft of the bull....

At 3:55 p.m., the band of Recreio dos Artistas opened the festivities by executing *Viva la Coruña*! This opening number

---

[5] Mouzinho de Albuquerque (1855-1902) and Paiva Couceiro (1861-1944) were both considered heroes of the Portuguese military campaigns of the end of the nineteenth century to subdue the Africans, in this case Mozambicans.–Trans.

was followed by a fanfare from the rival band Pátria e Liberdade, whose aim was to maintain the enthusiasm of the capacity crowds. Its echoes seemed to awaken the House of Madre de Deus from its torpor, nestled as it was within the bright blue of its facade and chapel, relics of the era of the admirals, who were raised there. Now the "very noble, loyal and always steadfast city of Angra do Heroísmo," or "The Bay of Heroism," had sunk into decadence; its bellicose shield and Great Cross of the Tower and Sword of Valor, Loyalty, and Merit had been compelled to yield the majority of the privileges that allowed Gaspar Frutuoso to call the city the "heart and soul of all the other islands" ("They did not leave us the Court of Appeals, nor the Central Lyceum; they want to deprive us of the Military Command of the Azores and its regimental band; they take everything to São Miguel! The only thing they haven't taken yet is the bishopric and the public fountain of Alto das Covas!..."). The House of Madre de Deus resigned itself, with melancholy disinterest, to becoming the horse-riding school that supplied the São João bullring with its share of gallantry and the streets of Angra with the white calm mount ridden by Morgado Vital and the fiery chestnut horse of *Senhor* João de Lemos Bettencourt, riding instructor to dandies and Amazons.

The bullfight, which was to benefit the eleven charities on the island, was assured a full house. The stands were packed; once in a while, one heard the sound of a board cracking. The doors to the last empty boxes were opened to allow passage to the socialite families of the island; some of them, assured of a place, came in with the chic and blasé look of the fashionably late. The groundskeepers sprinkled their last circles of water on the yellowish arena.

It was a modest bullring, built of pine and with its boxes partitioned by almagra-stained planks. But, filled with people, enlivened by the bells of the bullocks longing for their pastures, and with a band of white over the ocher of the *barreira* or ring fence, it seemed to reflect, with its crown of banderoles, the soul and passion of the Terceiran contaminated with *afición* during half a century of Spanish occupation. This feeling lent

410

credence to the admirable "spectral analysis of an archipelago" made by Antero de Quental in 1874, precisely two days after a notable tauromachic event:

> "[June 26, 1874].
> Dear Oliveira Martins:
> I'm writing to you from Terceira. Here in the Azores there is a proverb which runs: 'São Miguel, rich bourgeois; Terceira, poor aristocrats; Fayal, smart smugglers.' In fact, Terceira is an essentially Portuguese and *Peninsular* land: nobility, poverty, bullfights, sober and philosophic *insouciance*, enthusiasm, gallantry and braggadocio: in a word, the defects and qualities characteristic of Peninsular idealism, which you very well know and have already described. And this should suffice for you to realize how much I have enjoyed this place, and how I feel more Portuguese with each passing day, how much I have come to understand the national fiber and how much I feel the need to get in close quarters with the *collective soul*."

Finally, once the president of the bullfight had occupied his box, the sound of a bugle was heard and the bullfighters' entrance doors were thrown open and the horsemen, *cuadrilla*, and bull tacklers displayed in the ring their fan of plumes and gala outfits.

Availing themselves of the arrival of Moyanito's *cuadrilla*, hired this season by the ring management, the troupe called "The August 15th," caught a little short-handed, had reinforced their ranks with a large but poorly trained number of *banderilleros* and footmen. The *espada*, in a magnanimous gesture that very favorably impressed the crowd, renounced a portion of his fee. In these circumstances, the event would preserve its ancient aura of the "sport of kings," gaining in emotion what it might lose in authenticity. Moreover, five horsemen of the old guard, among them António Borges Leal Corte-Real and Mateus José da Rosa–the latter known as *Senhor* Matesinho of the

Zootechnical Post, dwarfish and upright in his saddle à la Revas mounted on his grayish, swan-necked steed with its teeth firmly holding the bit—had consented to embellish that much-awaited spectacle. On the subject of António Borges, people would say: "He's like a nail on a saddle! There's no denying he's the son of the Morgado José Borges, who used to race through the marshlands of Santana fearless of falling into a ditch...." And of "The Most Excellent João José Bettencourt e Vila," a man of culture, very affable, a consummate dandy both in the office and on the street, and a poet lost amidst cowbells and harnesses, it was claimed: "João doesn't stand a chance with the bulls because his horse is gelt, but he's our number-one expert on cattle-branding and horses. He likes animals so much that he has never married. When he dies, even the calving cows will moo in mourning for him!"

But only two members of this illustrious group of bullfighters were going to perform: a professional from the mainland (who alone wore a costume à la Louis XV), and an old amateur from Angra, very popular all over the island for his dandy garb and great gallantry and because he owned an array of taxi coaches. "Aren't you going to watch 'The August 15th?'"—the patrons would ask the barber. "José Dias is going to be one of the *picadores*. He hasn't set foot in the ring in over twenty years. He's going to be something!"

The first bull, reserved for the horseman featured in the publicity poster, came out full of fury and brawn but short on noble bearing. Somber and inane, he stuck, like a bull, to his *querencia*, his favorite spot in the ring. And José Dias, his first attempt having met with failure—perhaps in part as a result of the excessive eagerness with which he accepted the *banderilla* from Moyanito's pale, delicate hand (the horseman's own hand was, in contrast, tanned and calloused from holding the reins in the landaus) and also from having made prematurely that triumphant gesture of brandishing the dart in the middle of the arena in homage to the crowd—kept close to the fence, trying to calm his nervous and largely untried steed. His second attempt met with the same lack of success. Frightened, the cowardly horse fled

412

tangentially from where the bull stood, and its sudden leaps almost made José Dias lose his gray, round *picador's* hat. An increasing murmur of disappointment rose from the bleachers. A voice cried:

"Mr. President, get that bull out of there! It's no good!..."

"Tackle the bull! Tackle him!"

But a long "Shush" called the bleachers to order. José Dias made several other attempts, courageously tightening his circles around the bull, finally managing a daring and well-executed evasive move, which was surprising for an old man of sixty so long absent from the ring and even from handling horses. Moyanito, with the utmost effort, outdid himself with maneuvers there amidst his footmen, not sparing his own cape when the bull refused to charge. Reacting to the sometimes disastrous attempts by João Delgado *Mazzantini*–a local cobbler, crazy about bulls, who exchanged his awl and shoemaker's stirrup for the cape and goads, having once gone so far as to cover on foot the distance between Salamanca and Seville as a bullbreeder's valet and as a herder's apprentice–the bored and heartless spectators in the stands kept yelling:

"Get up close to the bull, Mazantim! This ain't shoemaking!"

"Out of the ring with you! Just get out...."

Resigned and looking askance at the jeerers, the footman withheld his cape. At last, an audible rumble of complaint rose from the stands, with some boos mixed in. Among the small groups of adepts, survivors of the Joseíto school and the golden age of the great Fernando de Oliveira, there were gestures of both disappointment and admiration for the horseman:

"The old man tries his best.... He's good!... It's the bull that doesn't charge!"

"I was right.... They shouldn't have put this bullfight together by rounding up bulls from all over the island! They should have gotten bulls from the breeder Morgado Barcelos... or Gaspar da Praia.... Even the worthless bullock José Francisco Aurora left–they even brought that one to the ring today!... an animal that's been used in a roped bullfight already!"

"I saw it myself! It was the fourth bull in the roped bullfight in São João de Deus last year. It gored the poor peanut vendor Quintinho, and tossed him in the air... right along with his basket, peanuts, popcorn, beard, measuring mug, everything!..."

Displeased, the president signaled to the bugle player, and the usual three calm, repeated notes were heard, indicating the end of that segment of the bullfight. That was when José Dias, seeing time and his reputation vanishing, zoomed diagonally across the arena; he raised his *banderilla* in the direction of a filled box, where a gentleman leaned on the railing with two ladies, one on either side; he stopped in front of the animal and then, advancing toward him, exposing the breast of his sweaty steed and blocking all exits to the cunning bull, yelled:

"Hey, bull! Hey, now!..."

His daring act paid off: the bull charged with his head lowered, snorting steam. The wood creaked, and the tip of the beribboned dart was buried quivering in the withers of the animal, which started running around the ring, bellowing, his tongue hanging out.

Instantly, the two bands broke into a paso doble and the entire crowd of spectators rose for a standing ovation. From the V.I.P. box, a lady enthusiastically threw a great bouquet of hydrangeas into the ring; a slim old man with a white moustache, standing discreetly behind her, threw a bunch of cigars. José Dias, hatless and radiant, was already riding around the arena soaking in the adulation.

"Who is it? Who is it?" several voices asked.

A perfumed young man who occupied one of the more expensive "shade" seats informed them:

"They are from São Jorge; it's the Baron da Urzelina."

"What about the girl who threw the flowers? Is she his daughter? She must be filthy rich!..."

"She's from Fayal, the daughter of that Dulmo who was here some years ago, during the first visit of the Azorean Brotherhood. Don't you remember? Come on! He never left Mariquinhas Cabiceira's tavern.... He seems to be a man who doesn't take well to drinking, if you catch my drift!..."

"She is a knockout! She must have quite a pair of legs!...
And, by the looks of it, the guy standing in the middle must be
her boyfriend...."

"No! They've been married for about three months; they're
going abroad for the rest of their honeymoon. The other girl is
his sister. The Baron da Urzelina is a very rich man! He owns
half of São Jorge. His daughter would be a nice catch for you...."

"What?! She's a beanpole.... She has a pretty face, but the
body is nothing to write home about. When it comes to the
body, it's the other one! I watched her getting out of the coach.
I could see her whole leg... all the way up to here!"

"Hey, you!... Listen here, buddy! Is that the way you talk
about ladies visiting Terceira?..."

"And what business is it of yours?"

"I'm asking if that's how one works for the Azorean
Brotherhood, making asinine cracks about someone else's
daughter?... Your tongue seems a little longer than that bull's;
but, if need be, it can be chopped off a little.... Remember that!"

"And who am I talking to, sir?" asked the other, blustering
and rising to his feet.

"Damião Serpa is the name. And we could finish this discussion here or wherever you prefer. That lady is from my
island and had to cross the São Jorge Channel with eight
whalemen, towed by a harpooned whale. And I bet that the
whalemen, despite being poor fishermen from Pico, would be
incapable of uttering half the stupid things that you've been
blubbering out... And she, despite being a lady in every sense
of the word, is woman enough to slap the face of a blowhard
like you...."

"Go screw!"

"You go screw, you rude little punk! And if you want to continue this conversation, let's step outside. I'm not about to cause
a scene here!"

A young fellow in a straw hat kept pulling his friend by the
coatflaps:

"Leave him alone!... These fops from Fayal think they can
really scare people...."

"I can scare both of you...," said Damião Serpa, placing a hand on his waist and remaining cool and collected. "I know that the people of Terceira are upstanding and hospitable. We just had the misfortune of running into two exceptions...."

The quarrel was drowned out amid the general uproar. Despite the danger involved in tackling a powerful and shrewd horse-fighting bull, the bugle marked the moment for the feat of tackling; and a courageous red-haired amateur, a gentleman who had been a cultural attaché in an embassy, brought the entire crowd to its feet once again with a great face-to-face tackle of the bull, which dragged him a distance of many meters as he held on, dangling helplessly from the animal's imposing head. When the bull had been driven from the ring into the pen, horseman and tackler, hand in hand, both modestly bestowing upon the other their mutual admiration, took a lap around the ring under a rain of flowers.

Happy and excited, Margarida had stood up, the better to take in the warm, colorful gaiety arising from the arena and to see the *rojo y gualdo* costumes of the *banderilleros*, the *mantones de Manilla*, and the *peinetas* of three ballerinas who worked in the nightclub Variedades–Esperanza, Consuelo, and Concha–and who, under the sobriquet of The Three Graces, turned the heads of all the local young men starved for adventure. Rising above all the others in the crowd was the din of voices, commentaries, soda pop, and pickled lupino beans coming from the casually dressed occupants of the cheaper "sun" area of the stands.

Gracefully, Moyanito had thrown his embroidered cape to the box occupied by an influential family from the city, where a respectable-looking elderly gentleman stood, as well as a girl who never took her eyes off Margarida through her binoculars. Once in a while she would turn toward a lady in a gray hat, probably her mother, and make some comment. But one of the swordsman's *banderilleros*, *El Revertito*, in order to countermand the attention the homage rendered to the illustrious visiting family had usurped, had draped his modest, short red cloak over the rim of the Baron da Urzelina's box; and Margarida artistically displayed it, as if it were a marvelous trophy. The attention of the whole audience demonstrated, in fact, that she was in her glory. She looked ravishing! She was wearing a mallow-colored silk dress a little loose around the shoulders and of a very simple cut. Above the white hat pulled a little over her eyes, the bird half-opening its wings seemed to have just perched itself on her brow, ready to take flight again at any moment. And the people occupying the box next to hers received from the slightly pale fire upon Margarida's cheeks—knowing, as they did, that she was on her honeymoon—an impression of perfect, spontaneous happiness, which only her eyes, sometimes a little sad, and her expression, by turns tense and relaxed, seemed to belie.

The bullfight continued with twists and turns of fate, Moyanito performing some impressive feats. The efforts of a raw young footman from the island, who evaded and taunted the bull with enthusiasm or *gana torera*, were much appreciated. But by the fourth bull, while José Vicente took his time with his *banderillas*, and Manzzantini readied his with much yelling and clumsy body movements, the "sun" crowd cupped their hands over their mouths and resumed the jeering:

"Get up in there, Mazantim! Yeah! Like that!... Come at him from the front. He can't see out of his rear eye! It's his blind spot!"

The baron, behind his ironic little moustache, was delighted with these scoffing remarks. He kept back at the edge of the box, always standing. André, not a great aficionado and worried about the time for the ship's departure, availed himself of the interval between bulls to go out to take a little fresh air and to watch the maneuvers in the bull pens. During the intermission, he went out for a while and then returned loaded with Alicante sugar-and-almond candy and *barquillos*. A huge sign, with crudely drawn letters and carried by Mazzantini and Vicente, made the rounds of the arena:

MAKE A DONATION TO THE OLD AND INVALID
BANDERILLERO JOSÉ DE SOUZA MORENO, EL MOYANO.

He was a poor black who had come to Angra as a domestic servant and who, overcome by the island's "bullfight fever," had donned a heavy red cape covered with beads the color of his own skin. Now, unsteady and mentally unfit, he was seen dragging his bullfighter's slippers in the taverns of Quatro-Cantos. The troupe of tacklers had taken advantage of the afternoon to extend to public charity a cape held by the young footmen. The former cultural attaché, who strode in front of them, had the look of a great lord in the act of receiving the prizes from a game in a large palatial hall.

During the entire afternoon, the baroness, finally wrested from her oratory and from her admitted inaction (the first miracle performed by her daughter-in-law), had kept her face turned away during the crucial moments of the bullfight, which she invariably deemed horrific. All she spoke about was the brutality of the whole affair and about her beloved tea that, since disembarking, she had to do without. And so, except for Clarinha, who watched the bullfight without repugnance but also not very spiritedly, Margarida was left with the spectacle of her father-in-law delighting in the most trivial catcall from the crowd and in the smiling presence of van Dam, who, on his way back to Holland with a few escudos in his pocket, witnessed the entire spectacle with the look of a child who has just received a fantastic toy as a present but does not yet know how to operate it.

The professional horseman opened the second half of the *corrida* by boldly attacking a Corvelos bull, black as pitch, that was a little slow but had the kind of quivering neck characteristic of the good stud animal; and to finish off the fight, the horseman drove in two short festively beribboned *banderillas*. Margarida, swept up in the excitement, had broken the morgue-like silence of the "shade" boxes and joined the rest of the audience in wild applause. Doubtlessly her bouquets, opportunely thrown into the ring, and her well-timed displays of enthusiasm had made the Baron da Urzelina's box the center of the crowd's attention for the entire afternoon, rendering the bullring itself the only other competing attraction. Her face, reflecting a spontaneous and unquestionable vivacity, seemed to mirror those of all the spectators.

418

By the ninth bull, the spectators' fervor reached its peak. After two admirable *quiebros*, executed almost improvisationally, Moyanito made for the *barreira* and crossed half the arena holding his cape as casually as you please, as if, having just finished shaving, he were about to open the door to go out with his coat on his arm. Then, after two *faenas* interrupted by the apathy that suddenly seized the bull, he performed a feat that was especially admirable for a mere fighter of young bulls like him: holding the cape at only one corner, with the rest wrapped gently around his feet, he stared the subdued bull straight in the eye and defiantly shook his pigtail with a sudden movement of his head. Two perfect *verónicas* and a stupendous *afarolada*, with both feet firmly together, crowned this assault. It practically brought down the house! Álvaro Duque–usually one of the most vociferous aficionados in Terceira but who now remained quiet–brought his joined fingers to his lips and, his back turned to the *barreira*, from which he seldom removed his elbows, blew a kind of kiss to the entire crowd which seemed to say it all:

"Bravo! Bravo!"

"*Muleta*! *Muleta*!" yelled the spectators.

Moyanito then went to fetch the red cloak and, as he made final preparations, signaled to his comrades to keep the bull occupied. But, as a rising breeze shook the cape and the bull gave little indication of being interested in the fight, Moyanito lifted his sword and, with the toe of his slipper, kicked some sand onto the edges of his fighting cloak, already a little damp from contact with the ground sprinkled by the footmen. While he took these precautionary measures, an authoritarian "Shut up, jackass!" put down a fool who kept screaming "It's the smell! The cloak smells!" A little on the defensive, Moyanito assumed his place in the arena close to the "shade" area.

The bull, despite being almost wedged between the sword and the wall, put on quite a display. One could hear the bull's snorting and the clash of the sword against his horns. Then, tracing an ever-tighter circle, Moyanito slid around the arena noiselessly, like a layman walking along an abandoned cloister. The beast, which normally would respond with a lively and low-headed charge, again started to raise his head to evade the bullfighter. Moyanito, signaling the tacklers to intervene, forced the bull to move from where he stood, applied a strong *muletazo*, and changing hands, finished with two natural *pases* executed from the left that drew enthusiastic *olés* from the spectators. The *espada* then considered the animal subdued enough to allow the bullfighter to lay his pale and steady hand over the white spot on the bull's forehead. Then, to adjust the muleta before executing the feigned killing of the bull, he disdainfully and lingeringly turned his back to the animal. That's when the beast, with lightning speed, treacherously charged the poor bullfighter, goring him in the waist and tossing him into the air like a bird.

A cry of terror rang through the bullring.

"The bull impaled him!"

"He's through!..."

The tackling footmen ran to the sad scene formed by the gladiator and the savage beast, but by then the bull had already reduced Moyanito to a dust-covered rag. Coiled up like a dead man, he still managed to raise his hands to protect his head. His shirt was torn under his arms; and his tattered underwear could be seen, all white, under his costume of lights; a portion of his abdomen lay exposed. Some in the stands thought they saw blood and a length of his intestines hanging out.

"Out of the ring! Out of the ring!" yelled the occupants of the "shade" stands to the circle of helpless capes.

"Cowards! Leaving the poor young man defenseless like that... a manly fighter like him!"

"Just look at Mazantim! The bastard is holding his cape over his shoulder... the damn ragdoll!"

"Couldn't he have helped him? Is that how you justify the twelve thousand escudos you're making?! Go back to your shoe store!"

Mazzantini, justifiably offended in seeing his honest attempts to save the bullfighter so misunderstood, kept wiping the sweat off his brow and gesturing toward the audience to signal that his conscience was clean.

420

"Ah! Mazantim!... Hang your head in shame, you gutless wonder!"

The *espada* was then carried to the bullfighters' entrance door. Surrounded by the sympathetic crowd, Moyanito, his body and arms hanging limp, looked like an unconscious child carried out by a fireman from a burning building, or like the Christ figure in a painting of the Lord's burial. In the boxes, some ladies had fainted and fallen to the floor; others, pale as ghosts, covered their faces with their hands. And because it was the last bull, the president could not cheer up the spectators by ordering the bands to vary their program.

"It seems he wasn't gored," someone said. "Dr. Manuel Vitorino has already checked him and believes he'll probably make it... Dr. Touret is also on his way to examine him. It appears that he is going to have to have an operation."

Like a huge pile of dry leaves that a sudden autumn gust whirls and scatters about, the masses dispersed and the arena was left empty of people and strewn with cushions. The Recreio band, true to convention and with its musicians all standing, started to play, trying to avoid a panic. But the paso doble, in homage to the courage and misfortune of Moyanito, came out sounding as ponderous and sad as a funeral march.

Clarinha had been one of the women who fainted; but, thanks to the salts that André gave her to smell, she quickly came to. The baroness, crossing herself, felt more than justified in her opinion that it would have been better to remain aboard ship; looking a little farther into the future, she could see other ill-omened adventures ahead. In a dead silence, the baron prudently and gently guided his family down the aisles. Stunned, van Dam kept repeating his foreigner's exclamation:

"*Ich bin baff! Ich bin baff!*" And, having changed the title by which he addressed Margarida, he added: "Isn't it trrrue, *mefrouw*?..."

While the baron made way for the disheartened families now leaving their boxes, whose steps caused the somewhat unsteady boards to make a slow, hollow creaking sound, Margarida lingered awhile, leaning over the parapet, whence she commanded a view of the fields and houses of São Pedro, extending west to São Mateus and the sea. The notes from the paso doble still hung over the bullring and echoed through the sloping risers like a reverberating blast of hot air. But now, with the box doors as hermetically shut as the bent and sloppily whitewashed boards allowed for, the entire experience seemed like a nightmare, as if, miraculously unhurt, she had just gotten out of a car that had plunged over a precipice and been demolished. She could not shake the image of the horseman mounted on the elegant, nervous steed brushing by the bull, the beribboned *bande-rilla* raised in oblation toward the box she occupied, and the triumphant charge of the dark savage beast with a little flag stuck in his loins. And her memory shifted back to the wooden horse she had seen in a corner of the old sacristy in Velas... the hurt she experienced before the open telegram, comparable to the pain of the bull brutally jabbed by the well-aimed dart... the whaleboat towed by a great sperm whale that also carried, on its leviathan back, a fluttering little flag.... Except that neither Uncle Amaro nor Intavante, famous *matadores* of cetaceans, had ever enjoyed the thunderous glory accorded Moyanito, agile and golden as a wasp circling around an immobile gadfly. And unable to remove from her memory the image of the pitiful downed bullfighter, Margarida longed to be with Uncle Amaro in the cavern by the sea.

André came back and, feeling a little morose and impatient, said:

"Let's go, Margarida! Don't keep Mother waiting."

Slowly, Margarida rejoined the group waiting to get into a coach with its top down. Van Dam, fearing he might have to ride in front next to the coachman, declared that he preferred to mingle with the crowd; and Clarinha, to avoid bothering her parents and riding squeezed between her brother and her sister-in-law, opted to accompany the Dutchman on foot. R i d i n g in the coach, Margarida, in her voluntarily distant eyes, held as if engraved the last image she had gathered: beyond the dusty arena and off to the west, like a yellow spider there rose the stretched-out silhouette of São Jorge. The island did not entirely block the view of Pico, which, thanks to its fantastic height, could peek from under its leaden cloak over the sister island at its feet, thus allowing itself to be seen from Terceira. Thinking of the reception and of the cabin that awaited her on board, Margarida felt like she was taking leave of her life and of her family forever.

II

Darkness had fallen when Margarida left her cabin to go up to the passenger deck for some fresh air. To save coal during the eighty-mile crossing from Terceira to São Miguel, the *San Miguel* had departed early. The chalk message on the slate board over the gangway read: "DEPARTURE–10 P.M." Wearing a short knitted vest and with a travel beret over her pinned-up hair, Margarida toured the bridge. The ship had cut communications with land; at the third ring of the bell, the last visitors had descended to the awaiting vedette boats gently rocking in the spray that lapped the side of the ship. A tanned old seaman asked Margarida to please move aside to allow him to lift the gangplank ladder. André, who had joined Margarida and mingled a little with the passengers on the quarterdeck, approached the nook where his mother was sitting on a deck chair, and because the baroness was beginning to feel seasick, he pushed in his chair and lent her a solicitous arm to accompany her to her cabin. The baron was already in bed munching on raisins. And since the order prohibiting passengers from the ship's bridge had been kindly lifted in the case of the baron's family, van Dam and Clarinha had taken advantage of the fact to visit with Commander Vasconcelos, who was leaning on the railing of the upper deck with his customary cigarette holder between his teeth and flaunting his impressive beard à la Conrad's Captain MacWhirr.

Below, the bulwark was swarming with passengers waving good-bye to relatives crammed in the boats. Some were drying their tears with handkerchiefs. Margarida, leaning on the rails from where she could see the hatchway leading to the stowage areas, saw a poorly dressed woman standing next to a gaunt boy, who seemed to be suffering from some foot disease. The woman picked up a child and pointed to an old man standing in a boat that was beginning to pull out:

"Ask grandpa for his blessing. Can you see him? Over there... over there!..."

The old man, whose wet face was illuminated by the light from the port side of the ship, had pulled out his handkerchief and was waving his silent farewell. They probably were father and daughter.... Another island family in search of Eldorado. A week hence, the *Canopic*, of the White Star Line, would stop in Ponta Delgada to pick up passengers for Providence, Rhode Island. Margarida again toured the passenger deck and, coming face-to-face with Damião Serpa, who was about to go down to his cabin in second class, could not contain an expression of joy:

"You're here, too? How could we have traveled all the way from Velas in the same ship and not run into each other until now?"

Damião explained that he had not gotten out of his bunk except to go see the bullfight, and only at the last minute. It was because of his seasickness... something he was embarrassed to admit!

"Come on, that can't be, Damião! A sportsman like you... an *islander!...*"

"Well, it's the truth...."

"So you are going to Lisbon...?"

"No. I'm going to get off in São Miguel and wait for the *Canopic.*

"Really? So you're returning to America?... You've decided to leave our beloved Horta... the island that supplies soccer players for the Sport Club of Fayal. You were the backbone of the team on those afternoon scrimmages on the dock lawn...!"

Damião Serpa informed Margarida that he was not going back to America out on a lark. The Metapsychical Society was really growing and had rented space in an enormous skyscraper in Chicago.

"I see... I see.... The spirits hold a greater attraction for you than does a poor, devoted, faithful girl...."

"Who do you mean? Daisy?"

"Who else could I mean?..."

"That wasn't a serious relationship.... I mean... it was a simple flirtation... (I hope you understand what I mean.) Ancient history. The man Daisy was interested in was your Uncle Roberto. Your Uncle Roberto spoke much more directly than I to Daisy's Anglophile soul.... Now she looks like a poor widow!"

Margarida suddenly became somber and changed the subject:

"Are you going for a long stay?"

"Maybe for good.... Who knows!... But don't think that spiritism has gotten to me. No! What I am is a theosopher; or, better still, a metapsychotechnician... a general metapsychist. Besides, I have a financial stake. Yes.... In addition to my dedication to the goals of the Society (which, to me, are quite important, mind you), I'm going to be making eighty dollars a month...."

"And what about you, Margarida? I'm sorry... I still haven't extended my congratulations on your marriage. Of course, I haven't seen you since then.... It's been three months since the god Hymen stole you from our beloved Horta! As you can see, I'm not the only wayward sheep of our native city.... But your case is different. Without you, Horta will never be the same. Everything looks withered... unappealing...." Margarida smiled, looking at the tips of her shoes and at the deck floor. "Hand to God.... Even Pico seems to be sulking. One doesn't even feel like crossing the channel for a picnic in the vineyards! The last time we enjoyed one was when Luís Witton da Terra had his at the Areia Larga quinta. Imagine! Even the wine had turned to vinegar! The poor fellow didn't know, of course, that the wine had gone bad! Only when he raised his own glass and tasted it did he realize: 'Good God, this wine has turned bitter!' Everyone broke out laughing. Luís Witton then ordered other bottles of wine opened and the rest of the party turned out all right. We enjoyed the authentic 'pico' from Criação Velha... the one your father used to serve us at the Vineyards house! See?...

After you turned your back on Horta, even the wine went bad! But, forget all that, I really do wish to congratulate you!"

"Thanks so much...."

"André is really a wonderful guy and the old folks seem very pleasant. Of course, following the old customs... the customs of São Jorge... they can't let their children out of their sight even during their honeymoon.... If I am not being indiscreet, are you traveling abroad? For a long time?"

"I wouldn't exactly call it a honeymoon. You see... I've been married for three months already. If the phases of the moon of life were to be regulated by the phases of the real moon, we'd already easily be in the waning phase... And for me, the third time around to boot!"

"You're familiar with that old saying: *'The January moonlight is worth a sheep, but that of August surpasses all others?'*"

"Yes, I am. You're right; André is a wonderful man. We get along very well. Contrary to prevailing opinion, three months is plenty of time for a couple to get adjusted to each other. Besides, I had known him for over a year and under conditions favorable to making a well-considered decision. In everyday life, mutual respect is the main thing... don't you agree? As far as love (I mean, the emotion that leads to great "unbridled" passions and that we believe in when we're still naive... single and unattached...), that's another question. What's important is conjugal love. I can't explain it.... But it comes close to everything pure and serious that I have ever known in my life: a daughter's love for her parents, love for a friend... love of one's country... No... no! The latter is probably something else; it's more demanding than other types of love.... It was on account of it, and also the fickleness of fate, that I found myself, for example, leaving the Vineyards house to go spend a night in a São Jorge pigeon cavern, and I'd been towed there by a whale.... These adventurous situations are not part of conjugal love."

"Sometimes they are, Margarida...."

"No, they're not!... For a self-respecting person who's overcome any youthful romantic illusions, conjugal love is the anchor. With time and the strong esteem I feel for André, being a

426

married woman is like being one of those sailboats that were left to rot for months and months in Horta, tied to a buoy by the dock; or, if you prefer a more tragic comparison, like a dead person who finally finds peace and perpetual light in a grave that her family bought and keeps neatly trimmed.... This is, of course, aside from the issue of whether there's such a thing as life-or-death love in which moon-eyed young people are such firm believers. For this kind of love can only be discussed on a person-by-person basis and so it has nothing to do with what we're talking about now. And also because it doesn't last very long... It's like a straw fire.... It burns very hot but soon goes out."

Damião Serpa, keeping a little distance from Margarida, who was immersed in her monologue as if in the vapor that rises from the fields on certain mornings, was going to say something, one of those dreamy yet respectful statements that fall short of clear meaning. But he could only remark:

"So you're going to spend a long time traveling?"

"Yes. My father-in-law is going to Caldelas to seek a cure for an ailment, while I'm going to spend time with my sister Cecília, whom I miss very much. She was attending a private school but now is living with my aunt and uncle. Do you know them? It's Uncle Saavedra, who was promoted to captain of a frigate and now is cabinet chief to the minister of the Navy, so he can't leave Lisbon. As for my uncle, he prefers to be at sea. In that, he's very much like me...." And resting her hands on the rail as if she were vaulting on parallel bars, Margarida hummed:

> *O immense sea, immense sea,*
> *O bottomless and immense sea....*

Coming out of her reverie, as if turning on a switch in a dark room, she added: "Then we'll travel to Rome; and, while my in-laws remain for some time in Lourdes, which the baroness adores, my husband, my sister-in-law, and I are going to tour Europe. We'll visit Paris, Brussels, Amsterdam... maybe Warsaw...."

"What about London?"

"No, not London!" Margarida replied forcefully. "For the time being, England isn't in our travel plans. We'd rather go to Holland. Van Dam would be very disappointed if we didn't give him a chance to show us the canals and every single windmill one by one... And since he lives near Delft, he can help us find a nice little hotel."

"Lucky André!... I haven't seen him since the bullfight. Where do you suppose he's hiding?"

"I don't know.... Perhaps in his mother's cabin; she's feeling a little seasick; or chatting with Dr. Diogo, the ship's doctor."

Damião Serpa felt the dissipation of that ecstasy that had made him feel somber and immobile, almost alienated from himself, and tried to be humorous:

"By the looks of things, Margarida, you haven't changed a bit.... You leave your husband busy with family pleasures and stay here whiling away the time.... And why not! That's how I like to see you. And to realize that André is behaving like a truly modern husband makes me like him even more. And no wonder.... That explains how he was able to win the most outgoing and hard-to-please young woman on our island..."

"Do you think so?"

"So help me God...! For a while there, it seemed that you had found some enchanted prince on your path or had decided to enter a convent!..."

"You and your crazy notions...!"

"Especially since your Uncle Roberto arrived. Rumor had it that he had found a position for you in a London clinic. The girls in Horta were dying of envy! But I understand that it's difficult for you to talk about your uncle... I'm sorry. I forgot his death is still a sore subject for you... it happened so recently. What a shame! Roberto, even though he spent so little time in Fayal, is missed by everybody. His coming to the islands was like one of those visits made by Polish princes, who sometimes show up unexpectedly and with their simplicity and their curly beards win the hearts of young women. Your uncle was even more popular than the Prince of Monaco, since he always kept company with whalemen and wild-pigeon shooters... lost in the island caverns.... That was Roberto for you! He was the real enchanted prince.... And there is no doubt that he himself became enchanted!..." Damião then fell silent. They both leaned on the bulwark. The *San Miguel*, rocking from bow to stern, cut through the spray on its starboard side. Kitchen bilge water gushed through the scupper on the ship's side. Damião turned his back to the bulwark. "And you don't want me to refer to Horta as a desert... a cemetery! Without you... without your uncle..." And suddenly changing his tone of voice, he said, with childish vanity: "And now also without me... for, if I may say so, I'm not a bad guy myself...."

Margarida broke into a warm, frank smile, which showed her white teeth and blotted out the vague, mysterious look always latent in her eyes. Damião Serpa, feeling a little touched, seemed to be scrutinizing her, preparing some quip:

"Today you are a married lady... perhaps I should not be so bold as to tell you this... But we're old friends; the time we played together as children on the dock lawn gives me the right to mention certain things (do you remember... us playing war between dwarfs and giants; you and the Lemos sisters were the giants... João Garcia and I were the dwarfs... then, boom! One day you hit me in the head with a stone!...)."

"I can still see the blood streaming down your forehead!" said Margarida, reproducing the face that she, at ten years old, had made at that time. "And was I scared! I have always been like that, kind of crazy... taking fantasy for reality!..."

"You were quite a brat!..." And returning to his knack for frankness, he added: "Childhood friendship gives us certain rights... Those are the friendships that last the longest... the only ones that life never soils! And after I returned from America–my, how quickly time passes!–and we sometimes ran into you on Ocean Street... Espínola, João Garcia and I: The Three Musketeers, as the patrons of Yankee House called us.... But the fact is that you are getting more and more beautiful all the time!... And now that you've gotten married (and it's natural... one doesn't leave the single life behind without undergoing deep transformations...), with that look of yours (how shall I put it?...), a more grown-up look... more relaxed.... You look like one of those apparitions in our séances in Boston... you look like Grete Spiel, Ximenes' bride."

"How horrible!" exclaimed Margarida, laughing and turning pale. "You're comparing me to a ghost?..."

"That's because sometimes you don't seem to be of this world..."

Margarida had acquired a natural and somber look, like a plant that receives a ray of sun through a broken cloud that another cloud quickly snuffs:

"And perhaps I'm not.... But let's change the subject! Heard anything about gymnastics at the Club? And Lieutenant Espínola...?"

"Captain! Captain!..."

"So he's already been promoted?... I didn't know."

"He debuted his three stripes at João Garcia's wedding, about a week ago. He was the best man."

Almost effortlessly, Margarida made the gesture of surprise that people are wont to make when bombarded with implied bits of news:

"Oh!... So he did finally marry Honório's daughter? Lau...ra.... Now I forget her father's last name... and it's such a common name! It's actually our town founder's name, our Ulysses... Jos van Huertere. (Now I'm probably the only person from Fayal who knows how to pronounce it correctly: *Hêêêrtere... Hêêêrtere*....) Did you know that I've started to learn Dutch? From the technician at my father-in-law's creamery, van Dam. The Dutch language is only slightly different from Flemish, the language of our ancestors. Isn't it a shame that we're from a city with a Flemish name... bathed by Flamengos Creek... with ten percent of Flemish last names among its population... and there isn't a living soul in Fayal who knows a word of Flemish?" Damião Serpa, his arms crossed, let that wise torrent gush forth, with mixed feelings of admiration and genuine mystification. Stunned, it had not even occurred to him to come to Margarida's aid, as she struggled with her real or feigned amnesia regarding Honório's family name. "As for me, and it

430

isn't because of our Flemish last name (and, besides, Captain Fernão van Hulm wasn't exactly unknown...), but I have this craze for old... historical things.... There are, actually, even other more recent family reasons.... A blood cousin of my grandmother Margarida Terra, Francisco Bruyn (another strange family name!...), is buried in Flanders, in the Oogenbom cemetery. It seems that they loved each other like brother and sister.... And I, who don't have anyone who can teach me Flemish, am trying to learn Dutch, which is almost the same thing. Do you want to hear something in Dutch, just to hear how it sounds? It's the caption on an engraving of Angra, from the 16th century, a time when they still grew woad. The orange boats, which earned the Clarks the fortune that they would one day squander, came some time after the boats that carried the woad and lichen rocella to the dye mills.... *Glastu* and *persea azorica*... all drugs!... (I've become a pedantic bore, haven't I? We've got to have some kind of hobby, and I had some lessons in zoology and botany with Pretextato from the Weather Station, to while away the time... those seemingly endless last months I spent in Horta!). That plan of Angra was sketched by a Dutchman by the name of Linschoten... Jan Huygen Linschoten. And the work is huge and beautiful... this big. And it was engraved by a Mr. Baptista van Doetechum...." Damião Serpa still kept his arms crossed, with a little ironic twinkle dancing in his dark-brown eyes. Margarida, too, burst into laughter, a little at her own rant. "But do you want me to tell you what the caption is or not?... I memorized it, so I can get used to Dutch pronunciation. Van Dam, who can only read a little, brought some Dutch reviews about making cheeses and butter. *Affbeelding vande Stat Angra, met het Slot op het Eylant Tercera, welcke alle de Eylanden onderworpen zyn, diemen Azores oste de Vlaemsche Eylanden noemt....*"

"Please spare me!... Show a little compassion for a friend!" said Damião, graciously stretching out his arm, as if to place a hand over Margarida's mouth. "You're sure waxing linguistic today!"

"But did you notice?... did you? A person who knows English as well as you do and who was in contact with

431

Germans... Grete Spiel and all... you know, the spirit from the other world who you say looks a lot like me, should easily understand: *'diemen Azores oste de Vlaemsche Eylanden noemt...'* means 'from the Azores, also known as the Flemish Islands....' Jos van Huertere Islands.... From 'Huertere' the names Horta, Ultra, Utra, and Dutra were derived. That's it: Laura Dutra... that's the Honórios' family name. My, how forgetful I am these days! So, they did get married, did they?"

"Yes, they did... they did."

"I was told that they had broken up. But I heard that some three months ago.... Don't be surprised. I was never much aware of the goings-on and gossip in Horta. And now less than ever...."

Damião Serpa found the courage to say:

"This is a world of dashed hopes and missed opportunities, Margarida.... When all is said and done, João Garcia loved only one woman in his life–you."

Margarida, taking advantage of the fact that a servant was just passing by carrying a tray with a bottle of mineral water and a glass, called him:

"Did you see any member of my family walking around? The *Senhor* Baron or *Senhor* André Barreto...?"

"The baron has already retired to his cabin; but, if Your Excellency wishes, I can call his son. I saw him a while ago in the ballroom, with Miss Clara Barreto."

"Never mind... never mind! I have to go to my cabin." And turning to Damião Serpa, with a pleasant smile that seemed to draw a curtain over the past and open another onto the future: "Good night, then! I guess we'll see each other again.... And do believe that it was a great pleasure to run into you, Damião."

"Don't mention it!... The pleasure was all mine."

While Damião Serpa walked past the gangway on his way toward his second-class cabin, Margarida went down to her own cabin, and not finding André there, she looked into her in-laws' quarters. The baron and baroness had dozed off, and Margarida quietly drew the door curtain. Clarinha, who traveled in a cabin with only one other lady from Angra, told her that André was in the ship doctor's cabin, with Dr. Diogo and the purser. *Senhor*

Gil de Arruda was very fond of stories, and André was telling him about his hunting adventures. Clarinha had left them entertained with a navigational chart that the first mate had gotten from the bridge; André pointed out his pigeon-shooting escapades on the cliffs of the coast of São Jorge and mentioned the Portuguese names not included on the English chart. He even told the story about his climbing the Zimbreiro, in Praia do Almoxarife, during which he had almost killed João Garcia, whom he hadn't seen behind a rock.... When he had a captive audience, André could go on talking for hours...

Margarida, almost disheartened, climbed to the upper deck, busily rolling the beret that she held in her hands. The ship's first-class section lay astern. Originally built for greater tonnage, the ship had been shortened at the last minute, rendering it very unstable and giving it a squat, clumsy appearance. These invariable comments preceded and followed the ship's bimonthly voyages from island to island: "I hope so-and-so has a good trip! The *San Miguel* rocks something awful. The *Funchal*, even though it's smaller, is more stable on the waves...." Or these: "Do you want anything sent to Lisbon? I'm leaving tomorrow. In second class, of course!... The cabins in first class shake a lot because of the propellers... In rough sailing, the *San Miguel* is like a cradle... (the only consolation for those traveling in first class is that they can disguise their poverty...)."

All aglow with lights, the ship gained the high seas. Margarida walked around the ballroom. Seen from the outside, the opaque windows, ornamented with little bouquets that reminded her of the finger-drawn motifs upon the rain-soaked door of a coupé, overlooked a number of lined-up benches as in a deserted park. Peeking inside, she discovered a little couple sitting in a corner of a sofa. The girl was slim and pale, wearing a red blouse and a black skirt; he, strong and swarthy, hair parted in the middle, had his arm around her waist. An unattractive girl with long curly hair was seated at the piano. The notes from a waltz vanished in the racket of the propeller's muffled rattling. The young man stood up and, bending backward a little, reached out to the girl's hands, pulled her toward him and started waltzing, very slowly at first, and then faster and faster, only to slow down again, his eyes fixed on the ceiling as if he were meditating or praying. Margarida turned her head away and went to lean on the bulwark.

As the ship moved away from land, the city, seen close-up, looked ugly with its houses hidden behind Canta Galo, Misericórdia, and Rocha; and as the ship drew farther and farther from land, the city's outline, in the middle of the web of lights, took on ever more clearly the shape of a reclining mermaid. On the port side lay the dark, barren silhouettes of Cabras islets, like a whale followed by its feeble calf. On starboard, hemmed in by ramparts and pine trees, rose Mount Brasil, somber and massive.

Margarida lounged on that side of the deck. On the deck chair, an athletic-looking old man wearing a silk cap was napping with his mouth open, his glasses resting on his traveling blanket. At some distance from him, taking advantage of the light from the deck and the skylight that provided some ventilation for the dining room, sat a distinguished, sad, shabbily dressed young man holding a pencil, focusing his attention on a sheet of paper and counting on his fingers. Maybe a traveling salesman.... Maybe a poet.... But he was too melancholy to be a salesman.... Salesmen always wore elaborate moustaches and impressive suits, this one wore a little scruff of a beard and creaseless trousers.

The first-class waiter went by with a corkscrew in his hand. He spoke in a light São Miguel accent:

"Are you a first-class passenger?"

The young man stood up:

"No, I'm not.... I'm just killing time before turning in. I'm also waiting until Terceira drops out of sight...."

"Well, then, keep to your own class! The passengers from second and third classes are allowed here only while the ship is at port."

"I'm sorry...."

Margarida, noticing by his demeanor that the young man was shy and also to indicate her displeasure with the waiter's treatment of the passenger, intervened with a smile:

434

"Excuse me, young man... are you going to America?"

"I'm going to Coimbra. I'm in my second year of law school. And since I left two courses from last year to take this October, I'm going a little earlier...."

"These employees on the *San Miguel* tend to put on airs." The student kept a worried eye on the top of the staircase by which the waiter had disappeared. "Don't pay him any mind! Now you are a guest of mine; we're here just chatting.... If I'm not intruding, may I ask if you were writing poetry?... Are you from Terceira?"

"Yes, I'm from Fontinhas. I attended the Angra Seminary; *Senhor* Marquis da Praia and Monforte paid for my tuition; but since I discovered I wasn't cut out for the priesthood, I decided to quit...."

"You made the right decision! That was a very honest thing to do. And (pardon me, if I'm being indiscreet...), how did you manage to go study in Coimbra? I'm assuming that your parents are poor...."

"They're peasants. When I quit the seminary, I worked as a farm hand.... And you know...," said the young man, with the proud, sad smile of one who has learned the value of certain ridiculous ironies: "... I used to play the saxophone in the village band... and gave lessons at night to earn enough to buy some books...."

"And now you are a Coimbra student and a poet...."

"That's life for you.... The Marquis da Praia's nephew, knowing I felt bad about not going on with my education, lent his support. My father mortgaged his home and five acres of land. I'm planning to finish in three years."

"Do you intend to practice law?"

"Maybe not. Consul... that's what I'd like to be!"

"To guard the interests of our fellow Azoreans in America...? Consul in *Bastão* [6], *Betefete* [7]... as they say."

---

[6] Boston.–Author.

[7] New Bedford.–Author.

"I'd rather work in some country nearer to home... Say France or England."

"What about in Holland, then?... Do you know that I'm going to Delft?..."

"Oh... Delft!..."

"Yes. Between Rotterdam and The Hague. My father-in-law hired a Dutchman to supervise his creamery. I'm the Baron da Urzelina's daughter-in-law; you probably have heard of him.... I am from Fayal myself... Margarida Dulmo."

"Very pleased to meet you...," said the student, bowing. "It's odd!... Your last name is identical to that of a man who is supposed to have discovered an island north of Terceira, Captain Fernão Dulmo.... I read it in Drumond's *Annals*."

"Yes... I'm supposed to be his great-great-great-granddaughter. But we all are descendants of Adam... aren't we?"

The young man smiled also. His original awkwardness started to melt away under his ill-fitting coat, and his personality started to blossom. The waiter's head appeared again at the top of the staircase; throwing a rancorous glance at that artificial paradise set up by Margarida to lower his prestige, he slowly reentered the already empty and silent ballroom. Margarida, more and more interested in the student from Fontinhas, pressed for information:

"But... really now! Are you a poet?" And looking at the edge of the sheet that the young man, in haste, had hidden in his pocket, she added: "So you think I'm not worthy of your sharing that little secret with me?... We are both islanders... We are here by ourselves, away from everybody.... Come, read me some of your poems. No one else will hear you!"

The young man, almost trembling, stared suspiciously at Margarida. Then, pulling out the sheet of paper, and with both of them drawing close to the light, he read:

> *I too, I too, keep my night vigil in the port*
> *That's so blue, despite the total darkness....*

The young man's voice was a little hoarse; his hand, suddenly daring and motioning like a preacher's, almost brushed

Margarida's hair. But the writing grew ever smaller and more tortured on the sheet of paper. The very poet seemed to have difficulty deciphering his own scribbles. Margarida, surprising herself with her own daring attitude and respecting the secret that seemed determined to remain locked in that chicken scratch, offered these words:

"How wonderful! My critical opinion isn't worth much, but believe me when I say I find those lines beautiful... You made the right decision in leaving the seminary. But you know... in poetry, it's perfectly legitimate to express the fear that others might forget us. It's a poetic license... that one takes with life, right?..."

Margarida became pale. As she drank in that minute, which seemed a gift from the gods, an ineffable truce in her natural destiny, she was about to let herself go and confide in that shy young man who had been scorned by a waiter. At that moment, though, the memory of the first line came to her, and she stopped herself just in time:

"'I too, I too, keep my night vigil in the port.' And please excuse me, for it's time for me to return to my cabin. Tomorrow I must get up very early so that we can visit the Lagoa das Sete Cidades and the volcano at Furnas... Good night! Mr.....? That is, if you don't mind telling me your name..."

"João Cardoso Pragana."

"... *Senhor* João Pragana."

Margarida, thinking of that stupendous name for a poet, [8] entered the ballroom, to allow time for the young man to reach the ship's bow. She did not feel like going down to her cabin, for she suspected she was not going to feel like sleeping. The little ballroom was totally deserted, with its somnolent mahogany furniture and brown upholstery. By the piano, in the corner of the sofa–a forgotten embroidered handkerchief. Since she had entered the ballroom to make the young man believe she was retiring to her cabin, Margarida recalled the times when Maria da Paz, the Lemoses, and she used to play hide-and-seek

---

[8] *Pragana* means "awn," the slender bristles on the head of wheat.–Trans.

in the abandoned rooms of the Granary and, with them and with other groups of Horta children, in the squares of sparse, green lawn by the dock, as Damião Serpa had just reminded her.

The *San Miguel* was now pitching quite a bit. And the movement of the propeller rattled the panes of the ballrooms's guillotine windows, which were equipped with fabric straps like those in the baron's coupé. Without any place to go but desperately wanting to go somewhere, anywhere, Margarida again left the ballroom; and only when she shook her hair and passed her hand over her head did she realize she needed to go out for some fresh air. She walked toward the parapet that separated the deck from the bow, and leaning her elbows on the edge, abandoned herself to the sensation of being carried away in a dream ship, whose white wake extended back into the distance and died toward the land she had left behind.

On the horizon, Angra had grown progressively smaller, reduced to a barely visible row of faint lights. In the middle of the handrail, behind the useless rudder controls, a little rotating dial, attached to a rope dragging obliquely along the surface of the water, drew her attention. It was the log. For the moment, the hand indicated but five or six thousand meters traveled; and Margarida, oblivious to everything around her, mechanically picked up the rope. That gesture seemed to interrupt the torsion of the apparatus, which, by means of some ingenious mechanism vibrating very far away, extracted from the waters the secret of distance. But when she again let go of the line, the pulsating gage returned to its original rhythm. Then the oscillation progressively slowed down as the *San Miguel* continued on its course like a fish that, following its instinct, searches for the waters whose density and temperature are most suitable to it. Repeating the experiment, Margarida was compelled to look at her own hand, which seemed to be playing with a marionette or engaged in trying to correct the ship's course. That's when she saw her beloved ring, the golden and emerald serpent she had inherited from Grandmother Margarida Terra, without her mother's ever having worn it. She had long ago lost one of the emeralds that formed the eyes of the beast; with the ring thus mutilated, she had once stood at the wall of her quinta speaking with João Garcia–who had beheld it while he held her hand in his as they sat on a garden bench in the quinta during a stormy night. She had allowed him to touch her hair and examine the scar from the great fall she had suffered when a child. And Margarida smiled bitterly. Yes... João Garcia, unlike the poet Pragana, had not attended the seminary. She was the one who, in a way, had attended a seminary! She was the one who wore a kind of tonsure and observed the astral chastity of a blind serpent, crushed on her finger by a maculate conception! That was why her mother used to say to people who noticed that indelible scar: "Do you see?... Scarred for life!"

Wearing this same mutilated ring, she had spoken to Uncle Roberto countless times on the Well terrace. Always calm and enigmatic, he had told her one afternoon, as he held her hand by her fingertips: "This serpent of yours is a second Camões, who was also blind in one eye!" Much later, just prior to her marriage, when the Baron da Urzelina had come to Horta to ask her father officially for her hand (that same hand that now held the line...), he had expressed his regrets that such a beautiful piece of jewelry should remain in such a state. Since Margarida had refused to have it repaired, André had asked her to lend it to him on the pretext that it would be used as a model for a ring that a friend of Clarinha's had commissioned from an Oporto jeweler. A few days later, her husband had returned it to her with two new emeralds; wrapped in a little cotton was the old emerald in a small jewelry case containing a necklace of rubies and diamonds, a wedding gift from her in-laws. Margarida had taken such offence at the gesture that she cried for days and days. And now, looking at her finger and seeing the painstakingly mounted emeralds adorning the head of the forked-tongued serpent, which seemed to have its eyes wide open, Margarida's eyes were likewise as big as saucers; and shaking her head three times, removing one of her shoes and then putting it on again with a quick flick of her foot, she was seized by an irrepressible fury. With her face burning and her eyes filled with tears, she brutally rubbed the ring against the rope braid until the two stones, first one then the other, were inexorably dislodged from their settings. Then, seized by a superstitious terror and not knowing how she was going to explain to her in-laws and husband the sad state of the ring, she carefully used the other hand to remove it from her ring finger. Considering for a moment the foam produced by the rudders and that serpent coiled and miserable like a dried worm, she hurled the ring into the sea.

With her eyes still staring at the ship's wake, Margarida felt a tender hand touching her shoulder and was startled.

"So that's where you've been, dear?... I've been looking all over for you.... I've searched the entire ship. It's time for you to retire.... See?... Look how red and swollen your eyes are! It was because of that grim scene with the bullfighter.... Or is it because you miss Horta?... Come, say something! Don't you want to go back to the cabin?..."

Margarida let him kiss her and whispered:

"Okay... Let's go, André! Give me your arm...."

André gently held her left hand; and tenderly searching for her wedding ring, he said, very startled:

"What the–?! You lost your ring?"

I was leaning over the bulwark and took it off my finger. I wasn't thinking... It fell into the sea."

André kissed her again:

"Don't worry.... We'll order another."

And taking her by the arm, he accompanied her as one might accompany a sick person. The sound of their slow unsynchronized steps resounded down the metal staircase leading to their cabin.

While Margarida prepared for bed, André went to his parents' cabin to say good night; and unable to stop thinking about his wife's grief, he could not resist telling them what had happened. Then he quickly undressed, climbed to the bunk above Margarida's, and turned off the brighter light.

In the dark, the baron asked:

"Are you already asleep, Angélica?"

"No. I'm saying my prayers.... I only have ten Hail Mary's to go before finishing the rosary. Don't disturb me!"

(Pause.)

"Are you awake, Angélica?"

"Yes, I am...."

"And what's your explanation for what happened to your daughter-in-law's ring?..."

"She is so unfortunate, the poor girl...."

"You're probably right.... But things like that don't happen to everybody. It has a lot to do with character.... This young lady is quite eccentric. Nice girl, pretty, very socially correct... but eccentric!"

"Don't say that, Caetano! She is so good to her husband... so polite to us!..."

"Yes... yes.... But eccentric... eccentric...! Even that enthusiasm of hers at the bullfight didn't square very well with me.... It's most likely fitting, very chic... but I didn't like it."

"Don't be silly, Caetano! Don't be ungrateful to God.... Do you know what I've been thinking?... There are people who don't have much luck in life.... Don't you remember how she came to our home... in that whaleboat... towed by that whale... and then within six days her uncle receiving the last rites and wrapped in a shroud!... And her difficult home life, with a debauched father... and her mother, a little crazy, always waiting hand and foot on her paralyzed grandfather.... It's actually amazing that she manages to stay so cheerful. Poor little angel!..."

Margarida, lying behind the draperies of her mahogany bunk, leading her husband to believe that she had fallen into the arms of Morpheus, kept staring at the wire mesh on the bunk above hers. Despite the dimness of the night-light that cast a purplish tinge upon the darkness of the cabin, Margarida felt blind... blind as the ring serpent that no belly of a fish would carry to a human table and which now, and like the *cucumaria of the abysses*, lay in the darkest depths of the sea.

Lisbon, 21 February 1944, 7:25 pm